7 DEADLY WONDERS

"... had me turning the pages so fast I had blisters on my fingers and my heart pounded so hard it sounded like a helicopter was landing on my roof! For stay-up-late, can't-put-down-ability, Reilly is the master."

—Brad Thor, national bestselling author of *Takedown*

HANG ON FOR THE RIDE OF A LIFETIME ... IN MATTHEW REILLY'S SENSATIONAL *NEW YORK TIMES* BESTSELLER!

"Adventure with a capital A. Matthew Reilly pulls out all stakes—and beats you over the head with them."
—James Rollins, *USA Today* bestselling author

"Ancient history, heart-stopping booby traps, and wild adventure ... a perfect book to jump-start your vacation beach reading."
—*Library Journal*

"Fun. ... Reilly keep[s] the action coming."
—*Kirkus Reviews*

This title is also available as an eBook

AREA 7

"Reilly . . . can inspire awe. How many heroes, after all, can kill an enemy aboard the space shuttle in outer space, then return to earth and dispatch another foe by pushing him into a pool full of meat-eating Komodo dragons all over the course of less than an hour?"
—*Publishers Weekly*

"Reilly's . . . most suspenseful blow-'em-up. The jet-boat chase through the blind chasms of Arizona's Lake Powell puts the Bond books to shame."
—*Kirkus Reviews* (starred review)

"Another action-packed adventure."
—*Booklist*

CONTEST

"Reilly hurls readers into an adrenaline-drenched thrill ride. Reilly's novel is almost impossible to put down."
—*Orlando Sentinel*

ALSO BY MATTHEW REILLY

MATTHEW REILLY

SEVEN DEADLY WONDERS

POCKET BOOKS

NEW YORK · LONDON · TORONTO · SYDNEY

POCKET BOOKS, a division of Simon & Schuster, Inc.
1230 Avenue of the Americas
New York, NY 10020

This book is a work of fiction. Names, characters, places, and incidents are products of the author's imagination or are used fictitiously. Any resemblance to actual events or locales or persons, living or dead, is entirely coincidental.

Copyright © 2006 by Karanadon Entertainment Pty Ltd.

Originally published in hardcover in 2006 by Simon & Schuster, Inc.

All rights reserved, including the right to reproduce this book or portions thereof in any form whatsoever. For information address Simon & Schuster, Inc., 1230 Avenue of the Americas, New York, NY 10020

ISBN-13: 978-1-4165-0506-8
ISBN-10:   1-4165-0506-7

This Pocket Books paperback edition January 2007

10 9 8 7

POCKET and colophon are registered trademarks of Simon & Schuster, Inc.

Cover design by Jae Song; Stepback illustration by Wayne J. Haag

Manufactured in the United States of America

For information about special discounts for bulk purchases, please contact Simon & Schuster Special Sales:
1-800-456-6798 or business@simonandschuster.com.

For Natalie

IN ANCIENT TIMES, AT THE PEAK

OF THE GREAT PYRAMID OF GIZA,

THERE STOOD A MAGNIFICENT

CAPSTONE MADE OF GOLD.

IT DISAPPEARED IN ANTIQUITY.

"A Collection of Wonders around the World"

TITLE OF A COLLECTION OF DOCUMENTS
WRITTEN BY CALLIMACHUS OF CYRENE,
CHIEF LIBRARIAN OF THE ALEXANDRIA
MUSEION, LOST WHEN THE FAMOUS
LIBRARY WAS DESTROYED IN 48 B.C.

Cower in fear, cry in despair,
You wretched mortals
For that which giveth great power
Also takes it away.
For lest the Benben be placed at sacred site
On sacred ground, at sacred height,
Within seven sunsets of the arrival of Ra's prophet,
At the high point of the seventh day,
The fires of Ra's implacable Destroyer will devour us all.

FORTY-FIVE-HUNDRED-YEAR-OLD
HIEROGLYPHIC INSCRIPTION FOUND ON
THE SUMMIT OF THE GREAT PYRAMID AT
GIZA IN THE PLACE WHERE THE
CAPSTONE ONCE STOOD.

"I have both held and beheld unlimited power and of
it I know but one thing. It drives men mad."

ALEXANDER THE GREAT

SEVEN DEADLY WONDERS

FIRST MISSION
THE
COLOSSUS

SUDAN
MARCH 14, 2006
SIX DAYS BEFORE TARTARUS

THE GREATEST STATUE IN HISTORY

IT TOWERED like a god above the mouth of Mandraki harbor, the main port of the island state of Rhodes, much like the Statue of Liberty does today in New York.

Finished in 282 B.C. after twelve years of construction, it was the tallest bronze statue ever constructed. At a stupendous 110 feet, it loomed above even the tallest ship that passed by.

It was crafted in the shape of the Greek sun god, Helios—muscled and strong, wearing a crown of olive leaves and a necklace of massive golden pendants, and holding a flaming torch aloft in his right hand.

Experts continue to argue whether the great statue stood astride the entrance to the harbor or at the end of the long breakwater that formed one of its shores. Either way, in its time, the Colossus would have been an awesome sight.

Curiously, while the Rhodians built it in celebration of their victory over the Antigonids (who had laid siege to the island of Rhodes for an entire year), the statue's construction was paid for by Egypt—by two Egyptian Pharaohs in fact: Ptolemy I and his son, Ptolemy II.

But while it took Man twelve years to build the Colossus of Rhodes, it took Nature fifty-six years to ruin it.

When the great statue was badly damaged in an earthquake in 226 B.C., it was again Egypt who offered to repair it: this time the new Pharaoh, Ptolemy III. It was as if the Colossus meant more to the Egyptians than it did to the Rhodians.

Fearing the gods who had felled it, the people of Rhodes declined Ptolemy III's offer to rebuild the Colossus and the remainder of the statue was left to lie in ruins for nearly nine hundred years—until A.D. 654 when the invading Arabs broke it up and sold it off in pieces.

One mysterious footnote remains.

A week after the Rhodians declined Ptolemy III's offer to reerect the Colossus, the *head* of the mammoth fallen statue—all sixteen feet of it—went missing.

The Rhodians always suspected that it was taken away on an Egyptian freighter-barge that had left Rhodes earlier that week.

The head of the Colossus of Rhodes was never seen again.

ANGEREB SWAMP, EASTERN SUDAN

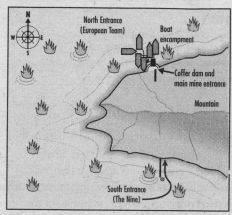

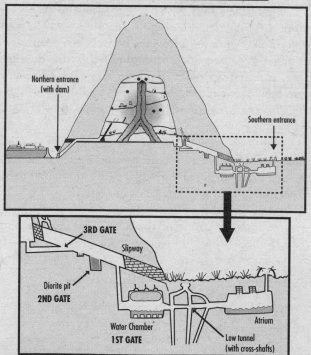

The nine figures raced through the crocodile-infested swamp on foot, moving fast, staying low.

The odds were stacked against them.

Their rivals numbered in excess of two hundred men.

They had only nine.

Their rivals had massive logistical and technical support: choppers, floodlights for night work, and boats of every kind—gunboats, houseboats, communications boats, three giant dredging barges for the digging, and that wasn't even mentioning the temporary dam they'd managed to build.

The Nine were only carrying what they'd need inside the mine.

And now—the Nine had just discovered—a *third* force was on its way to the mountain, close behind them; a much larger and nastier force than that of their immediate foes, who were nasty enough.

By any reckoning it was a hopelessly lost cause, with enemies in front of them and enemies behind them, but the Nine kept running anyway.

Because they had to.

They were a last-ditch effort.

The last throw of the dice.

They were the very last hope of the small group of nations they represented.

* * *

Their immediate rivals—a coalition of European nations—had found the northern entrance to the mine two days ago and were now well advanced in its tunnel system.

A radio transmission that had been intercepted an hour before revealed that this pan-European force—French troops, German engineers, and an Italian project leader—had just arrived at the Third Gate inside the mine. Once they breached that, they would be inside the Grand Cavern itself.

They were progressing quickly.

Which meant they were also well versed in the difficulties found inside the mine.

Fatal difficulties.

Traps.

But the Europeans' progress hadn't been entirely without loss: three members of their point team had died gruesome deaths in a snare on the first day. But the leader of the European expedition—a Vatican-based Jesuit priest named Francisco del Piero—had not let their deaths slow him down.

Single-minded, unstoppable, and completely devoid of sympathy, del Piero urged his people onward. Considering what was at stake, the deaths were an acceptable loss.

The Nine kept charging through the swamp on the south side of the mountain, heads bent into the rain, feet pounding through the mud.

They ran like soldiers—low and fast, with balance

and purpose; ducking under branches, hurdling bogs, always staying in single file.

In their hands, they held guns: MP7s, M16s, Steyr AUGs. In their thigh holsters were pistols of every kind.

On their backs: packs of various sizes, all bristling with ropes, climbing gear, and odd-looking steel struts.

And above them, soaring gracefully over the tree-tops, was a small shape, a bird of some sort.

Seven of the Nine were indeed soldiers.

Crack troops. Special forces. All from different countries.

The remaining two members were civilians, the elder of whom was a long-bearded sixty-five-year-old professor named Maximilian T. Epper, call sign: *Wizard*.

The seven military members of the team had some-what fiercer nicknames: *Huntsman, Witch Doctor, Archer, Bloody Mary, Saladin, Matador,* and *Gunman*.

Oddly, however, on this mission they had all acquired new call signs: *Woodsman, Fuzzy, Stretch, Princess Zoe, Pooh Bear, Noddy,* and *Big Ears*.

These revised call signs were the result of the ninth member of the team:

A little girl of ten.

The mountain they were approaching was the last in a long spur of peaks that ended near the Sudanese-Ethiopian border.

Down through these mountains, flowing out of Ethiopia and into the Sudan, poured the Angereb River. Its waters paused briefly in this swamp before continuing on into the Sudan, where they would ultimately join the Nile.

The chief resident of the swamp was *Crocodylus niloticus,* the notorious Nile crocodile. Reaching sizes of up to twenty feet, the Nile crocodile is known for its great size, its brazen cunning, and its ferocity of attack. It is the most man-eating crocodilian in the world, killing upwards of three hundred people every year.

While the Nine were approaching the mountain from the south, their EU rivals had set up a base of operations on the northern side, a base that looked like a veritable floating city.

Command boats, mess boats, barracks boats, and gunboats, the small fleet connected by a network of floating bridges and all facing toward the focal point of their operation: the massive coffer dam that they had built against the northern flank of the mountain.

It was, one had to admit, an engineering master-piece: a 110-yard-long, forty-foot-high curved retaining dam that held back the waters of the swamp to reveal a square stone doorway carved into the base of the mountain forty feet *below* the waterline.

The artistry on the stone doorway was extraordinary.

Egyptian hieroglyphs covered every square inch of its frame—but taking pride of place in the very center of the lintel stone that surmounted the doorway was a glyph often found in pharaonic tombs in Egypt:

Two figures, bound to a staff bearing the jackal head of Anubis, the Egyptian god of the Underworld.

This was what the afterlife had in store for grave robbers—eternal bondage to Anubis. Not a nice way to spend eternity.

The message was clear: do not enter.

The structure inside the mountain was an ancient mine delved during the reign of Ptolemy I, around the year 300 B.C.

During the great age of Egypt, the Sudan was known as "Nubia," a word derived from the Egyptian word for gold: *nub.*

Nubia: the Land of Gold.

And indeed it was. It was from Nubia that the ancient Egyptians sourced the gold for their many temples and treasures.

Records unearthed in Alexandria revealed that this mine had run out of gold seventy years after its founding, after which it gained a second life as a quarry for the rare hard stone, diorite. Once it was exhausted of diorite—around the year 226 B.C.—Pharaoh Ptolemy III decided to use the mine for a very special purpose.

To this end, he dispatched his best architect—Imhotep V—and a force of two thousand men.

They would work on the project in absolute secrecy for three whole years.

The northern entrance to the mine had been the main entrance.

Originally, it had been level with the waterline of the swamp, and through its doors a wide canal bored horizontally into the mountain. Bargeloads of gold and diorite were brought out of the mine via this canal.

But then Imhotep V had come and reconfigured it.

Using a temporary dam not unlike the one the European force was using today, his men had held back the waters of the swamp while his engineers had lowered the level of the doorway, dropping it *forty feet*. The original door was bricked in and covered over with soil.

Imhotep had then disassembled the dam and allowed the swamp waters to flood back over the new doorway, concealing it for over two thousand years.

Until today.

But there was a *second* entrance to the mine, a lesser-known one, on the south side of the mountain.

It was a back door, the end point of a slipway that had been used to dispose of waste during the original digging of the mine. It too had been reconfigured.

It was this entrance that the Nine were seeking.

Guided by the tall, white-bearded Wizard—who held in one hand a very ancient papyrus scroll and in the other a very modern sonic-resonance imager—they stopped abruptly on a mud mound about ninety yards from the base of the mountain. It was shaded by four bending lotus trees.

"Here!" the old fellow called, seeing something on the mound. "Oh dear. The village boys *did* find it."

In the middle of the muddy dome, sunk into it, was a tiny square hole, barely wide enough for a man to fit into. Stinking brown mud lined its edges.

You'd never see it if you weren't looking for it, but it just so happened that this hole was exactly what Professor Max T. Epper was searching for.

He read quickly from his papyrus scroll:

"In the Nubian swamp to the south of Soter's mine,
Among Sobek's minions,
Find the four symbols of the Lower Kingdom.
Therein lies the portal to the harder route."

Epper looked up at his companions. "Four lotus trees: the lotus was the symbol of the Lower Kingdom. Sobek's minions are crocodiles, since Sobek was the Egyptian crocodile god. In a swamp to the south of Soter's mine—Soter being the other name for Ptolemy I. This is it."

A small wicker basket lay askew next to the muddy hole—the kind of basket used by rural Sudanese.

"Those stupid, stupid boys." Wizard kicked the basket away.

On their way here, the Nine had passed through a small village. The villagers claimed that only a few days ago, lured by the Europeans' interest in the mountain, four of their young men had gone exploring in the swamp. One of them had returned to the village saying the other three had disappeared down a hole in the ground and not come out again.

At this point, the leader of the Nine stepped forward, peered down into the hole.

The rest of the team waited for him to speak.

Not a lot was known about the leader of this group. Indeed, his past was veiled in mystery. What *was* known was this:

His name was West—Jack West Jr.

Call sign: *Huntsman*.

At thirty-seven, he had the rare distinction of being both military *and* university trained—he had once been a member of the most elite special forces unit in the world, while at another time, he had studied ancient history at Trinity College in Dublin under Max Epper.

Indeed, in the 1990s, when the Pentagon had ranked the best soldiers in the world, only one soldier in the top ten had *not* been an American: Jack West. He'd come in at number four.

But then, around 1995, West disappeared off the international radar. Just like that. He was not seen at international exercises or on missions again—not even the allied invasion of Iraq in 2003, despite his experience there during Desert Storm in '91. It was assumed he had quit the military, cashed in his points and retired. Nothing was seen or heard of him for over ten years . . .

. . . until now.

Now, he had reemerged.

Supremely fit, he had dark hair and laser-sharp blue eyes that seemed perpetually narrowed. Apparently, he had a winning smile, but that was something rarely seen.

Today, like the rest of his team, he wore a decidedly nonmilitary uniform: a rugged caramel-colored canvas jacket, tattered cargo pants and steel-soled Salomon hiking boots that bore the scars of many previous adventures.

His hands were gloved, but if you looked closely at the left cuff of his jacket, you might catch a glimpse of silver steel. Hidden under the sleeve, his entire left forearm and hand were artificial, mechanical. How it came to be that way, not many people knew; although one of those who did was Max Epper.

Expertly trained in the art of war, classically trained in the lore of history, and fiercely protective of the little girl in his care, one thing about Jack West Jr. was clear: if anyone could pull off this impossible mission, it was him.

Just then, with a squawk, a small brown peregrine falcon swooped in from above the treeline and landed lightly on West's shoulder—the high-flying bird from before. It eyed the area around West imperiously, protectively. Its name, Horus.

West didn't even notice the bird. He just stared down into the dark square hole in the mud, lost in thought.

He brushed back some mud from the edge, revealing a hieroglyph cut into the rim:

"We meet again," he said softly to the carving.

He turned. "Glowstick."

He was handed a glowstick, which he cracked and tossed down the hole.

It fell for twenty feet, illuminating a pipelike stone shaft on its way down, before—*splonk!*—it landed in water and revealed—

Lots of crocodiles. Nile crocodiles.

Snapping, snarling, and grunting. Sliding over each other.

"More of Sobek's minions," West said. "Nice. Very nice."

Just then the team's radioman, a tall Jamaican with bleached dreadlocks, a heavily pockmarked face, and tree-trunk-sized arms, touched his earpiece in alarm. His real name was V. J. Weatherly, his original call sign *Witch Doctor,* but everyone here just called him *Fuzzy.*

"Huntsman," he said. "The Europeans just breached the Third Gate. They're inside the Grand Cavern. Now they're bringing in some kind of crane to overshoot the lower levels."

"Shit . . ."

"It gets worse. The Americans just crossed the border. They're coming in fast behind us. Big force: four hundred men, choppers, armor, with carrier-launched fighter support on the way. And the ground force is being led by the CIEF."

That really got West's attention.

The CIEF—the Commander-in-Chief's in Extremis

Force; pronounced "seef"—was America's very best special operations unit; a unit that answered only to the president and possessed the real-life equivalent of a license to kill. In recent years, however, it was said in hushed whispers that the CIEF had been systematically infiltrated by individuals *not* loyal to the president—but rather were servants of a shadowy group of people who operated behind the scenes in Washington, D.C. In any case, as West knew from hard experience, you didn't want to be around when the CIEF arrived.

He stood up. "Who's in command?"

Fuzzy said ominously, "Judah."

"I didn't think he'd come himself. Damn. Now we'd really better hurry."

West turned to his team.

"All right. Noddy—you've got sentry duty. Everybody else . . ."

He pulled an odd-looking helmet from his belt, put it on.

". . . it's time to rock and roll."

And so into the subterranean dark they went.

Fast.

A steel tripod was erected above the pipelike shaft, and, led by West, one after the other, eight of the Nine abseiled down it on a rope strung from the tripod.

One lone man, a dark-haired Spanish commando—once known as *Matador,* now *Noddy*—remained up top to guard the entrance.

THE ENTRY SHAFT

West sizzled down the drop rope, shooting past three steeply slanted cross shafts that intersected with the main shaft.

His falcon sat snugly in a pouch on his chest, while on his head he wore a weathered and worn *fireman's* helmet, bearing the badge FDNY PRECINCT 17. The battered helmet was fitted with a wraparound protective eye visor and on the left side, a powerful pen-sized flashlight. The rest of his team wore similar helmets, variously modified with flashlights, visors, and cameras.

West eyed the cross shafts as he slid down the rope. He knew what perils lay within them. "Everyone. Stay sharp. Do not, I repeat, do not make any contact with the walls of this shaft."

He didn't and they didn't.

Safely, he came to the bottom of the rope.

THE ATRIUM

West emerged from the ceiling at one end of a long, stone-walled room, hanging from his drop-rope.

He did not lower himself all the way to the floor, just kept hanging about eight feet above it.

By the eerie yellow light of his original glowstick, he beheld a rectangular room about 98 feet long. The room's floor was covered by a shallow layer of swamp water, water that was absolutely *crawling* with Nile crocodiles—not an inch of floor-space was crocodile-free.

And directly beneath West, protruding half out of the water, were the waterlogged half-eaten bodies of two twentysomething Sudanese men. The bodies lolled lifelessly as three big crocs took great crunching bites out of them.

"Big Ears," West said into his throat microphone, "there's a sight down here that's not PG-13. Tell Lily not to look down when you two reach the bottom of the rope."

"Righto to that, boss," came an Irish-accented reply over his earpiece.

West fired a luminescent amber flare down the length of the atrium.

It was as if the chamber came alive.

Deeply cut lines of hieroglyphs covered the walls, *thousands* of them.

And at the far end of the chamber, West saw his goal: a squat trapezoidal doorway, raised several feet off the watery floor.

The eerie yellow glow of the flare also revealed one other important feature of the atrium—its ceiling.

Embedded in the ceiling was a line of hand rungs, leading to the far raised doorway. Each rung, however, was lodged in a dark square hole that disappeared up into the ceiling itself.

"Wizard," West said, "I've got hand rungs."

"According to the inscription in Imhotep's tomb, we have to avoid the third and the eighth rungs," Wizard's voice said. *"Drop cages above them. The rest are OK."*

"Gotcha."

The Eight traversed the atrium quickly, swinging hand over hand down the length of the chamber, avoiding the two suspect hand rungs, their feet dangling just a few feet above the crocs.

The little girl—Lily—moved in the middle of the group, clinging to the biggest trooper of the Nine, her hands clasped around his neck, while he swung from rung to rung.

THE LOW TUNNEL

A long low tunnel led away from the atrium, heading into the mountain.

West and his team ran down it, all bent forward. Horus had been set free and she flew out in front of West, gliding down the passageway. Lily ran fully upright.

Water dripped from the low stone ceiling, but it hit their firemen's helmets and rolled off their curved backs, away from their eyes.

The tunnel was perfectly square—1.4 yards wide, 1.4 yards high. Curiously, these were exactly the same dimensions as the passageways inside the Great Pyramid at Giza.

Like the entry shaft earlier, this horizontal tunnel was intersected by three cross shafts: only these were vertical and spanned the entire width of the tunnel, cutting across it via matching holes in the ceiling and floor.

At one point, Lily's guardian, the large trooper named Big Ears, misstepped—landing on a trigger stone just before he leaped across one of the cross shafts.

He knew his mistake immediately and stopped abruptly at the edge of the shaft—

—just as a gushing waterfall of swamp water came blasting out of the upper hole, forming a curtain of water in front of him, before disappearing into the matching hole in the floor.

Had he jumped, the rush of water would have taken him and Lily down into the unknown depths of the lower hole.

"Careful, brother dearest," the team member in front of him said, after the water had passed. She was the only woman in the group and a member of the crack Irish commando unit, the Sciathan Fianoglach an Airm. Old call sign: *Bloody Mary.* New one: *Princess Zoe.* Her brother, Big Ears, was also a member of the SFA.

She reached out and caught his hand and with her help he leaped over the cross shaft, and with Lily between them, they took off after the others.

THE WATER CHAMBER (THE FIRST GATE)

The low tunnel opened onto a chamber the size of a small chapel. Incongruously, the floor of this chamber seemed to be made up of a lush carpet of green grass.

Only it wasn't grass.

It was algae. And beneath the algae, water—a rectangular pool of perfectly flat undisturbed water.

And no crocs. Not a single one.

At the far end of the chamber—beyond the long placid pool, just above the waterline—were three low

THE WATER CHAMBER

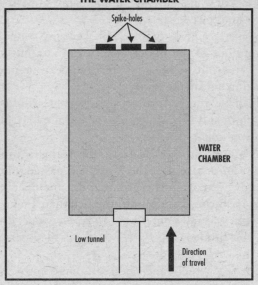

Spike-holes

WATER
CHAMBER

Low tunnel

Direction
of travel

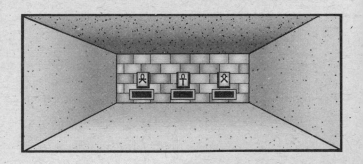

rectangular holes burrowing into the far wall, each roughly the size of a coffin.

An object floated in the pool near the entrance. West recognized it instantly.

A human body. Dead.

The third and last Sudanese man.

Breathless, Wizard came up alongside West. "Ah-ha, the First Gate. Ooh my, how clever. It's a false-floor chamber, just like we saw beneath the volcano in Uganda. Ah, Imhotep V. He always respected the classic traps . . ."

"Max . . ." West said.

"Ooh, and it's connected to a Solomon's Choice of spike holes: three holes, but only one is safe. This is some gate. I bet the ceiling is on rollers—"

"*Max.* You can write a book about it later. The state of the water?"

"Yes, sorry, ahem . . ." Wizard pulled a dipstick from a water-testing kit on his belt and dipped it into the algae-covered pool. Its tip quickly turned a vivid red.

Wizard frowned. "Extremely high levels of the bloodworm *Schistosoma mansoni.* Be careful, my friend, this water is beyond septic. It's teeming with *S. mansoni.*"

"What's that?" Big Ears asked from behind them.

"It's a microscopic bloodworm that penetrates the body through the skin or any exposed orifice, then lays eggs in the bloodstream," West answered.

Wizard added, "Infection leads to spinal cord inflammation, lower-body paralysis, and, ultimately, a cerebral aneurysm and death. Ancient grave robbers went mad after entering places like this. They blamed angry gods and mystical curses, but in all likelihood it was the *S. mansoni*. But at these levels, gosh, this water will kill you in minutes. Whatever you do, Jack, don't fall in."

"OK then," West said, "the jump-stone configuration."

"Right, right." The older man hurriedly pulled out a dog-eared notebook from his jacket pocket, started flipping pages.

A false-floor chamber was a fairly common booby trap in the ancient Egyptian world—mainly because it was very simple to build and exceedingly effective. It worked by concealing a safe pathway of stepping-stones beneath a false layer of liquid—which could be anything really: quicksand, boiling mud, tar, or most commonly, bacteria-infected water.

You defeated a false-floor chamber by knowing the location of the stepping-stones in it.

Wizard found the page he was after. "Okay. Here it is. Soter's Mine. Nubia. First Gate. Water chamber. Ah-ha. Five-by-five grid; the sequence of the jump stones is 1-3-4-1-3."

"1-3-4-1-3," West repeated. "And which spike hole? I'm going to have to choose quickly."

"Key of life," Wizard said, consulting his notebook.

"Thanks. Horus, chest." On command, the falcon immediately whizzed to West's chest and nestled in a pouch there.

West then turned to the assembled group behind him: "Okay, folks, listen up. Everyone is to follow me closely. If our friend Imhotep V follows his usual modus operandi, as soon as I step on the first stepping-stone, things are gonna get frantic. Stay close because we won't have much time."

West turned and contemplated the placid pool of algae-covered water. He bit his lip for a second. Then he took a deep breath.

Then *he jumped out into the chamber,* out over the surface of the pool, angling his leap way out to the left.

It was a long jump—he couldn't have just *stepped* that far.

Watching, Wizard gasped.

But rather than plunging into the deadly water, West landed lightly on the surface of the flat green pool—looking like he was walking on water.

His thick-soled boots stood an inch deep. He was standing on some kind of stepping-stone hidden underneath the algae-covered surface.

Wizard exhaled the breath he'd been holding.

Less obviously, West did, too.

But their relief was short-lived, for at that moment the trap mechanism of the water chamber came loudly and spectacularly to life.

The ceiling started lowering!

The *entire* ceiling of the chamber—a single great block of stone—began rumbling downward, descending toward the flat green pool!

The intention was clear: in about twenty seconds it would reach the waterline and block all access to the three low rectangular holes at the far end of the room.

Which left only one option: leap across the concealed stepping-stones and get to the correct rectangular hole before the lowering ceiling hit the waterline.

"Everyone! Move! Follow me step for step!" West called.

And so, with the ceiling lowering loudly above him, he danced across the chamber with big all-or-nothing jumps, kicking up splashes with every landing. If he misjudged even one stepping-stone, he'd land in the water, and it'd be game over.

His path was dictated by the grid reference Wizard had given him: 1-3-4-1-3, on a five-by-five grid. Which meant it looked like this:

		EXIT		
1	2	3	4	5
1	2	3	4	5
1	2	3	4	5
1	2	3	4	5
1	2	3	4	5
		ENTRY		

Direction
of travel

West reached the far wall of the chamber while his team crossed it behind him. The wide ceiling of the water chamber kept lowering above them all.

West eyed the three rectangular holes cut into the end wall. He'd seen these kind of holes before: they were spike holes.

But only one hole was safe, it led to the next level of the labyrinth. The other two would be fitted with sharp spikes that lanced down from the upper side of the rectangular hole as soon as someone entered them.

Each of the spike holes before him had a symbol carved above it:

Pick the right hole. While the ceiling lowered behind him, about to push his team into the water.

"No pressure, Jack," he said to himself. "Okay. Key of life, key of life . . ."

He saw the symbol above the left-hand hole:

Close, but no. It was the hieroglyph for magic. Imhotep V was trying to confuse the flustered, panicking explorer who found himself in this pressure-filled situation and didn't look closely enough.

"How's it coming, Jack?" Big Ears and the girl appeared beside him, joining him on the last stepping-stone.

The ceiling was low now, past halfway and still descending. No going back. He had to pick the right hole.

"West . . ." someone urged from behind him.

Keeping his cool, West saw the symbol above the center hole . . .

. . . and recognized it as the hieroglyph for *ankh,* or long life, otherwise known to the ancient Egyptians as "the key of life."

"It's this one!" he called.

But there was only one way to prove it.

He pulled his falcon from his pouch and handed it to the little girl. "Hey, kiddo. Take care of Horus for me, just in case I'm wrong."

Then he turned and crouch-dived forward, rolling *into* the center hole, shutting his eyes momentarily, waiting for a half dozen rusty spikes to spring down from its upper side and punch through his body—

—nothing happened.

He'd picked the right hole. Indeed, a tight cylindrical passage opened up in the darkness beyond the hole, bending vertically upward.

"It's this one!" he called back as he started ferrying his team into it, pulling them through.

Big Ears and Lily went first, then Wizard—

The ceiling was four feet off the water's surface.

Fuzzy and Zoe clambered up next.

The final two troopers in West's team rolled into the hole and last of all went West himself, disappearing into the rectangular hole just as the lowering stone ceiling rumbled past him and hit the surface of the water chamber with a resounding *boom*.

THE SLIPWAY AND THE SECOND GATE

The tight vertical passage from the spike hole rose for about forty feet before opening onto a long tunnel that sloped upward at a steep angle, boring up into the heart of the mountain.

West fired a new amber flare up into the tunnel.

It was the ancient slipway.

About the width of a car, the slipway was effectively a long straight stairway flanked by two flat stone trackways that abutted the walls of the tunnel. These trackways had once acted like primitive railway tracks: the ancient miners had slid giant containers filled with

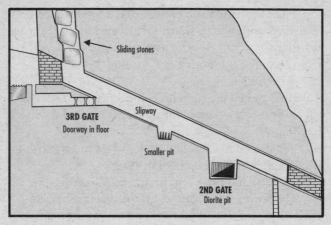

waste up and down them, aided by the hundreds of stone steps that lay in between them.

"Fuzz," West said, peering up the tunnel. "Distance?"

Fuzzy aimed a PAQ-40 laser range finder up into the darkness.

As he did so, West keyed his radio: "Noddy, report."

"The Americans aren't here yet, Huntsman," Noddy's voice replied, *"but they're closing fast. Satellite image puts their advance choppers fifty klicks out. Hurry."*

"Doing the best we can," West said.

Wizard interrupted: "Don't forget to tell Noddy that we'll be out of radio contact for the time the Warblers are initiated."

"You hear that?"

"I heard. Noddy, out."

Fuzzy's range finder beeped. "I got empty space for . . . five hundred feet."

West grimaced. "Why do I get the feeling it isn't empty at all?"

He was right.

The ascending slipway featured several traps: blasting waterfall shafts and some ankle-breaking trap holes.

But the Eight just kept running, avoiding the traps, until halfway up the inclined tunnel they came to the Second Gate.

The Second Gate was simple: a ten-foot-deep diorite pit that just fell away in front of them, with the ascending slipway continuing beyond it five yards away.

The lower reaches of the pit, however, had no *side* walls: it just had two wide yawning eight-foot-high passageways that hit the pit at right angles to the slipway. And who knew what came out of them . . .

"Diorite pit," West said. "Nothing cuts diorite except an even harder stone called *diolite*. Can't use a pickax to get yourself out."

"Be careful," Wizard said. "The Callimachus Text says this Gate is connected to the next one. By crossing this one, we trigger the Third Gate's trap mechanism. We're going to have to move fast."

"That's OK," West said. "We're really quite good at *that.*"

They ended up crossing the pit by drilling steel rock screws into the stone ceiling with pneumatic pressure guns. Each rock screw had a handgrip on it.

But as West landed on the ledge on the other side of the pit, he discovered that the first step on that side of the pit was one large trigger stone. As soon as he touched it, the wide step immediately sank a few inches *into* the floor—

—and *boom!* Suddenly the ground shook and everyone spun. Something large had dropped into the darkened tunnel up ahead of them. Then an ominous *rumbling* sound came from somewhere up there.

"*Shit!* The next Gate!" West called.

"Swear jar . . ." Lily said.

"Later," West said. "Now we *run*! Big Ears, grab her and follow me!"

Up the steep slipway they ran, keeping to the stairs inside the rails.

The ominous rumbling continued to echo out from the darkness above them.

They kept running, straining up the slope, pausing only once to cross a five-foot-long spiked pit that blocked their way. But strangely, the stone railway tracks of the slipway still flanked the pit, so they all crossed it rather easily by taking a light dancing step on one of the side rails.

As he ran, West fired a flare into the darkness ahead of them—

—and thus revealed their menace.

"It's a sliding stone!" Wizard called. "Guarding the Third Gate!"

A giant square-shaped block of granite—its shape filling the slipway perfectly and its leading face covered in vicious spikes—was sliding down the slipway, coming directly toward them!

Its method of death was clear: if it didn't push you into the spiked pit, it would slide over that pit on the stone runners and push you into the lower diorite pit . . . where it would fall in after you, crushing you, before whatever came out of the side passages made its big entrance.

Jesus.

Halfway between the sliding stone and the Eight, sunken into the angled floor of the slipway, was a doorway that opened onto a horizontal passage.

The Third and last Gate.

The Eight bolted up the slope.

The block gained speed—heading down the slope, propelled only by gravity and its immense bulk.

It was a race to the Gate.

West and Big Ears and the girl came to the doorway cut into the sloping floor, ducked inside it.

Wizard came next, followed by Fuzzy and Princess Zoe.

The sliding granite block slid across the top of the doorway just as the last two members of the team were approaching it.

"Stretch! Pooh! Hurry!" West called.

The first man—a tall, thin fellow known as Stretch— dived, slithering in under the sliding stone a nano-second before it completely covered the doorway.

The last man was too late.

He was easily the pudgiest and heaviest in the group. He had the olive skin and deep lush beard of a well-fed Arab sheik. His call sign in his own country was the rather mighty *Saladin,* but here it was—

"Pooh Bear! No! *Nooo!*" the little girl screamed.

The stone slid over the doorway, and despite a final desperate lunge, Pooh Bear was cut off, left in the slipway, at the mercy of the great block.

"No . . . !" West called, hitting the underside of the sliding stone as it went by, sweeping the helpless Pooh away with it.

"Oh dear, poor Zahir . . ." Wizard said.

For a moment, no one spoke.

The seven remaining members of the group stood in stunned silence. Lily started to sob quietly.

Then West blinked—something inside him clicking into action.

"Come on everyone. We've got a job to do and to do it we have to keep moving. We knew this wasn't going to be a cakewalk. Hell, this is only the beginning—"

He turned then, gazing at the horizontal corridor awaiting them. At its far end was a ladder cut into the end wall, a ladder that led up to a circular manhole cut into the ceiling.

White light washed down through the manhole.

Electric light.

Man-made light.

"—and it's about to get a lot worse. 'Cause we just caught up with the Europeans."

THE GRAND CAVERN

West poked his head up through the manhole to behold an absolutely *awesome* sight.

He was at the base of a gargantuan cavern situated right in the belly of the mountain, a cavern easily four hundred feet high.

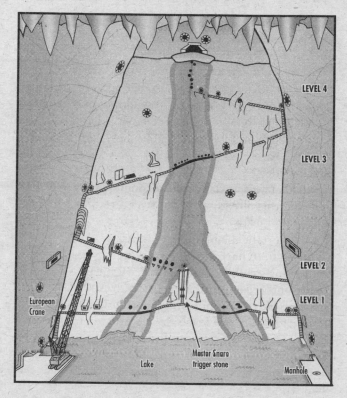

A former rock quarry, it was roughly triangular in shape, wide at the base, tapering to a point at the top.

West was at the extreme south end of the cavern, while opposite him at the northern end, a hundred yards away, were the Europeans: with their floodlights, their troops . . . and a half-built crane.

Without a doubt, however, the most striking feature of the cavern was its charcoal-colored diorite rock face.

The rock face rose for the full height of the cavern,

soaring into darkness beyond the reach of the Europeans' floodlights: a giant black wall.

As a quarry, the ancient Egyptians had mined this diorite seam systematically—cutting four narrow ledges out of the great wall, so that now the rock face looked like a thirty-story office building that had been divided into four steplike tiers. Each ledge ran for the entire width of the rock face, but they were perilously narrow: barely wide enough for two men to stand on side by side.

If that wasn't dangerous enough, Imhotep V had adapted this already-unusual structure into a masterpiece of protective engineering.

In short, he'd laid hundreds of traps all over it.

The four narrow ledges swung back and forth, each rising steadily before ending at a cut-into-the-rock ladder that led to the next level.

The only exception was the wall ladder between the first and second levels: it was situated in the exact center of the cavern, equidistant from the northern and southern entrances, as if Imhotep V was encouraging a race between rival parties who arrived at the same time.

Since each narrow ledge was cut from pure diorite, a grappling hook would be useless—it could never get a purchase on the hard black stone. To get to the top, one had to traverse *every level* and defeat the traps on each of them.

And how many traps there were!

Small arched forts dotted the great wall at irregular intervals, spanning each of the ledges, concealing traps.

Hundreds of basketball-sized wall holes littered the rock face, containing God-only-knew what kinds of lethal liquids. And where holes were not possible, long stone chutes slid snakelike down the rock face—looking a bit like upside-down chimneys that ended with open spouts ready to spew foul liquids over the unwary intruder.

Seeing the holes, West detected the distinctive odor of oil in the air—giving him a clue as to what might come out of some of them.

And there was the final feature.

The Scar.

This was a great uneven crevice that ran all the way down the rock wall, cutting across the ledges and the rock face with indifference. It looked like a dry river-bed, only it ran vertically not horizontally.

At the top of the cavern, it was a single thick crevice, but it widened toward the base, where it forked into two smaller scars.

A trickling waterfall dribbled down its length, from some unknown source high up inside the mountain.

To cross the Scar on any of the four ledges meant either tiptoeing across a foot-wide miniledge or leaping a small void . . . in both cases in front of wall holes or other shadowy recesses.

The trickling waterfall that rolled down the Scar fed a wide lake at the base of the rock face—a lake that now separated West and his team from the European force; a lake that was home to about sixty Nile crocodiles, all variously sleeping, sloshing, or crawling over each other.

And at the very top of the colossal structure: a small stone doorway that led to this mine's fabled treasure.

The head of an ancient wonder.

Peering over the rim of the manhole, West gazed at the Europeans and their half-finished crane.

As he watched, dozens of men hauled more pieces of the giant crane into the cavern, handing them to engineers who then supervised the attachment of the pieces to the growing machine.

In the midst of this activity, West spied the leader of the European expedition, the Jesuit, del Piero, standing perfectly erect, his hands clasped behind his back. At sixty-eight, del Piero had thinning slicked-down black hair, ghostlike gray eyes, deep creases on his face, and the severe expression of a man who had spent his life frowning at people.

But it was the tiny figure standing next to del Piero who seized West's attention.

A small boy.

With black hair and even blacker eyes.

West's eyes widened. He had seen this boy before. Ten years ago . . .

The boy stood at del Piero's side with his hands clasped behind his back, mimicking the imperious stance of the old Jesuit.

He seemed to be about Lily's age.

No, West corrected himself, *he was exactly Lily's age.*

* * *

West's gaze shifted back to the crane.

It was a clever plan.

Once finished, the crane would lift the Europeans up over the first ledge and land them on the second.

Not only did this allow them to avoid about ten traps, it also enabled them to avoid the most dangerous trap of all in this cavern:

The Master Snare.

West knew about it from the Callimachus Text, but del Piero and the Europeans could have become aware of it from other ancient texts written about Imhotep V.

While the other Imhoteps had their own signature traps, Imhotep V had invented the Master Snare, a trap that was triggered in advance of the system's innermost vault—thus making the final leg of the journey a matrix of trap-beating versus time. Or as Wizard liked to say, "Beating booby traps is one thing; beating them against the clock is another."

That said, the Master Snare was not so crude as to *destroy* the entire trap system. Like most of Imhotep's traps, it would reset itself to be used again.

No, in most cases the Master Snare left you in a do-or-die predicament: if you were good enough, you could take the treasure. If you weren't, you would die.

The Callimachus Text stated that the trigger stone for the Master Snare of this system lay in the very center of the first level, at the base of the ladder there.

Wizard appeared at West's side, peered out from the manhole. "Mmm, a crane. With that, del Piero and his men will avoid triggering the Master Snare. It'll give them more time up in the Holy of Holies. Very clever."

"No, it's not clever," West said flatly. "It's against *the rules.*"

"The rules?"

"Yes, the rules. This is all part of a contest that has been held for the last four thousand years, between Egyptian architects and grave robbers. And this contest has an honor code—we attack, Imhotep V defends. But by skipping a major trigger stone, del Piero is cheating. He's also showing his weakness."

"Which is?"

"He doesn't believe he can beat the Master Snare." West smiled. "But we can."

West dropped back down to the base of his ladder, turned to his team of six.

"OK, kids. This is what we've trained for. Leapfrog formation, remember your places. Lily, you're with me in the middle. Fuzzy, you're the point for the first disable. Then Big Ears, Zoe, and Stretch. Wizard, you'll have to cover for Pooh Bear, who was going to cover the fifth. I'll trigger the Master Snare."

Everyone nodded, game faces on.

West turned to Wizard. "OK, Professor. You got those Warblers ready? Because as soon as we break cover, those Europeans are going to open fire."

"Ready to go, Huntsman," Wizard said, holding up a large gunlike object that looked like an M203 grenade launcher. "I'll need maybe four seconds before you can make a break for it."

"I'll give you three."

Then they all put their hands into the middle, team-style, and called *"Kamaté!,"* after which they broke, with Wizard leading the way up the ladder, venturing into the fray . . .

Wizard popped up out of the manhole, his grenade launcher raised. He fired it three times, each shot emitting a loud puncturelike *whump*.

Phump!-Phump!-Phump!

The rounds that burst out of the grenade launcher *looked* like grenades, but they weren't grenades—fat and round and silver, they fanned out to three corners of the giant cavern, little red pilot lights on them blinking.

The Europeans heard the first shot and by the third had located Wizard.

A French sniper on the cabin of the crane swung his rifle round, drew a bead on Wizard's forehead, and fired.

His bullet went haywire.

It peeled downward almost as soon as it left the barrel of the Frenchman's rifle—where it struck an unfortunate croc square in the head, killing it.

The "Warblers" at work.

The three odd-looking silver rounds that Wizard had fired were more formally known as Closed Atmospheric Field Destabilizers (Electromagnetic), but everyone just called them "Warblers."

One of Wizard's rare *military* inventions, the Warblers created a magnetic field that disrupted the flight of high-subsonic metal objects—specifically bullets—creating a gunfire-free zone.

Wizard, one of the leading experts in electromagnetic applications, had sold the revolutionary technology to Raytheon in 1988 for $25 million, most of which went to the New York venture capitalist company that had bankrolled his research. Walking away with only $2 million, Wizard had sworn never again to work with venture capitalists.

Ironically, the U.S. Army—as always, thinking it knew better—ordered Raytheon to rework the Warbler system, creating *huge* problems that had stalled the program for over fifteen years. It had yet to enter active service.

Naturally, Wizard—a Canadian, not an American—had kept a few working prototypes for himself, three of which he was now using.

The Seven burst out from their manhole, one after the other, moving fast, heading for the nearest embedded ladder that led up to the first level.

As he ran at the back of the group, West set Horus free, and the little Peregrine falcon soared above the forward-moving group.

The Jamaican, Fuzzy, led the way—dancing along a narrow stone walkway that lay flush against the right-hand wall of the cavern. Pushed up against the walkway's low edge was a crush of crocodiles.

Fuzzy held in his hands a lightweight titanium bar welded in the shape of an X.

Halfway along its length, the walkway ended briefly at a small void. In the center of this void was a raised square stepping-stone that also stood flush against the wall and an inch above the croc-filled water.

Cut into the stone wall immediately *above* this stepping-stone was a dark hole about a meter in diameter.

Fuzzy didn't miss a beat.

He leaped from the walkway onto the stepping-stone—

—and immediately heard a rush of water from up inside the wall hole, accompanied by a low crocodilian growl—

—at which point he jammed his titanium X-bar into the wall hole and hit a switch on the bar.

Thwack!

The X-shaped bar expanded with a powerful spring-loaded motion, so that suddenly it was wedged tightly in the mouth of the circular wall hole.

Not a second too soon.

An instant later, a burst of water gushed out of the wall hole, immediately followed by the jaws of a massive crocodile that slammed at tremendous speed *into* the X-bar!

The croc roared angrily but its jaws were caught against the X-bar, unable to get past. The rush of water sprayed all around Fuzzy, but didn't knock him over.

"Trap One! Clear!" he called.

The others were already there with him, moving fast, and as Fuzzy kept watch over the writhing croc trapped in the wall hole, they danced safely by.

Now Big Ears went ahead, racing forward to disable the next trap, while the rest of them followed, step-jumping past Fuzzy, heading for the ladder at the base of the giant rock face.

* * *

The Europeans could only watch in helpless amazement as the Seven raced along the opposite wall to the base of the rock face.

Alone among them, Francisco del Piero eyed West—eyed him with an ice-cold gaze; watched him running with Lily at his side, gripping her hand.

"Well, well, well," del Piero said. "Who have you got there, Captain West . . ."

The Seven hit the base of the rock face.

The building-sized wall towered above them, black as the night.

Big Ears had already done his work, disabling two hand-chopping traps halfway up the rock-cut ladder.

Now Princess Zoe leapfrogged ahead. She moved with great athleticism, easily the match of the men. About thirty, she had shoulder-length blond hair, freckles, and the luminous blue eyes that only Irish girls possess.

Onto the first level she flew, raising two aerosol cans as she did so, filling two wall holes with a dense, expanding foam. Whatever evils had been in those wall holes were caught by the foam and neutralized.

No sooner had she done this than she was leapfrogged by the seventh member of the group, the tall, thin trooper named Stretch. Once known as Archer, he had a long, sanguine, bony face. He hailed from the deadly Israeli sniper unit, the Sayeret Matkal.

Stretch arrived at the right-side arm of the Scar,

where he triggered a huge trap from a safe distance: a bronze cage that fell out of a dark recess in the Scar and clattered down to the lake.

Had any of the team been walking on the foot-wide miniledge in front of the recess, the cage would have caught them and taken them down to the lake, either to be eaten by the crocs or drowned under the weight of the cage itself.

Now West and Lily took the lead, crossing the miniledge across the Scar, stepping out onto the center section of the first level.

Here they found the trigger stone for the Master Snare at the base of the wall ladder leading up to Level 2. West made to step on it—

"Captain West!"

West froze in midstride, turned.

Del Piero and his troops were staring up at him from the base of their half-finished crane, holding their useless guns stupidly in their hands.

"Now, Captain West, please think about this before you do it!" Del Piero called. "Is it *really* necessary? Even if you trigger the Master Snare, you are only postponing the inevitable. If you do somehow get the Piece, we'll kill you when you try to leave this mountain. And if you don't, my men will just return after the Snare has run its course and we will find the head of the Colossus and the Piece of the Capstone it contains. Either way, Captain, we get the Piece."

West's eyes narrowed.

Still he didn't speak.

Del Piero tried Wizard. "Max. Max. My old colleague, my old friend. Please. Reason with your rash young protégé."

Wizard just shook his head. "You and I chose different paths a long time ago, Francisco. You do it your way. We'll do it ours. Jack. Hit the trigger."

West just stared evenly down at del Piero.

"With pleasure," he said.

And with that he *stomped* on the trigger stone set into the floor at his feet, activating the Master Snare.

The spectacle of Imhotep's Master Snare going off was sensational.

Blasting streams of black crude oil shot out from the hundreds of holes that dotted the cavern: holes in the rock face and its sidewalls.

Dozens of oil waterfalls flowed down the rock face, cascading over its four levels. Black fluid flooded out from the sidewalls, falling a clear two hundred feet down them into the croc lake.

The crocs went nuts, scrambling over each other to get away from it—disappearing into some little holes in the walls or massing on the far side of the lake.

In some places on the great tiered rock face, oil came *spurting* out of the wall, forced out of small openings by enormous internal pressure.

Worst of all, a *river* of the thick black stuff came pouring down the main course of the Scar, a cascade that tumbled down the vertical riverbed, overwhelming the trickle of water that had been running down it.

And then the clicking started.

The clicking of many stone-striking mechanisms mounted above the wall holes.

Striking mechanisms made of flint.

Striking mechanisms that were designed to create sparks and . . .

Just then, a spark from one of the flints high up on the left sidewall touched the crude oil flowing out from the wall hole an inch beneath it.

The result was stunning.

The superthin waterfall of oil became a superthin waterfall of *fire* . . .

. . . then this flaming waterfall hit the oil-stained lake at the base of the cavern and set it alight.

The lake blazed with flames.

The entire cavern was illuminated bright yellow.

The crocs screamed, clawing over each other to get to safety.

Then more oilfalls caught alight—some on the sidewalls, others on the rock face, and finally, the great sludge waterfall coming down the Scar—until the entire Grand Cavern looked like Hell itself, lit by a multitude of blazing waterfalls.

Thick black smoke billowed everywhere—smoke that had no escape.

This was Imhotep's final masterstroke.

If the fire and the traps didn't kill you, smoke inhalation would, especially in the highly prized upper regions of the cavern.

* * *

"Fools!" Del Piero raged. Then to his men: "What are you standing there for! Finish the crane! You have until they get back to the second level to do so!"

West's team was now moving faster than ever, leapfrogging each other beautifully amid the subterranean inferno.

Up the rock face they went, first to the left along the second level, crossing the left arm of the Scar before the thick fire-waterfall got there, dodging wall holes, jumping gaps in the ledge, nullifying the traps inside the arched forts that straddled the narrow walkway.

Droplets of fire were now raining down all around them—spray from the oilfalls—but the fiery orange drops just hit their firemen's helmets and rolled off their backs.

Then suddenly West's team ran past the unfinished arm of the Europeans' crane and for the first time that day, they were in front.

In the lead in this race.

Up the wall ladder at the end of Level 2, on to Level 3, where they ran to the right, avoiding some chute traps on the way and coming to the fiery body of the Scar. Here West fired an extendable aluminum awning into the Scar's flame-covered surface with his pressure gun.

The awning opened lengthways like a fan, causing the fire-waterfall to flow *over* it, sheltering the miniledge. The team bolted across the superthin ledge.

Then it was up another ladder to the fourth level—

the second-highest level—and suddenly six ten-ton *block boulders* started raining down on them from way up in the darkness above the giant rock face.

The great blocks boomed as they landed on the diorite ledge of Level 4 and tumbled down the rest of the massive tiered wall.

"Get off the ladder!" West yelled to the others. "You can't dodge the boulders if you're on it—"

Too late.

As West called his warning, a boulder smacked horribly into the last man on the ladder, Fuzzy. The big Jamaican was hurled back down the rock face.

He landed heavily on the third level—setting off a trap of spraying flaming oil (it looked like a flame-thrower) but he snap-rolled away from the tongue of fire—in the same motion avoiding a second boulder as it slammed down on the ledge an inch away from his eyes!

His roll took him off the ledge, but Fuzzy managed to clasp onto the edge with his fingertips, avoiding the thirty-foot drop down to Level 2.

The final wall ladder was embedded in the center of the Scar itself, flanked by two fiery waterfalls.

Wizard erected another awning over the miniledge leading to the ladder, then allowed West and Lily to rush past him.

"Remember," Wizard said, "if you can't get the Piece itself, you must at least note the inscription carved into it. OK?"

"Got it." West turned to Lily. "It's just us from here."

They crossed the miniledge, came to the rough stone-carved ladder.

Drops of fire rained down it, bouncing off their firemen's helmets.

Every second or third rung of the ladder featured a dark gaping wall hole of some kind, which West nullified with "expand-and-harden" foam.

"Jack! Look out! More drop stones!" Wizard called.

West looked up. "Whoa shit . . . !"

A giant drop boulder slicked with oil and blazing with flames roared out of a recess in the ceiling directly above the ladder and came free-falling toward him and Lily.

"Swear jar . . ." Lily said.

"I'll have to owe you."

West quickly yanked an odd-looking pistol from his belt—it looked like a flare gun, with a grossly oversize barrel. An M225 handheld grenade launcher.

Without panic, he fired it up at the giant boulder free-falling toward them.

The grenade shot upward.

The boulder fell downward.

Then they hit and—*BOOM!*—the falling boulder exploded in a star-shaped shower of shards and stones, spraying outward like a firecracker, its pieces sailing *out and around* West and Lily on the ladder!

West and Lily scaled the rest of the ladder, flanked by flames, until finally they were standing at the top of the Scar, at the top of the giant rock face, past all the traps.

They stood before the trapezoidal door at the peak of the fire-filled cavern.

"OK, kiddo," he said. "Now it's just you and me. You remember everything we practiced?"

She loved it when he called her kiddo.

"I remember, sir," she said.

And so with a final nod to each other, they entered the holy inner sanctum of Imhotep V's deadly labyrinth.

THE INNERMOST CAVE

And still the traps didn't stop!

A wide low-ceilinged chamber met them: its ceiling was maybe two yards off the floor . . . *and getting lower.*

The chamber was about thirty meters wide and its entire ceiling was lowering! It must have been one single piece of stone and right now it was descending on the dark chamber like a giant hydraulic press.

If they'd had time to browse, West and Lily would have seen that the chamber's walls were *covered* with images of the Great Pyramid—most of them depicting the famous pyramid being pierced by a ray of light shooting down from the Sun.

But it was what lay beyond the entry chamber that seized West's and Lily's attention.

At the far end of the wide entry chamber, in a higher-ceilinged space, stood a giant mud-covered *head.*

The head was absolutely enormous, at least sixteen feet high, almost three times as tall as West.

Despite the layer of mud all over it, its features were stunning: the handsome Greek face, the imperious eyes, and the glorious golden crown fitted above the forehead.

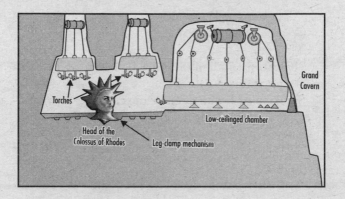

It was the head of a colossal bronze statue.
The most famous bronze statue in history.
It was the head of the Colossus of Rhodes.

Right in front of it, however, separating the great
bronze head from the low-ceilinged entry hall, was a
moat of perfectly calm crude oil that completely surrounded the Colossus's head.

The great god-sized head rose up from this oil
pool like a creature arising from primordial slime. It
sat on no holy pedestal, no ceremonial island, no
nothing.

Suspended *above* the pool was an extra problem:
several flaming torches now blazed above it, lit by
ancient flint-striking mechanisms. They hung from
brackets attached to the end of the entry hall's lowering
ceiling—meaning that very soon they would touch the
oil pool . . . and ignite it . . . cutting off all access to the
Colossus's head.

"Time to run," West said.

"You bet, sir," Lily replied.

They ran.

Down the length of the entry hall, beneath its wide lowering ceiling.

Smoke now began to enter the chamber from outside, creating a choking haze.

They came to the oil moat.

"If Callimachus is correct, it won't be too deep," West said.

Without missing a step, he strode into the pool—plunging to his waist in the thick, goopy oil.

"Jump," he said to Lily, who obliged by leaping into his arms.

They waded across the moat of oil—West striding with Lily on his shoulders—while above them the fiery torches continued their descent toward the pool, the entry hall's ceiling coming ever lower.

With his exit fast diminishing, Jack West Jr. stopped a few yards short of the head of the Colossus of Rhodes.

It towered over him, impassive, covered in centuries of mud.

Each of its eyes was as big as Lily was.

Its nose was as big as he was.

Its golden crown glimmered, while three trapezoidal golden pendants hung from a chain around its neck.

The pendants.

Each was about the size of a fat encyclopedia and trapezoidal in shape. Embedded in the exact center of each pendant's upper surface was a round diamondlike crystal.

On the slanting front side of each pendant was a series of intricately carved symbols: an unknown language that looked kind of like cuneiform.

It was an ancient language, a dangerous language, a language known only to a chosen few.

West gazed at the three golden pendants.

One of them was the Second Piece of the Golden Capstone, the minipyramid that had once sat atop the Great Pyramid at Giza.

Comprised of seven horizontal pieces, the Golden Capstone was perhaps the greatest archaeological artifact in history—and in the last month, it had become the subject of the greatest worldwide treasure hunt of all time. This piece, the Second, was the segment of the Golden Capstone that sat one place below the fabled First Piece, the small pyramid-shaped pinnacle of the Capstone.

Three pendants.

But only one was the correct one.

And choosing the correct one, West knew, was a do-or-die proposition that all depended on Lily.

He had to take one more step forward to reach them and that meant triggering the final trap.

"OK, kiddo. You ready to do your thing? For my sake, I hope you are."

"I'm ready," Lily said grimly.

And with that, West stepped forward and—

—*chunk!*—

—an unseen mechanism *beneath* the surface of the oil pool clamped tightly around his legs, pinning them in an ancient pair of submerged stone stocks.

West was now immobile . . . within easy reach of the three pendants.

"OK, Lily," he said. "Go. Make your choice. And stay off me, just in case you're wrong."

She leaped from his arms, onto the half-submerged collarbone of the great statue just as—

Whoosh!

A huge ten-ton drop stone *directly above* West came alight with flames and . . . lurched on its chains!

Imhotep V's final trap in the quarry mine was what is known as a "reward trap." It allowed the rightful claimant to the Second Piece to have it, *if* they could identify the correct one.

Choose the right "pendant" and the flaming drop stone remained in place and the submerged leg clamps opened. Choose the wrong one, and the drop stone fell, crushing you *and* igniting the oil pool.

Lily stared at the strange text on each pendant. It looked extremely odd, this little girl evaluating the incredibly ancient symbols.

West watched her, tense, expectant . . . and suddenly worried.

"Can you read it?" he asked.

"It's different from the other inscriptions I've read . . ." she said distractedly.

"What—?" West blanched.

Abruptly Lily's eyes lit up in understanding. "Ahh, I get it. Some of the words are written *vertically*."

Then her eyes narrowed . . . and focused. They blazed in the firelight, scanning the ancient symbols closely now.

To West, it seemed as if she had just entered a trancelike state.

Then the flaming drop stone above him creaked again. He snapped to look up.

The torch-riddled ceiling above the moat kept lowering.

Smoke was now billowing into this area from the main cavern.

West swiveled to see the entry chamber behind him getting smaller and smaller . . .

Lily was still in her trance, reading the runes intently.

"Lily . . ."

"Just a second . . ."

"We don't have a second, honey." He eyed the hazy smoke-filled chamber closing behind them. The smoke was getting denser.

Then, abruptly, one of the flaming torches attached to the descending ceiling dislodged from its bracket . . .

. . . and fell.

Down toward the oil moat where West stood helpless!

"Oh, God no—" was all he had time to breathe.

The flaming torch dropped through the air, into the oil moat—

—before, six inches off the surface, it was plucked from the air by the swooping shape of Horus, his falcon.

The little bird gripped the flaming torch in its talons, before it dropped it safely in the closing entry hall.

"Why don't you leave it to the last second next time, bird," West said.

Sitting now, Horus just returned his gaze, as if to say: *Why don't you stop getting into stupid predicaments like this, human.*

In the meantime, Lily's eyes glinted, staring now at the symbols on the rightmost of the three pendants:

She read in a low voice:

"Beware. Atone.
Ra's implacable Destroyer cometh,
And all will cry out in despair,
Unless sacred words be uttered."

Rama
Rath

Then Lily blinked and returned to the present.

"It's this one!" she said, reaching down for the pendant she had just read.

West said, "Wait, are you sure—"

But she moved too quickly and lifted the golden pendant from its shallow recess on the Colossus's neck.

The flaming drop stone lurched.

West snapped up and winced, waiting for the end.

But the drop stone didn't fall and—*chunk!*—suddenly his legs were released from their submerged bonds.

Lily had picked the right one.

She jumped happily back into his arms, holding the

heavy golden trapezoid like a newborn baby. She threw him a winning smile.

"That felt really weird."

"It looked really weird," West said. "Well done, kiddo. Now, let's blow this joint."

THE OUTWARD CHARGE

Back they ran.

West charged through the waist-deep oil pool, pushing hard with every stride, the torch-edged ceiling lowering above him.

They hit the floor of the entry hall as the lowering ceiling hit three feet in height.

The smoke coming in from outside was now choking, dense.

Lily crouch-ran across the wide low-ceilinged space, while Horus swooped through the haze.

West was the slowest, scrambling on all fours, slipping every which way in his oil-slicked boots, until at the very end of the chamber, as the ceiling became unbearably low, he dived onto his belly, sliding headfirst for the entire last four meters, emerging just as the ceiling hit the floor with a resounding *boom* and closed off the Colossus's chamber.

Wizard was waiting for them outside on Level 4.

"Hurry! Del Piero's men have almost finished their crane—they'll be on Level 2 any second now!"

LEVEL 4

The other members of the team—Big Ears, Stretch,

and Princess Zoe—were waiting on Level 4, covering the first three traps on the way back down.

When he reached them, West handed Big Ears the priceless golden trapezoid, which the big man placed inside a sturdy backpack.

Down the giant rock wall they went, again in leapfrog formation, sliding down ladders, dancing across booby-trapped ledges, all the while dodging flaming waterfalls and fire-rain. Giant drop stones now fell constantly from the upper regions of the cave, tumbling dangerously down the rock face, blasting through the smoke.

LEVEL 3

West scooped up Fuzzy as they came to the third level. "Come on, old friend," he said, hoisting the big Jamaican onto his shoulder.

They ran down the sloping ledgeway, across the face of the third level, covering their mouths to avoid inhaling the smoke.

The Europeans had almost finished their crane by now. It was lined with armed men, all waiting for the last piece of the crane to be screwed into place, thus giving them access to the second level—where they would cut off West and his team.

The last piece of the crane fell into place.

The Europeans moved.

LEVEL 2

West led the way now, leaping down onto Level 2 ahead of Fuzzy, where he landed like a cat—

—and was confronted by a crossbow-wielding French paratrooper, the first member of the European force to step off the now-finished crane.

Quick as a gunslinger, West drew a Glock pistol from one of his thigh holsters, raised it and fired it at the French trooper at point-blank range.

And for some reason *his* bullet defied Wizard's Warblers and slammed into the Frenchman's chest, dropping him where he stood.

No blood sprayed.

In fact, the man didn't die.

Rubber bullet.

West fired another rubber round—similar to those used by police in riot situations—at the next French paratrooper on the nearby crane, just as the Frenchman pulled the trigger on his crossbow.

West ducked and the arrow bolt missed high, while his own shot hit its mark, sending the French commando sailing off the crane and into the lake below, still crowded with panicking crocodiles.

Screams. Splashing. Crunching. Blood.

"Move!" West called to his crew. "Before they switch to rubber rounds, too."

Now everyone in his team had their guns drawn and as they passed the crane's arm, they traded shots with the two dozen French paratroopers on it.

But they got past the crane just as fifteen French

paratroopers came streaming off it, and headed down
to Level 1—

LEVEL 1

—where they saw the Europeans' *second* effort to cut
them off.

Down on the ground level, a team of German
Army engineers had almost finished building a temporary floating bridge across the croc lake—in an attempt
to get to West's manhole entrance on the southern side
of the cavern before West and his team did.

They had two segments of the bridge to put in
place, segments that were being brought across the
half-finished bridge at that very moment.

"Go! Go! Go!" West called.

The flaming cavern—already alive with smoke
and flames and falling boulders—was now zinging
with crossbow bolts and rubber bullets.

The aluminum crossbow bolts were only mildly af-
fected by the Warblers—they flew wildly, but their first
few meters of flight were still deadly.

West's team were running across Level 1, racing the
bridge-builders on the ground level.

Big Ears carried Lily. West helped Fuzzy. Princess
Zoe and Stretch fired at the paratroopers behind them,
while Wizard—coughing against the smoke—led the
way, nullifying the traps ahead of them. Above them,
Horus soared through the hazy black air.

They had just reached the ladder at the far right-
hand end of Level 1 when suddenly a stray French

crossbow bolt hit Big Ears in the shoulderblade, knocking him off his feet—causing him to stumble forward onto his face and . . .

. . . fall off the edge of the ledge, dropping Lily over it!

Lily fell.

Thirty feet.

Into the oily water near the base of the ladder, not far from the walkway that hugged the right-hand wall of the cavern.

By chance she landed in both a croc-free and a fire-free space.

But not for long. The crocs weren't far away, and no sooner had her splash subsided than a large one saw her and charged straight for her.

Big Ears was dangling over the edge of Level 1 directly above her, helpless. "I can't get to her!"

"I can!" another voice called.

West.

He never missed a step.

Running full tilt, he just leaped off the edge of Level 1 and sailed in a high, curving arc through the air toward the croc lake below.

The big bull croc that was charging at Lily never saw him coming. West landed square on its back, a mere foot away from Lily, and the two of them—man and croc—went under the black water's surface with a great splash.

They surfaced a second later, with the frenzied croc bucking like a bronco and West on its back, gripping it in a fierce headlock.

The croc growled and roared, before—*crrrrack*—

West brutally twisted its neck, breaking it. The croc went limp. West jumped clear, whisking Lily out of the water and onto the walkway flanking the lake not a moment before six more crocs attacked the carcass of the dead one.

"Th . . . thanks," Lily gasped, wiping oil from her facc and still shaking.

"Anytime, kiddo. Anytime."

GROUND LEVEL

The rest of the team joined them on the walkway.

Now Fuzzy *and* Big Ears were injured. But they were still mobile, helped along by Zoe and Wizard, while West and Lily were covered by Stretch.

They all hopscotched over the stepping-stone and its wall hole—inside which the trapped croc still writhed behind Fuzzy's X-bar—and dashed for their manhole, just as thc German engineers brought the final piece of their temporary bridge into place.

Forty armed German troops waited for the bridge to be completed. Some fired wayward crossbow shots at the Seven, while others jammed newly found rubber-bullet magazines into their MP7 submachine guns and started firing.

West and Lily came to the manhole. In they went. The others followed, while Stretch covered them all. Big Ears went in . . . then Fuzzy . . . Wizard . . . Zoe and . . .

. . . the final piece of the bridge fell into place . . .

. . . as Stretch jumped into the manhole and the army of Germans charged over the bridge and the chase through the slipway system began.

THE ANTECHAMBER (OUTWARD BOUND)

Being the last person in a retreating formation sucks. You're covering the rear, the bad guys are right on your ass, and no matter how loyal your team is, there's always the risk of being left behind.

By the time the tall and lanky Stretch had landed in the long antechamber beneath the manhole, the others were already entering the slipway at the far end.

"Stretch! Move it!" West called from the slanted doorway. "Zoe's gone ahead to trigger another sliding stone to run interference for us!"

As if to confirm that, a familiar *whump* echoed out from the upper regions of the slipway, followed by the rumble of a new sliding stone grinding down the slope.

Stretch bolted toward the slipway—as a dozen wraithlike figures rained down the manhole behind him, entering the antechamber.

Gunfire.

Rapid-fire.

Freed from the effects of the Warblers, the Europeans were now gladly employing live ammunition.

Stretch was done for.

He was still five steps away from the safety of the slipway when the first few Germans behind him went down in a hail of withering fire.

For just as they had fired, so too had someone else, someone standing guard in the doorway to the slipway.

Pooh Bear.

Holding a Steyr AUG assault rifle.

The heavy-bearded Arab—who had last been seen getting cut off behind the previous sliding stone—waved Stretch on.

"Come on, Israeli!" Pooh Bear growled. "Or I'll gladly leave you behind!"

Stretch staggered the last few steps into the slipway and past Pooh Bear just as a dozen bullet sparks exploded out all around the stone doorway.

"I thought you were dead," Stretch said, panting.

"Please! It'll take more than a *rock* to kill Zahir al Anzar al Abbas," Pooh Bear said in his deep gruff voice. "My legs may be stout, but they can still run with some speed. I simply outran the rock and took cover in that spiked pit, and let it pass over me. Now move!"

THE SLIPWAY

Down the slipway the Eight ran, dancing around the edge of the small spiked pit—the air filled with the rumble of the new sliding stone—then over the diorite pit that was the Second Gate. The cracked and broken remains of the first sliding stone from before lay strewn about its base.

The Eight swung over the diorite pit, hanging from the steel handholds they'd drilled into the rock ceiling earlier.

"Noddy!" West called into his radio mike when he landed safely on the other side. "Do you copy?"

There was no answer from Noddy, their man guarding the swamp entrance.

"It's not the Warblers!" Wizard called. "There must be someone jamming us—"

He was cut off by six Germans who raced into the slipway and opened fire—

—not a moment before the large spike-riddled sliding stone loomed up behind them, rumbling over the doorway to the antechamber!

The six Germans ran down the slipway, chased by the sliding stone.

When they came to the spiked pit, one panicked and lost his balance and fell in, chest first—impaling himself on the vicious spikes sticking up from the stone pit.

The others got to the larger diorite pit of the Second Gate too late.

Two managed to grip West's steel handholds for a couple of swings before all five of the remaining German troops were either impaled on the spikes on the leading edge of the sliding stone or jumped into the diorite pit to avoid those spikes just as—*whoosh!*—a blast of churning white water shot across the pit, sweeping them away, screaming.

West's team raced ahead now. The sliding stone had given them the lead they needed.

Having been blocked off momentarily behind it, and having not experienced the slipway before, the remainder of the German troops were more cautious.

West's team increased their lead.

They swept down the tight vertical shaft to the spike hole where West had correctly chosen the Key of

Life, the ceiling of the Water Chamber having reset itself . . .

Still no radio contact with Noddy.

Across the Water Chamber, its stepping-stones still submerged beneath the algae-covered pool . . .

Still no radio contact.

Crouch-running down the length of the low tunnel, leaping over its cross shafts . . .

And finally they came to the croc-filled atrium with its hand rungs in the ceiling and the vertical entry shaft at its far end.

"Noddy! Are you out there?" West called into his radio. "I repeat, Noddy, can you hear me—"

Finally, he got a reply.

"Huntsman! Hurry!" Noddy's Spanish-accented voice replied suddenly in his earpiece, loud and hard. *"Get out! Get out now! The Americans are here!"*

Two minutes later, West emerged from the vertical entry shaft and found himself once again standing in the mud of the mountain swamp.

Noddy was waiting for him, visibly agitated, looking anxiously westward. "Hurry, hurry!" he said. "They're coming—"

Shlat!

Noddy's head exploded, bursting like a smashed pumpkin, hit by a high-speed .50 caliber sniper round. His body froze for a brief moment before it dropped to the ground with a dull smack.

West snapped to look westward.

And he saw them.

Saw two dozen high-speed swampboats sweeping out of the reeds some 300 yards away, covered by two Apache helicopters. Each swampboat held maybe ten special forces troops, members of the CIEF.

Then suddenly on one of them the muzzle of a Barrett sniper rifle flashed—

—West ducked—

—and a split second later the bullet sizzled past his ears.

"Get Stretch up here!" he yelled, as his team emerged from the hole in the mud.

Stretch was pushed up.

"Give me some sniping, Stretch," West said. "Enough to get us out of here."

Stretch pulled a vicious-looking Barrett M82A1A sniper rifle off his back, took a crouching pose, and fired back at the American hovercraft.

Crack. Sizzle.

And 200 yards away, the American sniper was hurled clear off his speeding swampboat, his head snapping backward in a puff of red.

Everybody was now up and out of the hole.

"Right," West said. "We make for our swamprunners. Triple time."

The Eight raced across the swamp, once again running on foot through the world of mud.

They came to their swampboats, hidden in a small glade, covered by camouflage netting.

Their two boats were known as "swamprunners," shallow-draft, flat-bottomed, steel-hulled boats with giant fans at their sterns, capable of swift speeds across swamps of unpredictable depth.

West led the way.

He jumped onto the first swamprunner and helped the others on after him.

When everyone was on board the two boats, he turned to grab the engine cord—

"Hold it *right there,* partner," an ice-cold voice commanded.

West froze.

They came out of the reeds like silent shadows, guns up.

Eighteen mud-camouflaged CIEF specialists, all with Colt Commando assault rifles—the lighter, more compact version of the M16—and dark-painted faces.

West scowled inwardly.

Of course the Americans had sent in a *second* squad from the south, just in case—hell, they'd probably found his boats by doing a satellite scan of the swamp, then just sent this squad, which had just come out and waited.

"Damn it . . ." he breathed.

The leader of the CIEF team stepped forward.

"Well would you look at that. If it isn't *Jack West* . . ." he said. "I haven't seen you since Iraq in '91. You know, West, I still don't know how you got away from that Scud base outside Basra. There musta been three hundred Republican Guards at that facility and yet you got away—*and* managed to destroy all those mobile launchers."

"I'm just lucky, I guess, Cal," West said evenly.

The CIEF leader's name was Sergeant Cal Kallis and he was the worst kind of CIEF operative: an assassin who liked his job. Formerly from Delta, Kallis was a grade-A psycho. Still, he wasn't Judah, which meant West still held out a hope of getting out of there alive.

At first Kallis completely ignored West's comment. He just whispered into a throat mike: "CIEF Command. This is Sweeper 2-6. We're a klick due south of the mountain. We got 'em. Sending you our position now."

Then he turned to West, and spoke as if their conversation had never been interrupted:

"You ain't lucky anymore," he said slowly. Kallis

had cold black eyes—eyes that were devoid of pity or emotion. "I got orders that amount to a hunting license, West. Leave no bodies. Leave no witnesses. Something about a piece of gold, a very valuable piece of gold. Hand it over."

"You know, Cal, when we worked together, I always thought you were a reasonable guy—"

Kallis cocked his gun next to Princess Zoe's head. "No you didn't and no I wasn't. You thought I was 'a cold-blooded psychopath'—they showed me the report you wrote. The Piece, West, or her brains learn how to fly."

"Big Ears," West said, "give it to him."

Big Ears unslung his backpack, threw it into the mud at Kallis's feet.

The CIEF assassin opened it with his foot, saw the glistening golden trapezoid inside.

And he smiled.

Into his throat mike, he said: "Command. This is Sweeper 2-6. We have the prize. Repeat, we have the prize."

As if on cue, at that moment two U.S. Apache helicopters boomed into identical hovers in the air above West and his team.

The air shook. The surrounding reeds were blown flat.

One chopper lowered a harness, while the other stood guard, facing outward.

Kallis attached the pack holding the Piece to the harness. It was winched up, and that helicopter quickly zoomed off.

Once it was gone, Kallis touched his earpiece, getting some new instructions. He turned to West . . . and grinned an evil grin.

"Colonel Judah sends his regards, West. Seems he'd like to have a word with you. I've been instructed to bring you in. Sadly, everybody else dies."

Quick as a rattlesnake, Kallis then reasserted his aim at Princess Zoe and squeezed the trigger—just as the remaining Apache helicopter above him exploded in a fireball and dropped out of the sky, hit by a Hellfire missile from . . .

. . . the Europeans' Tiger attack helicopter.

The charred remains of the Apache smashed to the ground right behind the ring of CIEF troops—crashing in a heap, creating a giant splash of swampwater—in the process scattering the CIEF men as they dived out of the way.

The Tiger didn't hang around—it shot off after the other Apache, the one with the Piece of the Capstone in it.

But its missile shot had done enough for West.

Principally, it allowed Princess Zoe to leap clear of Kallis and dive onto the nearest swamprunner just as West started it up and yelled: "Everybody out! Now!"

His team didn't need to be told twice.

While the Delta men around them clambered back to their feet and fired vainly after them, West's two swamprunners burst off the mark and disappeared at speed into the high reeds of the swamp.

Kallis and his men jumped into their nearby swampboats—four of them—and gunned the engines.

Kallis keyed his radio, reported what had happened to his bosses, finishing with: "What about West?"

The voice at the other end was cold and hard, and the instructions it gave were exceedingly odd: "You may do whatever you want with the others, Sergeant, but Jack West and the girl must be allowed to escape."

"Escape?" Kallis frowned.

"Yes, Sergeant. Escape. Is that clear?"

"Crystal clear, sir. Whatever you say," Kallis replied.

His boats roared into action.

West's two swamprunners skimmed across the swamp at phenomenal speed, banking and weaving, propelled by their huge turbofans.

West drove the lead one; Stretch drove the second.

Behind them raced Kallis's four swampboats, bigger and heavier, but tougher—the men on their bows firing hard.

West was making for the far southern end of the swamp, twelve miles away, where a crumbling old road had been built along the shore of the vast water field.

It wasn't a big road, just two lanes, but it was made of asphalt, which was crucial.

"Sky Monster!" West shouted into his radio mike. "Where are you!"

"Still in a holding pattern behind the mountains, Huntsman. What can I do for you?" came the reply.

"We need exfil, Sky Monster! Now!"

"Hot?"

"As always. You know that paved road we pinpointed earlier as a possible extraction point?"

"The really tiny potholed piece-of-shit road? Big enough to fit two Mini Coopers side by side?"

"Yeah, that one. We're also going to need the pickup hook. What do you say, Sky Monster?"

"Give me something hard next time, Huntsman. How long till you get there?"

"Give us ten minutes."

"Done. The Halicarnassus *is on its way."*

The two swamprunners blasted across the water field, ducking the constant fire from the four pursuing CIEF swampboats.

Then suddenly, geyser explosions of water started erupting all around West's boats.

Kallis and his team had started using mortars.

Bending and banking, West's swamprunners weaved away from the explosions—which actually all fell a fraction short—until suddenly the road came into view.

It ran in an east-to-west direction across the southern edge of the swamp, an old blacktop that led inland to Khartoum. Like many of the roads in eastern Sudan, it actually wasn't that bad, having been built by the Saudi terrorists who had once called these mountains home, among them a civil engineer named Bin Laden.

West saw the road, and risked a smile. They were going to make it . . .

At which moment, three more American Apache helicopters arrived, roaring across his path, shredding the water all around his boats with blazing minigun fire.

The Apaches rained hell on West's two boats.

Bullets ripped up the water all round them as the boats sped through the swamp.

"Keep going! Keep going!" West yelled to his people. "Sky Monster is on the way!"

But then fire from one of the Apaches hit Stretch's turbofan. Smoke billowed, the fan clattered, and the second swamprunner slowed.

West saw it instantly—and knew what he had to do.

He pulled in alongside Stretch's boat and called: "Jump over!"

A quick transfer took place, with Stretch, Pooh Bear, Fuzzy, and Wizard all leaping over onto West's swamprunner—the last of them, Wizard, leaping across a split second before one of the Apaches let fly with a Hellfire missile and the second swamprunner was blown out of the water, disappearing in a towering geyser of spray.

Amid all this mayhem, West kept scanning the sky above the mountains—and suddenly he saw it.

Saw the black dot descending toward the little road.

A black dot that morphed into a birdlike shape, then a planelike shape, then finally it came into focus and it was revealed to be a huge aircraft.

It was a Boeing 747, but the most bizarre 747 you would ever see.

Once upon a time, it had been a cargo plane of some sort, with a rear loading ramp and no side windows.

Now it was painted entirely in black, dull black, and it bristled with irregular protrusions that had been added to it: radar domes, missile pods, and most irregularly of all: revolving gun turrets.

There were four of them—one on its domed roof, one on its underbelly, and two nestled on its flanks, where the plane's wings met its fuselage—each turret armed with a fearsome six-barreled Gatling minigun.

It was the *Halicarnassus*. West's very own plane.

With a colossal roar, the great black jumbo jet swooped downward, angling for the tiny road that bordered the swamp.

Now with all eight of his people on one swamprunner, West needed help, and the *Halicarnassus* was about to provide it.

Two missiles lanced out from its belly pods, missing one Apache by inches, but hitting the one behind it.

Boom. Fireball.

Then the great plane's underside minigun blazed to life, sending a thousand tracer rounds sizzling through the air all around the third Apache, giving it the choice of either bugging out or dying. It bugged out.

West's lone swamprunner swept alongside the straight roadway, raced parallel to it. The road was elevated a couple of feet above the water, up a low, gently sloping bank.

At the same moment, above and behind West's boat, the big 747 *landed* on the little country road!

Its wheels hit the road, squealing briefly before rolling forward with its outer tires half off the road's

edges. The big jet then taxied down the roadway—
coming alongside West's skimming swamprunner, its
wings stretching out over the waters of the swamp.

The *Halicarnassus* was coasting, rolling.

West's boat was speeding as fast as it could to
keep up.

Then with a bang, the loading ramp at the back of
the 747 dropped open, slammed down against the roadway behind the speeding plane.

A second later, a long cable bearing a large hook at
its end came snaking out of the now-open cargo hold. It
was a retrieval cable, normally used to snag weather
balloons.

"What are you going to do now, my friend!" Pooh
Bear yelled to West above the wind.

"This!"

As West spoke, he jammed his steering levers hard
left, and the swamprunner swept leftward, bouncing
up the riverbank *and out of the water,* dry-sliding on its
flat-bottomed hull onto the bitumen road close behind
the rolling 747!

It was an incredible sight: a big black 747 rolling
along a country road, with a *boat* skidding and sliding
along the road right behind it.

West saw the loading ramp of the plane, very close
now, just a few yards in front of his sliding boat. He also
saw the slithering retrieval cable bumping and bouncing on the road right in front of him.

"Stretch! The cable! Snag it!"

At the bow of the dry-sliding swamprunner, Stretch
used a long snagging pole to reach out and grab the
retrieval cable's hook. He got it.

"Hook us up!" West yelled.

Stretch did so, latching the cable's hook around the boat's bow.

And suddenly—*whap!*—the swamprunner was yanked forward, pulled along by the giant 747!

Dragged now by the *Halicarnassus,* the swamprunner looked like a water-skier being pulled by a speedboat.

West yelled into his radio, "Sky Monster! Reel us in!"

Sky Monster initiated the plane's internal cable spooler, and now the swamprunner began to move gradually forward, hauled in by the cable, pulled closer and closer to the loading ramp.

While this was going on, the 747's belly-mounted gun turret continued to swing left and right, raining hell on Kallis's pursuing swampboats and the two remaining Apaches, keeping them at bay.

At last, West's swamprunner came to the loading ramp. West and Pooh Bear grabbed the ramp's struts, held the boat steady.

"OK everyone! All aboard!" West yelled.

One after the other, his team leaped from the swamprunner onto the lowered loading ramp— Wizard with Lily, then Zoe helping Fuzzy, Stretch helping Big Ears, and finally Pooh Bear and West himself.

Once West had landed on the loading ramp, he unhooked the swamprunner and the boat fell away behind the speeding 747, tumbling end over end down the little black road.

Then the loading ramp lifted and closed, and the 747 powered up and pulled away from the American

Apaches and swampboats. It hit takeoff speed and rose smoothly into the air.

Safe.

Clear.

Away.

The *Halicarnassus* flew south over the vast Ethiopian highlands.

While the others collapsed in the plane's large main cabin, West went straight up to the cockpit where he found the plane's pilot: a great big hairy-bearded New Zealand Air Force pilot known as *Sky Monster*. Unlike the others in the group, this had actually been his call sign *before* he'd joined the team.

West gazed out at the landscape receding into the distance behind them—the swamp, the mountain, the vast plains beyond it—and thought about del Piero's Europeans engaging the superior American force. Del Piero would have little luck.

The Americans, as always the last to arrive but the greatest in brute force, had allowed West and the Europeans to squabble over the Piece, to lose men finding it, and then like opportunistic lions, they'd muscled in on the hyenas and taken the prize.

And as the *Halicarnassus* soared into the sky away from the danger, West gazed at the large American force now gathered at the western edge of the swamp.

A disquieting thought lingered in his mind.

How had the Americans even known about this place?

The Europeans had a copy of the Callimachus Text, and of course, they had the boy. But the Americans, so far as West knew, had neither.

Which meant there was no way they could have

known that this was the resting place of the Colossus of Rhodes.

West frowned.

Was his team's cover blown? Had the Americans discovered their base and followed them here? Or worse: was there a traitor in his team who had given their position away with a tracing beacon?

In any case, Judah now knew that West was involved in this treasure hunt. He might not know exactly who West was working for, but he knew West was involved.

Which meant that things were about to get very intense.

Safe at last, but without their prize, West's plane sped away to the south, disappearing over the mountains.

Exhausted, dirty, and saddened by the loss of Noddy— the Spaniard had been a loyal team member—West retired to a small bunkroom in the aft section of the plane.

He collapsed into his bunk and no sooner had his head hit the pillow than he was asleep.

He slept deeply, his dreams filled with vivid visions—of booby-trapped chambers, stone altars, chants and screams, waterfalls of lava, and of himself running frantically through it all.

The interesting thing was, these dreams weren't the product of West's imagination.

They had actually happened, ten years previously . . .

THE
VOLCANO

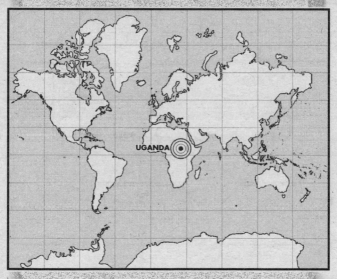

NORTHEASTERN UGANDA
MARCH 20, 1996
TEN YEARS EARLIER

THE BIRTHING CHAMBER
KANYAMANAGA VOLCANO, UGANDA

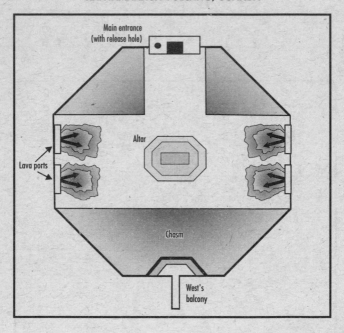

INSIDE THE KANYAMANAGA VOLCANO
UGANDA, AFRICA
MARCH 20, 1996, 11:47 A.M.

The images of West's dreams:

West running desperately down an ancient stone passageway with Wizard at his side, toward the sounds of booming drums, chanting, and a woman's terrified screams.

It's hot.

Hot as hell.

And since it's inside a volcano, it even *looks like* Hell.

It is just the two of them—plus Horus of course. The team does not even exist at this time.

Their clothes are covered in mud and tar—they've survived a long and arduous path to get here. West wears his fireman's helmet and thick-soled army boots. Ten years younger, at age twenty-seven, he is more idealistic but no less intense. His eyes are narrow, focused. And his left arm is his own.

Boom-boom-boom! go the drums.

The chanting increases.

The woman's screams cut the air.

"We must hurry!" Wizard urges. "They've started the ritual!"

They pass through several booby-trapped passageways—each of which West neutralizes.

A spray of sticky foam into a stiletto-firing wall trap.

Ten disease-carrying molossid bats burst forth from

a dark ceiling recess, fangs bared—only to have Horus launch herself off West's shoulder and plunge into their midst, talons raised. A thudding midair collision. Squeals and shrieks. Two bats smack down against the floor, brought down by the little falcon.

That splits the bats and the two men dash through them, Horus catching up moments later.

Then a false floor threshold chamber.

It's just like the one in the Sudan, only instead of green algae-covered water concealing the stepping-stones, here it is a pool of steaming-hot water—warmed from below by geothermal vents.

But Wizard has the jump-stone configuration and West crosses the chamber quickly, his thick-soled boots splashing on the steaming surface.

He's confronted by a long downward-sloping shaft. It's like a hundred-yard-long stone pipe, steeply slanted, big enough for him to fit if he sits down.

Boom go the drums.

The evil chanting is close now.

The woman's frenzied screams are like nothing he has ever heard: pained, desperate, primal.

West shoots a look to Wizard, still balancing his way across the water chamber.

The older man waves him on. "Go! Jack! Go! Get to her! I'll catch up!"

West leaps feet-first into the pipe shaft and slides fast.

Five traps later, he emerges from the bottom of the long stone pipe on . . .

. . . a balcony of some kind.

A balcony that overlooks a large ceremonial cavern.

He peers out from the balcony's railing and beholds the horrifying sight.

The woman lies spread-eagled on a rough stone altar, tied down, legs spread wide, writhing and struggling, *terrified*.

She is surrounded by about twenty priestlike figures all wearing hooded black robes and fearsome jackal masks of the Egyptian god Anubis.

Six of the priests pound on huge lion-skin drums.

The rest chant in a strange language.

Incongruously, surrounding the circle of robed priests, all facing outward, are sixteen paratroopers in full battle-dress uniforms. They are French, all brandishing ugly FN-MAG assault rifles, and their eyes are deadly.

Beyond all this, the chamber itself catches West's attention.

Cut into the very flesh of the volcano, it branches off the volcano's glowing red core and is octagonal in shape.

It is also ancient—very ancient.

Every surface is flat. The stone walls are so perfectly cut they look almost alien. Sharp-edged rectangular pipe holes protrude from the sidewalls.

Hieroglyphics cover the walls. In giant letters above the main door, the biggest carving reads:

"Enter the embrace of Anubis willingly, and you shall live beyond the coming of Ra. Enter against your will, and your people shall rule for but one eon, but you shall

live no more. Enter not at all, and the world shall be no more."

Interestingly, the raised pattern on the high ceiling exactly matches the indentations on the floor fifty feet below.

The ceiling also features a tiny vertical shaft bored into it—in the exact center, directly above the altar.

This ultranarrow vertical shaft must reach all the way to the surface because right now, a beam of noon-day sunlight—perfectly vertical, laser-thin, and dazzlingly bright—shines down through the tiny hole, hitting . . .

. . . the altar on which the woman lies.

And one other thing:

The woman is pregnant.

More than that.

She is in the process of giving birth . . .

It is obviously painful, but it's not the only reason for her screams.

"Don't take my child!" she cries. "Don't . . . you . . . take . . . my . . . baby!"

The priests ignore her pleas, keep chanting, keep drumming.

Separated from the ceremonial chamber by a chasm fifty feet wide and God-only-knows how deep, West can only stare helplessly at the scene.

And then, suddenly, a new cry joins the wild cacophony of sounds.

The cry of a baby.

The woman *has given birth . . .*

The priests cheer.

And then the chief priest—he alone is dressed in red robes and wears no mask—pulls the child from the woman's body and holds it aloft, illuminated by the vertical laser beam of sunlight.

"A boy!" he cries.

The priests cheer again.

And in that moment, as the chief priest holds the child high, West sees his face.

"Del Piero . . ." he breathes.

The woman wails, "Please God, no! Don't take him! No! *Noooo!*"

But take him they do.

The priests sweep out the main entrance on the far side of the chamber, crossing a short bridge, their cloaks billowing, the boy held tightly in their midst, flanked by the armed paratroopers.

As they do, the noonday sun moves on and the dazzling vertical laser beam of light vanishes.

The chief priest—Francisco del Piero—is the last to leave. With a final look, he stomps on a trigger stone in the main doorway and then disappears.

The response is instantaneous.

Spectacular streams of lava come blurting out of the rectangular holes in the walls of the cavern. The lava oozes across the floor of the chamber, heading toward the central stone altar.

At the same time, the ceiling of the chamber starts *lowering*—its irregular form moving toward the matching configuration on the floor. It even has a special indention in it to accommodate the altar.

The woman on the altar doesn't notice.

Either from emotional torment or loss of blood, she just slumps back onto the altar and goes still, silent.

Wizard arrives at West's side, beholds the terrible scene.

"Oh my God, we're too late," he breathes.

West stands quickly.

"It was del Piero," he says. "With French paratroopers."

"The Vatican and the French have joined forces . . ." Wizard gasps.

But West has already raised a pressure gun and fires it into the lowering ceiling of the chamber. The piton drives into the stone. A rope hangs from it.

"What on Earth are you doing?" Wizard asks, alarmed.

"I'm going over there," West says. "I said I'd be there for her and I failed. But I'm not going to let her get crushed to nothing."

And with that, he swings across the gaping chasm.

The ceiling keeps lowering.

The lava keeps spreading across the floor from either side, approaching the altar.

But with his quick swing, West beats it, and he rushes to the middle of the chamber, where he stands over the body of the woman.

A quick pulse check reveals that she is dead.

West squeezes his eyes shut.

'I'm so sorry, Malena . . ." he whispers, ". . . so sorry."

"Jack! Hurry!" Wizard calls from the balcony. "The lava!"

The lava is thirty feet away . . . and closing on him from both sides.

Over at the main entrance, a waterfall of oozing lava pours out of a rectangular hole *above* the doorway, forming a curtain across the exit.

West places his hand on the woman's face, closes her eyes. She is still warm. His gaze sweeps down her body, over the sagging skin of her abdomen, the skin over her pregnant belly now rumpled with the removal of the child formerly there.

Then for some reason, West touches her belly.

And feels a tiny little kick.

He leaps back, startled.

"Max!" he calls. "Get over here! *Now!*"

* * *

A gruesome yet urgent image: flanked by the encroaching lava and the steadily lowering ceiling, the two men perform a Caesarian delivery on the dead woman's body using West's Leatherman knife.

Thirty seconds later, Wizard lifts a *second* child from the woman's slit-open womb.

It is a girl.

Her hair is pressed against her scalp, her body covered in blood and uterine fluid, her eyes squeezed shut.

West and Wizard, battered and dirty, two adventurers at the end of a long journey, gaze at her like two proud fathers.

West in particular gazes at the little infant, entranced.

"Jack!" Wizard says. "Come on! We have to get out of here."

He turns to grab their loosely hanging rope—just as the spreading lava reaches it and ignites it with a *whoosh!*

No escape that way.

Holding the baby, West spins to face the main entrance.

Fifty feet of inch-deep lava blocks the way.

And then there's the curtain of falling lava blocking the doorway itself.

But then he sees it, cut into the left side of the stone doorframe: *a small round hole* maybe a handspan wide, veiled by the same waterfall of superheated lava.

West says, "How thick are your soles?"

"Thick enough for a few seconds," Wizard replies. "But there's no way to switch off that lavafall."

"Yes, there is." West nods over at the small hole.

"See that hole. There's a stone dial inside it, hidden behind that curtain of lava. A cease mechanism that switches off the lavafall."

"But Jack, anyone who reaches in there will lose their—"

Wizard sees that West isn't listening. The younger man is just staring intently at the wall hole.

West bites his lip, thinking the unthinkable.

He swallows, then turns to Wizard: "Can you build me a new arm, Max?"

Wizard freezes.

He knows it's the only way out of this place.

"Jack. If you get us out of here, I promise you I'll build you a better arm than the one you were born with."

"Then you carry her and let's go." West hands the baby to Wizard.

And so they run, West in the lead, Wizard and the baby behind him, across the inch-deep pool of slowly spreading lava, crouching beneath the descending ceiling, the thick soles of their boots melting slightly with every stride.

Then they arrive at the lava-veiled doorway, and with no time to waste, West goes straight to the small hole next to the doorframe, takes a deep breath and—

—thrusts his left arm into the hole, up to the elbow, *through* the waterfall of lava!

"*Ahhhh!*"

The pain is like nothing he has ever known. It is excruciating.

He can see the lava *eating* through his own arm like a blowtorch burning through metal. Soon it will eat all the way through, but for a short time he still has feeling in his fingers and that's what he needs, because suddenly he touches something.

A stone dial inside the wall hole.

He grips the dial, and a moment before his entire lower arm is severed from his body, Jack West Jr. turns it and abruptly all the lavafalls flowing into the chamber stop.

The ceiling freezes in mid descent.

The lavafall barring the doorway dries up.

And West staggers away from the wall hole . . .

. . . to reveal that his left arm has indeed been severed at the elbow. It ends at a foul stump of melted bone, flesh, and skin.

West sways unsteadily.

But Wizard catches him and the two of them—plus the child—stumble out through the doorway where they fall to the floor of a stone tunnel.

West collapses, gripping his half arm, going into shock.

Wizard puts the baby down and hurriedly removes West's melting shoes—before also removing his own a bare second before their soles melt all the way through.

Then he dresses West's arm with his shirt. The red-hot lava has seared the wound, which helps.

Then it is over.

And the final image of West's dream is of Wizard and himself, sitting in that dark stone tunnel, spent and exhausted, with a little baby girl between them, in the belly of an African volcano.

And Wizard speaks:

"This . . . this is unprecedented. Totally unheard of

in all recorded history. Two oracles. *Twin* oracles. And del Piero doesn't know . . ."

He turns to West. "My young friend. My *brave* young friend. This complicates matters in a whole new way. And it might just give us a chance in the epic struggle to come. We must alert the member states and call a meeting, perhaps the most important meeting of the modern age."

A
MEETING
OF NATIONS

COUNTY KERRY, IRELAND
OCTOBER 1996
SEVEN MONTHS LATER

To the untrained eye, it seemed like just another lonely old farmhouse on a hilltop overlooking the Atlantic. To the trained eye, however, it was something else entirely. The experienced professional would have noticed no less than twenty heavily armed Irish commandos standing guard around the estate, scanning the horizon.

To be sure, this was an unusual setting for an international meeting, but then again this was not a meeting that the participants wanted widely known.

The state of the world at that time was grim. Iraq had been chased out of Kuwait, but now it played cat-and-mouse games with UN weapons inspectors. Europe was furious with the United States over steel tariffs. India and Pakistan, already engaged in a phony war, were both on the verge of entering the Nuclear Weapons Club.

But all these were *big* ticket issues, and the small group of nations gathered together today were not big ticket players in world affairs. They were small countries; mice, not lions; relative minnows of world affairs.

Not for long.

The mice were about to roar.

Six delegations now sat in the main sitting room of the farmhouse, waiting. Each national delegation consisted of two or three people—one senior diplomat, and one or two military personnel.

The view out through the windows was breathtaking—a splendid vista of the wild waves of the Atlantic smashing against the coast—but no one at this gathering cared much for the view.

The Arabs checked their watches impatiently, frowning. Their leader, a wily old sheik from the United Arab Emirates named Anzar al Abbas, said: "There's been no word from Professor Epper for over six months. What makes you think he'll even come?"

The Canadians, typically, sat there calmly and patiently, their leader simply saying, "He'll be here."

Abbas scowled.

While he waited, he flipped through his briefing kit and started rereading the mysterious book extract that had been provided for all the participants at the meeting.

It was headed "The Golden Capstone" . . .

THE GOLDEN CAPSTONE

From: *When Men Built Mountains: The Pyramids* by
        Chris M. Cameron (Macmillan, London, 1989)

Perhaps the greatest mystery of the pyramids is the most obvious one: the Great Pyramid at Giza stands nine feet shorter than it should.

For once upon a time at its peak sat the most revered object in all of history.

The Golden Capstone.

Or as the Egyptians called it, the *Benben*.

Shaped like a small pyramid, the Capstone stood nine feet tall and was made almost entirely of gold. It was inscribed with hieroglyphics and other more mysterious carvings in an unknown language, and on one side—the south side—it featured the Eye of Horus.

Every morning it shone like a jewel as it received the first rays of the rising sun—the first earthly object in Egypt to receive those sacred rays.

The Great Capstone was actually made up of seven pieces, its pyramidal form cut into horizontal strips, creating six pieces that were trapezoidal in shape and one, the topmost piece, that was itself pyramidal (small pyramids such as this were called *pyramidions*).

We say that the Capstone was made *almost* entirely of gold, because while its body was indeed crafted from solid gold, it featured a thin borehole that ran vertically down through its core, in the exact center of the Capstone.

This hollow was about two inches wide and it cut downward through each of the seven pieces, punching holes in all of them. Embedded in each of those circular holes could be found a crystal, not unlike the lens of a magnifying glass. When placed in sequence those seven crystals served to concentrate the Sun's rays on those days when it passed directly overhead.

This is a crucial point.

Many scholars have noted that the construction of the Great Pyramid by the pharaoh Khufu curiously coincides with the solar event known as the Tartarus Rotation. This phenomenon involves the rotation of the Sun and the subsequent appearance of a powerful sunspot that comes into alignment with the Earth.

Accomplished Sunwatchers that they were, the

Egyptians certainly knew of the Sun's rotation, sunspots, and indeed of the sunspot that we call "Tartarus." Aware of its intense heat, they called it "Ra's Destroyer." (They also knew of the smaller sunspot that precedes Tartarus by seven days, and so labeled it "the Destroyer's Prophet.")

The last Tartarus Rotation occurred in 2570 B.C., just a few years after the Great Pyramid was completed. Interestingly, the next Rotation will occur in 2006, on March 20, the day of the vernal equinox, the time when the Sun is perfectly perpendicular to the Earth.

Those theorists who link the construction of the pyramid to Tartarus also claim that the Capstone's unique "crystal array" has the ability to capture and harness solar energy, while the more outrageous authors claim it possesses fabulous paranormal powers.

Having said this, however, it should be noted that the Golden Capstone only sat atop the Great Pyramid for a very short time.

The day after the Tartarus Rotation of 2570 B.C., the Capstone was removed and taken to a secret location where it rested for over two thousand years.

It has since disappeared from history altogether, so that now all that remains of it is an ominous inscription found on the empty summit of the Great Pyramid at Giza itself.

Cower in fear, cry in despair,
You wretched mortals
For that which giveth great power
Also takes it away.
For lest the Benben be placed at sacred site

On sacred ground, at sacred height,
Within seven sunsets of the arrival of Ra's prophet,
At the high point of the seventh day,
The fires of Ra's implacable Destroyer
will devour us all.

A door slammed somewhere. Abbas looked up from his reading.

Footsteps.

Then the sitting room door opened, and through it stepped—

Professor Max T. Epper and Captain Jack West Jr.

Epper wore a classic academic's tweed coat. His beard back then was just as white and long as it would be ten years later.

West wore his miner's jacket and some brand-new steel-soled boots. His ice-blue eyes scanned the room, sharp as lasers, ever watchful.

And his left arm ended at the elbow.

Everyone noticed it.

Whispers rippled across the room.

"The ones who found the Scrolls of the Museion . . ." one of the Arabs whispered.

"Epper is Professor of Archaeology at Trinity College in Dublin, a brilliant fellow, but he also has doctorates in physics and electromagnetics . . ."

"And Huntsman?"

"He *was* military, but not anymore. Worked alongside the Americans in Iraq in '91."

"What on earth has happened to his arm?"

Abbas stood up. "Where is the girl, Maximilian? I thought you were bringing her."

"We left her at a secure location," Epper said. "Her

safety at this juncture is of paramount importance. Her actual presence at this meeting, my old friend, Anzar, is not."

Epper and West sat down at the table, joining the six delegations.

Epper sat with the Canadians.

West sat alone, attaching himself to none of the six countries at the table. *He* was the seventh delegation. His home nation had sent no other representative, having decided that his presence at this meeting was sufficient.

That nation: Australia.

The host, the leader of the Irish delegation, General Colin O'Hara, formally opened the meeting.

"My friends, welcome to Ireland, and to a meeting of tremendous significance. I will get directly to the point. Six months ago, members of a European military-archaeological team found the pregnant wife of the Oracle of Siwa in her hideaway in Uganda. It is not known how they found her, but we do know that the leader of the European expedition was the eminent Vatican historian Father Francisco del Piero. Del Piero's specialty is ancient Egyptian religious practices, particularly Sun worship.

"In accordance with the dictates of an ancient Egyptian Sun cult, del Piero and his team took the pregnant woman to a remote volcano in Uganda on the day of the vernal equinox, March 20.

"At noon on the day of the equinox, by the so-called pure light of the Sun, in a chamber cut into the flank of the volcano, the Oracle's wife gave birth to a son, whom del Piero immediately abducted.

"Del Piero and his military escorts then left, leaving the mother to die inside the chamber.

"But then something most unexpected occurred.

"After Dr. del Piero's team had departed, the Oracle's wife gave birth to *another* child, a girl. Through the extraordinary efforts of Professor Epper and Captain West, this baby girl was recovered, alive and well . . ."

There was, of course, more to it than that, West thought as he listened.

He and Epper had actually found the Oracle's wife a day *before* the Europeans. Her name was Malena Okombo and she had been living in hiding, in fear of her abusive husband, the present-day Oracle of Siwa. Pregnant with the Oracle's heir (or heirs), she had fled from his fists and rages, the petulant rages of a spoiled man. West had sympathized with Malena immediately, promised to look after her. But then the Europeans had arrived the following day in great numbers and abducted her—leading to the incident at the volcano.

O'Hara was still talking: "It is this extremely fortunate occurrence—the birth of a second Oracle—that brings us together today. Professor Epper, if you will . . ."

Epper stood up. "Thank you, Colin." He addressed the assembled delegates. "Ms. Kissane, gentlemen. Our seven small nations come together today at a pivotal moment in history.

"The actions of Father del Piero and his men in Uganda can mean only one thing, a most dangerous thing. The Europeans are making their move. After two thousand years of searching, they have just secured the key to discovering the greatest, most sought-after treasure in human history: the Golden Capstone of the Great Pyramid."

"Allow me to elaborate," Epper said.

"As you will have read in your briefing materials, there was once a magnificent Golden Capstone that sat atop the Great Pyramid. It, however, was removed from the apex of the structure soon after the Great Pyramid was completed, staying there for less than a year.

"It is not mentioned in any Egyptian records after that time nor is its final resting place known.

"Over the ages since then, the Golden Capstone has been the subject of countless myths and legends. The Persian King, Cambyses, tried to find it at the Siwa Oasis in the Western Desert, only to lose fifty thousand men in the attempt, consumed in a sandstorm of unusual ferocity.

"Julius Caesar tried to locate it, but failed. Napoleon brought an entire army to Egypt to find it, and failed. The tale of Jason and the Argonauts and their attempt to acquire a mystical, all-powerful 'Golden Fleece'—written by Appollonius of Rhodes— is widely believed to be a thinly veiled allegory for the search for the Golden Capstone.

"But all the legends have one thing in common. In all of them the Capstone is said to possess unusual properties. It is said to be a source of immense power; it is said to contain the secret to perpetual motion; it is said to be a solar polarizer, capable of absorbing the rays of the Sun.

"And then, of course, there are the occult myths: that the Capstone is a talisman of evil, forged in a bloody ceremony by occultist priests; that the nation that claims it as its own and keeps it in its lands will be unconquerable in battle; that it is a piece of alien technology brought to Earth thousands of years ago as a gift from a higher civilization."

The representative of New Zealand said: "And now the European Union wants it—"

"Ahem," O'Hara said. "These nations do *not* represent the European Union. Ireland and Spain are members of the EU, and Father del Piero does not act in our name. While it calls itself an EU mission, it is really a coalition of four 'Old European' states: France, Germany, Italy, and the Vatican."

At the mention of France, the New Zealander visibly stiffened. Relations between New Zealand and France had been tense ever since the bombing by French agents of the Greenpeace boat, the *Rainbow Warrior,* in Auckland Harbor in 1985. "Old Europe then. My point is if Old Europe wants the Capstone, you can be assured that her enemies are aware of this—"

"They are," Abbas said firmly. "The Americans are already putting together a rival expedition spearheaded by Marshall Judah and the CIEF, and backed by the Caldwell Group."

"Wait a second," the head of the Jamaican delegation said. "America and Europe are *enemies*?"

"As only ex-friends can be," Epper said. "Through

the vehicle of the EU, Old Europe has been waging economic warfare on the United States for the last five years. It began when the Europeans accused America of subsidizing its steel industry and shutting European producers out of its market."

Canada nodded. "And ex-friends, like ex-wives and ex-husbands, make for the bitterest of foes. Europe and America despise each other. And their enmity will only get worse over time."

Epper said, "Which is why we are all here today. Our seven small nations are not the enemies of the United States or Old Europe. Indeed, we have fought by their side on many previous occasions. But on this matter, we have decided that we cannot sit idly by while these so-called Great Powers engage in a battle for the most powerful artifact known to humankind.

"No. We are gathered here today because we believe that the Capstone should not belong to *any* one superpower. Its power is simply too great. In short, we are here to save the world."

"So what about the baby girl—" Abbas asked.

Epper held up his hand. "In a moment, Anzar, in a moment. Just a little more background first. Throughout history, the Capstone has been sought by many powerful individuals: Julius Caesar, Augustus Caesar, Richard the Lionheart, Napoleon, Lord Kitchener and, most recently, by Adolf Hitler and the Nazis. It is worshipped by organizations such as the Templars and the Freemasons, and—this will surprise some—the Catholic Church. All of them believe the same thing: whosoever finds the Capstone and performs an ancient ritual with it, will rule the Earth for a thousand years."

The room was silent.

Epper went on.

"Only one man in history is believed to have actually held the Capstone in his possession and harnessed its awesome power. He is also the one who, according to legend, broke the Capstone into seven pieces—so that no one man could ever have it whole again. He then had those pieces spread to the distant corners of the world, to be buried within seven colossal monuments, the seven greatest structures of his age."

"Who?" Abbas said, leaning forward.

"The only man ever to rule the entire world of his era," Epper said. "Alexander the Great."

"Seven colossal monuments?" Abbas said suspiciously. "You're talking about the Seven Wonders of the Ancient World? Alexander had the seven pieces of the Capstone buried within the Seven Wonders?"

"Yes," Epper said, "although in his lifetime, they weren't *known* as the Seven Ancient Wonders. That label was coined later, in the year 250 B.C. by Callimachus of Cyrene, the Chief Librarian of the Library at Alexandria. Why, at the time of Alexander's death in 323 B.C., only five of the Seven Wonders had actually been built."

"My ancient history is a little rusty," Abbas said, "can you remind me of the Seven Wonders, please?"

It was the young Irish woman who answered him, quickly and expertly: "In order of construction, they are: the Great Pyramid at Giza, the Hanging Gardens of Babylon, the Temple of Artemis at Ephesus, the Statue of Zeus at Olympia, the Mausoleum at Halicarnassu, the Lighthouse at Alexandria, and the Colossus of Rhodes."

"Thank you, Zoe," Epper said.

"I thought the Hanging Gardens were a myth," Abbas said.

Epper said, "Just because something has not been *found* yet does not make it a myth, Anzar. But we digress. In his lifetime, Alexander visited all five of the existing Wonders. The last two Wonders—the Light-

113

house and the Colossus—would be built by his closest friend and general, Ptolemy I, who would himself later become Pharaoh of Egypt.

"This creates a curious coincidence: taken together, these two titans of their age visited *all seven* of the sites that would subsequently be called the Seven Ancient Wonders of the World.

"Sure enough, soon after their deaths, the concept of seven 'great' structures came into being.

"But don't be fooled. This was no coincidence at all. As I've said, the idea of *the* Seven Wonders of the World was first espoused by Callimachus of Cyrene in 250 B.C. He did this in a text called *A Collection of Wonders around the World* now known simply as the Callimachus Text.

"Callimachus, however, was not publishing some idle list. He was a man who knew everything about Alexander, Ptolemy, *and* the Golden Capstone.

"By pinpointing these seven structures—and let's be honest, there were other just-as-impressive monuments in existence at the time that were not included—Callimachus was drawing a map, a clear and specific map to the location of the pieces of the Golden Capstone."

"According to the Callimachus Text, the Capstone was cut into pieces like so." Epper drew a pyramid on the whiteboard and cut across it horizontally, dividing it into seven bands.

"Seven pieces: one pyramidal tip, six trapezoidal base pieces, all of varying sizes, which we number from the top down, one through seven. Then they were hidden in each of the Seven Wonders."

"Wait," Abbas said, "the Seven Wonders of the Ancient World have long since fallen, been disassembled, or simply disappeared. How can we find these pieces in structures that no longer exist?"

Epper nodded. "This is a good point. Apart from the Great Pyramid, *none* of the Seven Wonders has survived to the present day. The Callimachus Text, however, has.

"And let me make something else clear: while it bears his name, Callimachus was not the only person to write it. His Text is a compendium of writings from many writers, all of them members of a secret cult who updated it and revised it over the course of 1500 years. They *did* keep track of every Wonder, even after they fell, and by extension they kept track of every piece of the Capstone. Allow me to explain."

"There is a well-known story about Alexander the Great. Before he embarked on his campaign in Persia, Alexander visited an Oracle at the desert oasis of Siwa in Egypt. During this visit the Oracle confirmed Alexander's belief that he was a god, no less than the son of Zeus.

"Less well known, however, is the *gift* that the Oracle is said to have given Alexander when he departed Siwa. It was never seen, but according to the historian, Callisthenes, it occupied 'a whole covered wagon that required eight donkeys to draw it.'

"Whatever this gift was, it was heavy. Very heavy.

Alexander would take it in its shrouded wagon with him on his all-conquering campaign across Persia."

"You believe the Oracle gave the Capstone to Alexander?" Abbas said.

"I do. I further believe that during that campaign, Alexander systematically hid those pieces at the five then-existing Wonders. He then left the last two pieces with his trusted friend, Ptolemy I, who as we know would go on to build the last two Ancient Wonders.

"For you see, this 'Oracle at Siwa' was more than just a seer. The Oracle was—and is to this day—the High Priest of an ancient Sun cult known as the Cult of Amun-Ra. Interestingly, Egyptian records knew this cult by another name: the Priests of the Capstone. That's right. They are the ones who placed the Golden Capstone on the apex of the Great Pyramid. They are also the ones who took it down.

"This Cult of Amun-Ra has endured to the present day, under many guises. For instance, the Knights of St. John of Malta, and some sections of the Catholic Church.

"The Freemasons, too, have long attached great significance to the Great Pyramid—and are often accused of being a thinly veiled reincarnation of the Cult of Amun-Ra. Indeed, one very famous Freemason, Napoleon Bonaparte, was initiated into the order's highest ranks *inside* the King's Chamber of the Great Pyramid.

"Other famous individuals who have been associated with the Cult of Amun-Ra include Thomas Jefferson, Frederic-Auguste Bartholdi, the designer of the Statue of Liberty, Dr. Hans Koenig, the famous Nazi archaeologist, and the American vice president Henry Wallace, the man behind the now infamous inclusion of a capstone-bearing pyramid on the U.S. one-dollar bill.

"For our purposes, it should be noted that *all* of the Chief Librarians of the Library at Alexandria were key members of the Cult—among them Apollonius of Rhodes and Callimachus of Cyrene."

Epper continued. "As time passed and each Wonder fell, Callimachus's successors in the Cult of Amun-Ra kept careful watch over the pieces of the Capstone, recording their resting places in the Callimachus Text.

"For example, when the Colossus of Rhodes was toppled by an earthquake, Egyptian cultists spirited away its head, rescuing the Capstone Piece on its neck-piece. The Colossus's new resting place was then noted in the Callimachus Text—but in a secret language.

"And here, Anzar, lies the importance of the little girl.

"You see, Callimachus and his successors wrote all of their entries in an ancient language, a language unlike any other in the history of man, a language that has defied translation for over 4,500 years, even by modern supercomputers.

"It is a mysterious language known as the Word of Thoth.

"Now, we believe that Father del Piero possesses a Vatican copy of the Callimachus Text—copied in secret by a Vatican spy in the thirteenth century. But he cannot translate it. And so he went in search of the one person in the world capable of reading the Word of Thoth: the Oracle of Siwa.

"For while Alexander has come and gone, the Oracle of Siwa lives to this very day, albeit in hiding somewhere in Africa.

"In a single unbroken line spanning more than four thousand five hundred years, the Oracle—male or female, the Oracle can be either—has always spawned one child. And the Oracle's offspring have inherited the preternatural 'sight' associated with the Oracle, thus becoming the next one.

"The extent of this 'sight' has been debated over the years, but one talent peculiar to the Oracle has been documented by Egyptian, Greek, and Roman writers alike: the Oracle of Siwa is the only person alive who is *born* with the ability to read the Word of Thoth.

"Since Callimachus's followers died out sometime in the fourteenth century, the Oracle is now the only person on Earth who can decode the Callimachus Text and thus reveal the locations of the Seven Ancient Wonders."

"As we have just heard, led by Francisco del Piero, the European coalition did not locate the Oracle himself, but they did find his pregnant wife, which is just as well: the Oracle, a foul, distasteful man by all accounts, was killed two months later in a drunken accident. Had he been located sooner, this mission would have been significantly easier and could have started immediately.

"In any case, now the Europeans have a newborn Oracle—a boy which means that when he reaches sufficient age, he will be able to decode the Text. According to ancient sources, a new Oracle begins to command his or her abilities around the age of ten.

"Once del Piero has the ability to decode the Callimachus Text, his European force will commence upon the greatest treasure hunt in history: a search for the seven pieces of the Golden Capstone."

The Irish woman, Zoe Kissane, leaned forward: "Only on this occasion, by some fluke, the Oracle's wife gave birth to twins. And we have the other child: a girl."

"Correct," Epper said. "And now it becomes a race. A race based solely on the maturation of two children. As they grow, they will learn to command their abilities, and when they are able to read the Word of Thoth, they will be able to decipher the Callimachus Text."

* * *

"Which means the girl's well-being is of the utmost importance," O'Hara said. "She is to be guarded around the clock, nurtured, and brought to maturity, so that when the time comes, she can translate the Text and guide us to the Wonders before the Europeans or the Americans can get them."

Epper nodded in agreement. "Make no mistake, people. The odds are against us. Our rivals from America and Old Europe are already employing hundreds of scientists in pursuit of this goal. When the time comes, they will send entire armies after those seven pieces.

"We do not have their resources, or their numbers. But having said that, we are not entirely without advantages.

"First. Aiding our quest is the fact that the two superpowers do not know we are embarking on it. They don't know we have the girl.

"And second: we are not after the entire Capstone. We only need to get one piece. If we do that, we deprive our adversaries of the power of the entire Capstone. Granted, getting just one piece will be a titanic task."

Epper scanned the room.

"This is a weighty responsibility, too weighty for one nation alone to bear. Which is why we have all come together today, a group of small nations who are prepared to join forces to combat the great powers of our time. And so the following course of action is proposed: each member of this group of nations will provide one soldier to share in the guardianship of the girl—both in her growth and in our ultimate quest to find one piece of the Capstone.

"But I warn you. This will be a long mission, a mission of years, not months. It will also be one of constant vigilance, self-sacrifice, and discipline. The group of chosen soldiers will accompany Captain West and me to the safehouse where the girl is now being kept. There we shall guard her and raise her, in absolute secrecy, until she is ready to fulfil her destiny."

Six of the delegations formed into huddles, whispered among themselves. Since he was his own delegation, West didn't need to discuss anything with anyone.

At length, they reconvened, each nation presenting its selected guardian.

Canada already had Max Epper.

Sheik Abbas said, "On behalf of the United Arab Emirates, I offer the services of my second son, Captain Zahir al Anzar al Abbas."

The trooper who had been sitting beside Abbas for the duration of the meeting stood. He was a rotund fellow, short and round—some would say chubby—with a bushy black beard and turban.

"Captain Zahir al Anzar al Abbas, heavy arms, explosives, 1st Commando Squadron, at your command. Call sign: *Saladin*."

Then the Spaniards' representative stood: tall, handsome and athletic, he looked like Ricky Martin, only tougher. "Lieutenant Enrique Velacruz. Unidad de Operaciones Especiales, Spanish Marines. Underwater destruction and demolition. Call sign: *Matador*."

The Jamaicans introduced a tall dreadlocked fellow named Sergeant V. J. Weatherley, call sign: *Witch Doctor*.

The New Zealanders offered a big hairy-faced NZAF pilot nicknamed *Sky Monster*.

Last of all, the Irish proffered two representatives, one of whom was the only woman to join this special multinational unit.

They sent Zoe Kissane and the giant fellow who sat at her side, her brother, Liam. Both hailed from the famed Irish commando unit, the Sciathan Fianoglach an Airm.

She introduced herself: "Sergeant Zoe Kissane, hostage rescue, advanced medical. Call sign: *Bloody Mary*."

He did too: "Corporal Liam Kissane, also hostage rescue, bomb disposal, heavy arms. Call sign: *Gunman*."

And there they stood, around the wide table, the eight chosen representatives of seven small nations who were about to embark on the mission of their lives.

They would acquire a ninth member soon—Stretch, from Israel—but he would not be a member of their choosing.

They prepared to leave. A plane was waiting to take them out of Ireland and to the secret safehouse.

At the door, Abbas spoke to his son, Saladin, in Arabic. One word kept arising: "*bint*."

The short fat trooper nodded.

As he did so, West stepped past them, walking out the door.

"If you're going to talk about her," he said, "please stop calling her 'the girl.' She has a name, you know."

"You named her?" Saladin said, surprised.

"Yes," West said. "I named her Lily."

They commenced their journey to the safehouse.

It was in Africa, in Kenya, but for secrecy's sake they took a long circuitous route to get there, taking several flights over several days.

On one of these flights, Saladin said to Epper, "At the meeting we were given an extract from a book. It told of the Capstone and the Tartarus Sunspot. What is this Tartarus Sunspot and what relationship does it bear to the Great Pyramid and its Capstone?"

Epper nodded. "Good question. It is a most curious relationship, but one that takes on a new level of importance at this time."

"Why?"

"Because in ten years' time, in March 2006, we will see the second great turning of the Sun, a solar event that has not occurred in over four thousand five hundred years."

The big-bearded Arab frowned. "The second great turning of the Sun? What is that?"

"Although you can't see it, our Sun actually spins on its own axis, much as the Earth does. Only it doesn't turn in a flat even rotation as we do. Rather, it rocks slowly up and down as it spins. As such, every four thousand to five thousand years, a certain section of the Sun—a sunspot known as the Tartarus Sunspot—comes into direct alignment with our planet. This is a bad thing."

"Why?"

"Because the Tartarus Sunspot is the single hottest point on the surface of the Sun," Zoe Kissane said, coming over and sitting down. "The ancient Greeks named it after one of the two realms of their Underworld. The nicer realm was Elysian Fields: it was a place of eternal happiness. The nasty one, a cursed land of screaming, flames, and punishment, was known as the Tartarus Plains."

"Global temperatures have been rising steadily for twenty years now," Epper said, "because the Tartarus Sunspot is approaching. When it shines directly upon the Earth, as it has done before, for about two weeks, temperatures will rise to unbearably high levels, around 110 degrees Celsius.

"Rainforests will shrivel. Rivers will boil. Humankind will have to move indoors for that time. It will be a literal scorching of the Earth, but it is survivable.

"The problem is: the polar ice caps will melt, causing massive global floods. The oceans will rise by perhaps fifty feet. Many coastal cities worldwide will be severely damaged. But as I say, all that is survivable, given due warning."

"OK . . ." Saladin said.

Epper wasn't finished. "Now, we have geological records of similar mass global water risings in the past—specifically in the years 15000 B.C., 10500 B.C., and 6500 B.C.

"The flood of 15000 B.C. is believed to have been the giant oceanic movement that flooded the Persian Gulf; while the flood of 10500 B.C. is widely acknowledged as the 'Great Flood' mentioned in religious texts worldwide: Noah's flood in the Bible, the floods mentioned in ancient Sumerian texts; even the Australian aborigines refer to a Great Flood in their Dreamtime folklore.

"The most recent global flood, that of 6500 B.C., broadly correlates with the worldwide episode of water rise known as the Flandrian transgression, where entire coastlines were submerged by about seventy feet."

Epper leaned forward to make his point: "All three of these major global floods occurred during a Tartarus Rotation.

"The thing is," he raised a finger, "in 2570 B.C., during the most recent Tartarus Rotation, *no such mass global flooding took place*."

Saladin frowned. "You're saying that something stopped the cataclysm. Something to do with the pyramids?"

"Yes," Epper said. "It's complicated but, you see, prior to King Djoser in 2660 B.C. the Egyptians *never* built pyramids. And after Menkaure in 2503 B.C. they stopped building giant ones. The fact is: for a period of 160 years, the Egyptians went on an absolute frenzy of pyramid-building, the high point of which was the Great Pyramid. *And then they never did it again*.

"They just stopped . . . immediately after the Tartarus Rotation of 2570 B.C. Later Egyptian architecture was certainly impressive and colossal—*but it didn't involve pyramids*."

"So you think the Egyptians knew something about the coming of this Tartarus Sunspot?" Saladin said. "What, were they visited by aliens or something and told to build the Great Pyramid and put this special Capstone on it?"

Epper just raised his bushy eyebrows theatrically. "I don't know why the Egyptians started building pyramids. But they did. In a rush and on a scale never seen before then and not seen since. And for some reason, the Tartarus Sunspot had no effect on planet Earth in the year 2570 B.C. The Great Pyramid was built, the sunspot passed—harmlessly—and the Egyptians took down the Golden Capstone, hid it, and stopped building pyramids."

"So how do you explain it?" Saladin asked.

"Putting aside for the moment all the occultist literature, I believe the crystals in the Capstone are the key. I think the Capstone is a polarizer, a crystal array that absorbs the superhot rays of the Tartarus Sunspot, rendering them harmless."

"And the occultist literature? These tales about obtaining global power for a thousand years."

Epper's face became grave. "The scientist in me scoffs at them. But something else gives me pause before discarding them completely. I've seen enough in my life to know that some things defy scientific explanation.

"The inscription on the summit of the Great Pyramid tells of placing the 'Benben' *at sacred site, on sacred ground, at sacred height* within seven days of the arrival of the minor sunspot, Ra's Prophet.

"This is a reference to an ancient ritual, a ritual passed down through the Cult of Amun-Ra, a ritual to be performed at the arrival of the Tartarus Sunspot. This ritual involves the intoning of a sacred incantation—the words of which are carved *into* the very Pieces of the Capstone.

"But this ritual can be performed in *two* ways: one

for good, the other for ill. With the Capstone in place atop the Great Pyramid, if you utter the noble incantation—known as the ritual of peace—the world will be spared the wrath of Tartarus and life will go on. This is also to our advantage: if we fail in our quest to obtain a Piece of the Capstone, we could yet be able to utter the good incantation over the replaced Capstone."

"And the evil spell?" Saladin asked hesitantly.

Epper's face went grim.

"The evil incantation—the ritual of *power*—will also spare the world from the blaze of Tartarus by capturing the Sun's rays in the Capstone's crystal array, but at a terrible price.

"For, according to the ancient texts, when the entire Capstone is placed on the summit of the Great Pyramid at noon on the seventh day and a designated amount of pure soil from one nation is placed in a crucible inside it *and* the ritual of power is uttered, 'all earthly power' will be invested in that nation for a thousand years."

Epper stared at Saladin. "The Capstone is the ultimate test of mankind's mettle. In the face of cataclysm, it can be used selflessly for the universal good, or it can be used selfishly, to attain absolute power."

"Or there is the third option," Saladin said. "Our option. If we obtain a single Piece of this Capstone and withhold it, we condemn the world to two weeks of catastrophic weather and floods, but not a thousand years of slavery. A lesser-of-two-evils argument, Dr. Epper?"

"Something like that," Epper said quietly. "Either way, my Arab friend, the fate of the world now depends on our efforts."

A GIRL
NAMED LILY

VICTORIA STATION, KENYA
1996–2006

Within days of the historic meeting, the team was in Kenya—living and working and training—at a remote farm-station near the Tanzanian border. On a clear day, to the south they could see the mighty cone of Kilimanjaro peeking above the horizon.

Far from the Western World.

Far from their enemies.

The farm—very deliberately—had wide flat treeless pastures stretching for two miles in every direction from the central farmhouse.

There would be no unexpected visitors to this place.

The team raised few eyebrows among the locals.

To the Kenyans, Victoria Station was just another working farm, populated by a few foreigners, all working for the old man, Epper, and his lovely wife, Doris. Gray-haired, patient, and kind, she had come from Canada to join her husband on this mission and provide a much-needed grandmotherly figure on the farm.

Of course, the locals soon became aware of a baby girl on the property—every now and then, Doris or a worker from the farm would come into town to buy baby food, formula milk, diapers, and sometimes toys.

But the Kenyans simply assumed that the olive-skinned girl was the daughter of the young blond woman at the farm, who in turn was presumably the wife of one of the men.

The locals, however, never noticed that every single night, there were always two members of the team patrolling the perimeter of the property.

Lily grew up quickly.

Indeed, she transformed rapidly from a happy gurgling baby into an inquisitive toddler who on taking her first steps became an absolute security nightmare.

It was not uncommon to see seven crack commandos frantically upturning chairs, couches or hay bales trying to find a giggling little girl who could disappear seemingly at will.

Then she began to talk and to read.

Inevitably, she was the product of many influences.

When she saw Saladin kneeling toward Mecca, she asked him what he was doing. It was he who taught her about Islam—only growing tongue-tied once when, as a four-year-old, she asked him why Islamic women had to wear head-covering burqas.

"If they do not wear the burqa, men will not . . . er . . . respect them," Saladin said, clearing his throat.

"Zoe doesn't wear a burqa," Lily said.

Several members of the team were eating nearby at the time: Zoe, Epper, and West. Smiling, Zoe looked expectantly at Saladin, waiting for his answer.

"Well, no, she doesn't, because she is not a Muslim."

"But you can see her face, right?" Lily asked.

"Yes . . ."

"Which means, according to Islam, you mustn't respect her."

Saladin blushed bright pink. "Well, no . . . I do respect Miss Zoe. Very much."

"Then why do all Muslim women have to wear these burqa things?"

Saladin was helpless.

It was Zoe who saved him. "Not all men are as gentlemanly as Zahir, Lily. They can't control their urges as well as he can."

"Urges?" Lily asked, zeroing in on the new word.

Zoe said, "And *that* is a topic we will address when you're a little older."

All this time, a sheet of paper hung in the kitchen, attached by a magnet to the refrigerator—on it were seven boxes, filled with a strange kind of writing, reproductions of the seven main verses in the Callimachus Text.

It looked like this:

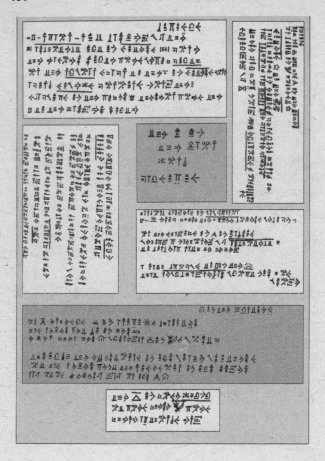

It was positioned so that Lily saw it every day when she went to get her morning juice. When she asked what it said, Doris Epper answered: "We don't know. We're hoping that one day you'll be able to tell us."

When she hit five years of age, Max Epper took charge of her schooling, teaching her math, science, ancient history, and languages—with an emphasis on Latin, Greek, and the ancient form of writing, cuneiform.

It turned out she had a singular aptitude for languages, learning them quickly and fluidly—with almost unnatural ease.

By age seven, she had mastered Latin and Greek.

By eight, she was deciphering Egyptian hieroglyphics.

By nine, she had outstripped Epper in his knowledge of cuneiform—translating all three of the ancient languages from the Bisitun Monument.

Not to mention the modern languages she was learning just by speaking with her multinational guardians. She particularly loved the difficult Gaelic tongue spoken by her Irish protectors, Zoe and Liam Kissane.

Epper was a wonderful teacher.

Lily just adored him—loved his wise old face, his kind blue eyes, and the gentle yet clever way he taught.

And so she renamed him *Wizard*.

Every day, she would race to his schoolroom in the east wing of the farmhouse to learn new and interesting things.

Poems like "The Charge of the Light Brigade" were acted out with verve and energy.

Simple arithmetic was illustrated with farming examples.

And science was a blast—literally. For Wizard had all manner of crazy homemade inventions in his workshop at the farm. Gadgets and tools that emerged from his dabblings in electromagnetism and foam poxies.

He once told Lily that a long time ago he had worked at a laboratory called Sandia in the United States, and that it was a secret place where they made secret things.

She liked that. Secret things.

She got along with the team members in different ways.

Although she herself wasn't a very girly girl, Zoe taught Lily some necessary girly things—like brushing her hair, filing her nails, and how to make boys do her bidding.

Matador, the Spanish trooper, spent a lot of time in the gym they'd set up in the smaller barn. At first he let Lily watch him work out. Then, as she grew bigger, he let her sit on one end of a plank of wood while he bench-pressed it, balancing her mass with lead weights at the other end, lifting her high into the air. She loved that.

Witch Doctor, the Jamaican commando, taught her how to tread in silence—they would terrorize Doris Epper, sneaking up on her when she dozed on the veranda in the afternoon sun.

But the soldier she bonded with most was Zoe's brother, Liam, call sign Gunman.

Gunman was a big guy, broad and tall, easily six-foot-three—with a wide honest face, a fully shaven head, and large jug ears.

He wasn't all that smart, but he was a great commando.

With Lily, though, he just clicked—perhaps because they were of an equal intelligence level, even though he was twenty-four and she was just a kid.

They watched movies and read books together.

They played the video game *Splinter Cell* endlessly in dual-player mode—killing baddies left, right, and center, coordinating their moves with loud shouts and commands. They actually made a good team, winning the inaugural "Victoria Station Dual-Player *Splinter Cell* Competition," defeating Wizard and Zoe in a hard-fought final.

They went on adventures around the station—including one visit to a giant hangar concealed in the western hills of the property, inside of which they found the towering *Halicarnassus*.

Lily gazed in awe at the great 747, and felt a thrill of excitement when she walked up to it, touched it and read a peculiar inscription on its underbelly: "PRESIDENT ONE—AIR FORCE OF IRAQ."

But most of all, no one would ever forget the famous tea party held on the front lawn one summer, with Mister Bear, Little Dog, Big Dog, Barbie, Lily, and Gunman—huge Gunman, all six-foot-three of him, hunched over on a tiny plastic chair, sipping from a plastic teacup, allowing Lily to pour him another cup of imaginary tea.

Everyone on the team saw it—watching from inside the farmhouse, alerted by a whisper from Doris. The thing was: no one ever—*ever*—teased Gunman about the incident.

This was unusual.

They were soldiers. They could and did make fun of each other on a regular basis, but for some reason, Gunman's relationship with Lily was off-limits.

Well, except for the time he and Lily broke into Aziz's workshop in the big barn, took a plasticine-like substance from his lockbox and used it to blow up Barbie's campervan.

Both Gunman and Lily caught hell for that.

And so, gradually, the team became a family—a family centered around the protection and nurturing of one little girl.

Of course, Lily loved the attention—like when she discovered ballet and put on a one-girl show to a cheering audience of seven commandos and two grandparent-like figures.

And still every day, when she appeared in the kitchen for breakfast, whoever happened to be there at the time would turn to see if she noticed the sheet of paper magnetized to the fridge.

But then one day, when she was seven, there was a commotion.

As the team had been eating breakfast, a radio squawked: *"All units. This is Sentry One, I have an intruder coming in through the main gate."*

Everyone leaped up, alarmed at the presence of an outsider, worried that other nations might know of their mission.

The intruder turned out to be a lone man—tall and thin, with a sanguine face—walking casually down the dirt road from the main gate.

Three hidden guns were trained on him as he rang the doorbell.

Wizard answered the door. "Can I help you, young man?"

"Indeed you can, Professor Epper," the thin man said. He had a dry pale face, with high cheekbones and deep hollow eye sockets.

Wizard blanched, did a double take.

The intruder's gray eyes never blinked. He knew that he had just chilled Wizard to the very bone.

"Professor Max T. Epper," he said, "Professor of Archaeology at Trinity College, Dublin, and the representative of Canada on a secret eight-nation task force protecting the daughter of the Oracle at Siwa, with a view to obtaining the lost Capstone of the Great Pyramid. My name is Lieutenant Benjamin Cohen, call sign

Archer, formerly of the Sayeret Matkal, now of the Israeli Mossad. I've been sent by my government to join your task force."

West stepped out from behind Wizard.

"Why hello, Jack," Archer said familiarly. "Haven't seen you since Desert Storm. Heard about what you did at that SCUD base outside Basra. Very nice. And Israel appreciated your efforts; although we still don't know how you got out. My bosses said you were involved in this, which was why they sent me. They thought you would accept me more than you would a total stranger."

"They were right, Ben," West said. "It's the only thing keeping you alive right now."

"Don't shoot the messenger."

"Why not?" West said and for the briefest of moments, Archer's confident air faltered.

West said, "I don't like having my hand forced, Ben, and you've got us over a barrel here."

Archer said seriously, "This is big, Jack. Affairs of state. Fate of the world and all that. This confrontation between Europe and the U.S. has been coming for a long time. Let's just say, Israel always likes to be involved. If it makes you feel better, I have orders to place myself under your direct command."

West pondered this a moment.

Then he said, "No contact with home. No reporting back to Mossad until the mission is achieved."

"I *have* to report back sometime—"

"No reporting back to Mossad until the mission is achieved or I blow your brains out right now, Ben."

Archer held up his hands, smiled. "Can't argue with that. You've got a deal."

The team was stunned—but they knew they didn't have any choice in the matter.

Either they allowed Archer to join their team or the Israelis would just advise the Americans of their mission.

How the Israelis had discovered them, they didn't know—but then Mossad *is* the most ruthless and efficient intelligence service in the world. It knows everything.

What was also apparent, however, was that Israel did *not* want to see the Capstone fall into the hands of either America or Europe—which meant Israel had an interest in the mission succeeding. That was good.

The big question, however, was what Israel planned to do at the end of the mission. Could Archer and Israel be trusted then?

At first, hardly anyone even spoke to Archer—which the ever-cool Israeli didn't seem to mind at all.

But no man is an island, and one day he joined West as he carried out some repairs on the station . . . and so began the process of becoming part of the team.

And slowly, over the course of many months, by working and sweating and training with the others, he became accepted as one of them.

One member of their little community, however, always regarded Archer with great suspicion.

Saladin.

As an Arab and a Muslim, he distrusted the Israeli intensely, but he also knew that Archer's presence in Kenya was now a given.

He would often say that while he had to accept Archer's presence, he didn't have to like it.

As all this was happening, Lily's development was proceeding apace.

She was always inquisitive, always watching.

Watching Saladin go off into the big barn and disappear inside his explosives workshop. He was so sweet and cuddly, she renamed him Pooh Bear.

Watching the new man, Archer, go out to the western paddock and practice firing his ultralong Barrett sniper rifle at far-off targets—and hitting the target *every single time*. She watched him closely, even when he disassembled his rifle. He was so tall and thin, she started calling him Stretch. (She also noticed that Pooh Bear and Stretch hardly ever even spoke. She did not know why.)

Watching Witch Doctor do chin-ups. From an early age, she had loved his wild dreadlocked hair. He became Fuzzy.

Watching the two youngest troopers, Matador and Gunman, jog together, train together, and drink together. This earned them their new call signs: Noddy and Big Ears.

And, of course, watching Zoe.

Idolizing Zoe.

Being the only twentysomething female Lily knew, it wasn't unexpected that Zoe would become her feminine role model.

And Zoe Kissane was a good role model. She could

outlast the men in fitness tests, outwit most of them at dinner-table discussions, and she could often be found studying history books deep into the night.

It was not uncommon to find Lily sitting in an armchair late at night beside Zoe, fast asleep with a book open, trying to imitate the pretty Irishwoman.

Naturally, Lily called her Princess Zoe.

But above all, the one person Lily enjoyed watching most was Jack West Jr.

She would never forget the day in 2000 when Wizard had presented West with a shiny new silver arm.

With Zoe assisting, Wizard spent the whole day attaching the high-tech arm to West's left elbow, pausing every now and then to frown and say something like, "The arm's CPU is experiencing interference from somewhere. Zahir, would you turn off the television set, please." Eventually, he changed some frequencies on the arm's central processing unit and it worked to his satisfaction.

The four-year-old Lily had watched them keenly as they worked.

She was aware that West had lost his arm on the day she was born, in the process of saving her life, so she really wanted his new arm to work.

At the end of the day, the arm was on, and West flexed his new metal fingers. His new hand could actually grip things far more tightly and firmly than his natural right hand could.

True to his word, Wizard had built West an arm that was better than the one he'd been born with.

* * *

Other things about West intrigued Lily.

For one thing, of all the team at the farm, he hung out with her the least.

He didn't play with her.

He didn't teach her any special subject.

He would spend most days in his study, poring over old books *really* old books with titles like *Ancient Egyptian Building Methods, Imhotep and the Architects of Amun-Ra,* and one *really* old scroll titled in Greek: *A Collection of Wonders around the World.*

Lily loved his study.

It had lots of cool stuff arrayed around its walls: sandstone tablets, a crocodile skull, the skeleton of some apelike creature Lily couldn't recognize, and hidden in one corner, a glass jar filled with a very strange kind of rusty red sand. On a secret mission of her own late one night, she discovered that the jar's lid was sealed tight, too tightly for her to open. It remained a mystery.

There was also a medium-sized whiteboard attached to the far wall, on which West had scribbled all sorts of notes and pictures. Things like:

> *HOWARD CARTER (1874–1939):*
> *Found Tutankhamen's tomb; also discovered Queen Hatshepsut's unused tomb (KV20) in Valley of the Kings in 1903. Empty tomb, never used. Unfinished carving on tomb's east wall is only known picture of Capstone atop Great Pyramid receiving vertical shaft of sunlight:*

After this West had noted: *"Queen Hatshepsut: only female pharaoh, prolific obelisk builder."*

One note on the board, however, caught Lily's eye.

It was at the very bottom corner of the whiteboard, under all the others, almost *deliberately* out of the way. It read simply: **"4 MISSING DAYS OF MY LIFE— CORONADO?"**

Once, late at night, she had seen West staring at those words, tapping his pencil against his teeth, lost in thought.

Whenever West worked in his study, his falcon always sat loyally on his shoulder—alerting him with a squawk when anyone approached.

Lily was intrigued by Horus.

She was an absolutely stunning bird, proud in her bearing and laserlike in her intensity. She didn't play with Lily—despite Lily's continued efforts to coax her.

Bouncing balls, fake mice, nothing Lily used could draw the falcon out into play. No, whatever silly thing Lily did to get her attention, Horus would just stare back at her with total disdain.

Horus, it seemed, cared for only one person.

Jack West.

This was a fact Lily would confirm through experimentation. One day, when once again Horus would not be drawn from West's shoulder, Lily threw her rubber mouse *at West*.

The falcon moved with striking speed.

She intercepted the tossed mouse easily—in midair halfway between Lily and West—her talons clutching the toy rodent in twin viselike grips.

Dead mouse.

Lesson learned.

But research was not the only thing West did.

It didn't escape Lily's notice that while she was busy studying in her classroom, Huntsman would often disappear into the old abandoned mine in the hills beyond the western paddock, not far from the airplane hangar. Strangely, he would wear an odd uniform: a fireman's helmet and his canvas jacket. And Horus always went with him.

Lily was strictly forbidden from going into those caves.

Apparently, Wizard had built a series of traps in the

mine tunnels—traps based on those in the ancient books that he and West studied—and Huntsman would go in there to test himself against the traps.

Lily found Jack West Jr. to be a bit of a mystery.

And she wondered at times, as children do, if he even liked her at all.

But one thing Lily *didn't* know was just how closely she herself was being observed.

Her progress with languages was being carefully monitored.

"She continues to excel," Wizard reported, just after she turned nine. "Her transliteration skills are like nothing I have ever seen. And she doesn't even know how good she is. She plays with languages the way Serena Williams plays with spin on a tennis ball—she can do things with it, twist it this way and that, in ways you or I can't even begin to imagine."

Big Ears reported, "She's physically fit, good endurance. If it ever becomes necessary, she can run six miles without breaking a sweat."

"And she knows every inch of my study," West said. "She sneaks in there once a week."

Zoe said, "I know it isn't mission-related, but she's actually becoming quite good at something else: ballet. Watches it on cable. Now I know lots of little girls *dream* of becoming prima ballerinas, but Lily is actually very good at it, especially considering she's self-taught. She can hold a toe pose unaided for close to twenty seconds—which is exceptional. The kid just loves ballet, can't get enough of it. It's a girl thing. Think you can get some ballet DVDs the next time you go to Nairobi, Wizard?"

"Certainly."

"Ballet, you say . . ." West said.

It then came as a surprise to Lily when she arrived at breakfast one day—again ignoring the sheet on the fridge—and found West waiting for her in the kitchen, alone, dressed and ready to go somewhere.

"Hey, kiddo. Want to go out for a surprise?"

"Sure."

The surprise was a private plane trip to Cape Town and a visit to a performance of *The Nutcracker* by the South African Royal Ballet.

Lily sat through the entire performance with her mouth agape, her eyes wide with wonder, entranced.

West just looked at her the whole time—and maybe once, just once, he even smiled.

Years went by.

In 2001, she saw the first *Lord of the Rings* movie. That Christmas, Sky Monster, proud of the New Zealand–born team behind the film, gave her the three books by Tolkien and read them with her.

By the time the third film had come and gone in 2003, Lily and Sky Monster had reread the books to within an inch of their lives.

And from those readings of *The Lord of the Rings,* Lily got her own call sign.

Sky Monster bestowed it on her, naming her after her favorite character in the epic.

Eowyn.

The feisty shieldmaiden from Rohan who kills the Witch-King of Angmar, the Ringwraith whom no *man* can kill.

Lily loved her call sign.

And still, every day, she would enter the kitchen and get her juice—and see the sheet of paper with the strange writing on it stuck to the fridge door.

Then one morning, a few days before her tenth birthday, she looked at the uppermost box on it and said, "Huh. I get it now. I know what that says."

Everyone in the kitchen at the time—Doris, Wizard, Zoe, and Pooh Bear—whirled around instantly.

"What does it say, Lily?" Wizard said, gulping, trying not to show his excitement.

"It's a funny language, uses letters and pictures to create sounds. It says,

"Colossus.
Two entrances, one plain, one not,
Carved by the fifth Great Architect,
Out of Great Soter's tenth mine.
The easier route lies below the old mouth. Yet
In the Nubian swamp to the south of Soter's mine,
Among Sobek's minions,
Find the four symbols of the Lower Kingdom.
Therein lies the portal to the harder route."

The next day, the entire team left Victoria Station on board the *Halicarnassus,* bound for the Sudan.

* * *

That same day the Sun rotated on its axis and the small sunspot that the Egyptians called Ra's Prophet appeared on its surface.

In seven days, on March 20, the Tartarus Rotation would occur.

THE
LIGHTHOUSE

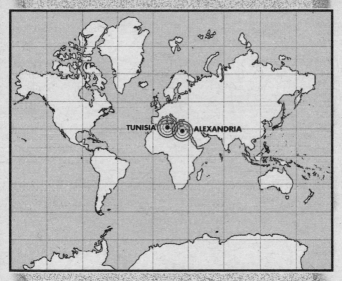

TUNISIA • ALEXANDRIA

TUNISIA
MARCH 15, 2006
FIVE DAYS TO TARTARUS

THE PHAROS

As a Wonder of the World, the Lighthouse at Alexandria has always been, terribly unfairly, the perennial runner-up.

It is second in height to the Great Pyramid of Giza—by a mere ninety-five feet.

It stood, intact and functioning, for sixteen hundred years, until it was hit by a pair of devastating earthquakes in A.D. 1300. Only the Great Pyramid survived for longer.

But ultimately it would defeat the Pyramid on one important count: it was useful.

And because it survived for so long, we have many descriptions of it: Greek, Roman, Islamic.

By today's standards, it was a skyscraper.

Built on three colossal levels, it stood 384 feet high, the equivalent of a forty-story building.

The first level was square—broad, solid, and powerful. The foundation level.

The second level was octagonal and hollow.

The third and uppermost level was cylindrical and also hollow—to allow for the raising of fuel to the peak.

At the summit of the tower stood its crowning glory. Sostratus's masterpiece: the mirror.

Ten feet high and shaped like a modern satellite dish, the mirror was mounted on a sturdy base and could rotate 360 degrees. Its concave bronze shape reflected the rays of the Sun to warn approaching ships of the dangerous shoals and submerged rocks just off Alexandria.

By night, a huge bonfire was lit in front of the mirror, allowing the great lighthouse to send its beam twelve miles out into the darkened sea.

Interestingly, like the Colossus of Rhodes a few years later, it was built at the request of Ptolemy I of Egypt—Alexander the Great's close friend and general.

The *Halicarnassus* roared toward Kenya.

The huge black 747 with its bristling array of missiles and gun turrets cut a mean figure in the sky. It looked like a gigantic bird of prey—death on wings.

Inside it, West's multinational team was still recovering from their disastrous mission in the Sudan.

In the main cabin of the jumbo, West, Wizard, Lily, and Pooh Bear all sat in contemplative silence. The cabin was fitted with couches, some tables, and wall consoles for radio and communications gear.

Wizard stood. "I'd better call the Spanish Army attaché. Tell them about Noddy."

He went to a nearby wall console, grabbed the secure sat phone there, started dialing.

West just stared into space, replaying in his mind everything that had gone wrong in the Sudan.

Lily sat with Pooh Bear, gazing at the team's original copy of the Callimachus Text.

As for the others, Fuzzy and Big Ears were in the infirmary in the rear of the plane, being treated by Zoe; and Sky Monster was up in the cockpit, flying the plane, with Stretch keeping him company.

In the main cabin, Lily scanned another entry of the Callimachus Text. The symbols on the page were ancient, alien.

Then suddenly she squealed, "Hey!"

West snapped up. Wizard also spun.

"This entry here. I couldn't understand it before, but for some reason, I can now. It's more complex than the last one. Uses new symbols. But I can read it now."

"What's it say?" West leaped to her side.

Lily read it aloud:

"The Pharos.
Look for the base that was once
the peak of the Great Tower
In the deepest crypt of Iskendur's Highest Temple,
Soter's illustrious House to the Muses,
Among the works of Eratosthenes the measurer,
Hipparchus the stargazer,
And Archimedes and Heron the machine makers,
There you will find ~~it~~ EUCLID'S INSTRUCTIONS
Surrounded by Death."

Lily frowned. "The word 'it' has been crossed out and replaced with 'Euclid's Instructions.' I don't know what they are."

"I do," Wizard said, reaching for a high-tech stain-less-steel trunk behind him. It opened with a vacuum-sealed *hiss*. The trunk was fitted with many pigeonholes, each pigeonhole containing an ancient scroll. Wizard's collection was huge; there were at least two hundred tightly rolled scrolls.

"Now where is that index? Ah, here it is." Wizard pulled a computer printout from a sleeve in the trunk's lid. On it was a very long typewritten list. "Now, Euclid's Instructions . . . Euclid's Instructions. I'm sure I saw that title once before. Ah, good, there we are. Just a moment."

Wizard proceeded to rummage through his scrolls. As he did so, West typed out Lily's translation of the Text.

Stretch entered the main cabin, noticed the activity immediately. "What's going on?"

"We may have had a development," West said. He read one line from the translation. " 'Soter's illustrious House to the Muses.' A House to the Muses is a 'museion' or 'museum.' Soter was Ptolemy I. *Soter's House to the Muses* is the Library at Alexandria, otherwise known as the Museion."

"So," Pooh Bear said, "in the deepest crypt of the Alexandria Library, among those works mentioned, we'll find 'the base that was once the peak of the Lighthouse,' whatever that is. I thought the Library was destroyed in antiquity."

"It was," Zoe said, coming into the lounge. "By the Romans in 48 B.C. The Biblioteca Alexandrina was the center of all learning in the ancient world, possessed of over seven hundred thousand scrolls and the writings of some of the greatest thinkers in human history, and the Romans *razed it to the ground*."

She saw West's translation. "God. Look at those names. It's like a Who's Who of history's greatest minds. Eratosthenes: he calculated the circumference of the Earth. Hipparchus mapped the constellations. Archimedes figured out volume and was a prolific inventor. And Heron. Well. Heron invented geared cogwheels and a primitive steam engine *two thousand years* before James Watt was even born."

Pooh Bear asked, "And now?"

Zoe sighed. "The Library is gone. Long since buried

underneath modern-day Alexandria. They know where it stood—and the Egyptian government recently built a new Library not far from the old site—but the Romans did their work well. Just as they had done with Carthage a hundred years previously, the Library was removed from existence. Not a single brick, text, or crypt remains."

"So all its scrolls were destroyed, then?"

"Many were, but a large portion of them were spirited away from the Library in the days before the Roman invasion. The scrolls were reputedly taken to a secret location, deep in the Atlas Mountains—and to date, have never been officially found."

When Zoe said this last sentence, she threw West and Wizard a sideways look.

"Not everyone announces it to the world when they find something important," West said.

"*What*—?" Pooh Bear said, whirling to face the scrolls Wizard was rummaging through. "Are you telling me that those scrolls are—"

"Ah-ha! Here it is!" Wizard exclaimed.

He extracted an ancient scroll from a pigeonhole. It was beautifully made, with ornate rollers at each end and thick cream-colored parchment.

Wizard unrolled it, read it.

"Hmmm. Greek text. Handwriting matches that of other known Euclidian texts. One of the greatest mathematicians in history, Euclid. He created plane geometry, you know, a grid with an x and y axis, which we now call Euclidian Geometry. This scroll is undoubtedly written by him, and its title is simply *Instructions*. Which makes it Euclid's Instructions, I suppose."

"What does it say?" Pooh Bear asked.

Wizard scanned the scroll. "It just seems to restate some of Euclid's more mundane discoveries. No reference to any ancient wonder or Golden Capstone."

"Damn," West said.

"Bugger," Zoe said.

"Wait a second . . ." Wizard held up his hand. "Look at this."

He had unfurled the scroll to its edges, revealing a small handwritten notation at the extreme bottom of the parchment, right where it met the lower roller.

Written across the bottom of the scroll were a few lines of text, not in classical Greek, but in another language: the cuneiform-like strokes of the Word of Thoth. It read:

"Lily?" Wizard said.

Lily scanned the ancient document for a moment, then read it aloud:

> *"Base removed before the Roman invasion,*
> *Taken to Hamilcar's Forgotten Refuge.*

Follow the Deadly Coast of the Phoenicians
To the inlet of the two tridents,
Where you will behold the easier entrance to
The sixth Great Architect's masterwork.
The Seventh has lain there ever since."

"There's that word again," Pooh Bear said, "base. Why do they call it a base?"

But West wasn't listening. He turned to Wizard, his face alive with excitement. "The Callimachus Text doesn't give the location of the Pharos Piece . . ."

"No," Wizard said. "This scroll does. And this is the only copy. Which means—"

"—neither the Europeans nor the Americans can possibly know where this Piece rests. Max, we've got a clear run at this one."

They stared at each other in amazement.

"Holy shit," West said, smiling. "We might just have a chance in this race."

The *Halicarnassus* zoomed through the dawn, arriving at the northern coast of Libya, soaring over the frothy white line where the waters of the Mediterranean meet the shores of the North African desert.

Inside it, West, Wizard, and Zoe were making swift progress on Euclid's Instructions.

"The Phoenicians was another name for the people of Carthage—the trading state annihilated by Rome in the Third and last Punic War. The state of Carthage approximated modern-day Tunisia, directly south of Italy, across the Mediterranean," Wizard said.

"And Hamilcar is Hamilcar Barca," West said, "father of Hannibal and commander of the Carthaginian forces in the First Punic War. I didn't know he had a refuge, let alone a forgotten one."

Zoe commented, "Hamilcar died in Spain in 228 B.C., between the First and Second Punic Wars. He must have ordered the construction of a faraway fortress and never lived to see it."

Wizard was on his computer: "I'm checking my database for any references to 'Hamilcar's Refuge.' But I've already found this: the 'Deadly Coast' was a name used by Alexandrian sailors to describe the coast of modern-day Tunisia. For a hundred miles the shore is all cliffs—four hundred feet high and plunging vertically into the sea. Major shipwreck area even in the twentieth century. Oh dear. If your ship goes down close to the shore, you can't climb out of the water because of the cliffs. People have been known to die within an arm's length of dry land. No wonder the ancient sailors feared it."

West added, "And the sixth Great Architect is Imhotep VI. He lived about a hundred years after Imhotep V. Clever trap builder; fortified the island-temple of Philae near Aswan. Known for his predilection for concealed underwater entrances. There are *six* at Philae alone."

Stretch said, "Wait a moment. I thought the Egyptian civilization was finished by the time of the Punic Wars."

"A common misconception," Wizard said. "People tend to think that the ancient Greek, Roman, and Egyptian civilizations existed separately, one after the other, but that's not true, not at all. They *coexisted*. While Rome was fighting Carthage in the Punic Wars, Egypt was still flourishing under the Ptolemies. In fact, an independent Egypt would continue to exist right up until Cleopatra VII, the famous one, was defeated by the Romans in 30 B.C."

"So what are these two tridents?" Pooh Bear asked.

"My guess is they are rock formations just out from the coastal cliffs," Wizard said. "Markers. Triple-pointed rock formations that look like tridents, marking the location of the Refuge."

"One hundred miles of sheer-cliffed coast." Pooh Bear groaned. "It could take *days* to patrol that kind of terrain by boat. And we don't have days."

"No," West said. "We don't. But I'm not planning on using a *boat* to scan that coastline."

* * *

An hour later, the *Halicarnassus* was soaring high above the Tunisian coast, traveling parallel to it, heading westward, when suddenly its rear loading ramp opened and a tiny winged figure leaped out of the plane and plummeted down through the sky.

It was a man.

West.

Shooming headfirst down through the air, his face covered by a wickedly aerodynamic oxygen-supplying full-face helmet.

But it was the object on his back that demanded attention.

A pair of lightweight carbon-composite *wings*.

They had a span of 8.5 feet, upturned wingtips, and in their bulky center (which covered a parachute), they possessed six compressed-air thrusters that could be used to sustain a gliding pattern when natural glide failed.

West rocketed down through the sky at a forty-five-degree angle, his bullet-shaped winged body slicing through the air.

The Deadly Coast came into view.

Towering yellow cliffs fronted onto the flat blue sea. Giant, immovable. Waves crashed against them relentlessly, exploding in gigantic showers of spray.

West zoomed lower, hitting 110 mph, before at around 800 feet . . .

. . . he swooped upward and entered a slower, more serene glide pattern.

Now he soared, three hundred feet above the waves of the Mediterranean, parallel to the massive coastal cliffs.

He was flying near the Tunisian-Libyan border, a particularly desolate stretch of the North African coastline. Broad flat sand plains stretched away from the sheer cliffs of the coast. About a klick inland, those plains rammed up against a mountain range made up of a few extinct volcanoes that ran parallel to the shore.

It was a land devoid of life. Desolate. Depressing. A place where nothing grows.

As he flew, West scanned the cliffs, searching for any rock formations on them that resembled a pair of tridents.

After ten minutes of gliding, he lost his natural glide pattern, so he ignited a compressed-air thruster. With a sharp *hiss-wapp,* it lifted him to a higher altitude, allowing him to glide for longer.

Then after about forty minutes—and three more compressed-air assists—he saw them.

Two rock-islands positioned about fifty meters out from the coastal cliff face, their rocky shapes each resembling a three-fingered human hand pointing toward the sky.

Or a trident.

Two tridents.

The section of cliff immediately behind the two tridents looked particularly forbidding—vertical and rough, with the upper section of the great cliff partially overhanging its base. Very difficult to scale.

"Wizard! Come in!" West called into his radio mike. "I've found them!"

An hour later, the *Halicarnassus* had landed on the flat sandy plain, dropped off a Land Rover four-wheel drive from its belly, and lifted off to take up a holding pattern a hundred miles to the south.

Bouncing along in the Land Rover, the team joined West—now standing on the windswept cliff overlooking the two tridents. The team numbered seven, since the injured Fuzzy had stayed in the *Halicarnassus* with Sky Monster, along with Horus. Big Ears, however, was there and still mobile, thanks to a cocktail of painkillers.

Technically, they were in Tunisia. The landscape was empty and dry. There wasn't a village or human settlement for fifty miles in any direction.

In fact, the landscape could better be described as a moonscape: the flat sand plain, the occasional meteorite crater, and of course the chain of mountains guarding the landward approach about a half mile inland.

"You know," Big Ears said, "they filmed *Star Wars* in Tunisia. The Tatooine scenes."

"I can see why," West said, not turning from the view of the sea. "It's totally alien."

Wizard came alongside West, handed him a printout. "This is the only reference my database has for Hamilcar's Refuge. It's a hand-drawn schematic found in a worker's hut in Alexandria, an Egyptian worker who must have worked on Imhotep VI's reconfiguration of Hamilcar's Refuge."

The papyrus sheet bore a carefully crafted hand-drawn sketch on it:

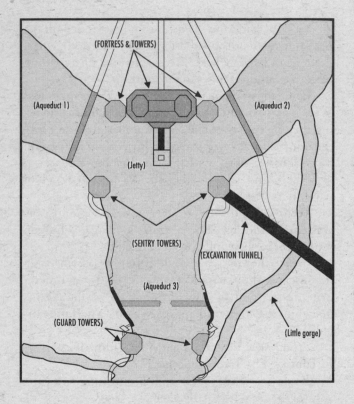

It was hard to tell exactly what the image depicted. Cut off at the top and bottom, it didn't seem to show the entire structure.

"Aqueducts and guard towers," West said, "and a

filled-in excavation tunnel. Jesus, this place must be huge." He scanned the landscape all around him, but saw nothing but barren desert and the harsh coast. "But if it's so huge, where the hell is it?"

He checked his printout of the Euclidian clue:

Follow the Deadly Coast of the Phoenicians
To the inlet of the two tridents,
Where you will behold the easier entrance to
The sixth Great Architect's masterwork.
The Seventh has lain there ever since.

"The inlet of the two tridents," he read aloud. "We've found the two tridents, so there's supposed to be an inlet here. But I don't see one. It's all just one seamless coastline."

It was true.

There was no bay or inlet in the coast anywhere nearby.

"Just hold on a moment . . ." Epper said.

He dug into his rucksack and extracted a tripod-mounted device.

"Sonic resonance imager," he said, erecting the tripod on the sand. He then aimed it *downward* and hit a switch. "It'll show us the density of the earth beneath our feet."

The sonic resonance imager pinged slowly.

Piiiing-piiiing-piiiing.

"Solid sandstone. All the way to the imager's depth limit," Wizard said. "As you'd expect."

Then he swiveled the imager on its tripod and aimed it at the ground a few yards to the west, the section of coastline directly in line with the two tridents—

Ping-ping-ping-ping-ping-ping . . .

The imager's pinging went bananas.

West turned to Wizard. "Explain?"

The old man looked at his display. It read:

TOTAL DEPTH: 26.2 ft.

SUBSTANCE ANALYSIS: SILICON OVERLAY
18.0 ft.; GRANITE UNDERLAY 8.2 ft.

Wizard said, "Depth here is twenty-six feet. Mix of hard-packed sand and granite."

"*Twenty-six* feet?" Pooh Bear said. "How can that be? We're *three hundred* feet above sea level. That would mean there's two hundred eighty feet of empty air beneath that section of ground—"

"Oh, no way . . ." West said, understanding.

"Yes way . . ." Wizard said, also seeing it.

West looked back inland at the sand plain stretching to the nearest mountain a half mile away. The sand *appeared* to be seamless. "Amazing the things you can do with a workforce of ten thousand men," he said.

"What? *What?*" Pooh Bear said, exasperated. "Would you two mind telling the rest of us mere mortals what in the blazes you're talking about?"

West smiled. "Pooh. There *was* once an inlet here. I imagine it was a narrow crevice in the coastal cliffs that cut inland."

"But it's not here now," Pooh said. "How does *an entire inlet* disappear?"

"Simple," West said. "It doesn't. It's still here. It's just been hidden. Concealed by the labor of ten thousand workers. The keepers of the Capstone put a roof over the inlet, bricked in the entrance, and then covered it all over with sand."

THE COAST OF TUNISIA

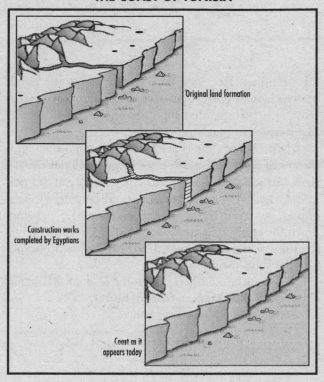

Original land formation

Construction works
completed by Egyptians

Coast as it
appears today

Five minutes later, Jack West Jr. hung from the Land Rover's winch cable fifty feet down the face of the coastal cliff, suspended high above the waves of the Mediterranean Sea.

He probably could have blasted through the eight meters of sand and granite with conventional explosives, but using explosives was risky when you did not know what lay beneath you—it could close off tunnels or passageways in the system below; it could even bring down the entire structure, and West's team didn't have the time or the manpower to sift through a thousand tons of rubble for months.

West now aimed Wizard's sonic resonance imager at the vertical cliff face in front of him.

Ping-ping-ping-ping-ping-ping . . .

Once again the imager's pinging went wild.

The display read:

> TOTAL THICKNESS: 13.5 ft.
> SUBSTANCE ANALYSIS: SANDSTONE
> OVERLAY 5.25 ft.; GRANITE UNDERLAY
> 8.2 ft.

West gazed at the cliff face in wonder. It looked exactly like the rest of the coastline: same color, same texture; rough and weatherworn.

But it was a hoax, a ruse, an entirely *artificial* cliff.

A false wall.

West smiled, called up. "It's a false wall! Only thirteen feet thick. Granite, with a sandstone outer layer."

"So where is the entrance?" Zoe asked over West's radio.

West gazed straight down the sheer cliff face—at the waves crashing at its base.

"Imhotep VI reconfigured this one. Remember what I said before: he was known for his concealed underwater entrances. Haul me up and prep the scuba gear."

Minutes later, West again hung suspended from the Land Rover's superlong winch cable, only now he had been lowered all the way down the false cliff face. He dangled just a few meters above the waves crashing at its base.

He was wearing a wetsuit, full face mask, and a lightweight scuba tank on his back. His caving gear— fireman's helmet, X-bars, flares, ropes, rock-screw drill, and guns—hung from his belt.

"OK! Lower me in, and do it fast!" he called into his throat mike.

The others obeyed and released the cable's spooler, lowering West *into* the churning sea at the base of the cliff.

West plunged underwater—

—and he saw it immediately.

The vertical cliff continued on under the surface, but about six meters below the surface it stopped at a distinctly man-made opening: an enormous square

doorway. It was huge. With its bricked frame, the doorway looked like a great airplane hangar door carved
into the submerged rock face.

And engraved in its upper lintel was a familiar
symbol:

West spoke into his face mask's radio. "Folks. I've
found an opening. I'm going in to see what's on the
other side."

Guided by his Princeton-Tec underwater flashlight,
West swam through the doorway and into an underwater passage that was bounded by walls of granite
bricks.

It was a short swim.

About thirty feet in, he emerged into a much wider
area—and instantly felt the tug of unusually strong
tidal motion.

He surfaced in darkness.

While he couldn't see beyond the range of his flashlight, he sensed that he was at one end of a vast internal
space.

He swam to the left, across the swirling tide, to a
small stone ledge. Once he was out of the water and on
the ledge, he fired a flare into the air.

The dazzling incandescent flare shot high into the
air, higher and higher and higher, until it hovered nearly
250 feet above him and illuminated the great space.

"Mother of God . . ." he breathed.

At that very same moment, the others were peering down the cliff face outside, waiting for word from West.

Suddenly, his crackly voice came in over their radios: *"Guys. I'm in. Come on down and prepare to be amazed."*

"Copy that, Huntsman," Zoe said. "We're on our way."

Lily stood a short distance from the group, staring inland, out across the plain.

As the others started shouldering into their scuba gear, she said, "What's that?"

They all turned—

—in time to see a C-130 Hercules cargo plane bank lazily around in the sky high above them, and release about a dozen small objects from its rear.

The objects sailed down through the air in coordinated spiraling motions.

Parachutes. Soldiers on parachutes.

Heading straight for their position on the cliff top!

The Hercules continued on, touching down on the plain several klicks to the east, stopping near one of the larger meteor craters over there.

Wizard whipped a pair of high-powered binoculars to his eyes—zoomed in on the plane.

"American markings. Oh, Christ! It's Judah!"

Then he tilted his binoculars upward to see the incoming strike team directly above him.

He didn't need much zoom to see the Colt Commando assault rifles held across their chests and the black hockey helmets they wore on their heads.

"It's Kallis and his CIEF team! I can't imagine how, but the Americans have found us! Everybody, move! Down the cable! Into the cave! Now!"

Exactly six minutes later, a pair of American combat boots stomped onto the spot where Wizard had just been standing.

Cal Kallis.

In front of him stood the abandoned Land Rover with its winch cable stretched out over the edge of the cliff face and down to the waves four hundred feet below.

Kallis looked out over the edge just in time to see the last two members of West's team vanish under the waves with scuba gear on.

He keyed his radio mike. "Colonel Judah, this is Kallis. We've just missed them at the sea entrance. Immediate pursuit is a viable option. Repeat, immediate pursuit is viable. Instructions?"

"Engage in pursuit," the cold voice at the other end said. *"Instructions are as before: you may kill any of the others, but not West or the girl. Go. We'll enter via the second entrance."*

Wﬞest's team surfaced inside the dark cave behind the false cliff.

As soon as his head broke the surface, Wizard called, "Jack! We've got trouble! The Americans are right behind us!"

One by one, West hauled the others out of the water and onto the small stone ledge to the left.

"*How?*" he said to Wizard.

"I don't know. I just don't know."

West scowled. "We'll figure it out later. Come on. I *hate* having to rush through uncharted trap systems and now we've got to. Get a look at this place."

Wizard looked up at the cavern around them.

"Oh my . . ." he gasped.

HAMILCAR'S REFUGE (OVERHEAD VIEW)

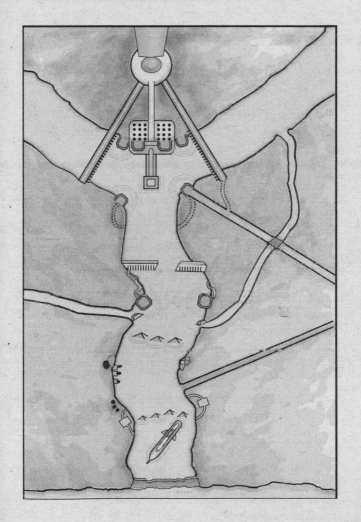

Wizard stared in wonder at the sight. So did the others.

Through sheer force of will, Imhotep VI had indeed constructed a *ceiling* over the natural inlet—turning it into a most unique cavern.

It wasn't wide, maybe twenty meters on average, fifty at the widest. But it was long, superlong. Now lit by many flares, it was revealed to be a narrow twisting chasm that stretched away into darkness for several hundred meters.

Its sidewalls were sheer and vertical, plunging into the water. Spanning the upper heights of these walls, however, were massive beams of granite—each the size of a California redwood—laid horizontally side by side across the width of the inlet, resting in perfectly fitted notches dug just below ground level.

At some time in the distant past, this granite ceiling had been covered over with sand, concealing the entire inlet.

Behind West's team stood the great wall that sealed the inlet off from the sea. Four hundred feet tall, it was a colossal structure, strong and proud, and on this side its giant granite bricks had not been camouflaged to match the coastline. It looked like a massive brick wall.

Of immediate importance to West and his team, however, was what lay behind this wall.

The roofed chasm.

Cut into the sheer cliffs on either side of the chasm's central waterway were a pair of narrow ledgelike paths.

The two paths ran in identical manner on either side of the twisting, bending chasm—perfect mirror images of each other. They variously rose to dizzying heights as long bending stairways or descended below the waterline; they even delved momentarily into the walls themselves before emerging again farther on. At many points along the way, the paths and staircases had crumbled, leaving voids to be jumped.

The waterway itself was also deadly. Fed by the surging tide outside, small whirlpools dotted its length, ready to suck down the unwary adventurer who fell in, while two lines of toothlike boulders blocked the way for any kind of boat.

Spanning the watercourse was a beautiful multi-arched aqueduct bridge built in the Carthaginian style, but sadly it was horribly broken in the middle.

As a final touch, vents in the walls spewed forth plumes of steam, casting an ominous haze over the entire scene.

Wizard raised a pair of night-vision binoculars to his eyes and peered down the length of the great chasm.

The world went luminescent green.

In deep shadow at the far end of the cavern, only partially visible beyond its twists and turns, he saw a structure. It was clearly huge, a fortress of some kind, with two high-spired towers and a great arched entrance, but because of the bends in the chasm and the haze, he couldn't see it in its entirety.

"Hamilcar's Refuge," he breathed. "Untouched for over two thousand years."

"Maybe not," West said. "Look over there."

Wizard did, and his jaw dropped.

"My goodness . . ."

There, wrecked against some rocks in the middle of the waterway, lying half-in, half-out of the water, was the great rusted hulk of a World War II–era submarine.

Emblazoned on its conning tower, corroded by time and salt, was the Nazi swastika and the gigantic number: *"U-342."*

"It's a Nazi U-boat . . ." Big Ears breathed.

Zoe said, "Hessler and Koenig . . ."

"Probably," Wizard agreed.

"Who?" Big Ears asked.

"The famous Nazi archaeological team: Herman Hessler and Hans Koenig. They were experts on the Capstone, and also founding members of the Nazi Party, so they were buddies of Hitler himself. In fact, with Hitler's blessing, they commanded a top secret scientific expedition to North Africa in 1941, accompanied by Rommel's Afrika Korps."

Big Ears said, "Let me guess, they were after the Capstone, they disappeared and were never heard from again?"

"Yes and no," Zoe answered. "Yes, they were after the Capstone; and yes, Hessler never returned, but Koenig did, only to be caught by the British when he arrived, on foot, in Tobruk, staggering out of the desert, starving and almost dead from thirst. I believe he was handed over to the Americans, who asked to interrogate him. Koenig would ultimately be taken back to the States with a bunch of other German scientists, where I believe he still lives."

West turned to Wizard. "How far behind us is Kallis?"

"Five minutes at the most," Wizard said. "Probably less."

"Then we have to get cracking. Sorry, Zoe, but you'll have to continue the history lesson on the way. Come on, people. Dump your bigger scuba tanks, but keep your pony bottles and your masks—we might need them." A pony bottle was a small handheld scuba tank with a mouthpiece. "Wizard, fire up a Warbler or two."

THE FIRST STAIRCASE (ASCENDING)

West and his team took the left-hand cliff path.

It quickly became a staircase that rose and twisted up the left-hand wall like a slithering snake. After a minute of climbing, West was eighty feet above the swirling waterway below.

At two points along the ascending stone staircase there were four-foot gaps that preceded stepping-stone-like ledges.

And facing onto those ledges were wall holes just like the one that Fuzzy had neutralized at the base of the quarry in Sudan.

West didn't know what deadly fluid these wall holes spewed forth, for the Nazis had—very conveniently—neutralized them long ago, riveting sheets of plate steel over the holes, then laying steel catwalk-gangways over the gaps in the stairs.

West danced across the first catwalk-bridge and past the sealed wall hole.

Whump!

A great weight of some unseen liquid banged against the other side of the steel plate, trying to burst

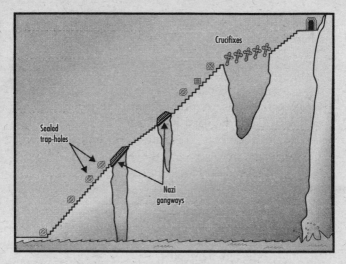

its way through. But the plate held, and West and his team ran by it.

No sooner were they past the second plugged-up wall hole than—

Zing-smack!

A bullet sizzled past their heads and ricocheted off the wall above them.

Everyone spun.

To see a member of Kallis's CIEF team hovering in the water at the base of the great wall, his Colt rifle raised and aimed.

The CIEF man let fly with a spray on full auto.

But Wizard had initiated a Warbler in Big Ears's backpack and the bullets fanned outward, away from the fleeing group.

More CIEF men surfaced at the base of the false

wall—until there were three, six, ten, twelve of them gathered there.

West saw them.

And once all his people were past the two gaps in the rising staircase, he jimmied the two Nazi gangways free, sending them free-falling into the water eighty feet below. Then he used his X-bar like a crowbar to lever off the Nazi plate covering the second wall hole. The plate came free, exposing the wall hole.

Then West took off after the others.

THE CRUCIFIXES

Up they ran, following the narrow winding staircase that hugged the left-hand cliff.

About 150 feet up, they came to a wider void in the stairs, about twenty feet across.

Some handholds had been gouged out of the cliff face, allowing one to climb sideways across the void, resting one's feet on a two-inch-wide miniledge.

Strange X-shaped hollows—each the size of a man—lined the wall of the void, curiously in synch with the handholds.

"Crucifixes," Wizard said as West caught up. "Nasty. Another of Imhotep VI's favorites."

"No choice then. I'll go up and over," West said.

Within seconds, he was free-climbing up the cliff face, gripping cracks in its surface with only his finger-tips, crossing it sideways above the trap-laden void.

As he climbed, Wizard peered anxiously at the pursuing CIEF team. They were themselves trying to negotiate the two stepping-stone ledges fifty yards below.

West landed on the other side, and quickly strung a rope—with a flying fox attached to it—across the void.

The CIEF team got past the first stepping-stone ledge.

West pulled the others across the void on the flying fox. First Lily, then Zoe, Big Ears, and Wizard.

One of the Delta men leaped onto the second stepping-stone ledge—and a gush of superheated *mud* came blasting out of the now-exposed wall hole there and enveloped him.

The mud was a deep dark brown; thick, viscous, and heavy. It was volcanic mud. It seared the skin from the man's body in an instant before its immense weight hurled him down to the water eighty feet below.

Wizard's eyes goggled. "Oh my . . ."

The remaining CIEF men were more cautious, and they skirted the wall hole carefully.

In the meantime, Stretch and—last of all—Pooh Bear were hauled across the wider void on the flying fox.

No sooner had Pooh Bear's feet touched solid ground than the first member of the pursuing CIEF team arrived at the other side of the void, only twenty feet away!

West immediately cut his team's rope, letting it fall into the abyss, and took off around the next bend.

The first CIEF man, energized by how close he was to his enemy, immediately set about using the handholds gouged into the wall of the void.

It happened when his hands hit the second and third handholds.

Like slithering tentacles, two bronze manacles

came springing out of the wall and clasped tightly around his wrists.

Then, a great man-sized bronze cross *fell out* of the X-shaped recess in the wall, *right in front of* the hapless CIEF man.

And the operation of the crucifix trap suddenly became apparent to the CIEF trooper: the manacles were attached to the big heavy cross and he was now held tight by them.

He shrieked as the cross tipped out of its recess and fell 150 feet straight down the sheer cliff face, plunging into the water at the bottom with a gigantic splash . . .

. . . where it sank, taking the CIEF man with it.

He screamed the whole time, right up to the point where the weight of the cross took him under.

West and his team ran.

THE SINKHOLE CAVE

It was probably the first time in history someone could claim to have been *helped* by Adolf Hitler's Nazi regime, but it was largely the Nazis' bridge-building efforts from sixty years previously that kept West and his team ahead of Kallis's men.

At the next bend in the chasm, halfway up the high vertical wall, the ledge path bored *into* the cliff face, cutting the corner.

The short tunnel there took them to a square, diorite-walled sinkhole cave, twenty feet across and thirty feet deep. Steaming, bubbling volcanic mud—heated by a subterranean thermal source—filled the entire base of the sinkhole. The tunnel continued on the opposite side of the cave.

But the Nazis had once again bridged this gap—so West's crew ran across the bridge, then promptly kicked it into the sinkhole behind them.

THE SECOND STAIRCASE (DESCENDING)

They emerged on the other side of the bend—where they fired some new flares—and beheld a steep staircase that plunged down the curving wall of the chasm before them, hugging it all the way down to the water at its base.

Indeed, the staircase seemed to continue *into* the water . . . right into the mouth of a swirling whirlpool.

But yet again, the Nazis had bridged this peril with a gangway.

West flew down the stairs—running beneath a large and rather ominous wall hole mounted above the tunnel's doorway.

"Jack!" Wizard called. "Trigger stones! Find them and point them out for the rest of us, will you!"

West did so, avoiding any step that was askew or suspicious, and identifying it for the next person in their line.

Their progress was slowed at two places along the staircase—where the stairs had decayed and fallen away, meaning they had to make precarious jumps over the voids.

It was just as the last man in their line—Pooh Bear—was leaping over the second void that another CIEF trooper appeared at the top of the staircase!

Pooh Bear jumped.

The CIEF man charged.

And in his hurry, Pooh Bear landed awkwardly . . . and slipped . . . and fell, dropping clumsily onto his butt, and landing squarely on a trigger stone.

"Blast!" Pooh Bear swore.

Everyone froze, and turned.

"You stupid, stupid Arab . . ." Stretch muttered.

"Stretch . . . not now," West snapped.

An ominous rumbling came from the wall hole at the top of the long, curving staircase.

"Let me guess," Stretch said, "a big round boulder is going to roll out of that hole and chase us down the stairs, just like in *Raiders of the Lost Ark.*"

Not exactly.

Three wooden boulders, each three feet in diameter and clearly heavy, came rushing out of the hole in quick succession—and each was fitted with hundreds of out-ward-pointed bronze *nails*.

They must have weighed 200 pounds each and they bounded down the stairway, booming with every im-pact, bearing down on the team.

West scooped up Lily. "Go! *Go! Go!*"

The team bolted down the stairs, chased by the nail-ridden boulders.

So did the lone CIEF trooper.

West came to the base of the stairs, to the Nazi gangway balanced across the whirlpool there at an odd angle.

He sprang across it, leading Lily by the hand, fol-lowed by Zoe and Big Ears, then Wizard and Stretch.

But the CIEF man was also fleet-footed and,

chased by the nail boulders, he hurdled the two voids easily and almost caught up with Pooh Bear, running last of all, red-faced and breathless.

But at the final moment, Pooh dived forward, leaping full stretch onto the gangway. The CIEF man did the same, but in the instant he leaped into the air, the first of the nail boulders *slammed* into him, piercing his body with at least twenty jagged nails, and swept him into the whirlpool at the base of the stairs, closely followed by the other two boulders, which bounced off the gangway's handrails and away into the water.

"Ouch . . ." said Pooh Bear, lying on the gangway.

"Come on, Pooh!" West called. "No time for resting now."

"Resting? Resting! Pity those of us who don't have your energy, Captain West." And so with a groan, Pooh Bear hauled himself up and took off after the others.

THE DROWNING CAGE

Crossing the Nazi gangway, they arrived at a sizable stone platform separated from the next large stepping-stone by a five-foot-wide gap of water.

A further five feet beyond that stepping-stone was another staircase, going upward. However, this staircase was difficult to access—its first step lay seven feet *above* the swirling water, an impossible leap.

The biggest problem, however, lay above the stepping-stone itself.

A great cube-shaped cage was suspended above it, ready to drop the moment someone landed on it.

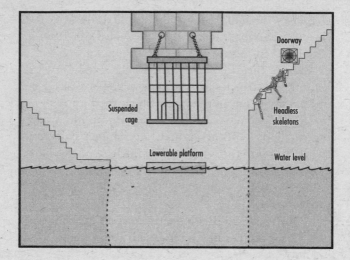

"It's a drowning cage," Wizard said. "We jump onto the stepping-stone and the cage traps us. Then *the whole platform* lowers into the water, cage and all, drowning us."

"But it's the only way across . . ." Zoe said.

Stretch was covering the rear. "Figure something out, people. Because Kallis is here!"

West spun—

—to see Kallis emerge from the sinkhole cave at the top of the staircase behind them.

"What do you think, Jack?" Wizard asked.

West bit his lip. "Hmmm. Can't swim around it because of the whirlpools. And we can't climb up and around it: the wall here is polished smooth. There just doesn't seem to be any way to avoid it . . ."

Then West looked over at the ascending staircase *beyond* the drowning cage's stepping-stone.

Three Nazi skeletons lay on it—all headless. But beyond them, he saw something else:

A square doorway sunk into the wall, covered in cobwebs.

"There *is* no way to avoid it," he said aloud, "so don't avoid it. Wizard. The Templar Pit in Malta. Where we found the Museion scrolls. It's just like that. You have to enter the trap in order to pass it."

Stretch urged, "Some action, people. Kallis is halfway down the stairs . . ."

Zoe said to West: "Enter the trap in order to pass it? What do you mean?"

"Hurry *up,* people . . ." Stretch said. "Warblers don't work at point-blank range."

West spun to see Kallis gaining on them, still with nine more men, only thirty yards away and closing.

"OK everyone," he said, "you have to trust me on this one. No time to go in groups, we have to do this together."

"A bit all or nothing, isn't it, Jack?" Zoe said.

"No other choice. People, get your pony bottles ready. Then we all jump onto that stepping-stone. Ready . . . go!"

And they all jumped together.

The eight of them landed as one on the wide stepping-stone—

—and immediately, the great cage above it dropped, clanging down around them like a giant mousetrap, trapping them under its immense weight—

—and the entire ten-foot-wide stepping-stone began *to sink* into the swirling depths of the water-way!

"I hope you're right, Jack!" Zoe yelled. She grabbed the pony bottle from her belt, put its mouthpiece to her mouth. Breathing from a pony bottle is just like breathing a regular scuba tank, except it only has enough air for about three minutes.

The cage went knee deep in water.

West didn't answer her, just waded over to the wall side of the cage and checked its great bronze bars.

And there he found it—a small archway cut into the cage's wall-side bars, maybe three feet high, large enough for a man to crawl through.

But the stone wall abutting that side of the cage was solid rock. The little arch led nowhere . . .

The cage sank farther into the swirling water and the little arch went under.

Waist deep.

Big Ears lifted Lily into his arms, above the swirling waterline.

On the stairway behind them, Cal Kallis paused, grinned at their predicament.

"*Jack* . . ." Zoe called, concerned.

"*Jack* . . ." Wizard called, concerned.

"It has to come," West whispered to himself. "It has to—"

The cage went two-thirds under, and as it did so, West cracked a glowstick, put his pony bottle to his mouth, and ducked under the choppy surface.

* * *

Underwater.

By the light of his glowstick, West watched the cage's bars slide past the stone wall . . .

Solid rock.

Nothing but solid rock flanked the cage on that side.

It can't be, his mind screamed. *There has to be something down here!*

But there wasn't.

There wasn't anything down there.

West's heart began to beat faster. He had just made the biggest mistake of his life, a mistake that would kill them all.

He resurfaced inside the swirling cage.

The water was chest deep now, the cage three-quarters under.

"Anything down there?" Zoe called.

West frowned, stumped. "No . . . but there should be."

Stretch shouted, "You've killed us all!"

Neck deep.

"Just grab your pony bottles," West said grimly. He looked to Lily; held high in Big Ears's arms. "Hey, kiddo. You still with me?"

She nodded vigorously—scared out of her wits. "Uh-huh."

"Just breathe through your pony bottle like we practiced at home," he said gently, "and you'll be all right."

"Did you mess up?" she whispered.

"I might have," he said.

As he did so, he locked eyes with Wizard. The old man just nodded: "Hold your nerve, Jack. I trust you."

"Good, because right now I don't," West said.

And with that, the great bronze cage, with its seven trapped occupants, went completely under.

With a muffled *clunk,* the cage came to a halt, its barred ceiling stopping exactly three feet below the surface.

The underwater currents were extremely strong. On the cage's outermost side, the silhouette of a whirlpool could be seen: a huge inverted cone of downward-spiraling liquid.

Pony bottle to his mouth, West swam down to check the little arch one final time . . .

. . . where he found something startling.

The little arch had stopped perfectly in line with a small dark opening in the stone wall.

Shape for shape, the arch matched the opening exactly, so that if you crawled through the arch, you escaped *into* the submerged wall.

West's eyes came alive.

He spun to face the others, all trapped in the submerged cage with pony bottles held to their mouths, even Lily.

He signaled with his hands:

Wizard would go first.

Then Big Ears with Lily. Zoe, Stretch, Pooh Bear, and West last of all.

Wizard swam through the arch, holding a glowstick in front of him, and disappeared into the dark opening in the wall.

West signaled for Big Ears to wait—wait for Wizard to give them all clear.

A moment later, Wizard reappeared and gave an enthusiastic OK sign.

So through the little arch they went, out of the cage and into the wall, until finally only Jack West Jr. remained in the cage.

No one saw the relief on his face. He'd made the call, and almost killed them all. But he'd been right.

Kicking hard, he swam out of the cage, his boots disappearing into the tiny opening.

The opening in the wall quickly turned upward, becoming a vertical shaft, complete with ladder handholds.

This shaft rose up and out of the sloshing water before opening onto a horizontal passage that led *back* to the main chasm, emerging—unsurprisingly—at the cobweb-covered doorway a few steps up the ascending staircase, the same doorway West had observed earlier.

As they stepped out from the passage, West saw Kallis and his men arriving at the base of the previous staircase, stopped there by the now-resetting cage.

Lying on the steps in front of West were the three headless Nazi skeletons he had spied before.

Wizard said, "Headless bodies at the *bottom* of a stairway mean only one thing: blades at the top somewhere. Be careful."

Retaking the lead, West gazed up this new stairway. "Whoa. Would you look at that . . ."

At the top of the stairs was a truly impressive structure: a great fortified guard tower, leaning out from the vertical cliff two hundred feet above the watery chasm.

The ancient guard tower was strategically positioned on the main bend of the chasm. Directly opposite it, on the other side of the roofed chasm, was its identical twin, another guard tower, also jutting out from its wall, and also possessing a stairway rising up from a drowning cage down at water level.

West had taken one step up this stairway when—

"Is that you, Jack!" a voice called.

West spun.

It hadn't come from Kallis.

It had come from farther away.

From the other side of the chasm.

West snapped round.

And saw a *second* American special forces team standing on the path on the other side of the chasm, on the platform preceding the drowning cage on that side.

They had emerged from a side doorway in the rock wall opposite, *twenty-four men* in total.

At their head stood a man of about fifty, with steely black eyes and, gruesomely, *no nose*. It had been cut off sometime in the distant past, leaving this fellow with a grotesque misshapen stump where his nose should have been.

Yet even with this glaring facial disfigurement, it was the man's clothing that was his most striking feature right now.

He wore steel-soled boots just like West did.

He wore a canvas jacket just like West did.

He wore a belt equipped with pony bottles, pitons, and X-bars, just like West did.

The only difference was his helmet—he wore a lightweight caver's helmet, as opposed to West's fireman's helmet.

He was also older than West, calmer, more confident. His small black eyes radiated experience.

He was the one man West feared more than any other on Earth. The man who had been West's last field commander in the military. The man who had once left West for dead on the plains outside Basra in Iraq.

He was a former commander of Delta Team Six, the best within Delta, but was now, thanks to the machinations of some very powerful men, the commanding officer of the CIEF, the very best special forces unit in the world and a power unto itself.

He was Colonel Marshall Judah.

COMPARATIVE POSITIONS IN HAMILCAR'S REFUGE

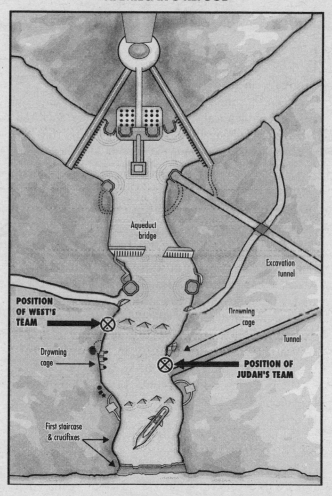

Aqueduct bridge

Excavation tunnel

POSITION OF WEST'S TEAM

Drowning cage

Drowning cage

Tunnel

POSITION OF JUDAH'S TEAM

First staircase & crucifixes

In their current positions, West and his team were marginally ahead of Judah.

Given that the paths running on either side of the chasm were identical, West's team was one trap ahead. Judah had yet to pass the drowning cage on his side, and had just stepped out onto the base of the descending stairway over there, in doing so setting off—

—three nail-studded boulders.

The three boulders tumbled down the stairway toward Judah and his men.

Judah couldn't have cared less.

He just nodded to three of his men, who quickly and competently erected a sturdy tripodlike barricade between their team and the oncoming nail boulders.

The titanium-alloy barricade blocked the entire width of the stairway and the boulders slammed into it one after the other, each one being deflected by the sturdy barricade and bouncing harmlessly away into the water.

Judah never took his eyes off West.

"How are those dreams going, Jack? Still trapped in that volcano?" he called. "Still haunted by the chants and the drums?"

On his side of the chasm, West was stunned. *How could Judah know that . . .*

It was exactly the response Judah had wanted. He smiled a thin, cold smile. "I know even more than that, Jack! More than you can possibly suspect."

West was rattled—but he tried not to show it.

It didn't work.

Judah nodded at the fireman's helmet now back on West's head. "Still using that fireman's hat, Jack? You know I never agreed with that. Too cumbersome in tight places. It always pains a teacher to see a talented student employing foolish methods."

West couldn't help himself—he glanced up at his helmet.

Judah followed through, driving home his edge "Looks like we've got something of a race on our hands here, Jack. Think you can outrun me? Do you seriously think *you* can outrun *me*?"

"Everybody," West said quietly to his people, not taking his eyes off Judah. "We have to run. Fast. Now. Go!"

West's team bolted up their stairs, heading for the guard tower at its peak.

Judah just nodded calmly to his men, who immediately began erecting a long gangway to bypass their drowning cage and reach the ascending stairway on their side of the chasm.

The race was on.

THE GUARD TOWER AND THE GORGE

West and his team ran up their stairway.

Just before the guard tower, a narrow gorge cut across their path. It was maybe fifteen feet across, with sheer vertical sides. This little gorge actually sliced all the way across the *main* chasm, and as such, had a twin over on the other side.

And once again, the Nazis had been helpful. It seemed that the ancient Carthaginians had built a complex chain-lowered *drawbridge* to span the gorge—a drawbridge that the Nazis had managed to lower into place, spanning the void.

Taking any luck they could get, West and his team sprinted across the ancient drawbridge, and arrived at the guard tower high up on the next bend in the chasm.

There was a ladder hewn into the guard tower's curved flank, a ladder that wound *around* the outside of the structure, meaning they had to free-climb two hundred feet above nothing but the swirling waters below.

Two head-chopping blades sprang out from slits in the wall ladder, but West neutralized them with sticky foam, and his team, roped together, successfully climbed around the gravity-defying guard tower.

On the other side of the chasm, Judah's long lightweight bridge fell into place and his men ran across it, completely avoiding their drowning cage, reaching the base of their ascending staircase.

The wall ladder on the outside of West's guard tower brought his team up onto its balcony.

A tight tunnel in the back of the balcony delved into the chasm wall itself and emerged on the other side of the bend, where West fired off three self-hovering flares . . .

. . . to gloriously reveal the far end of the chasm and their goal.

"*Holy* shit . . ." Big Ears gasped.

"Swear jar," Lily said instantly.

Standing there before them in all its splendor, towering above the waterway, lording over it, easily fifteen stories tall and jutting out from the far-facing rock wall, was a gigantic ancient fortress.

The steaming vents of the chasm gave the fortress a grim haunting look.

A supersolid box-shaped keep formed the core of the structure, with a giant gaping archway in its exact center. This central section was flanked by two soaring defensive towers, high-spired pinnacles in the darkness. The style of these towers matched that of the guard tower that West had just passed through—only these were taller, stretching all the way up from the water.

Stretching downward from the Great Arch in the center of the keep was a wide, guttered rampway that lanced all the way down to the waterway, ending at a flat stone jetty. At least 130 feet in length, with stairs nestled in its center, the rampway resembled the step ramps on Hatshepsut's mortuary temple near the Valley of the Kings.

Never finished and never used for its intended purpose—and long since concealed by an ingenious Egyptian architect—this was Hamilcar's Refuge.

West snatched his printout from his pouch, examined it:

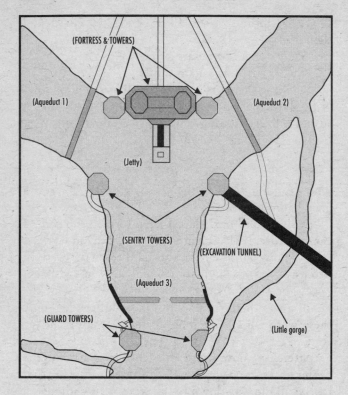

Just like on the ancient drawing, the chasm before him ended at a Y-junction, splitting into two diverging channels. The Refuge sat nestled in the V at the top of the Y, facing the long upright "stem."

Two more spirelike "sentry towers" sat on either side of the stem, facing the two towers of the Refuge itself.

As if all this weren't colossal enough, the Refuge featured two more soaring aqueduct bridges to add to the broken one in the main chasm—two hundred feet high and made of many bricked arches.

These two new bridges spanned the Y-channels of the waterway, but unlike the one crossing the main chasm, they were whole and intact.

It was Zoe who noticed the rock wall behind the Refuge.

"It slopes *backward*," she said. "Like the cone of a—"

"Come on, we don't have time," West urged them on.

The final stretch of the chasm featured a descending stairway followed by an *ascending* ramp. The ramp slithered up the left-hand wall of the chasm, bending with every curve. Curiously, it bore a low upraised gutter on its outer edge, the purpose of which was not readily apparent.

Of course, this stairway-ramp combination was mirrored on Judah's side of the chasm.

West and his team charged down their descending stairway, avoiding a couple of blasting steam vents on the way.

In the meantime, Judah's team had just crossed their little gorge and arrived at their guard tower.

They started climbing around it.

THE ASCENDING RAMP

An unusually high stepping-stone separated the base of the descending stairway from the base of the ascending ramp. It jutted out from the wall about thirty feet above the waterway.

The guttered ascending ramp rose above West and his team, stretching upward for a hundred yards, ending at the left-hand sentry tower. It was four feet wide, enough for single file only, and a sheer drop to the right of it fell away to the swirling waters below.

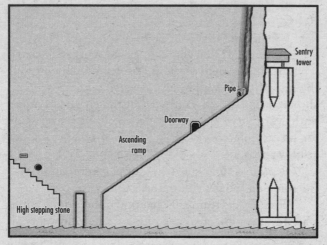

The ramp featured two openings along its length: one two-thirds of the way up that looked like a doorway; the second all the way at the very top of the ramp, that looked more like a *pipe*.

Ominously, a wispy thread of steam issued out from the pipe, dissipating as it spread into the chasm.

Wizard was enthralled. "Ooh, it's a Single-Exit Convergence Trap . . ."

"A what?" Pooh Bear said.

West said, "He means it's a race between us and

whatever liquid comes out of that pipe. We have to get to the doorway before the liquid does. I assume the high stepping-stone triggers the contest."

"What kind of liquid?" Big Ears asked.

Wizard said, "I've seen crude-oil versions. Heated quicksand. Liquid tar . . ."

As Wizard spoke, West stole a glance back at Judah's men.

They were climbing around the outside of their guard tower, high above the waterway, moving in a highly coordinated way—far faster than his team had.

The first CIEF man climbed over the balcony and disappeared inside the tower.

"No time to ponder the issue," he said. "Let's take the challenge."

And with that he jumped onto the stepping-stone and bounced over onto the ascending ramp.

No sooner had his foot hit the stepping-stone than a blast of superhot volcanic mud vomited out from the pipe at the top of the ramp. Black and thick, the mud was so hot it bore thin streaks of golden red magma in its oozing mass.

The ramp's gutter instantly came into effect.

It funneled the fast-oozing body of superheated mud down the ramp, toward West's team!

"This is why we train every day," West said. "Run!"

Up the ramp the seven of them ran.

Down the ramp the red-hot mud flowed.

It was going to be close—the ramp was obviously constructed in favor of the mud.

But West and his team were fit, prepared. They bounded up the slope, heaving with every stride, and they came to the doorway set into the wall just as the mud did and they charged in through it one after the other, West shepherding them through, diving in himself just as the volcanic mud slid by him, pouring down the ramp, where it ultimately tipped into the waterway at the bottom, sending up a great hissing plume of steam.

Judah's team, close behind West's, handled their ramp in a different way.

They sent only one man up it: a specialist wearing a large silver canister on his back and holding a device that looked like a big-barreled leafblower.

The specialist raced up the ramp and beat the flowing mud to his doorway, where instead of disappearing inside the doorway, he fired his big "leafblower" *at the ramp*.

Only instead of hot air, the device he held spewed forth a billowing cloud of supercooled liquid nitrogen, which instantly turned the leading edge of the mudflow into a solid crust that acted like a dam of sorts, funneling the rest of the oncoming mud off and over the outer edge of the ramp!

This allowed Judah and his team to just stride up their ramp in complete safety, heading for the sentry tower on their side—moving ever forward.

In stark contrast, West and his team arrived in their sentry tower breathless and on the run.

"Even if we get this Piece of the Capstone," Stretch said, "how can we possibly get it out? How can we get it past the Americans? And if it's a large Piece, it'll be nine feet square of near-solid gold—"

Pooh Bear scowled. "Always argue the negative, don't you, Israeli. Sometimes I wonder why you even bothered to come on this mission."

"I came to keep an eye on all of you," Stretch retorted.

Wizard said, "If we can't *get* the Piece, we at least need to *see* the Piece. Lily has to see the positive incantation carved into its upper side."

West ignored them all.

He just peered out from the balcony of the sentry tower, down at the Great Arch of the Refuge.

He eyed the jetty at the bottom end of the guttered rampway stretching down from the Great Arch. The jetty stood at a point exactly halfway between the two sentry towers, and it was covered by a small four-pillared marble gazebo. The vertical distance from West's balcony to the little gazebo: 150 feet.

"Big Ears. I need a flying fox to that gazebo."

"Got it."

Big Ears whipped out his M16, loaded a grappling

hook into its underslung grenade launcher, aimed, and fired.

The hook whizzed out across the chasm, arcing high through the air, its rope wobbling through the air behind it. Then it shot downward, toward the marble gazebo on the jetty, until—*thwack!*—the hook whip-lashed around one of the gazebo's pillars and took hold.

"Nice shot, brother," Zoe said, genuinely impressed.

Big Ears looped his end of the hook's rope around a pillar in the sentry tower's window and the rope went taut—creating a long steep zipline that stretched down and across the chasm, from the high sentry tower down to the low jetty.

"Lily," West said, "you're with me from here. Grab on. We go first."

Lily leaped into West's arms, wrapped her hands around his neck. West then slung a compact handlebar-like flying fox over the rope and pushed off—

—and the two of them sailed out over the immense chasm, across the face of Hamilcar's Refuge, tiny dots against the great ancient fortress—

—before they slid to a perfect halt on the surface of the little jetty that lay before the dark, looming structure.

"OK, Zoe, come on down," West said into his radio.

Zoe whizzed down the rope on her own flying fox, landing deftly next to West and Lily.

"Wizard, you're nex—" West said.

Bam!

Gunshot.

It echoed loudly across the great chasm.

West spun, saw one of Judah's snipers aiming a long-barreled Barret rifle out from their sentry tower's balcony . . . and suddenly realized that he was no longer within the protective range of the Warbler.

But strangely no bullet impact hit near him, Zoe, or Lily.

And then the realization hit West.

The sniper wasn't aiming for them.

He was aiming at the—

"Damn it, no . . ."

Bam!

Another shot.

Ping! Shwack!

The flying fox's *rope* was severed right in its middle and went instantly slack, cut clean in two. It dropped, limp, into the water.

And suddenly West, Zoe, and Lily were out on the jetty, all on their own, completely separated from the rest of their team.

"No choice now," West said grimly. Then, into his radio: "Big Ears, Pooh Bear, Stretch. Give us some cover fire. Because in four seconds we're gonna need it!"

Exactly four seconds later, right on cue, a withering barrage of gunfire blazed out from Judah's sentry tower.

A wave of bullets hammered the marble gazebo where West, Zoe, and Lily were taking cover.

Impact sparks exploded all around them.

But then the reply came from West's team, on their tower: roaring fire, aimed at the opposite sentry tower.

Bullets zinged back and forth across the main chasm, between the two towers.

The cover fire had its intended effect: it forced Judah's men to cease firing briefly and thus gave West the opening he needed.

"OK, now!" he yelled to Zoe and Lily.

Out of the gazebo they ran, up the wide, guttered rampway that gave access to the fortress, tiny figures against the enormous ancient citadel.

They flew up the stairs and, to the sound of gunfire outside, disappeared inside the dark yawning entrance to Hamilcar Barca's long-abandoned Refuge.

They entered a high-ceilinged many-pillared hall. The pillars ran in long sideways lines, so that the hall was exceedingly wide but not very deep.

It was absolutely beautiful—every column was ornately decorated, every ghostlike statue perfectly cut. It was also curiously Roman in its styling—the heavy-trading Carthaginians had been incredibly similar to their Roman rivals. Perhaps that was why they had been such bitter enemies over three bloody Punic Wars.

But this hall was long deserted. Its floor lay bare, covered in a layer of gray ash.

It had also been modified by the Ptolemaic Egyptian engineers.

A wide ascending tunnel bored into the earth behind the fortress, continuing in a straight line from the Great Arch's entry rampway. Indeed, this tunnel and the rampway were connected by a flat path that crossed the pillared hall and also featured raised gutters on its edges.

Zoe said, "Looks like these gutters are designed to funnel some kind of liquid that flows out from the tunnel's core, through this hall, and down the front ramp."

"No time to stop and stare," West said. "Keep moving."

They ran across the stupendous hall, dwarfed by its

immense pillars, and entered the gently sloping tunnel sunk into its innermost wall.

At the same time, outside in the chasm, Big Ears, Stretch, Wizard, and Pooh Bear were engaged in their fierce gun battle with the CIEF unit over in the other sentry tower.

"Keep firing!" Wizard yelled above the din. "Every moment we keep Judah pinned down is another moment Huntsman has inside the Refuge—"

He was abruptly cut off as, all of a sudden, the entire chasm shook and shuddered.

For a moment, he and the others stopped firing.

So did Judah's men—in fact, they started to abandon their position on their sentry tower.

"What is this . . . ?" Big Ears eyed the cavern around him.

"It feels like an earthquake . . ." Pooh Bear said.

"It's not an earthquake," Wizard said, realizing.

The next instant, the source of the great rumbling burst out of the wall at the base of Judah's sentry tower, just above the waterline of the main chasm itself.

It was a M113 TBV-MV (Tunnel-Boring Vehicle, Medium Volume). The military equivalent of a commercial tunnel-boring engine, it was in truth an M113A2 bridge-laying vehicle that had been adapted for tunnel-making.

The size of a tank, it had a huge pointed nose that whizzed around and around, screwlike, obliterating everything in its path. Chewed-up rock and dirt was "digested" through the center of the vehicle and disposed out the rear. It also bore on its roof a foldable mechanical bridge.

The tunnel-boring vehicle poked out through the wall at the base of the sentry tower and stopped, its drill bit still spinning, only twenty horizontal meters from the jetty that West had ziplined down to.

"They drilled through the filled in excavation tunnel . . ." Wizard breathed in awe. "How clever. It wouldn't have given a modern tunnel borer much resistance."

"It helps if you have the logistics," Stretch said.

"Which they do," Pooh Bear said.

At that moment, the tunnel-boring vehicle engaged its internal engines to fold forward the steel bridge on its roof. The mechanical bridge unfolded slowly, stretching out in front of the tunnel borer until it was fully flat and extended. At which point, it touched down lightly against the jetty twenty meters away.

The American tunnel and the jetty were now connected.

"Man, they're good . . ." Big Ears said.

A second later, Judah's team rushed across the bridge, guns up, having raced down the internal stairs of their sentry tower.

They fired up at Wizard's men as they crossed the metal bridge.

Big Ears and the others tried to halt them with more cover fire, but it was no use.

Judah's men were across the waterway and racing up the rampway into Hamilcar's Refuge.

They were going in, only a minute behind West, Zoe, and Lily.

West, Zoe, and Lily raced up the ascending tunnel behind the fortress, guided by glowsticks.

As he ran, West noticed large clumps of dried solidified mud clinging to the edges of the rampway. He frowned inwardly. *Dried mud? How had it come to be here?*

"*Jack! Zoe!*" Wizard's voice called in their earpieces. "*Judah's crossed over the waterway! I repeat, Judah has crossed the waterway! He's right behind you!*"

After about a hundred meters of dead-straight, steadily rising tunnel, they emerged in a high dome-ceilinged chamber—

—and froze.

"What the—" Zoe breathed. "There are *two* of them . . ."

The chamber was perfectly circular and it reeked of gaseous sulfur, the smell of volcanoes. It was also distinctly holy, reverential, a shrine.

Alcoves lined its curved walls—housing broken and decayed Carthaginian statues—while on the chamber's far side rose a wide granite dam, behind which simmered a wide pool of bubbling volcanic mud, the source of the foul sulfurous odor.

And lying on the floor before West, Lily, and Zoe were six skeletons of long-dead Nazi soldiers. All were hideously deformed: the bottom half of each man was missing, their legs simply gone. Indeed, the lower ends of their spinal columns seemed to have *melted* . . .

Beyond the grisly skeletons, however, was the main feature of the holy chamber.

Rising in the chamber's exact center, ten feet above the floor of the perfectly round room, was an elevated platform, fitted with a flight of wide rising steps, and on it—to West's surprise—lay not one but *two* Ancient Wonders.

Mounted atop the islandlike platform, aimed upward like a satellite dish, stood the fabled Mirror of the Lighthouse of Alexandria.

It was completely covered in gray volcanic ash, but its outline was unmistakable. With its wide fifteen-foot dish, it was simply *astonishing* in its beauty.

West's eyes, however, fell immediately to its base.

Its solid trapezoidal base, also covered in a layer of gray ash.

Suddenly something made sense. the continual use of the word "base" in the texts he had followed to get here. He recalled the original clue to the location of the Pharos Piece:

> *Look for the base that was once the peak of the Great Tower*

And Euclid's Instructions:

> *Base removed before the Roman invasion, Taken to Hamilcar's Forgotten Refuge.*

The Mirror of the Lighthouse was a wonder unto itself, but its base—its plain trapezoidal base—was of immensely greater value.

Its base was the Seventh Piece of the Golden Capstone.

But there was a second monument standing proudly atop the platform—next to the Mirror, on the right-hand side.

It was a huge octagonal marble pillar, standing upright, eight feet in height and seven feet in circumference. Its upper portions had long since been hacked away, but its lower section was perfectly intact.

And just like the Mirror, its base was trapezoidal.

It was *another* Piece of the Capstone.

"Oversized octagonal pillar . . ." Zoe said, her mind racing. "Only one ancient structure was known to possess oversized octagonal pillars—"

"The Mausoleum at Halicarnassus," West said. "Lily hasn't been able to read its entry yet, but I bet when she does, the Callimachus Text will say that its Piece is with the Pharos Piece. When you find one, you find the other. Zoe, we just hit the jackpot. We just found two Pieces of the Capstone."

"We have to do something!" Pooh Bear growled.

"What *can* we do?" Stretch sighed. "They're done for. This mission is over. I say we save ourselves."

They were still in their sentry tower, having watched Judah's force enter the Refuge.

"Typical of you, Israeli," Pooh said. "Your first instinct is always self-preservation. I don't give up so easily, or give up on my friends so easi—"

"Then what do you suggest, you stupid stubborn Arab?"

But Pooh Bear had gone silent.

He was staring out to the left of the fortress, out toward the high multiarched aqueduct that spanned the channel on that side of the Y-junction.

"We cross that," he said determinedly.

In the holy chamber, West approached the central island.

In addition to the two priceless treasures standing on it, one other thing was visible atop the raised island: a seventh Nazi skeleton, lying all on its own, curled in the fetal position on the topmost step.

Unlike the others, this skeleton was not deformed in any way. It was whole and intact, still wearing its black SS uniform. Indeed, its bones were still covered in decaying flesh.

West approached the island and its flight of steps cautiously—the whole flight was probably just one great big trigger stone.

He scanned the skeleton.

Saw a pair of spindly wire-framed glasses still sitting on its nose, saw the red swastika armband, saw the purple amethyst ring on its bony right hand, the ring of a Nazi Party founding member.

"Hessler . . ." he gasped in recognition. It was Hermann Hessler, the Nazi archaeologist, one half of the famed Hessler-Koenig team.

Oddly, the skeleton's right hand was outstretched, seemingly *reaching* down the steps, as if it had been Hessler's last earthly movement, grasping for . . .

. . . a battered leather-bound notebook that lay on the bottom step.

West grabbed the notebook, flipped it open.

Pages of diagrams, lists, and drawings of each of the Ancient Wonders stared back at him, interspersed with German notes written in Hermann Hessler's neat handwriting.

Suddenly, his earpiece roared to life:

"Jack! Zoe!" Wizard's voice called. *"You have to hide! Judah's going to be there any moment now—"*

West spun, just as a bullet sizzled out of the entry tunnel behind him and whizzed over his head, missing his scalp by inches.

"You two, that way!" he ordered Zoe and Lily to the left side of the doorway, while he himself scampered to the right of the stone doorframe, peered back, and saw dark shadows rising up the tunnel, approaching fast.

Decision time.

There was no way he could get to the podium containing the Lighthouse's Mirror and the Mausoleum's Pillar before Judah's force arrived. No way to allow Lily to glimpse their carved incantations.

His eyes scanned the chamber for an escape.

There was some open space on the far side of the island, but it offered no escape: only the wide granite dam that held back the pool of superhot mud lay over there—presumably waiting to be set off by the trigger-stone steps.

And in an instant, it all made sense: the rising tunnel with the clumps of dried mud at its edges, the guttered path in the hall below and the similarly guttered stairs down at the Great Arch: this molten mud, when released from its dam, would flow *around* the raised island containing the Mirror and Pillar and then down through the Refuge, all the way to the water in the chasm, killing any crypt raiders in the process and protecting the two Pieces.

The half-bodied Nazi skeletons, melted at the waist, now also made sense: they'd been killed trying to outrun the mud. Hessler himself must have been trapped atop the podium as it had been surrounded by the stuff. He had then died in perhaps the worst way of all—of starvation, in the dark, alone. His buddy, Koenig, must have escaped somehow and trekked across the desert to Tobruk.

Among the many statue alcoves that lined the circular wall of the chamber, West also saw two smaller openings on either side of the main entry doorway.

They were low, arched tunnels, maybe three feet

high—and elevated slightly above the floor of the chamber by about two feet.

West didn't know what they were, and right now he didn't care.

"Zoe! That little tunnel! Get Lily out of here!"

Zoe swept Lily into the low, arched tunnel on their side of the doorway, while West himself charged over to the right-hand one and peered down it.

The low tunnel disappeared downward in a long dead-straight line.

"No choice," he said aloud.

He ducked inside the little arched tunnel—just as Zoe and Lily did the same on the other side of the chamber—a bare second before Judah's force swept into the holy chamber.

At that exact same moment, four tiny figures were hustling across the superhigh aqueduct bridge that spanned the left arm of the Y-junction.

Led by the frumpy but determined Pooh Bear, they looked like a team of tightrope walkers. But they made it across and disappeared into the small yard-high arched tunnel on the far side.

Marshall Judah stepped into the domed chamber and gazed up at the Mirror and the Pillar.

He grinned, satisfied.

His eyes searched the area for West—scanning the many alcoves, nooks, and crannics.

No sign of him. Yet.

He called: "I know you're in here, Jack! My, my, twice in two days. Looks like you've failed again . . ."

His men fanned out, searching the chamber, guns up.

West backed down his little arched tunnel, praying that the darkness concealed him.

As he moved, he drew his H&K pistol from his thigh holster and aimed it up the tunnel—when with startling suddenness, a CIEF trooper appeared at the top of the tunnel, gun up!

West's finger balanced on his trigger—firing might save him momentarily, but it would also give away his position . . .

But the trooper didn't fire.

He just peered down the tunnel, squinting, searching.

He couldn't see West . . .

But then the CIEF trooper reached for the pair of night-vision goggles hanging from his belt.

* * *

At the same time, in the domed chamber itself, Marshall Judah was evaluating the podium island in the middle of the room with a portable X-ray scanner.

The staircase giving access to the island was indeed one great big trigger stone. And the domed roof was solid diorite—offering no purchase for drilled handholds.

The situation was clear, and typical of Imhotep VI: to get onto the raised island, you had to trigger the trap.

Which meant Judah and his men would have to be quick.

"Gentlemen," he said. "It is an Imhotep VI, Type 4 trap. Time will be short. Prepare the rollers. I want an eight-man lifting team for the Mirror Piece, and a four-man team for the Pillar Piece."

"Do you want us to take the Mirror and the Pillar themselves?" one lieutenant asked.

"I don't give a shit about the Mirror and the Pillar. All I want are the Pieces," Judah snapped.

The CIEF men got into position.

They brought forward two six-wheeled "roller units"—to convey the heavy Pieces out.

"OK, here we go," Judah said.

And with those words, he trod on the first step of the staircase, setting off the deadly trap mechanism.

At that moment, several things happened.

The trooper who had been peering down West's tunnel placed his night-vision goggles to his eyes—and immediately saw West, crouched in the tunnel like a trapped animal.

The trooper whipped up his Colt Commando, pulled the trigger—

Bam!

Gunshot.

From West.

The trooper dropped dead, hit right between the eyes.

In the chamber, three other CIEF men saw their comrade go down and they charged for the right-hand arched tunnel, leading with their guns.

But at the exact moment the CIEF trooper fell, Judah had stepped on the stairway, setting off its trap mechanism.

And the mighty nature of that trap meant he didn't see the CIEF trooper behind him fall.

For as Judah stepped onto the trigger stone, the great granite dam at the far end of the chamber instantly began to lower, *releasing the pool of boiling volcanic mud behind it into the chamber!*

With a titanic *whoosh,* the foul stinking body of mud oozed over the lowering dam and began to fan out slowly into the round chamber.

Judah's men rushed forward, clambering up onto the central island, where they pushed the Mirror and Pillar from their bases.

The spreading body of mud split into two fat fingers that oozed around both sides of the island . . .

A quick wipe to each base revealed its glittering golden surface beneath the layer of ash.

Then the two CIEF teams grabbed the two bases, moving fast.

The two fingers of mud were two-thirds of the way around the island now and moving quickly, ready to devour anything that lay in their paths . . .

Leaving the Pharos's Mirror and the Mausoleum's Pillar lying pathetically on their sides on the island, Judah's team bounded off the raised platform, returning to the chamber's main doorway just as the two creeping fingers of molten mud enveloped the base of the island and touched, surrounding the island completely, sealing it off.

But the mud continued to flow, spreading ever *outward* . . .

Judah's eight-man A-team loaded the Mirror's base onto one of the six-wheeled rollers—a couple of them noting that unlike the other Piece, the Pharos Piece had a human-shaped indentation carved into its underside. Curious. But they didn't have time to examine it now.

The B-team loaded the Mausoleum Piece onto their roller.

And then they were off, led by Judah, racing back down the entry tunnel with the two large golden trapezoids in their midst.

By this time, the three CIEF men who had seen West's victim fall arrived at the right-hand arched tunnel—but with the spreading mud closing in behind them.

Guns up, they peered down the tunnel—saw West; trapped, dead to rights—and pulled their triggers . . .

. . . only to be assailed by a withering volley of gunfire from somewhere behind them.

The three CIEF men convulsed in grotesque

spasms, erupting in a thousand blood spurts, peppered by automatic gunfire.

The volley of gunfire had come from the *left*-hand arched tunnel, on the other side of the main entrance, where Pooh Bear and Big Ears now stood, their Steyr AUG and MP7 submachine guns still smoking!

Guided only by Wizard's incomplete sketch of the Refuge, they had guessed—correctly—that their aqueduct's tunnel led to the same place the fortress's main ascending tunnel led to.

West ran to the top of his tunnel, peered out, saw his lifesaving teammates on the other side of the lava-filled chamber—saw Lily and Zoe safely in their midst.

He would have yelled his thanks, but he arrived there just in time to see the spreading body of mud reach his tunnel's raised entrance and *swallow* the corpses of the four CIEF men as it went by.

The molten mud seared right through their bodies, liquefying them in an instant, before oozing over them, *absorbing them* into its mass.

It was the same on the other side of the chamber— the creeping body of mud had just flowed across the entrance to Pooh Bear's little tunnel and was now heading quickly toward the main doorway of the domed chamber.

The effect was simple.

West was now cut off from both his comrades on the far side of the chamber *and* from the main entrance.

And the level of the flowing mud river was *rising*.

Any second now, it would rise up over the lips of the two arched aqueduct tunnels . . . and flow down them!

From the look on his face, Pooh Bear had seen this, too.

"Pooh Bear! Get out of here!" West called.

"What about you!" Pooh yelled back.

West nodded back down his aqueduct tunnel. "No other option! I have to go this way!"

"Jack!" Wizard called.

"What!"

"Judah used a tunnel-boring vehicle to drill *through* the old filled-in excavation tunnel! They must be planning to take the Pieces out that way! Check your sketch! You may still be able to get a look at the Pieces! All may not be lost!"

"I'll do my best!" West nodded at the expanding mud pool. "Now get out of here! Call Sky Monster! Get to the *Halicarnassus*! I'll catch up somehow!"

And with that, West's team split, went their separate ways, disappearing into the two arched tunnels on either side of the domed chamber—the chamber whose perfectly round floor was now little more than a lake of stinking dark mud, a lake that surrounded a raised island containing the only existing remains of two Ancient Wonders, now lying discarded and broken on their sides.

West bolted down his aqueduct tunnel as fast as his legs could carry him. It was long and tight and dead straight.

In the main tunnel of the fortress, Marshall Judah and his two teams were also hustling, pushing their six-wheeled rollers—bearing the two Pieces of the Capstone—down the slope.

They rushed through the many-pillared hall of the fortress before they emerged in the chasm and raced down the guttered rampway that stretched down from the front of the Refuge.

While in the left-hand aqueduct tunnel, Pooh Bear, Big Ears, Stretch, Wizard, Zoe, and Lily also rushed headlong through their own tight dark passageway.

All three groups ran for good reason—for in the domed chamber high behind them, the radially expanding mud lake finally reached the edge of the round room and began to rise up and over the lips of the three tunnels . . .

. . . at which point it flooded rapidly down each of them!

Three surging fingers of mud roared down the three sloping tunnels.

Since they were tight and small, the two rivers of

mud flowing down the aqueduct tunnels moved faster than the one flowing down the wider main tunnel:

As he ran, West turned to see the glowing orange-red liquid pouring down the tunnel behind him. It moved powerfully, relentlessly, as if it had a will of its own, a will bent on destroying any living thing in its path.

Then, abruptly, West burst out into open space—and found himself standing on the high aqueduct bridge that spanned the right-hand arm of the Y-junction.

The bridge was very high—at least two hundred feet—long, and very narrow, barely wide enough for one person to stand on. For it was not made for human crossing. Its surface wasn't even flat; rather it contained a sunken two-foot-wide channel for mud to flow across.

"Oh man . . ." he breathed.

He stepped out onto the high aqueduct bridge, and suddenly saw Judah's men appear on the jetty far below him, pushing their pair of six-wheeled rollers across their foldout metal bridge. In the recently bored tunnel on the other side of their bridge, the big tunnel-boring vehicle's front screw was now folded open, waiting to be loaded. Judah was going to use the tunnel-boring vehicle to carry the Pieces out.

West remembered Wizard's newsflash from before.

"Check the sketch . . ." he said.

With a glance back at the oncoming mud, he snatched his printout of the ancient sketch.

OK, I'm here. He saw the right-hand aqueduct, labeled *Aqueduct 2.*

Max was right. This aqueduct bridge linked up with the excavation tunnel—the same tunnel that Judah had reopened with his tunnel borer and was now using to get the Pieces out.

West looked up.

If he hurried, he might be able to . . .

He bolted, raced out across the high aqueduct bridge—while far below him, Judah's CIEF team loaded their tunnel-boring vehicle with the two golden trapezoids.

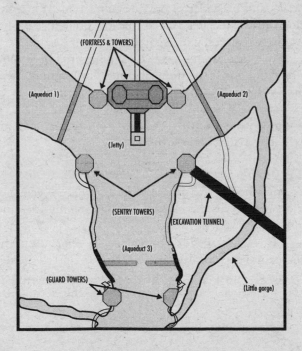

* * *

On the other side of the Y-junction, Pooh Bear emerged from his aqueduct tunnel—just in time to see the aqueduct bridge in front of him get hit, spectacularly, by a rocket-propelled grenade . . . right in the middle!

One of Judah's men had been waiting for them, keeping an eye on the bridge through the crosshairs of an RPG launcher.

The RPG hit the multiarched bridge in the exact center. A huge explosion billowed outwards, hurling bricks and blasted rock in every direction. When the cloud dissipated it revealed that the aqueduct bridge was in two pieces, with a gaping void in its middle.

Pooh Bear spun—saw the long finger of dark mud stretching down the tunnel behind him, coming inexorably closer.

And now he and his team had nowhere to go, no bridge to escape across!

"This is terrible," he breathed.

West dashed across his aqueduct bridge unseen, but still pursued by the elongated finger of mud behind him.

He reached the little tunnel on the other side of the chasm and disappeared into it at speed—just as Judah's people clamped shut the folding front section of their M113 tunnel borer and withdrew the temporary bridge.

Judah shouted, "CIEF units, fall in! We're leaving!"

The tunnel-boring vehicle was like a tank, with tracked wheels and a box-shaped armored body. The main hold of the body was hollow since it usually held troops. When used as a tunnel borer, however, it conveyed crushed rock through its body and disposed of it out the rear, laying it against the walls of the tunnel as hard-packed dirt.

Now that the tunnel had been bored, the hold of the M113 was being used to house the two Pieces of the Capstone.

Four armed CIEF men sat in there, guarding the Pieces.

The rest of Judah's force leaped into four cage-framed Light Strike Vehicles—dune buggies essentially—to escort their prize out of the excavation tunnel.

By this time, Cal Kallis and his team, who had been on West's side of the main chasm, had crossed the main chasm via the broken aqueduct and joined Judah.

"Mr. Kallis," Judah said, pointing up at Pooh Bear's team, trapped up on the partially destroyed left-hand aqueduct. "West's people do not leave this place alive. I want snipers taking them down one at a time if necessary. Join us when you're done."

Then Judah turned and jumped into one of the chase cars.

The CIEF convoy fired up their engines and moved off into the tunnel—two of the small LSVs in front, followed by the big M113 tunnel borer, then the other two LSVs behind.

They left Cal Kallis and his men at the mouth of the tunnel, standing at the waterline—eyeing Pooh Bear's trapped team.

Pooh Bear spun to check the mud behind him. It was close now—only thirty feet away and approaching fast.

The aqueduct bridge before him offered no escape.

But about twenty meters across the cliff face from him was one of the Refuge's high-spired towers—and it was connected to Pooh Bear's bridge by an inch-thin ledge.

"This way!" he ordered the others.

And so they edged out across the ledge, standing on their tiptoes, Wizard, Zoe and Lily, Stretch, and Big Ears, and finally Pooh Bear, who stepped off the remains of the aqueduct bridge a bare second before the stream of mud shot past him, flowed out over the bridge, and fell—gloriously, as a waterfall of thick dark mud—off the newly formed void in its middle, down to the waterway two hundred feet below.

Moments later, an even larger body of mud came roaring out of the main entry of Hamilcar's Refuge. It moved fast, pouring down the rampway and out over the jetty, before it tipped out into the waterway, kicking up a hissing geyser of steam.

The huge geyser shot up into the air, its cloudy haze positioned directly *between* Pooh Bear and Kallis, giving Pooh Bear several valuable seconds of movement.

But then the haze from the geyser began to dissipate and Kallis's snipers opened fire with a vengeance.

* * *

West ran through darkness. Alone.

Guided only by the light of a single glowstick.

His little tunnel was tight, only big enough for him to run through bent over.

After about a hundred yards, however, he heard engine noises up ahead and suddenly—

—he burst out into a wider tunnel, with hard-packed walls of dirt and wide enough for a tank to pass through. Low mounds of dirt lay at regular intervals along the center of the roadway—mounds left behind by the tunnel borer. A long line of fading American glowsticks had been left along its length to illuminate the way back.

It was the excavation tunnel.

The engine noises came from his right, from over a crest in the sloping roadway—the sound of light car engines and the deep-throated diesel roar of the tunnel-boring vehicle.

Judah and his CIEF team.

Approaching fast.

West chucked his glowstick and, thinking fast, quickly rolled out *onto the roadway.*

He rolled into the middle of the tunnel, lying lengthways in a dark shadowy spot, pressing himself close to one of the dirt mounds in the center of the road, half-burying himself in the dirt.

Judah's convoy rose above the crest, headlights blazing.

The lead Light Strike cars whizzed by West on either side, avoiding the dirt mound by inches, before . . .

. . . the great M113 Tunnel-Boring Vehicle thundered over the crest and rumbled right over the top of West, its huge tracked wheels clanking by on either side of his body!

No sooner was it over him than West quickly whipped out his MP7 submachine gun and using its grip as a hook, latched it over a pipe on the underbody of the TBV—and suddenly he was swept along with it, hanging from the huge vehicle's underbelly!

He had to work fast.

He guessed that he had about thirty seconds till they came to the gorge—the narrow gorge that cut across the excavation tunnel: his escape route.

Vastly outnumbered and outgunned, he could never hope to beat all of Judah's CIEF force and take the Pieces. Working alone, there was no way he could carry the two huge Pieces anyway.

The thing was, he didn't want to *carry* them—he just needed to *see* them and take a couple of quick photos of the carvings on their upper sides.

West clambered forward along the underside of the moving tunnel borer, pulling himself forward hand over hand, until he came to the front of the great lumbering vehicle—where he climbed up and over its bow and commenced his one-man war against the CIEF.

Marshall Judah sat in the passenger seat of one of the rear LSVs, keeping an eye on his tunnel borer up ahead.

He never saw West disappear under it—nor did he

see West climb forward along its underbelly to its front bumper—nor did he see West shoot its driver right between the eyes and leap inside the driver's hatch.

No, all Judah saw was several sudden lightning flashes of gunfire flaring within the big tunnel borer— before he saw it veer out of control to the left and grind horribly against the left-hand wall of the tunnel!

The big vehicle crunched against the wall, still moving forward but losing speed, and as it did so, more flashes could be seen flaring within it—only these weren't muzzle flashes from guns, they were different, almost like . . . *camera* flashes.

Then the big tunnel borer regained its alignment and pulled away from the wall, continuing on down the tunnel, where it rumbled across a sturdy ancient stone bridge that spanned a thirty-foot-wide cross gorge. The drop to the watery floor of the gorge was about eighty feet.

Judah couldn't be sure, but as he watched the tunnel borer race across the bridge, he could have sworn he saw a figure leap off its roof and drop into the narrow black gorge, splashing into the water below.

Either way, as soon as it was across the ancient bridge, the tunnel borer again lurched leftward, crunching against the wall, before grinding to a slow labored halt about ninety yards down the tunnel.

The escort cars converged on it, unloaded their men, guns up—

—and found the two golden Pieces still in it, safe and sound.

The driver of the M113 and the four CIEF guards in it were all dead, shot to bits. Their blood covered the walls of the hold. All had got their guns out—but not a single one of them had got a round off.

Judah just gazed at the human wreckage inside the tunnel-boring vehicle, the work of Jack West Jr.

"West, West, West . . ." he said to the air. "You always were good. Perhaps the best pupil I ever had."

Then he reorganized his men and the convoy shot off down the tunnel again, safe and away.

Sniper rounds slammed into the cliff all around Pooh Bear's team as they tiptoed across the cliff face to the fortress's left-hand tower.

The Warbler in Big Ears's backpack was working admirably—bending the bullets away—and one by one, Pooh's team made it to the high-spired tower attached to the fortress.

Far below them, superheated mud continued to flow out the mouth of the great citadel, while above them, the dark ceiling of the chasm was close, barely twenty feet above the peak of their tower.

Then, abruptly, Kallis's men stopped firing.

Pooh Bear exchanged a worried look with Wizard.

Change of tactics.

A brutal change of tactics.

Frustrated by the electromagnetic field of the Warbler, Kallis and his team started firing RPGs at the tower.

It looked like a fireworks display: long hyper-extending fingers of smoke lanced upward from their tunnel, streaking up toward the mighty ancient citadel.

"Oh my Lord," Wizard breathed. "The Warbler won't work against RPGs! RPGs are too heavy to divert magnetically! Somebody do something—"

It was Stretch who came up with the answer.

Quick as a flash, he unslung his sniper rifle, aimed and fired *at the first oncoming RPG*!

The bullet hit the RPG a bare thirty feet from the tower and the RPG detonated in midflight, exploding just out of reach of the tower.

It was an incredible shot. A single shot, fired under pressure, hitting a high-velocity target in *midflight*!

Even Pooh Bear was impressed. "Nice shot, Israeli. How many times can you do that?"

"As long as it takes for you to figure out a way out of here, Arab," Stretch said, eyeing a second incoming RPG through his sights.

Pooh Bear evaluated their position. Their aqueduct was shattered, uncrossable. The main entrance to the fortress was filled with flowing mud. No dice there. And the main chasm, with its traps and deadly whirlpools, was guarded by Kallis's CIEF team.

"Trapped," he said, grimacing in thought.

"Isn't there *any* way out of here?" Big Ears asked.

"This place was sealed long ago," Wizard said.

They all stood in silence.

"Why not go up?" a small voice suggested.

Everyone turned.

It was Lily.

She shrugged, pointed at the "planked" granite ceiling not far above the pinnacle of their tower. "Can't we go out that way? Maybe with one of Pooh Bear's demolition charges?"

Pooh Bear's frown became a grin. "Young lady, I like your style."

A minute later, as Stretch kept the incoming RPGs at bay, Pooh Bear fired a grappling hook up at the high ceiling of the chasm, almost directly above his tower.

The hook he fired was a rock-penetrating climbing hook—but instead of rope, attached to it was a Semtex-IV demolition charge.

The climbing hook slammed into the granite ceiling, embedded itself in it.

One, one thousand . . .

Two, one thousand . . .

Three—

The Semtex charge went off.

Fireball. Explosion. Dustcloud.

And then, with an almighty *craaaack!* one of the granite planks that formed the chasm's ceiling broke in two, and fell from its place, tumbling out of the ceiling formation. It was easily as big as a California redwood tree, and the great granite plank created a huge splash as it hit the waterway far below.

A cascade of sand streamed in through the newly formed rectangular opening in the ceiling, followed by a blazing beam of sunlight that illuminated the tower and lit up the chasm in an entirely new way.

Pooh Bear and the others had completely lost track of time, of how long they'd been in the chasm system. It was actually just after noon.

Kallis's men were still firing RPGs. And Stretch was still picking them off, shot for shot.

Once the Semtex charge had created its opening in the ceiling, Big Ears fired a second grappling hook—only this one *did* have a rope attached to it.

The hook flew up through the big rectangular hole in the ceiling, disappearing up into the daylight, where it landed and caught hold of something.

"Up we go!" Pooh Bear called. "Big Ears. You first. Stretch, you're last."

"As always . . ." Stretch muttered.

"Wizard, call the *Halicarnassus,* send them a pickup signal."

"What about Huntsman?" Lily asked.

"I'll catch up with you all later," a voice said in their earpieces.

West's voice.

"I've got pictures of the Pieces," he said. *"But I can't get back to you guys at the fortress. I'll have to get out another way. I'll call you later."*

And so up the rope they went, climbing into the blinding daylight, all the while protected by Stretch's incredible sniping skills.

When at last Stretch himself had to go, he bolted for the rope, latched on to it and started climbing.

Almost immediately, an RPG slammed into the tower beneath him and with an awesome *booooom,* the left-hand tower of Hamilcar's Refuge burst outward in a star-shaped spray of giant bricks and shattered rock—bricks and rock that sailed far out into the chasm before plunging down into the waterway below.

And when the smoke cleared, the tower stood deprived of its pinnacle, its upper reaches charred and broken, its high-spired balcony simply gone. The great tower had been decapitated.

All that remained in its place was a rectangular hole in the ceiling, through which glorious sunshine now streamed.

Pooh Bear and his team had escaped.

The *Halicarnassus* would pick them up ten minutes later, swooping down to the desert plain for a rapid extraction.

There was, however, no further word from West.

Indeed, as the *Halicarnassus* soared away from the American forces massed around a crater two miles west of the covered Refuge, all contact with West appeared lost.

For the remainder of that day, no one would hear a word from Jack West Jr.

At 2:55 A.M. the next morning, West finally sent a pick-up signal—from a position *sixty miles north* of the concealed inlet that housed Hamilcar's Refuge, a position that put him out in the middle of the Mediterranean Sea!

It was a small Italian resort island, conveniently possessing its own airstrip.

The staff at the resort would long recall the night a dark 747 jumbo jet touched down unannounced on their airstrip and performed a brilliant short-runway landing procedure.

They didn't know what the plane was, or why it had landed briefly on their island.

Two days later, one of their diving expeditions would find a sixty-year-old World War–II-era Nazi U-boat lying aground on a rocky reef just off the southern tip of the island, a submarine that had not been there two days previously.

Its conning tower blazed with the number *"U-342."*

It would become one of the resort's favorite dive spots from then on.

His face dark and grim, West strode into the *Halicarnassus*'s main cabin and without stopping or speaking to any of the assembled team—including Lily—he grabbed Wizard by the arm and hauled him into the back office of the plane with the words: "You. Me. Office. *Now*."

West slammed the door and whirled around.

"Wizard. We've got a mole in our team."

"What?"

"Fool me once, shame on you. Fool me twice, shame on me," West said. "*Twice* now Judah and his Americans have arrived at our location only hours after we got there. The Sudan wasn't conclusive, since they could have tracked the Europeans there. But Tunisia was different. First, the Europeans weren't in Tunisia. Second, even if Judah has a copy of the Callimachus Text, he couldn't have found Hamilcar's Refuge. He needed Euclid's Instructions to find it and *we* have the only copy in existence. They followed us there. Someone on our team *led them there*. Sent up a tracing signal, or somehow got a message out to Judah."

Wizard's face fell. The thought of a rat in their ranks actually pained him—he felt like they had all become something of a family. "Jack. We've been working with these people for *ten years.* How could any of them undermine our mission now?"

"Stretch hasn't been with us for ten years. He's only been with us for three. And he wasn't a part of the original team. He crashed the party, remember. And he represents Israel, not the coalition of the minnows."

Wizard said, "But he's really become a part of the team. I know he and Pooh Bear have Arab-Israeli issues, but I'd say he's blended in rather well."

"And if he hasn't been making secret reports to the Mossad, I'll eat my own helmet," West said.

"Hmmm, true."

West threw out another option: "Pooh Bear? The Arab world is five hundred years behind the West. They'd love to get their hands on the Capstone, and Pooh's uncle the Sheik was unusually keen for the United Arab Emirates to be involved in this mission."

"Come on, Jack, Pooh Bear would step in front of a runaway bus to save Lily. Next theory."

"Big Ears trained with Judah at Coronado in the States a few months before our mission began—"

"Freight train," Wizard said simply.

"What does that mean?"

"If Pooh Bear would step in front of a bus to protect Lily, then Big Ears would step in front of a freight train to save her. And as I recall, you yourself also once went to a U.S.-sponsored training course at Coronado Naval Base in the States, a course conducted by Marshall Judah and the CIEF. That's not even mentioning your mysterious work with him in Desert Storm."

West slumped back in his chair, thought about it all. The problem with a multinational team like theirs was the motivations of its members—you just never knew if members had the team's interests at heart or their own.

"Max. This is not what we need. We're going up against the two biggest fish in the world and getting our asses kicked. We're hanging on by our fingertips."

He took a deep breath.

"I can't believe I'm going to do this: conduct surveillance on my own team. Max, set up a microwave communications net around this plane. A net that will catch all incoming and outgoing signals. If someone's communicating with the outside world, I want to know about it when it happens. We gotta plug this leak. Can you do that?"

"I will."

"We keep this to ourselves for the time being, and we watch everyone."

Wizard nodded. "I've got another issue for you."

West rubbed his brow. "Yes?"

"While you were getting away from Tunisia on that U-boat, I set Lily to work on the Callimachus Text again. It's odd, she says that the language of the Text gets more and more difficult. But at the same time she herself is progressing in skill: sections that she couldn't read yesterday, she can suddenly comprehend today. It's as if the very language of the Text is determining the order in which we can find the Pieces."

"Uh-huh. And . . ."

"She's read the next three entries—the Mausoleum one came next and it just said, 'I lie with the Pharos.' The next two entries concern the Statue of Zeus at Olympia and the Temple of Artemis at Ephesus.

"Following on from the ones we've already translated these new entries confirm a curious pattern: the Text is guiding us through the Seven Wonders of the Ancient World from the youngest Wonder to the oldest. The Colossus, the most recently built, came first, then the Pharos, then the Mausoleum. The next two, those of the Statue of Zeus and the Temple of Artemis, are the next oldest Wonders in the progression."

"The Middle Wonders," West said, nodding. "And you say Lily has now read the entries for them?"

"Yes. And in doing so, she has revealed some very serious problems."

Wizard told West the situation.

After he'd done so, West sat back in his chair and frowned, deep in thought.

"Damn . . ." he said. Then he looked up. "Assemble everyone in the main cabin. It's time to make a tough decision."

The entire team gathered in the main cabin of the *Halicarnassus*.

They sat in a wide circle, variously sitting on couches or at the desklike consoles that lined the walls. Even Sky Monster was there, leaving the plane to fly on autopilot for a while.

West spoke.

"OK, here's the state of play. We're oh-for-two after two efforts at the plate. In those two missions, three Pieces of the Capstone have been unearthed and we have none of them.

"But we're not completely dead yet. We may not have got any of the Pieces, but so long as we keep seeing the Pieces and accumulating the lines of the Positive Incantation carved into them, we still have a chance, albeit a very slim one."

"Very, *very* slim," Stretch said.

West threw Stretch a look that would've frozen water. Stretch retreated immediately. "Sorry. Go on."

West did. "So far the Callimachus Text has been an excellent guide. It has led us accurately to the Colossus and to the Pharos Pieces, and the Mausoleum Piece.

"But now," West said seriously, "now Lily has managed to translate the next two entries, and we have a problem."

"What?" Zoe asked, worried.

"Our enemies may already have the next two Pieces."

* * *

West projected Lily's translation of the next two entries of the Callimachus Text onto a pull-down screen.

They read:

The Statue of cuckolded Zeus,
Cronos's Son, the false deity.
While his statue was immense, his power was illusory.
No thunderbolts did he wield, no wrath did he bear,
No victory did he achieve.
Indeed, it was only the Victory in his right hand
that made him great,
Oh winged woman, whither didst thou fly?

The Temple of the Huntress,
In heavenly Ephesus.
The sister of Apollo, Ra's charioteer,
Has never let go of her Piece,
Even when her Temple burned
on the night of Iskendur's birth.
Through the exertions of our brave brothers,
It has never left the possession of our Order.
Nay, it is worshipped every day
in our highest temple.

Zoe saw the first problem immediately. "There are no *clues* in these verses . . ." she said with dismay.

"There's nothing for us to go on," Fuzzy said.

"More than that," Stretch said, "the writers of the first verse didn't even know where the Statue of Zeus *went.* This is a total dead end."

"You always argue the negative, don't you, Israeli?"

Pooh Bear scowled. "After all they've done, have you no faith in Wizard and Huntsman?"

"I believe in what is achievable," Stretch shot back.

"Gentlemen. Please," Wizard cut in. He turned to Stretch. "It's not a *total* dead end, Benjamin. Close, but not total. The Zeus verse is indeed disappointing, as it offers no clues at all to the location of its Piece.

"But the verse about the Temple of Artemis—the goddess of the hunt and in Greek lore, Apollo's sister—is actually quite clear about the location of its Piece of the Capstone.

"It states that, through the efforts of its priests over the ages, the Artemis Piece has never left the possession of the Cult of Amun-Ra. It even gives us an exact location: the highest temple of the Cult of Amun-Ra. Unfortunately, this means that the Piece is almost certainly already in the hands of our European competitors."

"What do you mean?" Sky Monster asked. "I didn't realize that the Cult of Amun-Ra was still around. I thought it died out. What is it and where is its 'highest temple?' "

"Why, Sky Monster," Wizard said, "the Cult of Amun-Ra is most certainly alive and well. Indeed, it is one of the most widespread religions in the world today."

"A religion?" Big Ears asked. "Which one?"

Wizard said simply: "The Cult of Amun-Ra, my friend, is the Roman Catholic Church."

"Are you saying that the Catholic Church—*my* Catholic Church, the church I have attended all my life—is *a Sun cult?*" Big Ears asked in disbelief.

Very Irish and hence very Catholic, he spun to face West—who just nodded silently, as if it was the most obvious thing in the world.

"Come on," Big Ears said. "I read *The Da Vinci Code,* too. It was a fun book with a great conspiracy theory, but this is something else."

Wizard shrugged. "Although its everyday followers don't know it, the Catholic Church is indeed a thinly veiled reincarnation of a very ancient Sun cult."

Wizard counted the points off his fingers:

"The virgin birth of the Christ character is a direct retelling of the Egyptian legend of Horus—only the names have been changed. Look at the vestments Catholic priests wear: emblazoned with the Coptic Cross. But two thousand years before that symbol was the Coptic Cross, it was the Egyptian symbol, *ankh,* meaning life. Look at the Eucharistic chamber on any altar: it is in the shape of a dazzling golden *Sun.* And what is a halo? A Sun disc.

"Go to Rome and look around. Look at all the obelisks—the ultimate symbols of Sun worship, pointing up at their deity. They are all genuine Egyptian obelisks, transported from Egypt to Rome by Pope Sixtus V and erected in front of *every major church* in the

253

city, including St. Peter's Basilica. There are more obelisks in Rome than any other city in the world, including any Egyptian city! Why, Liam, you tell me, what word do you say at the end of every single Catholic prayer you utter?"

"Amen," Big Ears said.

"The Ancient Egyptians had no vowels in their writing. *Amen* is simply another way of spelling *Amun*. Every time you pray, Liam, you intone the most powerful god of ancient Egypt: Amun."

Big Ears's eyes went wide. "No way . . ."

Zoe brought the conversation back to the point: "But the Artemis verse says that its Piece is *worshipped every day* in the Cult of Amun-Ra's *highest temple*. If what you say is true, then the highest temple of the Roman Catholic Church would be St. Peter's Basilica in the Vatican in Rome."

"That is my conclusion too," Wizard said.

"Welcome to Problem No. 1," West said. "If the Artemis Piece is in St. Peter's Basilica, it could be *anywhere* in there. The cathedral itself is a behemoth, the size of about seven football fields, and beneath it is a labyrinth of tombs, crypts, chambers, and tunnels. For all we know, it could be on display in a crypt, worshipped every day by only the most senior cardinals, or it could be embedded in the floor of the main cathedral, twenty feet underground. Searching for a golden trapezoid in there would be like searching for a needle in a mountain of haystacks. It could take years, and we don't have years."

"And Problem No. 2?" Zoe asked.

Wizard said, "The Zeus piece. As you said before,

this verse gives us absolutely nothing. Beyond the usual legends *we have no way of knowing where it is*."

A silence fell on the room. This situation had not been anticipated. The Callimachus Text had served them so well so far, none of them had thought that it would completely fail them on the later Pieces.

"So what do we do?" Zoe asked.

"There is one option," West said solemnly. "But it's not one that I'd take lightly."

"And that is . . . ?"

"We get outside help," West said. "Help from an expert on the Capstone, perhaps the greatest living expert on it. A man who has devoted his life to pursuing it. A man who knows more about the Seven Ancient Wonders than anyone else alive."

"Sounds like a guy we should have consulted ten years ago," Fuzzy said.

"We would have if we could have," Wizard said, "but this man is . . . *elusive*. He is also psychotic."

"Who is he?" Sky Monster asked.

"His name is Mullah Mustapha Zaeed . . ." West said.

"Oh no, this is outrageous—" Stretch sat upright.

"The Black Priest of Kabul—" Pooh Bear breathed.

West explained for the others.

"Zaeed is Saudi by birth, but he's been linked to dozens of Islamic fundamentalist terrorist groups as far afield as Pakistan, Sudan, and Afghanistan, where he was sheltered by the Taliban until September 11, 2001. A qualified mullah, he's a teacher of fundamentalist Islam—"

"He's an assassin," Stretch spat, "responsible for the deaths of at least twelve Mossad agents. Zaeed's been on the Red List for fifteen years." The Mossad Red List was a list of terrorists whom any Mossad agent was permitted to shoot *on sight* anywhere around the world.

"If the Mossad can't find him, how on Earth are we going to find him at such short notice?" Zoe asked.

West looked to Stretch as he spoke. "Oh, the Mossad knows where he is, they just can't get to him."

The tight-lipped expression of Stretch's face said this was true.

"So where is he then?" Pooh Bear asked.

West turned to Stretch.

Stretch practically growled as he spoke. "Mustapha Zaeed was picked up by U.S. forces during Operation Enduring Freedom, the invasion of Afghanistan after 9/11, the one that toppled the Taliban regime. In early 2002, Mustapha Zaeed was taken to Camp X-Ray, the temporary terrorist prison at Guantanamo Bay, Cuba. He's been there ever since."

"Guantanamo Bay," Zoe repeated. "Cuba. The most heavily guarded, most secure military compound *in the world*. And what—we're just going to stroll in there and walk out with a known terrorist?"

West said, "Naval Station Guantanamo Bay is designed for two things: to keep the Cubans from retaking it; and to keep prisoners *in*. Its guns are pointed landward and inward. That leaves us one open flank—the sea side."

Zoe said, "I'm sorry, but are you seriously thinking of sneaking into Guantanamo Bay and busting out one of its inmates?"

"No," West said, standing. "I'm not planning on *sneaking* in at all. No, I suggest we do the one thing the Americans least expect. I suggest we launch a frontal assault on Guantanamo Bay."

THIRD MISSION
THE BATTLE OF GUANTANAMO BAY

CUBA

GUANTANAMO BAY, CUBA
MARCH 17, 2006
THREE DAYS BEFORE TARTARUS

CUBA

100 MILES

GUANTANAMO BAY

U.S. NAVAL STATION
GUANTANAMO BAY, CUBA

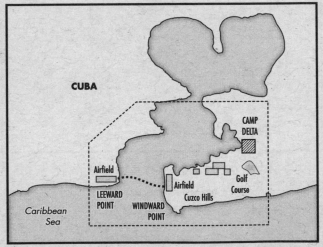

CUBA

CAMP DELTA

Airfield

Airfield

Cuzco Hills

Golf Course

LEEWARD POINT

WINDWARD POINT

Caribbean Sea

Naval Station Guantanamo Bay is a true historical oddity.

Born out of two treaties between the United States and Cuba made in the early twentieth century—when the U.S. had Cuba over a barrel—Cuba essentially leases a small chunk of its southeastern coast to America at the obscenely low rent of $4,085 a year (the actual price mentioned in the treaty is "$2,000 in gold per year").

Since the treaty can only be terminated by the agreement of *both* parties—and since the U.S. has no intention of agreeing to such a termination—what it amounts to is a permanent military outpost on Cuban soil.

The bay is situated at the extreme southern tip of Cuba, opening onto the Caribbean Sea, facing away from America. Occupying both of its promontories is the U.S. base, and it is very small—maybe four miles deep by six miles long; its twisting and turning landside fence line barely fifteen miles in length.

After all that, its most well known feature (apart from the Tom Cruise movie *A Few Good Men*) is its status in international law: for as far as international law is concerned, Guantanamo Bay does not exist. It floats in a kind of legal limbo, free of the constraints of the Geneva Convention and other troublesome treaties.

Which was exactly why the United States chose it as a prison for the seven hundred "stateless combatants" that it captured in Afghanistan during Operation Enduring Freedom.

The bay itself bends northward like a fat, slithering snake, bounded by dozens of inlets and marshy coves. Its western side is known as Leeward, and it contains little of interest except for the base's airstrip, Leeward Point Field.

It is on the eastern side of the bay—Windward—where all the real activity takes place. This is where the various Marine barracks and prison complexes are situated. An inactive airfield, McCalla Field, occupies the eastern side of the harbor entrance. Farther inland, there are administrative buildings, a school, shops, and a housing estate for the Marines who live on base.

Further inland still, at Radio Range, in the dead heart of Naval Station Guantanamo Bay, you will find Camp Delta. (Camp X-Ray, with its notorious open-air chain-link cages, was always intended to be temporary. In April 2002, all of its detainees were shipped to the newly constructed Camp Delta, a more permanent complex.)

Camp Delta is made up of six detention camps: Camps 1, 2, 3, 4, Echo, and Iguana. Camp 3 is the "SuperMax" facility. Only the most dangerous prisoners live in Camp 3.

Prisoners like Mullah Mustapha Zaeed.

In short, Camp Delta, nestled in the center of the world's most heavily fortified base, is a maze of cinder-block buildings and chain-link fences, all topped with razor wire and guarded by stony-faced U.S. Army Military Police.

It is a forbidding installation, one of the bleakest places on Earth.

And yet after all that, only a quarter of a mile from the Camp's outermost razor-wire fence is something you would find only in an American military base, a golf course.

With two heavily defended airfields to choose from, naturally West aimed for the golf course.

"I know Gitmo . . ." he said, standing in the cockpit of the *Halicarnassus* as it roared down through the night sky, descending on Guantanamo Bay.

After a quick refueling in friendly Spain, they had soared off over the Atlantic, commencing the five-hour flight to Cuba.

". . . I went there once, after some wargames Australia did with the CIEF. Believe it or not, I actually played on the golf course—Christ, a golf course on a military base. Thing is, there aren't many trees and the last few holes—the sixteenth, seventeenth, and eighteenth—run end to end, separated only by low bushes. They're wide and straight and long, about five hundred yards each. About runway length. What do you say, Sky Monster? Think you can do it?"

"Can I?" Sky Monster scoffed. "My friend, give me something harder next time!"

"Great." West turned to leave the cockpit. "See you down on the ground."

* * *

Ten minutes later, West strode into the lower hold of the *Halicarnassus,* dressed entirely in black and wearing his back-mounted carbon-fiber wings.

Zoe was waiting for him, also dressed in black, also wearing a wing set. The tight formfitting bodysuit brought out the best in her slender figure. Lean and shapely, Zoe Kissane was beautiful and *fit.*

"I hope you're right about this," she said.

"Surprise is the key. Their guns are pointed at the Cubans and at their seven hundred prisoners. The Americans don't think anyone is stupid enough to take Guantanamo Bay head-on."

"Nope. Only us," Zoe said.

"Have you checked out Stretch's satellite image of Camp Delta?"

"Three times," Zoe said. "The intel from Mossad says that Zaeed is in hut C-12 of Camp 3, solitary confinement. Hope we can spot it in the dark. Is there anything Mossad doesn't know?"

"Mossad knows what my aunt Judy eats for breakfast." West checked his watch. "We're eight minutes out. Time to fly."

Moments later, the rear ramp of the 747 rumbled open and they leaped out of it together, disappearing into the night sky.

Inside the *Halicarnassus* itself, every battle station was manned.

Big Ears, Fuzzy, Pooh Bear, and Stretch all sat in

the great black plane's four gun turrets—Big Ears and Pooh Bear on the wing-mounted turrets; Fuzzy on the underbelly, and Stretch up on the 747's domed roof.

Their six-barreled miniguns were currently loaded with superlethal 7.62mm armor-piercing tracer rounds—but they had special instructions from West as to what to use later, when the battle got really hot.

Wizard, Lily, and Horus had been dropped off at a safe island location nearby—it was far too dangerous to bring Lily on this mission.

The *Halicarnassus* thundered through the night sky.

It flew without lights, so it was little more than a dark shadow against the clouds; and it had long ago been stripped of its transponder—so it gave off no electronic signature.

And its black radar-absorbent paint, the same as that used on the B.2 Stealth Bomber, deflected any radar scans the Americans projected from Gitmo.

It was a ghost.

A ghost the American forces at Guantanamo Bay would not know existed until it was right on top of them.

In the end, it was a pair of night sentries who saw it—or, rather, *heard* it—first. They were posted on one of the most far-flung sentry towers on the base, on a remote headland overlooking the ocean about two klicks east of Windward Point, near the Cuzco Hills.

They saw the huge black shadow come roaring in

low over their heads, zooming in from the south, from over the Caribbean Sea.

They called it in immediately.

And so the alert went out, and the 3,000-strong American force at Guantanamo Bay declared war on Jack West Jr. and his team.

The *Halicarnassus* shot low over the Cuzco Hills, bearing down on the rumpled moonlit landscape of Guantanamo Bay. It was 3:45 in the morning.

Then the big 747 banked sharply to the left and disappeared below the tree line . . .

. . . landing right on the fairway of the sixteenth hole of the Guantanamo Bay Golf Course, its wing lights blazing to life as it did so!

The plane's massive tires ripped up the pristine fairway, churning up great ragged chunks of grass, its glaring wing lights lighting up the way. It romped down the sixteenth fairway, rumbled onto the seventeenth.

The stand of bushes separating the seventeenth from the eighteenth hole loomed in front of it, and Sky Monster called out on his radio: "Gunners! Mow 'em down!"

All four of his gunners responded immediately— and they let fly with a blazing barrage of tracer fire, a barrage that ripped mercilessly through the stand of trees, cutting through each at the base so that just as the last tree fell, the *Halicarnassus* blasted over the top of its stump and rumbled down the eighteenth fairway.

Klaxons and alarms wailed all over Guantanamo Bay. Flashing lights erupted everywhere.

Marines leaped out of their beds.

Guard tower sentries scanned the perimeter down the barrels of their M16s.

Spotlights searched the sky for more aircraft.

The word went out: they were being attacked . . . *from the golf course!*

Two crack teams of Recon Marines were dispatched to the golf course, while Black Hawk helicopters and a much larger force was assembled to follow up behind them.

And every single jail on the base was instantly placed into lockdown—every gate was double-locked via computer, every guard post sentry team was doubled.

It was chaos.

Pandemonium.

And in all the chaos and confusion that had followed the *Halicarnassus*'s spectacular landing on the golf course, no one noticed the two black-winged figures that descended over Gitmo with graceful silent swoops, landing lightly and silently on the flat concrete roof of hut C-12 in Camp 3 of Camp Delta.

West detonated a Semtex charge on the roof of the cinder-block cabin, blasting a hole in it big enough for him to fit through.

He jumped down through the hole—

* * *

—and landed in darkness on the roof of a cube-shaped wire-mesh cage. A blowtorch made short work of the cage's roof and West leaped down into it—

—to see a skeletal wraithlike figure come rushing out of the darkness at him, arms outstretched!

West pivoted quickly and sent Zaeed thudding into the wall, where he pinioned the terrorist and shone his barrel-mounted flashlight right into the man's eyes.

By the light of the flashlight, Zaeed looked positively *scary*.

The terrorist's beard and hair had been shaved off, leaving him with a crude stubble on both his angular chin and his scalp. He was thin, malnourished. And his eyes—those eyes—they were hollow, sunken into his skull, accentuating his overall appearance of a living skeleton. They blazed with madness.

"Mustapha Zaeed?"

"Ye-yes . . ."

"My name is West. Jack West Jr. I'm here to offer you a one-time deal. We get you out of here, and you help us find the Seven Wonders of the Ancient World and from them, the Golden Capstone of the Great Pyramid. What do you say?"

Any resistance Zaeed still harbored disappeared in an instant at the mention of the Wonders. In his wild eyes, West saw several things at once: recognition, comprehension, and naked ravenous ambition.

"I will go with you," Zaeed said.

"Then let's move—"

"Wait!" Zaeed shouted. "They implanted a microchip

in my neck! A locator! You have to extract it, or they'll know where you've taken me!"

"We'll do it on the plane! Come on, we've got to run!" West called above the sirens. "Zoe! Rope!"

A rope was hurled into the hut from the hole in the roof, and together West and Mustapha Zaeed scrambled up it, out of the cell.

Over at the golf course, the two teams of Recon Marines arrived to behold the *Halicarnassus* standing on the ruins of the shed that had once been their clubhouse, illuminating the area for a full five hundred yards with a dozen outward-pointed floodlights.

Blinded by the dazzling lights, the Marines spread out around the big black 747, raised their guns—

—just as a withering volley of gunfire erupted from the *Halicarnassus*'s four revolving gun turrets.

The volley of bullets slammed into the Recon Marines, sent them flying backward through the air, slamming them into trees and vehicles.

But they weren't dead.

The bullets were rubber bullets, like those West and his team had used in the quarry in Sudan.

West's instructions to his team had been simple: *you only kill someone who wants to kill you. You never ever kill men who are just doing their job.*

And as far as West was concerned, he had no quarrel with the Marine guards at Guantanamo Bay—only with their government and its shadowy backers.

The rubber bullets, however, had another effect on the Recon Marines—it made them think this was an *ex-*

ercise; an elaborate surprise in the dead of night designed by their superiors to test their response.

And so they actually became *less* lethal. They concentrated on surrounding and containing the plane, rather than destroying it.

But then, to their surprise, the big black 747 started moving again, rolling around in a tight circle until it was pointed back up the eighteenth fairway.

Then with its guns still blazing, the big plane's engines fired up. The roar they made was absolutely deafening in the night.

Then the great plane started rumbling *back up* the fairway, having unloaded not a single trooper, having done—seemingly—absolutely nothing.

But then came the most amazing sight.

Two *winged* figures came shooting over the tree-tops from behind the Recon Marines—black-clad figures wearing carbon-fiber wing sets—chasing after the fleeing 747, firing compressed-air thrusters on their backs. They flew in a series of long swoops, like hang gliders powered by the odd thrust of compressed air.

And as the Marines saw the winged figures more closely, their hearts sank for they now understood that this hadn't been an exercise at all.

For one of the low-flying winged intruders carried a *man* harnessed to his chest: a shaven-headed man still dressed in the bright orange coveralls of a Camp 3 detainee.

This was a jailbreak . . .

The two winged figures swooped in low over the right-hand wing of the rolling *Halicarnassus,* where they landed deftly and ran inside an emergency door which swung shut behind them.

Then the *Halicarnassus* picked up speed and thundered down the two fairways and, just before it hit the woods at the far end, it lifted off, taking to the air.

Three Black Hawk choppers followed for a short while, firing after it in vain, but they could never hope to keep up with the fleeing 747.

A couple of F-15 strike fighters would be dispatched ten minutes later, but by the time they were in the air and on the right heading, the ghostly 747—defying their radar scans and transponder searches—was gone.

It was last seen heading south, disappearing somewhere over Cuba's nearest neighbor to the south.

Jamaica.

An hour later, in another part of the world, a digital teleprinter printed out an intercepted radio transmission:

TRANS INTERCEPT:
SAT BT-1009/03.17.06-1399
A40-TEXT TRANSMISSION
FROM: USAF SECURE FREQUENCY, ASWAN MILITARY AIRFIELD (EGYPT)
TO: UNSPECIFIED DESTINATION, MARYLAND (USA)
VOICE 1 (USA): PRESIDENT IS BECOMING INCREAS-INGLY ANXIOUS, COLONEL. AND HIS MOOD WAS NOT LIFTED BY A REPORT THAT JUST CAME IN FROM GITMO: SOMEONE JUST BROKE A TERROR-IST OUT OF CAMP DELTA, A SAUDI NAMED ZAEED WHO WE'VE DISCOVERED HAS CONNECTIONS WITH THE CAPSTONE PROJECT.
VOICE 2 (EGYPT): IT WAS WEST. HE'S BOLD, I'LL GIVE HIM THAT. HE MUST HAVE HIT A SNAG AND DE-CIDED HE NEEDED ZAEED.
VOICE 1 (USA): DOES HE? DO WE NEED THIS ZAEED?
VOICE 2 (EGYPT): NO. WE GOT ALL WE NEEDED FROM MUSTAPHA ZAEED WHILE HE WAS UNDER.
[LONG PAUSE]
VOICE 1 (USA): COLONEL JUDAH, SHOULD WE BE NERVOUS? THE PRESIDENT IS GROWING UNCOM-FORTABLE WITH YOUR METHODS. HE'S DISTANC-

ING HIMSELF FROM US. AGAINST OUR ADVICE, HE HAS ORDERED THAT A DRAFT "ADDRESS TO THE NATION" BE WRITTEN, CONCERNING THE EVACUATION OF THE COASTAL CITIES, JUST IN CASE YOU DON'T SUCCEED.

VOICE 2 (EGYPT): TELL HIM WE WILL SUCCEED. TO DATE, EVERYTHING HAS GONE ACCORDING TO PLAN. WEST IS CONTAINABLE AT ANY TIME WE CHOOSE, BUT IT'S ALSO VERY USEFUL TO HAVE HIM RUNNING AROUND. AND THE EUROPEANS HAVE ACTED JUST AS WE ANTICIPATED. TELL THE PRESIDENT TO GO AHEAD AND WRITE HIS SPEECH, BUT HE'LL NEVER HAVE TO USE IT. JUDAH, OUT.

A GIRL
NAMED LILY

PART TWO

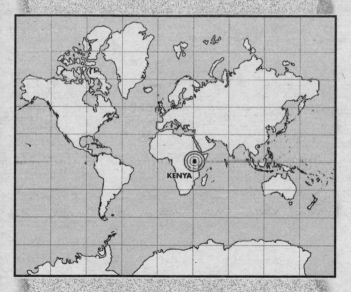

KENYA

VICTORIA STATION, KENYA
2003–2006

Throughout the team's time in Kenya, a large glass jar sat on top of the kitchen bench.

It was the "Swear Jar." Every time a member of the team was caught swearing or cursing in front of Lily, they had to put a dollar in it.

And since they were soldiers, it was nearly always full. The proceeds of the Swear Jar went toward toys or books or ballet clothes for Lily.

Naturally, since it was she who would ultimately benefit from their indiscretion, Lily loved catching team members swearing. It became commonplace for any curse heard around the station to be followed by her voice chiming: "Swear Jar!"

She was also given pocket money in return for doing chores around the farm.

It was West's and Wizard's idea. They wanted her upbringing—already highly unusual—to appear, at least to her, as normal as possible. Doing chores with the other team members—gathering wood with Big Ears; helping Pooh Bear clean his tools; and in a very momentous occasion, feeding Horus for West—made her feel like she was contributing; made her feel like she was part of a family. It also just made her a nice kid.

* * *

As she grew older, however, she grew increasingly curious, and she began to learn more about the team around her.

She learned, for example, that Pooh Bear was the second son of the most powerful sheik in the United Arab Emirates.

And that Wizard had once studied to be a Catholic priest but never went through with it.

She also discovered that Zoe had once been reassigned from the armed forces to study archaeology under Wizard at Trinity College, Dublin.

Apparently, Jack West had studied there with her—having also been sent by his home country to learn from the Canadian professor.

West's home country.

Lily was ever curious about Australia. It was a curious nation, full of contradictions. Eighty percent of its enormous landmass was made up of desert, yet it also possessed supermodern cities like Sydney, famous beaches like Bells and Bondi, and superb natural formations, like Ayers Rock and the Great Barrier Reef, which—she discovered—had been named as one of the Seven *Natural* Wonders of the World.

As she grew older, however, Lily developed more sophisticated questions about Australia, including its place in international relations. Australia only had a population of 20 million people, so despite its physical size, globally speaking it was a small country.

And yet while its military was equally small, one particular part of it was world-renowned: Australia was the home of what was widely acknowledged to be the best special forces unit in the world, the SAS—West's former regiment.

Another thing piqued her interest: during the twentieth century, Australia had been one of America's closest and most loyal allies. In World War II, Korea, Vietnam, Kuwait, Australia had always been the first country to stand beside the United States.

And yet not now.

This perplexed Lily, so she decided to ask West about it.

One rainy day, she went into his study, and found him working in darkness and silence (with Horus perched on his chair-back) staring at his computer screen, chewing on a pen, deep in thought.

Lily strolled around his office, idly touching the books on the shelves. She saw his whiteboard with the words "4 MISSING DAYS OF MY LIFE—CORONADO?" still written on it. She also noticed that the sealed glass jar with the rusty red dirt in it had been removed.

He didn't acknowledge her presence, kept staring at his computer monitor.

She came round behind him, saw the image on his screen. It was a digital photo of some giant hieroglyphics carved into a wall somewhere. Lily translated them quickly in her head:

ENTER THE EMBRACE OF ANUBIS WILLINGLY, AND
    YOU SHALL LIVE BEYOND THE COMING OF RA.
ENTER AGAINST YOUR WILL, AND YOUR PEOPLE
    SHALL RULE FOR BUT ONE EON, BUT YOU
    SHALL LIVE NO MORE.

ENTER NOT AT ALL, AND THE WORLD SHALL BE
NO MORE.

"What do you reckon?" West asked suddenly, not
turning to face her.

Lily froze, put on the spot. "I . . . I don't know . . ."

West swiveled. "I'm thinking it's about death and
the afterlife, in the form of an address from Amun to
the Jesus-like character, Horus. 'The embrace of Anubis' is death. If Horus accepts his death willingly, he
will rise again and confer a benefit on his people. A bit
like Christ dying on the cross. But enough of that.
What brings you here today, kiddo?"

A vigorous discussion followed about Australian-
American relations—about the rise of America as a sole
superpower, and the concerns of Australia that its
friend was becoming something of a global bully.
"Sometimes a good friend," West said, "has to show
tough love. It's also much better to get taught a difficult
lesson from your friend than from your enemy."

West then abruptly changed the subject. "Lily,
there's something I have to tell you. When all this
comes to a head, if it turns out as I hope it will, I'm
probably going to have to go away for a while—"

"Go away?" Lily said, alarmed.

"Yes. Lie low for a while. Go someplace where no
one can find me. Disappear."

"Disappear . . ." Lily gulped.

"But I want *you* to be able to find me, Lily," West
said, smiling. "Now, I can't tell you where I'm going,
but I can point you in the right direction. If you can
solve this riddle, you'll find me."

He handed her a slip of paper, on which was written:

My new home is home to both tigers and crocodiles.
To find it, pay the boatman,
take your chances with the dog and journey
Into the jaws of Death,
Into the mouth of Hell.
There you will find me, protected by a great villain.

"And that, kiddo, is all I'll say. Now scram."

Lily scampered out of the study, gripping the slip of paper.

She would pore over West's riddle for months—even going so far as to punch every word of it into Google—trying to figure it out.

She had other questions, however, which *were* answered.

Such as where West had acquired Horus.

"Horus's former owner was once Huntsman's teacher," Wizard said, as the two of them sat outside in the brilliant African sunshine.

"He was a nasty man named Marshall Judah. Judah was an American colonel who taught Jack how to be a better soldier at a place called Coronado.

"Judah would walk around the Coronado base with Horus on his shoulder, yelling at the troops. And as an example to them, he would beat Horus if she didn't perform as she had been trained. He would say, 'the only way to get obedience is through discipline and brute force!'

"Huntsman didn't like this. Didn't like seeing Judah being so cruel to the falcon. So when West left Coronado, he stole the bird from her cage in Judah's office. Ever since, Jack has treated Horus with kindness and love, and she returns his affection tenfold.

"Lily, as you grow up, you'll find that some people in this world are not very nice at all. They favor cruelty over kindness, power over sharing, anger over understanding.

"These people think only of themselves. They seek to rule over others, not for others' sakes, but for their own desire for power. Lily, one day you are going to be very powerful—*very* powerful—and I hope that if you learn nothing else from us here, you learn that the truly great people think of others first and themselves last.

"For an example of this, look no further than Huntsman and Horus. A beaten bird will obey a cruel master out of fear. But a kind master, it will die for."

One day, Lily was helping Wizard organize some of his ancient scrolls.

She loved all his old stuff—the parchments, the tablets. To her, they held within them all the mysteries of ancient faraway times.

On that particular day Wizard was collating everything he had on a series of Egyptian architects all named *Imhotep*.

Lily noticed some design plans for a quarry-mine in a place called Nubia, with four rising levels and lots of water-driven booby traps. Marked on the plans were descriptions of all the traps, and in the case of a set of concealed stepping-stones, five numbers written in Egyptian hieroglyphics: **1-3-4-1-4**. Wizard placed those plans in a file marked "Imhotep V."

She also saw a really old drawing that looked like an ancient game of Snakes and Ladders. It was titled:

Waterfall Entrance—Refortification by Imhotep III in the time of Ptolemy Soter and it looked like this:

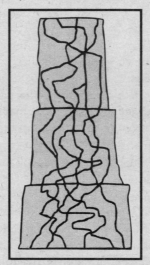

Wizard noticed Lily's interest, so he taught her things about the various Imhoteps.

Imhotep III, for instance, lived during the time of Alexander the Great and his friend, Ptolemy I, and he was known as "the Master Moat Builder"—he had been known to divert entire rivers in order to provide his structures with uncrossable moats.

"This waterfall entrance," Wizard said, "must have been a beautiful decorative cascade at a palace in ancient Babylon, near modern-day Baghdad in Iraq. The lines dictate the course of the flowing water. Sadly, in all the excavations of Babylon over the years, it has never been found. Such a shame."

Lily spent the rest of that day curled up behind

some boxes in the corner of Wizard's study, reading all manner of parchments, absolutely rapt.

She hardly even noticed when Zoe came in and started chatting with Wizard. It was only when West's name came up that she started listening more closely.

Zoe said, "It's been good to see him again. Although he seems to have changed since we studied together in Dublin. He's become even quieter than he already was. I also hear he's quit the Army."

Lily listened, although she never looked up from the parchment she appeared to be reading.

Wizard leaned back. "Gosh, Dublin. When was that—1989? You two were so young. Jack's been down a long road since then."

"Tell me."

"He quit the Army soon after Desert Storm. But to understand why, you have to understand why he joined the Army in the first place: both to please and to spite his father.

"Jack's father was a great soldier in his time, but Jack was better. His father had wanted him to join the military straight after high school, but Jack wanted to study, to go to university. But he acquiesced to his father's wishes ... and quickly became a much more formidable soldier than his father had ever been.

"Jack rose through the ranks, was fast-tracked to the SAS regiment. He particularly excelled at desert missions; he even set a new record on the desert survival course, lasting forty-four days without being captured.

"But unlike his father, Jack didn't like what they were turning him into: a killing machine, an *exception-*

ally good killing machine. His superiors knew this, and they were worried that he'd quit—that was when they sent him to study with me in Dublin. They hoped it would satisfy his intellectual needs for the time being and he'd stay on with the regiment. And I suppose it did satisfy him, for a time."

"Hold on a minute," Zoe said. "I need to backtrack for a moment. Jack told me once that his father was American. But he joined the *Australian* Army?"

"That's right," Wizard said. "Thing is, Jack's *mother* is not American. To please his father, he joined the military, but to spite his father, he joined the military of his mother's birth nation: Australia."

"Ah . . ." Zoe said. "Go on."

Wizard said, "Anyway, as you know, Jack's always had a sharp mind, and he started to look at Army life critically. Personally, I believe he just enjoyed studying ancient history and archaeology more.

"In any case, things started to go downhill when Jack's superiors sent him to a series of multinational special forces exercises at Coronado in 1990—exercises hosted by the Americans at their SEAL base, where they invited crack teams from all their allies to take part in high-end wargames. It's a huge opportunity for smaller nations, so the Australians sent West. In 1990, the exercises were hosted by none other than Marshall Judah, who instantly saw Jack's potential.

"But something happened at Coronado that I don't know about fully. Jack was injured in a helicopter accident and lay unconscious in the base hospital for four days. The four missing days of Jack West's life. When he woke up, he was sent back home, no serious damage done, and after a few months, he was back on active duty—just in time for Desert Storm in 1991.

"Jack West was one of the first men on the ground in Iraq in 1991, blowing up communications towers. After two weeks, however, he found himself serving under Judah. Seems Judah had personally asked the Pentagon to request that Jack be reassigned to him. Australia—ever loyal to the Americans—complied.

"And so Jack West Jr. made his name in Desert Storm. Did some incredible things deep behind enemy lines, including that miraculous escape from the SCUD base in Basra where, it should be said, Judah and the Americans had left him for dead.

"But when it was all over and he was back home, he walked into the office of his commanding officer, Lieutenant General Peter Cosgrove, and informed him that he would not be renewing his contract with the regiment.

"Now Cosgrove and I have known each other for a long time. He's a very clever fellow and, through me, he was aware of *this* upcoming mission and he thought fast, and came up with a way of keeping West happy but also keeping him in the fold: he assigned West to me, as part of a long-term open-ended mission, to take part in archaeological research connected to the discovery of the Capstone.

"That was how West and I came to work together again. That was how we came to be the ones who found the scrolls from the Alexandria Library and, ultimately, Lily and her ill-fated mother. And that's why West is here on this mission."

After discussing a few more unrelated topics, Zoe left.

Wizard returned to his work . . . at which moment, he seemed to remember that Lily was still in the corner, behind the boxes. He turned to face her.

"Why, little one, I'd clean forgotten you were here. You've been as quiet as a mouse over there. I don't know if you heard any of that, but if you did, excellent. It's important that you know about our friend, Huntsman, because he's a good fellow, a very good fellow. And although he doesn't say it, he's incredibly fond of you—in fact, he has been since the moment he first held you in his arms inside that volcano. He cares about you more than anything else in the world."

That had been a big learning day for Lily.

Infinitely more fun, however, was the day she learned about the origins of West's plane.

The *Halicarnassus* had long been a source of curiosity to her. From the moment she'd been old enough to comprehend jumbo jets—and how much they cost—it struck her as exceedingly odd that one man could own his very own 747.

"Where did you get your plane?" she asked him at breakfast once.

Others around the table at the time suppressed laughs: Zoe, Stretch, and Wizard.

West actually looked a little sheepish. "Don't tell anyone, but I stole it."

"You *stole* it? You stole an entire airplane! Isn't it wrong to steal?"

"Yes, it is wrong," Zoe said. "But Huntsman stole the *Halicarnassus* from a very bad man."

"Who?"

"A man by the name of Saddam Hussein," Wizard said. "The former president of Iraq, a very horrible individual. Huntsman stole it from him back in 1991."

"Why did you steal Mr. Hussein's plane?" Lily asked.

West paused before answering, as if he was choosing his words carefully.

"I was near a place called Basra, and I was in a lot of trouble. And Mr. Hussein's plane was the only way for me to get out alive. He kept it there in case it ever became necessary for him to escape his country." West winked. "I also knew that he had a lot of other planes scattered all over Iraq for the very same purpose."

"Why do you call it the *Halicarnassus*? Is it named after the Mausoleum that was at Halicarnassus?"

West smiled at her easy grasp of the ancient names. "I'm not sure, but I think it is. Mr. Hussein called it the *Halicarnassus* and I just kept the name because I liked it. I'm not sure why he called it that, but Mr. Hussein was a guy who liked to think he was a great Persian ruler, like Mausollos or Nebuchadnezzar. Only he wasn't like them at all. He was just a big bully."

West turned to Wizard. "Hey, speaking of the *Halicarnassus*, that reminds me: how is the refit going? Have you attached those Mark 3 retrogrades yet?"

"Almost done," Wizard answered. "We've got her weight down by a third, and all eight external retrograde thrusters have been attached and are testing well. As for the Mark 3s, they fit the 747's existing engines beautifully—the balance on the Boeing is really quite exceptional, great for VTOL, if you have the fuel. Sky Monster and I will be doing some testing this Saturday, so wear your earplugs."

"Will do. Keep me informed."

Lily didn't know what they were talking about.

Oh, and Lily's interest in ballet continued.

She put on many shows—shows that took place on a little stage with drawable curtains. Each performance was greeted with great applause by the whole team.

At one such show, Lily announced with a flourish that she would attempt to hold a difficult tiptoe pose for a whole minute. She made it to forty-five seconds, and was bitterly disappointed.

Everyone applauded anyway.

As families do.

THE BLACK PRIEST OF KABUL

AIRSPACE ABOVE THE ATLANTIC OCEAN
MARCH 17, 2006
THREE DAYS BEFORE THE ARRIVAL OF TARTARUS

Twelve hours after its brazen assault on Guantanamo Bay, after lying low in a remote Jamaican Air Force hangar outside Kingston—where it had picked up Wizard, Lily, and Horus—the *Halicarnassus,* now refueled and replenished, soared once again over the Atlantic, heading back toward Europe and Africa, back into the fray.

Once again, everyone sat in the main cabin, arrayed in a wide circle.

The focal point of the circle: Mullah Mustapha Zaeed, the Black Priest of Kabul.

Immediately after their escape from Guantanamo Bay, West had grabbed an AXS-9 digital spectrum analyzer—a wandlike device used to sweep a room for bugs—and waved it over Zaeed's body.

Sure enough, at the terrorist's neck, the wand had gone berserk, beeping wildly, indicating that there was indeed a GPS locator microchip buried under Zaeed's skin.

Surgery wasn't necessary. West was able to neutralize the chip with an electromagnetic pulse from a disabling gun, turning the locator chip into a dead piece of plastic.

And so now Zaeed was here, in the main cabin—and while everyone gazed warily at the terrorist, he just stared straight at Lily.

He eyed her the way a hyena eyes an injured baby deer—with hunger, desire, and a kind of stunned disbelief that such a delightful meal could be right here in front of him.

His general appearance was frightening—despite the fact that he had been bathed and was now dressed in clean clothes.

With his shaved head, sharp stubble-covered chin, hollow eyes, and wiry physique, he seemed more ghost than man, a walking skeleton. Three years of solitary confinement at Camp Delta will do that to you.

And in the clear light of the cabin, a peculiar feature became apparent: half of Zaeed's left ear, the whole bottom half, the entire lobe, had been *cut off*.

The spell broke, and he scanned West's multinational team.

"Mmm. How interesting, how very interesting," he said. "The mice are roaring. Taking on the two lions of the world: Europe and America."

He looked at Wizard. "I see Canada. And Ireland." He nodded at Zoe. "Fellow scholars of the ancient texts."

His voice went low as he saw Stretch: "And I see Israel. Why Katsa Cohen, the master sniper, nice to see you again. The last time we met was in Kandahar, at two thousand yards. And it was a rare miss on your part."

Stretch scowled, showing his extreme distaste for Mustapha Zaeed.

Zaeed pointed at his half ear. "You were a few inches wide."

"I won't be next time," Stretch growled.

"Now, now, Katsa. I am your guest, and a valuable one at that. After all the trouble you went to to get me, *Jew*"—Zaeed's eyes turned to ice—"you should be more courteous."

He spun, aiming his wild eyes at Pooh Bear.

"Ah, a good Muslim. You are Sheik Anzar Abbas's son, are you not? The great Captain Rashid Abbas, commander of the elite UAE First Commando Regiment . . ."

"I fear I am not," Pooh Bear replied. "Rashid Abbas is my brother. I am *Zahir* Abbas, a humble sergeant and the sheik's second son."

"The Sheik is a noble servant of Allah," Zaeed bowed respectfully. "I honor you as his kin."

Finally, Zaeed rounded on West, who sat with Horus on his shoulder.

"And you. John West Jr. *Captain* John West Jr. of the Australian SAS. The Huntsman. A name that floats around the Middle East like a wraith. Your feats have become the stuff of legend: your escape from Basra angered Saddam for years, you know. Till the day he was captured, he wanted that plane back. But then you vanished for a very long time. Disappeared off the face of the Earth. Most unusual—"

"Enough," West said. "The Wonders: Zeus and Artemis. Where are they?"

"Oh, yes, I am sorry. The Wonders. And Tartarus

approaches, too. Mmmm. Forgive me, Captain West, but I haven't yet grasped the basis of your belief that I will even *want* to help you in this cause."

"The United States of America already has three pieces of the Capstone," West said simply. "They are well equipped and well informed, and well on their way to securing the entire Capstone. How's that?"

"Good enough," Zaeed said. "Who leads the U.S. force? Marshall Judah?"

"Yes."

"A formidable foe. Clever and cunning. And murderous. Although did you know he has a curious weakness?"

"What?"

"A fear of heights. But I digress. Brief me on your progress so far. You are using the Callimachus Text, I presume. Which means you found the Colossus first? Was it the rightmost pendant?"

"Yes . . . it was," West said, surprised.

"Mmmm. And then came the Pieces from the Pharos and the Mausoleum, no?"

"How did you know they'd be found in that order?"

Zaeed sighed dramatically. "This is elementary. The Callimachus Text is written in the Word of Thoth—a most ancient and complicated language. The language itself contains within it seven levels of increasing complexity, dialects, if you will. Your young reader here"—he indicated Lily—"can only read one entry at a time, can't she? This is because each entry in the Callimachus Text is written in an increasingly difficult dialect of the Word of Thoth. The Colossus entry is written in 'Thoth I,' the easiest dialect of the Word of

Thoth. The Pharos Piece is in 'Thoth II,' slightly harder. The Oracle will ultimately be able to read all seven dialects, but not instantly."

"You can read the Word of Thoth?" Wizard asked, incredulous.

"I can decipher its first four dialects, yes."

"But how?"

"I taught myself," Zaeed said. "With discipline and patience. Oh, I forget, in the decadent West, *discipline* and *patience* are no longer attributes that warrant respect."

"How did you know the Mausoleum Piece would be entombed with the Pharos Piece?" Zoe asked.

"I have spent the last thirty years acquiring every scroll, carving, and document relating to the *Benben* that I could find. Some are famous, like the Callimachus Text, of which I possess a ninth-century copy, others less so—written by humble men who merely wanted to record the marvelous deeds they had done, like constructing great roofs over entire ocean inlets, or carrying marble pillars into the hearts of dormant volcanoes. My collection is vast."

"The Callimachus Text is unhelpful on the Zeus and Artemis Pieces," West said. "Zeus is lost. And we believe Artemis is somewhere in St. Peter's Basilica, but we don't know exactly where. Do you know where they are?"

Zaeed's eyes narrowed. "The passage of time and many wars have scattered these two Pieces, but yes, I believe I do know their resting places."

P ooh Bear leaned forward. "If you know so much, why have you yourself not gone in search of these Pieces before?"

"I would have if only I had been able, my Muslim friend," Zaeed said smoothly. "But I fear I was not as nimble then as I am now." As he said this, Zaeed rolled up his right pant leg, to reveal hideous scarring and fire-melted skin on his lower leg.

"A Soviet fragmentation grenade in Afghanistan in 1987. For many years, I was unable even to walk on it. And a man with limited movement is useless in trap-laden quarries and inlets. While I retrained my withered muscles throughout the '90s, building them up again, I researched all I could about the Capstone. I was actually grooming a team of mujahideen in Afghanistan to hunt for the Pieces at the time of the attacks on New York and Washington, D.C. But then the September 11 attacks happened and Afghanistan was plunged into chaos. And I was captured by the Americans. But now my leg is strong."

"The Zeus and Artemis Pieces," West repeated. "Where are they?"

Zaeed grinned a sly smile. "Interestingly, these two Pieces that defy your search are neither hidden nor concealed. Both exist in plain sight—if only one knows where to look. The Artemis Piece, yes, it is indeed in St. Peter's in Rome, in no less than *the most holy place* of the Cult of Amun-Ra. As for the Zeus Piece . . ."

Zaeed leaned back in his chair, recited the appropriate verse from memory:

> *"No thunderbolts did he wield, no wrath did he bear,*
> *No victory did he achieve.*
> *Indeed, it was only the Victory in his right hand*
> *that made him great,*
> *Oh winged woman, whither didst thou fly?"*

Zaeed looked at West. "It was only *the Victory in his right hand* that made him great."

West followed his line of reasoning. "The Statue of Zeus at Olympia was said to hold in his right hand a smaller statue of *Winged Victory:* the Greek goddess Nike, a woman with wings coming out of her back, like an angel or the figurehead on the prow of a ship. And since the figure of Zeus was so immense, its statue of Winged Victory was said to be life-size."

Zaeed said, "Correct. And if it was Victory who made him great, we must look not for *Zeus's* statue, but the statue of Victory. Thus the verse asks: whither did she fly?

"Now, as I'm sure you know, many life-size statues of Winged Victory have been found around the ancient Greek world. But after a comprehensive study of the works of Phidias, the sculptor of the statue of Zeus, I have found only one statue of Victory that possesses the features of his superior level of artistry: fine lines, perfect form, and the rare ability to reproduce the appearance of *wet* garments in marble.

"The specimen I have found is the greatest surviving example of Greek sculpture in the world today, yet ironically, Western scholars still assign its construction to an unknown artist. It was found in 1863 by a French archaeologist, Charles Champoiseau—"

"Oh, no way . . ." Wizard gasped in understanding. "It's not . . ."

Zaeed nodded. "The very same. Champoiseau found it on the Greek island of Samothrace, and thus the statue now bears that island's name: the *Winged Victory of Samothrace.*

"It was brought back to France, where its genius was quickly appreciated, whence it was taken to the Louvre. There it has sat to this very day in pride of place on a great landing at the top of the Daru Staircase, underneath a high domed ceiling in the Denon Wing of the Louvre in Paris."

The *Halicarnassus* sped toward Europe.

It was decided that the team would split into two.

West would lead one subteam to Paris to go after the Zeus Piece, while Wizard would lead a smaller team to Rome, to chase the Artemis Piece. As for Zaeed, he would stay with Sky Monster on the *Halicarnassus,* bound and secured.

Everyone scattered around the plane, some to rest, others to research, others just to prepare for the missions ahead.

It happened that Pooh Bear found himself preparing his guns near Mustapha Zaeed, still handcuffed to his chair.

"Hello, my brother," Zaeed whispered. "May Allah bless and keep you."

"And you," Pooh Bear replied, more out of religious habit than because he meant it.

"Your father, the sheik, is a great man," Zaeed said. "And a fine Muslim."

"What do you want?"

"The presence of the Jew concerns me," Zaeed said simply, nodding at Stretch over on the far side of the main cabin. "I can understand your father aligning himself with these Westerners for convenience, but I cannot believe he would ally himself with the Jewish State."

Pooh Bear said, "The Israelis were not invited to

join this mission. They discovered us somehow—and threatened to reveal our mission unless we allowed them to join it."

"Is that so? How typical," Zaeed hissed. "Then I am doubly glad that you are here, my friend. The second assembling of the Capstone will be one of the greatest moments in all of human history. Before the end, all will show their true colors. When the time comes, Allah's brethren should stand together."

Pooh Bear just kept his eyes downcast.

In West's office in the rear of the plane, West, Wizard, Zoe, and Big Ears were gazing at the brown leather-bound diary West had found inside Hamilcar's Refuge: Hermann Hessler's notebook detailing his search for the Seven Wonders of the Ancient World during World War II.

Translating it from the German, they found several references that they understood:

> **WORD OF THOTH**—MULTIPLE DIALECTS OF
>   INCREASING DIFFICULTY . . . NEED TO
>   LOCATE THE ORACLE FOR PRECISE
>   TRANSLATION . . .
> *"Catholic Church = Cult of Amun-Ra."*
> **"COLOSSUS: THIRD NECKPIECE."**
> **MYSTERIOUS BUILDING EXPEDITION IN**
>   **85 B.C.**
> • IMHOTEP VI + 10,000 WORKERS;
> • ALL MARCHED WEST TO SECRET LOCATION
>   ON COAST NEAR CARTHAGE;

- **A WORKER'S PAPYRUS** FOUND AT ROSETTA MENTIONS THE MAN'S PARTICIPATION IN AN EXTRAORDINARY CONSTRUCTION PROJECT: THE COVERING OF AN ENTIRE COASTAL INLET AND THE FABRICATION OF A SECTION OF COAST.
- THE MEN WHO PLACED TWO COVERED TREASURES IN THE INNERMOST HOLY CHAMBER WERE ALL EXECUTED.
- *Pharos and Mausoleum Pieces???*

Accompanying these last entries was a teletyped order from Heinrich Himmler himself authorizing Hessler to use a U-boat to trawl the entire North African coast of the Mediterranean for the false section of coastline.

There were also some hand-drawn hieroglyphics that Wizard translated aloud:

THE CHOICE OF MAN

ONLY ONE OF THE TWO RITUALS MAY BE CHOSEN.
ONE BEGETS PEACE,
THE OTHER POWER.
ON THE FINAL DAY,
A CHOICE MUST BE MADE,
A CHOICE MADE IN THE PRESENCE OF RA HIMSELF
THAT WILL DETERMINE THE VERY FATE OF MEN.

Wizard leaned back. "It's a reference to the two incantations—the rituals. But only one of them can be performed when the Capstone is placed atop the Great Pyramid."

They also found other references, however, that they did not understand. Like these rather ominous inscriptions:

1ST INSCRIPTION FROM THE TOMB OF IMHOTEP III

WHAT AN INCREDIBLE STRUCTURE IT WAS,
CONSTRUCTED AS A MIRROR IMAGE,
WHERE BOTH ENTRANCE AND EXIT WERE
    ALIKE.
IT PAINED ME THAT MY TASK—WHAT
    WOULD BECOME MY LIFE'S
    MASTERWORK—
WAS TO CONCEAL SO MAGNIFICENT A
    STRUCTURE.
BUT I DID MY DUTY.
WE SEALED THE GREAT ARCHWAY WITH A
    LANDSLIDE.
AS INSTRUCTED, THE PRIESTS' ENTRANCE
    REMAINS OPEN SO THEY MAY TEND THE
SHRINES INSIDE—THE PRIESTS HAVE BEEN
    INFORMED OF THE ORDER OF THE
    SNARES.

2ND INSCRIPTION FROM THE TOMB OF IMHOTEP III

ONLY THE BRAVEST OF SOULS
SHALL PASS THE WELLS OF THE WINGED
    LIONS.

BUT BEWARE THE PIT OF NINGIZZIDA.
TO THOSE WHO ENTER THE SERPENT LORD'S
    PIT,
I OFFER NO ADVICE BUT THIS:
ABANDON ALL HOPE,
FOR THERE IS NO ESCAPE FROM IT.

*Winged Lions. Common Assyrian Statue
    Found in Persia/Mesopotamia.
Ningizzida: Assyrian God of Serpents &
    Snakes.
Possible Ref to the H.G. of Babylon???*

A few pages later there was a pair of scribbled pictures, simply titled "Safe Routes":

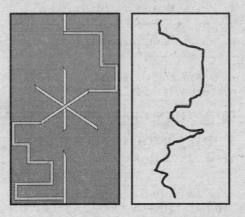

After this there was another translation, which caused Wizard to say, "Ooh, it's a reference to one of the rituals that must be performed on the final day."

It read:

THE RITUAL OF POWER

AT THE HIGH ALTAR OF RA,
UNDER THE HEART OF THE SACRIFICIAL
    ONE
WHO LIES IN THE ARMS OF VENGEFUL
    ANUBIS,
POUR INTO THE DEATH GOD'S HEART
ONE DEBEN OF YOUR HOMELAND.
UTTER THOSE ANCIENT EVIL WORDS
AND ALL EARTHLY POWER SHALL BE YOURS
FOR A THOUSAND YEARS.

"'One deben of your homeland?'" Big Ears frowned. "What's that supposed to mean?"

Zoe began, "A deben was an ancient Egyptian unit of measurement; about three and a half ounces. I imagine it means—"

But suddenly Wizard jumped up and gasped, seeing the next entry. It read:

FROM THE SECRET GOSPEL OF ST. MARK

AT DAWN ON THE DAY OF JUDGMENT,
THAT FINAL HORRIBLE DAY,
AT THE ONLY TEMPLE THAT BEARS BOTH
    THEIR NAMES,
THREAD THE POWER OF RA THROUGH THE
    EYES OF GREAT RAMESES'
TOWERING NEEDLES,
FROM THE SECOND OWL ON THE FIRST
TO THE THIRD ON THE SECOND . . .

... WHEREBY THE TOMB OF ISKENDUR WILL
BE REVEALED.
THERE YOU WILL FIND THE FIRST PIECE.

Beneath this entry, Hessler had scrawled:

*The Tomb of Iskendur—the Burial Place of
Alexander the Great. Alexander was
Buried with the First Piece!*

Wizard leaned back, his eyes wide.

"The Secret Gospel of St. Mark," Zoe exchanged a
look with West. "The Heretical Gospel."

"Explain," Big Ears said.

West said, "It's not widely known, but St. Mark actually wrote *two* gospels while he was in Egypt. The
first gospel is the one we all know, the one in the Bible.
The second gospel, however, caused an incredible stir
when he produced it, so much so that nearly every copy
was burned by the early Christian movement. And
Mark himself was almost stoned for it."

"Why?"

Zoe said, "Because this secret gospel recounted several *other* things Jesus did during his life. Rituals. Incantations. Bizarre episodes. The most infamous of
which was the so-called homosexual incident."

"The *what*!" Big Ears said.

Zoe said, "An episode in which Jesus went away
with a young man and, according to Mark, *initiated* the
young man into 'the ancient ways.' Some sensationalist
writers have interpreted this to have been a homosexual
experience. Most scholars, however, believe it was a rit-

ual of the Cult of Amun-Ra, which has subsequently been adopted as the initiation rite of the Freemasons, another sun-worshipping faith to have emerged from ancient Egypt."

West said, "Now do you understand why it's called the Heretical Gospel?"

"Yuh-huh," Big Ears said, "but wait, the Freemasons. I thought they were *anti*-Catholic."

"They are," Zoe said. "But the Freemasons hate the Catholic Church as only siblings can hate each other. They are like rival brothers, religions born from the same source. Just as Jerusalem is holy to both Judaism and Islam, so too do Catholicism and Freemasonry share a common source. They are simply two faiths born out of the one Mother Faith—Egyptian Sun worship. They just diverged in their interpretations of this Mother Faith somewhere along the way."

West patted Big Ears on the shoulder. "It's complicated, buddy. Think of it this way: America is a Masonic State; Europe is a Catholic State. And now they're both fighting for the greatest prize of their two faiths: the Capstone."

Big Ears said, "You say America is a Masonic State. I thought it was overwhelmingly Christian. The Bible Belt and all that."

Zoe said, "Just because the *population* is Christian, doesn't mean the *country* is. What is a country anyway? A group of people with a common heritage who band together for reasons of mutual prosperity and security. And that's the key word: *security*. You see, countries have armies; religions don't. And who commands the armed forces of the entity we call 'the United States'?"

"The elected president and his advisers."

"Exactly. So, America's *people* are indeed honest Christians; but America's *leaders* since George Washington have almost exclusively been Freemasons. Washington, Jefferson, Roosevelt, the Bushes. For over two hundred years, the Freemasons have used the armed forces of 'the United States of America' as their own personal army for their own personal purposes. Hey presto, a religion got itself an army, and the population never even knew."

West said, "You can see Masonic worship of the Capstone everywhere in America. Why, over the years, American Freemasons have built replicas of each of the Seven Ancient Wonders."

"No way . . ."

West counted them off on his fingers: "The Statue of Liberty, built by the leading French Freemason, Frederic-Auguste Bartholdi, replicates the Colossus of Rhodes almost exactly—she even holds a torch aloft just as the original statue did. The Woolworth Building in New York is disturbingly similar to the Pharos. Fort Knox is built according to the floor plan of the Mausoleum at Halicarnassus. The Statue of Zeus, a great figure seated on a throne, is the Lincoln Memorial. The Temple of Artemis: the Supreme Court Building.

"The Hanging Gardens of Babylon couldn't be exactly replicated, since no one knows what they looked like, so a special rambling garden was built and tended in their honor at the White House, first by George Washington, then Thomas Jefferson and, later, Franklin Roosevelt. The Catholic president, John F. Kennedy, tried to rip the garden up, but he never managed it entirely. And while he didn't survive, the garden did. It's had many names over the years, but we now call it the Rose Garden."

Big Ears folded his arms. "What about the Great Pyramid, then? I don't know of any monumental pyramids in the U.S.?"

"That's true," West said, "there are no giant pyramids in America. But when the Egyptians stopped building pyramids, do you know what they started building instead?"

"What?"

"Obelisks. The obelisk became the ultimate symbol of Sun worship. And America does indeed possess one colossal obelisk: the Washington Monument. Interestingly, it is five hundred fifty-five feet tall. The Great Pyramid is four hundred sixty-nine feet tall, eighty-six feet shorter. But when you take into account the height of the Giza Plateau at the point where the Great Pyramid stands—eighty-six feet—you will discover that the peaks of both structures sit at *the exact same height* above sea level."

While this conversation was going on, Wizard was gazing at the text in the notebook.

"The only temple that bears both their names . . ." he mused. Then his eyes lit up. "It's Luxor. The Temple at Luxor."

"Oh, yes. Good *thinking,* Max. Good thinking!" Zoe clapped him on the shoulder.

"It would certainly fit . . ." West said.

"What would fit?" Big Ears asked, again not understanding this code they were using.

"The Temple of Amun at Luxor in southern Egypt,

more commonly known as the Temple at Luxor," Zoe said. "It's one of the biggest tourist attractions in Egypt. The famous one with the giant pylon gateway, the two colossal seated statues of Rameses II, and the lone obelisk out in front. It stands on the east bank of the Nile in Luxor, or—as it used to be called—Thebes.

"The Luxor Temple was built by several older pharaohs, but Rameses II comprehensively rebuilt it and so claimed it as his own. It was also augmented, however, by none other than Alexander the Great. Which is why—"

"—it's the only temple in all of Egypt in which Alexander the Great is recorded *as a pharaoh*," Wizard said. "At Luxor alone, Alexander's name is carved in hieroglyphics and enclosed in a ringlike cartouche. *The only temple that bears both their names:* the Luxor Temple is indeed the only temple that bears both the names of Rameses II and Alexander."

Big Ears said, "So what about threading *the power of Ra through the eyes of Great Rameses' towering needles.*"

West said, "Towering needles are usually obelisks. The power of Ra, I'm guessing, is sunlight. Dawn sunlight on Judgment Day: the day of the Tartarus Rotation. This verse is telling us that on the day of the Rotation, the morning sun will shine through two matching holes in the obelisks to reveal the location of the tomb."

Big Ears turned to Zoe. "But I thought you said there's only one obelisk still standing at Luxor."

Zoe nodded. "That's right."

"So we're screwed. Without the two obelisks, we

can't see how the Sun shines through them, so we'll never be able to find Alexander's Tomb."

"Not exactly," Wizard said, his eyes gleaming at West and Zoe.

They both smiled back at him.

Only Big Ears didn't get it.

"What? *What?*"

Wizard said, "The second obelisk from the Temple at Luxor still exists, Big Ears, just not in its original location."

"So where is it?"

Wizard answered him. "Like many of the obelisks of ancient Egypt, it was given to a western nation. Thirteen obelisks went to Rome, taken by the Sun-worshipping Catholic Church. Two went to London and New York—the pair of obelisks known as Cleopatra's Needles. The second obelisk from the Temple of Luxor, however, was given to the French in 1836. It now stands in pride of place in the Place de la Concorde, in the very heart of Paris, about half a mile from the Louvre."

"The Zeus Piece *and* the obelisk," Zoe said. "Looks like it's going to be double trouble in Paris."

West leaned back in his seat.

"Paris," he said, "isn't going to know what's hit her."

FOURTH MISSION
THE
STATUE OF ZEUS
AND THE
TEMPLE OF ARTEMIS

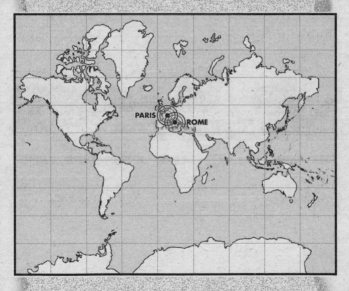

PARIS–ROME
MARCH 18, 2006
TWO DAYS BEFORE TARTARUS

THE PARIS OBELISK, PLACE DE LA CONCORDE, PARIS

Jack West Jr. sped around the huge multilaned traffic circle that surrounded the Arc de Triomphe, whipping through traffic in a rented four-wheel-drive SUV.

Lily sat in the passenger seat, while in the back were Pooh Bear, Stretch, and Big Ears.

They all sat in tense silence, as one does before an outrageously daring mission deep inside enemy territory.

The heart of Paris is shaped like a Christian cross.

The longer beam of this giant cross is the Champs-Élysées, which travels all the way from the Arc de Triomphe to the Palais de Louvre. The short horizontal transept of the cross ends with the National Assembly at one end and the stunning Church of St. Mary Magdalene at the other.

Most important of all is what lies at the junction of these two axes.

There one will find none other than the Place de la Concorde.

Made famous in the French Revolution as the venue for the executions of hundreds of noblemen and -women, the Place de la Concorde was the bloody home of the guillotine.

Now, however, standing in the exact center of this

plaza, in the exact center of Paris—the very *focal point* of Paris—stands a towering Egyptian obelisk.

The second obelisk from the Temple of Luxor.

Of all the obelisks in the world—whether still in Egypt or not—the Paris Obelisk is unique in one important respect:

The pyramidion at its peak is coated in gold.

Historians love this, because this was how obelisks appeared in ancient Egyptian times: the tiny pyramids on their peaks were coated with electrum, a rare alloy of silver and gold.

Interestingly, however, the golden pyramidion on the Paris Obelisk is only a very recent addition—it was added to the great stone needle in 1998.

"Pooh," West said as he drove, "you checked the catacombs?"

"I did. They're clear. The entry gate is under the Charles de Gaulle Bridge and the tunnel runs all the way under the Boulevard Diderot. Lock has been disabled."

"Stretch. The train?"

"TGV service. Platform twenty-three. Leaves at 12:44 p.m. First stop Dijon."

"Good."

As West drove down the Champs-Élysées, he eyed the wide boulevard ahead and beheld the Paris Obelisk, rising above the traffic, easily six stories tall.

He had climbing gear in his car—ropes, hooks,

pitons, carabiners—ready to scale the great needle and examine its upper reaches. He figured he'd look like just another reckless thrill-seeker and if he was fast enough, he'd be gone before the police arrived. After that, his team would proceed to the Louvre, for the larger, more dangerous mission.

Only then, as he drove closer, the traffic parted—

"Oh, no . . ." West breathed.

The entire lower half of the Obelisk was concealed by scaffolding. There were three stories of it, planklike levels shrouded with netting, like the scaffolding on a construction site.

And at the base of this temporary scaffold structure, guarding its only entrance, were six security guards.

A large sign in French and English apologized for the inconvenience as the Obelisk was covered for "essential cleaning work."

"They're *cleaning* it," Stretch scoffed. "A little convenient, don't you think? Our European rivals are onto this lead."

"The heretical Gospel of St. Mark is notorious. There are other copies of it around the world," West said. "Del Piero would surely have one. He must have already checked and measured the Obelisk and since he can't remove it from here, he's sealed it off, stopping us from doing the same. Which means—damn it—del Piero is one step short of locating Alexander's Tomb and getting the topmost Piece . . ."

West gazed at the scaffolding-enclosed Obelisk, rethinking, replanning, adapting.

"This changes things. Everyone. Switch of plans. We're not going to do the Obelisk first anymore. We're going to take the Louvre first, in the way we planned. Then we'll grab a look at the Obelisk on the way out."

"You have *got* to be kidding," Stretch said. "We're going to be running for our lives. Half the Gendarmerie will be on our asses by then."

"Confronting the Europeans at the Obelisk now will attract too much attention, Stretch," West said. "I was hoping to climb up and down it unnoticed. I can't do that now. But after we do what we plan to do at the Louvre, Paris is going to be in an uproar—a state of chaos that'll give us the cover we need to get past those guards at the Obelisk. And now that I think about it, our intended escape vehicle will also come in handy."

"I don't know about this . . ." Stretch said.

Pooh Bear said, "What you know or don't know is irrelevant, Israeli. Honestly, your constant doubting grates on me. You'll do as Huntsman says. He is in command here."

Stretch locked eyes with Pooh Bear, biting his tongue. "Very well then. I will obey."

West said, "Good. The Louvre plan remains the same. Big Ears: you're with Lily and me; we're going in. Pooh, Stretch: get the escape vehicle and make sure you're in position when we jump."

"Will do, Huntsman." Pooh Bear nodded.

Twenty minutes later, West, Lily, and Big Ears—gunless—strode through the metal detectors at the entrance to the Louvre.

The building's famous glass pyramid soared high above them, bathing the great museum's atrium in brilliant sunshine.

"I think I'm having another Dan Brown moment," Big Ears said, gazing up at the glass pyramid.

"They didn't do what we're going to do in *The Da Vinci Code*," West said ominously.

Lily provided the perfect cover: after all, how many snatch-and-grab teams enter a building holding the hand of a small child?

West's cell phone rang.

It was Pooh Bear. *"We have the exit vehicle. Ready when you are."*

"Give us ten minutes," West said and hung up.

Eight minutes after that, West and Big Ears were both dressed in the white coveralls of the Louvre's maintenance crew—taken from two unfortunate workers who now lay unconscious in a storeroom in the depths of the museum.

They entered the Denon Wing and ascended the impressive Daru Staircase. The staircase wound back and forth in wide sweeping flights, disappearing and reappearing behind soaring arches, before it revealed, standing proudly on a wide landing . . .

. . . the *Winged Victory of Samothrace*.

She was, quite simply, breathtaking.

The goddess stood with her chest thrust forward into the wind, her magnificent wings splayed out behind her, her wet tunic pressed against her body, perfectly realized in marble.

Six feet tall and standing on a five-foot-high marble mounting, she towered above the tourists milling around her.

Had her head not been missing, *Winged Victory* would almost certainly have been as famous as the *Venus de Milo*—also a resident of the Louvre—for by any measure, the artistry of her carving easily outdid that of the *Venus*.

The management of the Louvre seemed to recognize this, even if the public did not: *Winged Victory* stood high up in the building, proudly displayed up on the first floor, not far from the *Mona Lisa,* while the *Venus* stood in confined clutter on an underground level.

The marble mounting on which the great statue stood resembled the pointed prow of a ship, but this had never been a ship.

It had been the armrest of Zeus's throne; the broken-off tip of the armrest.

If you looked closely, you could see Zeus's gigantic marble *thumb* beneath *Winged Victory*.

The natural conclusion was mind-blowing: if *Victory* was this big, then the Statue of Zeus—the actual Wonder itself, now vanished from history—must have been absolutely *gigantic*.

Victory's position on the first floor of the Denon Wing, however, created a problem for West.

As with all the other key exhibits in the Louvre, all items on the first floor were laser-protected: as soon as a painting or sculpture was moved, it triggered an invisible laser, and steel grilles would descend at every nearby doorway, sealing in the thieves.

On the first floor, however, there was an extra precaution: the Daru Staircase, with all its twists and bends, could be easily sealed off, trapping any would-be thief *up on the first floor*. You could disturb *Victory,* but you could never take her anywhere.

Dressed in their maintenance coveralls, West and Big Ears strode up onto the landing and stood before the high statue of *Victory*.

They proceeded to move some potted trees arrayed around the landing, unnoticed by the light weekday crowd strolling past the statue.

West placed a couple of trees slightly to the left of *Victory,* while Big Ears placed two of the big pots far out of the way, over by the doorway that led south, toward the side of the Louvre that overlooked the River Seine. Lily stood by this doorway.

No one noticed them.

They were just workmen going about some unknown but presumably authorized task.

Then West grabbed a rolling REPAIR WORK IN PROGRESS screen from a nearby storeroom and placed it in front of *Victory,* blocking her from view.

He looked at Big Ears, who nodded.

Then Jack West Jr. swallowed.

He couldn't believe what he was about to do.

With a deep breath, he stepped up onto the marble podium that was Zeus's armrest and pushed the *Winged Victory of Samothrace*—a priceless marble carving twenty-two hundred years old—off its mount, to the floor.

No sooner had *Victory* tilted an inch off her mount than sirens started blaring and red lights started flashing.

Great steel grilles came thundering down in every doorway—*bam!-bam!-bam!-bam!*—sealing off the stairwell and the landing.

All except one doorway.

The southern doorway.

Its grille whizzed down on its runners—

—only to bang to a halt two feet off the ground, stopped by the two solid treepots that Big Ears had placed beneath it moments earlier.

The gateway route.

Victory herself landed in the two potted trees that West had placed to her left, her fall cushioned by them.

West rushed over to the upturned statue, and examined her feet, or rather the small cube-shaped marble pedestal on which her feet stood.

He pulled out a big wrench he'd taken from the maintenance room.

"May every archaeologist in the world forgive me," he whispered as he swung down hard with the wrench.

Crack. Crack. Craaaack.

The tourists on the landing didn't know what was going on. A couple of men stepped forward to investigate the activity behind the screen, but Big Ears blocked their way with a fierce glare.

After West's three heavy blows, the little marble pedestal was no more—but revealed within it was *a perfect trapezoid of solid gold,* maybe eighteen inches to a side.

The Third Piece of the Capstone.

It had been embedded in *Victory's* marble pedestal.

"Lily!" West called. "Get a look at this thing! In case we lose it later!"

Lily came over, gazed at the lustrous golden trapezoid, at the mysterious symbols carved into its top side.

"More lines of the two incantations," she said.

"Good. Now let's go," West said.

The Piece went into Big Ears' sturdy backpack and, with Lily running in the lead, suddenly they were off, sliding under the propped-open grille that led south.

No sooner were they through than West and Big Ears kicked the pot plants free, and the grille slammed fully shut behind them.

Running flat out down a long long corridor, legs pumping, hearts pounding.

Shouts came from behind them—shouts in French, from the museum guards giving chase.

West spoke into his radio mike: "Pooh Bear! Are you out there?"

"We're waiting! I hope you use the right window!"

"We'll find out soon enough!"

The corridor West was running down ended at a dramatic right-hand corner. This corner opened onto a superlong hallway that was actually the extreme southern flank of the Louvre. The hallway's entire left-hand wall was filled with masterpieces and the occasional high French window looking out over the Seine.

And right then, a second team of armed museum guards were running down it, shouting.

West hurled his huge wrench at the first French window in the hallway, shattering it. Glass sprayed everywhere.

He peered out the window.

To see Pooh Bear staring back at him, level with him, only a few feet away . . .

. . . standing on the open top deck of a double-decker bus!

Only one thing stands between the Louvre and the River Seine: a narrow strip of road called the Quai des Tuileries. It is a long riverside roadway that follows the course of the river, variously rising and falling—rising up to bridges and dipping down into tunnels and underpasses.

It was on this road that Pooh Bear's recently stolen double-decker bus now stood, parked alongside the

Palais de Louvre. It was one of those bright red open-topped double-deckers that drive tourists around Paris, London, and New York, allowing them to look up and around with ease.

"Well! What are you waiting for!" Pooh Bear yelled. "Come on!"

"Right!"

West threw Lily across first, then pushed Big Ears, with the Piece in his backpack, before finally jumping from the first-floor window onto the double-decker bus—just as the onrushing guards in the hallway started firing at him.

A second after his feet hit the open top deck of the bus, Stretch, in the driver's seat, hit the gas and the bus took off and the chase began.

The big red double-decker bus rocked precariously as Stretch threw it through the midday Paris traffic at speeds it was never meant to reach.

Police sirens could be heard in the distance.

"Go left and left again!" West yelled down. "Back around the Louvre! Back to the Obelisk!"

The bus took the bends fast, and West came down to look over Stretch's shoulder.

"When we get there, what then?" Stretch asked.

West peered forward—and saw the Obelisk appear beyond the rushing line of trees to their left, its base still shrouded by scaffolding.

"I want you to ram into the scaffolding."

The double-decker bus screamed onto the Place de la Concorde, almost tipping over with its speed.

The guards at the scaffolding surrounding the Obelisk realized just in time what it was going to do and leaped out of the way, diving clear a moment before the bus slammed into the near corner of the scaffold structure and obliterated a whole chunk of it.

The bus shuddered to a halt—

—and the tiny figure of Jack West could be seen leaping from its open top deck *onto* the second level of the scaffolding with some rope looped over his shoulder and climbing gear in his hands.

* * *

Up the scaffolding West ran, until he came to the top-most level and saw the Obelisk itself.

The size of a bell tower, it was totally covered in deeply engraved hieroglyphics. It soared into the sky high above him.

The hieroglyphs were large and carved in horizontal lines—approximately three glyphs to a line, depicting pharaonic cartouches, images of Osiris, and animals: falcons, wasps, and, in the second line from the very top, owls.

Using the deeply carved hieroglyphs as hand- and footholds, West clambered up the ancient Obelisk like a child scampering up a tall tree.

Stretch's voice exploded through his earpiece. *"West! I've got a visual on six police cars approaching fast along the Champs-Élysées!"*

"How far away?"

"About ninety seconds, if that . . ."

"Keep me posted. Although somehow I think we're going to have more to worry about than the Paris cops."

West scaled the great stone needle quickly, climbing higher and higher, until even the big red bus looked tiny beneath him.

He came to the top, more than seventy feet above the ground. The sun reflecting off the golden pyramidion at its peak was blinding.

He recalled the quote from Hessler's notebook:

THREAD THE POWER OF RA THROUGH THE
EYES OF GREAT RAMESES' TOWERING
NEEDLES,

FROM THE SECOND OWL ON THE FIRST
TO THE THIRD ON THE SECOND . . .
. . . WHEREBY THE TOMB OF ISKENDUR
WILL BE REVEALED.

"The third owl on the second obelisk," he said aloud.

Sure enough, on the second line of this obelisk—the second obelisk from Luxor—there were three carved owls standing side by side.

And near the head of the third one, was a small circle depicting the Sun.

He imagined that very few people in history had actually seen this carving up close, since it was designed to sit so high above the populace—but up close, the carved image of the disclike Sun looked odd, as if it were not a carved image but rather . . . well . . . a *plug* in the stone.

West grabbed the plug and pulled it free—

—to reveal a horizontal cavity roughly two fingers wide and perfectly round in shape, that bored *right through* the Obelisk.

Like a kid scaling a coconut tree, West clambered around the other side of the Obelisk's peak, where he found and extracted a second matching plug, and suddenly, looking through the borehole he could see right through the ancient Obelisk!

"West! Hurry! The cops are almost here . . ."

West ignored him, yanked from his jacket two high-tech devices: a laser altimeter, to measure the exact height of the borehole, and a digital surveyor's inclinometer, to measure the exact angle of the borehole, both vertically and laterally.

With these measurements, he could then go to Luxor in Egypt and re-create this obelisk "virtually," and thus deduce the location of Alexander the Great's Tomb.

His altimeter beeped. Got the height.

He aimed his inclinometer through the borehole. It beeped. Got the angles.

Go!

And he was away, sliding down the Obelisk with his feet splayed wide, like a fireman shooting down a ladder.

His feet hit the scaffolding just as six police cars screeched to a halt around the perimeter of the Place de la Concorde and disgorged a dozen cap-wearing Parisian cops.

"Stretch! Fire her up! Get moving," West called as he ran across the top level of the three-story scaffold structure. "I'll get there the short way!"

The bus reversed out of the scaffolding, then Stretch ground the gears and the big red bus lurched forward, just as Jack West took a flying leap off the top level and sailed down through the air . . .

. . . landing with a thump on the top deck of the bus, a second before it sped away toward the River Seine.

From the moment of their daring heist at the Louvre, other forces had been launched into action.

As one would expect, a theft from the Louvre instantly shot across the Paris police airwaves—airwaves that were monitored by other forces of the state.

What Stretch didn't know was that the Paris police

had been outranked at the highest levels *and been taken off this pursuit.*

The chase would be carried out by the French Army.

Just as West had anticipated.

And so, as the big red double-decker bus shot away from the Obelisk and its wrecked outer structure, the Parisian police didn't follow. They just maintained their positions around the perimeter of the Place de la Concorde.

Moments later, five green-painted heavily armed fast-attack reconnaissance vehicles *whooshed* past the cop cars and shot off after the great ungainly bus.

Horns honked and sirens blared as the double-decker bus roared down the Quai des Tuileries on the edge of the River Seine for the second time that day—weaving between the thin daytime traffic, blasting through red lights, causing all manner of havoc.

Behind it were the five French Army recon vehicles.

Each was a compact three-man scout car known as Panhard VBL. Fitted with a turbocharged four-wheel-drive diesel engine and a sleek arrow-shaped body, the Panhard is a swift and nimble all-terrain vehicle that looks like an armor-plated version of a sports four-by-four.

The Panhards chasing West were fitted with every variety of gun turret: some had long-barreled 12.7mm machine guns, others had fearsome-looking TOW missile launchers.

Within moments of the chase beginning, they were all over the speeding bus.

They opened fire, shattering every window on the bus's left-hand side—a second before the bus roared into a tunnel, blocking their angle of fire.

Two of the Army Panhards tried to squeeze past the bus inside the tunnel, but Stretch swerved toward them, ramming them into the wall of the tunnel, grinding them against it.

With nowhere to go, both Panhards skidded and

flipped . . . and rolled . . . tumbling end over end until they crashed to twin halts on their roofs.

On the upper deck, Pooh Bear and West rocked with every swerve, tried to return fire. Pooh spied one of the TOW missile launchers on one Panhard.

"They've got missiles!" he yelled.

West called, "They won't use them! They can't risk destroying the Piece!"

"*West!*" Stretch's voice came over their radios. "*It's only a matter of time before they seal off this road! What do we do!*"

"We drive faster!" West replied. "We have to get to the Charles de Gaulle Bridge—"

Shoom—!

—they blasted out of the tunnel, back into sunlight, just in time to see two French Army helicopters sweep into position above them.

They were two very different types of chopper: one was a small Gazelle gunship, sleek and fast and bristling with guns and missile pods.

The other was bigger and much scarier: it was a Super Puma troop carrier, the French equivalent of the American Super Stallion. Big and tough, a Super Puma could carry twenty-five fully armed troops.

Which was exactly what this chopper was carrying.

As it flew low over the top of the speeding double-decker bus, along the rising-and-falling roadway on the north bank of the Seine, its side door slid open and drop ropes were flung from within it—and the French plan became clear.

They were going to storm the bus—the *moving* bus!

At the same moment, three of the pursuing Panhards swept up alongside the bus, surrounding it.

"I think we're screwed already," Stretch said flatly.

But he yanked on his steering anyway—ramming into the Panhard to his right hard, forcing it clear off the roadway, right *through* the low guardrail fence . . . where it shot high into the air, wheels spinning, and went crashing down into the river with a gigantic splash.

Up on the top deck, West tried to fire at the hovering Super Puma above him, but a withering volley from the Gazelle gunship forced him to dive for the floor. Every single passenger seat on the top deck of the bus was ripped to shreds by the barrage of bullets.

"Stretch! More swerving please!" he yelled, but it was too late.

The first two daredevil French paratroopers from the Super Puma landed with twin thumps on the open top deck of the moving double-decker bus only a few feet in front of him.

They saw West instantly, lying in the aisle between the seats: exposed, done for. They whipped up their guns and pulled the trigg—

—just as the floor beneath them erupted with holes, bullet holes from a shocking burst of fire from somewhere *underneath* them.

The two French troopers fell, dead, and a moment later, Pooh Bear's head popped up from the stairwell.

"Did I get them? Did I get them? Are you OK?" he said to West.

"I'm all right," West said, hurrying down the stairs to the lower deck. "Come on, we've gotta get to the Charles de Gaulle Bridge before this bus falls apart!"

The rising-and-falling riverside drive that they were speeding along would normally have been a tourist's delight: after leaving the Louvre behind, the roadway swooped by the first of the two islands that lie in the middle of the Seine: the Ile de la Cité. Numerous bridges spanning the river rushed by on the right, giving access to the island.

If West's team continued along the riverside road, they would soon arrive at the Arsenal precinct—the area where the Bastille once stood.

After that came two bridges: the Pont d'Austerlitz and the Pont Charles de Gaulle, the latter of which sat beside the very modern headquarters of the Ministry of Economics, Finances, and Industry, which itself sat next door to the Gare de Lyon, the large train station that serviced southeastern France with high-speed trains.

The big red tourist bus whipped along the riverside road, weaving through traffic, ramming the pursuing Army cars with wild abandon.

It shot underneath several overpasses and over some raised intersections. At one stage the spectacular Notre Dame Cathedral whizzed by on the right, but this was perhaps the only tourist bus in the world that didn't care for the sight.

As soon as West had abandoned the upper deck of the bus, the French troops on the Super Puma above him went for it in earnest—despite Stretch's best efforts at evasive weaving.

And within a minute, they took the bus.

First, two troopers landed on the open top deck, whizzing down the drop-ropes suspended from the chopper. They were quickly followed by two more, two more, and two more.

The eight French troopers now moved to the rear stairwell of the bus, guns up, preparing to storm the lower deck . . .

. . . just as, downstairs, West called: "Stretch! They're crawling all over the roof! See that exit ramp up ahead! Roll us over it!"

Immediately ahead of them was another overpass, with an exit ramp rising to meet it on the right-hand side of the riverside drive. A low concrete guard-rail separated this ramp from the roadway which continued on underneath the overpass as a tunnel.

"What!" Stretch shouted back.

"Just do it!" West yelled. "Everybody, grab on to something! Hang on!"

They hit the exit ramp at speed, and rose up it briefly—

—at which moment Stretch yanked *left* on the steering wheel, and the bus lurched leftward, hitting the concrete guardrail and . . .

. . . tipped over it!

The double-decker bus overbalanced shockingly and rolled *over* the concrete fence, using the fence as a fulcrum. As such, the entire double-decker bus *rolled,* going fully upside down—off the exit ramp, *back down* onto the roadway proper—where it *slammed* down onto its open-topped roof . . .

. . . crushing all eight of the French troops on its roof!

But it wasn't done yet.

Since it had tipped over the dividing rail from a considerable height, it still had a lot of sideways momentum.

So the big bus *continued* to roll, bouncing off its now-crushed roof and coming upright once again, commencing on a second roll—only to bang hard against the far wall of the sunken roadway, which had the incredible effect *of righting the bus* and plonking it back on its own wheels, so that now it was traveling once again on the riverside drive and heading into the tunnel, having just performed a full 360-degree roll!

Inside the bus, the world rotated crazily, a full 360 degrees, hurling West's team—Lily included—all around the cabin.

They tumbled and rolled, but they all survived the desperate move.

Indeed, they were all still lying on the floor when West scrambled to his feet and launched into action.

He took the wheel from Stretch as their mangled and dented bus swept out of the tunnel and into the Arsenal district. Having seen what West was prepared to do to anyone who tried to storm his bus from above, the Super Puma just flanked them now, swooping low over the river parallel to the speeding bus.

And just then, the modern glass-and-steel towers of the Economics Ministry came into view up ahead.

"That bridge up ahead is the Pont d'Austerlitz," Pooh Bear said, peering over West's shoulder. "The Charles de Gaulle Bridge is the one after it!"

"Gotcha," West said. "Tell everybody to get their pony bottles and masks ready, then get to the doors. Go!"

Pooh Bear gathered everyone together—Lily, Stretch, and Big Ears—and they all clambered to the side and rear doors of the bus.

The bus swept past the Pont d'Austerlitz, roaring toward the next bridge: the Pont Charles de Gaulle. Like the Austerlitz before it, the Charles de Gaulle Bridge branched out to the right, stretching over the river; beyond it, the glass towers of the Economics Ministry stabbed into the sky.

The riverside drive rose to meet the Charles de Gaulle Bridge, providing West with a ramp of sorts.

And while every other car in Paris would have slowed as it climbed this exit ramp, West accelerated.

As such, he hit the Charles de Gaulle Bridge at phenomenal speed, whereupon the great battered double-decker tourist bus performed its last earthly feat.

It *exploded* through the low pedestrian fence on the far side of the bridge and shot out into the air above the Seine, flying in a spectacular parabolic arc, its great rectangular mass soaring through the sky, before its nose tipped and it began to fall, and West bailed out of the driver's compartment and the others leaped from the side and rear doors and the big bus slammed into the river.

As the bus hit the surface of the Seine, the four people on its doors went flying to the side of it, also crashing into the water, albeit with smaller splashes.

But to the shock of those in the two pursuing French helicopters, they never surfaced.

Underwater, however, things were happening.

Everyone had survived the deliberate crash, and they regrouped with West, all of them now wearing divers' masks and breathing from pony bottles.

They swam through the murky brown water of the river, converging on the cobblestoned northern wall of the Seine, underneath the Charles de Gaulle Bridge.

Here, embedded in the medieval wall, under the surface of the river, was a rusty old gate that dated back to the 1600s.

The padlock sealing it was new and strong, but a visit earlier that morning by Pooh Bear with a boltcutter had altered it slightly. The padlock hung in place, and to the casual observer, it would have looked intact. But Pooh Bear had cut it cleanly on the rear side, so that now he just pulled it off the rusty gate by hand.

Beyond the gate, a brick-walled passageway disappeared into the murky gloom. The team swam into the passageway—with the last person in the line, Big Ears, closing the underwater gate behind them and snapping a brand-new padlock on it, identical to the one that had been sealing it before.

After about twenty yards, the underwater passageway rose into a dry sewerlike tunnel.

They all stood in the sewer tunnel, knee deep in foul-smelling water.

"How very Gothic," Stretch said, deadpan.

"Christian catacombs from the seventeenth century," Pooh Bear said. "They're all over Paris, over one hundred seventy miles of tunnels and catacombs. This set of tunnels runs all the way along the Boulevard Diderot. They'll take us past the Economics Ministry, right to the Gare de Lyon."

West checked his watch.

It was 12:35 P.M.

"Come on," he said. "We've got a train to catch."

The three remaining French Army Panhards descended on the Charles de Gaulle Bridge, disgorging men. The big red bus was still actually half-afloat, but in the process of sinking.

The two choppers patrolled the air above the crash site, searching, prowling.

Curious Parisians gathered on the bridge to watch.

Extra commando teams were sent into the Ministry complex and also into the Gare d'Austerlitz, the large train station that lay directly across the Charles de Gaulle Bridge, on the southern side of the Seine.

Every train that hadn't yet departed from it was barred from leaving. As a precaution, trains from the Gare de Lyon—farther away to the north, but still a possibility—were also grounded.

Indeed, the last train to depart the Gare de Lyon

that day would be the 12:44 TGV express service from Paris to Geneva, first stop Dijon.

An hour later, now dressed in dry clothes, West and his team disembarked the train in Dijon, smiling, grinning, elated.

There they boarded a charter flight to Spain, where they would rendezvous with Sky Monster and the *Halicarnassus* and commence their journey back to Kenya.

But their smiles and grins said it all.

After two failed attempts — or three if you counted the Mausoleum Piece—they had finally obtained a Piece of the Capstone.

They were now in a position to bargain.

They were now well and truly in the game.

At the same time, twelve hundred miles away, in Rome, a long-bearded man wearing the all-black robes of a Catholic priest strode across the wide square in front of St. Peter's Basilica, the magnificent domed cathedral designed by Michelangelo, the most holy place of worship in the Roman Catholic Church.

With his long gray beard and stooping walk, Max Epper looked very much the part: an old and wizened priest, perhaps even an Eastern Orthodox one, making a pilgrimage to the Vatican.

With him walked Zoe and Fuzzy, and as they crossed St. Peter's Square in the midst of hundreds of tourists, Zoe gazed up at the gigantic stone obelisk that stood proudly in the exact center of the Square.

"Cult of Amun-Ra," Wizard said flatly, striding past the towering stone needle.

Zoe turned as she walked, gazing up at this *Egyptian* structure taking pride of place in front of the biggest Catholic church in the world.

She shrugged. "The Cult of Amun-Ra . . ."

They entered the Basilica.

Few man-made structures on earth can match St. Peter's Basilica for sheer scale. It is shaped like a giant crucifix—just like the center of Paris—and its famous dome soars three hundred feet above a glistening marble floor. Brilliant shafts of sunlight penetrate its impossibly high windows, as if sent by God himself.

Michelangelo's *Pieta* flanks one side of the main entrance. Giant statutes of saints stand in alcoves lining the main hall—St. Ignatius, St. Francis of Assisi—looming over the faithful.

It is designed to inspire awe.

But the most spectacular section of the great cathedral is to be found at its most holy place, the junction of the cross.

Here you will find the altar of St. Peter's, covered by a colossal four-pillared awning made of sturdy iron laced with gold. At the top of each tree-trunk-like pillar, you will find angels leaning outward, blowing trumpets, praising the Lord.

And beneath this awning is the altar.

"It looks so plain," Fuzzy said, gazing up at it.

He was right. The altar of St. Peter's was remarkably plain, just a large oblong block of marble mounted on a raised platform. At the moment, since it wasn't being used, it was covered by a simple red-white-and-gold cloth and some candles. A thick rope suspended from brass poles prevented the public from surmounting it.

"Yes," Wizard said. "Considering its importance, it is very plain."

"It's only important if Zaeed was telling us the truth," Zoe commented.

Before they had all split up on their separate missions, Zaeed had explained that the Artemis Piece of the Golden Capstone lay *embedded* in the altar at St. Peter's

Basilica. The trapezoid, he claimed, had been incorporated facedown in the otherwise solid marble altar—so that its base lay flush with the flat upper surface of the altar. To the uninitiated, it would just look like a square plate of gold on the flat surface, a square plate with a crystal in its center.

To the initiated, however, it would mean much more.

Wizard stared at the altar. "I imagine that only a handful of cardinals have ever been allowed to gaze upon the naked surface of this altar. Fewer still would know the true nature of the golden trapezoid embedded in it. All would be very senior, privileged initiates into the true history of the Church."

"So what do we do?" Zoe asked. "We can't just pull out a crowbar and prise the trapezoid from the altar in front of all these people."

"I only need to *look* at it," Wizard said. "To memorize the inscription if I can."

They were surrounded by tourists and uniformed Swiss Guards—and, Wizard guessed, many plainclothed guards, ready to grab anyone who tried to step onto the altar.

Anyone, except maybe a doddery old Orthodox priest.

"Run me some interference," Wizard said. "Here I go."

He moved quickly, gazing adoringly up at the awning above the altar, stepping close to the rope, seemingly rapt with wonder.

Then before anyone could stop him, Wizard stepped over the rope and up the steps . . .

. . . and stood behind the altar of St. Peter's, running

his hands across the flat surface of the big oblong block as if it were made of some holy substance itself.

Plainclothes Swiss Guards appeared at once, emerging from the crowds, converging on the altar.

Standing behind the great oblong block in the exact heart of the Basilica, Wizard swept aside the red cloth that covered the altar and beheld its bare upper surface.

What he saw was dazzling.

The flat surface of the altar was made of exquisite white marble, except in its very middle. Here Wizard saw, flush with the flat marble surface, a square-shaped section made of gold.

It was medium-sized, perhaps three feet to each side. And you couldn't tell it was a golden trapezoid, since only its base side was visible. But there in its exact center, was a small diamondlike crystal.

The Artemis Piece.

Wizard saw the inscriptions carved into the surface of the trapezoid:

His wide eyes flashed like camera lenses, attempting to memorize the inscriptions in the short window of time he had—

"Excuse me, Father, but you cannot step up here." Wizard was yanked away from the altar.

Two Swiss guards had grabbed him firmly by the arms and were removing him politely but forcibly.

At the same time another guard redraped the red cloth back over the altar top, concealing the golden trapezoid—although he seemed to do it merely to restore the order of the altar, not out of any sense that a great secret had been unveiled.

"I-I-I'm s-s-so sorry," Wizard stammered, feigning senility and offering no resistance. "I just wanted to f-f-feel the power of my Lord in all h-h-his glory . . ."

The lead guard escorting him off the raised stage assessed him more closely, saw Wizard's earnest eyes, his scraggly beard, his tattered robes, and he softened. "All right, old man. Get out of here. Just stay behind the rope next time."

"Th-th-thank you, my son."

The guard escorted Wizard back to the main doors.

As he walked, Wizard tried to contain his excitement. He had the Artemis inscription burned into his brain—which was the next best thing to getting the Piece itself. Soon, he, Zoe, and Fuzzy would be winging their way out of Rome's Leonardo da Vinci International Airport and heading for home.

Flanked by the guards, he stifled the smile that was beginning to spread across his face.

At that very same moment, in a darkened room elsewhere in the Vatican, someone else was watching Wizard on a small security monitor.

Francisco del Piero.

"I knew you would come, Max, my old colleague,"

del Piero said to the image on the screen. "That's why I did not remove the Piece from the altar. I knew it would bring you out into the open."

Del Piero turned to the Vatican Security Chief next to him. "They'll head for the airport. Follow them, but do not grab them yet. Monitor their radio transmissions. The old man will send a signal soon after he leaves St. Peter's to inform his teammates that he has succeeded in his mission. Let him send his message. *Then* seize him and his accomplices at the airport and bring them to me."

Minutes later, speeding through the streets of Rome in a rental car, heading for the airport, Wizard sent a short encrypted text message to Doris in Kenya.

It said:

> *Mission accomplished.*
> *On our way back now.*
> *Wizard*

Shortly after, his car arrived at the airport and swung into the parking lot—

—just as the air all around it was pierced by sirens and police cars appeared from every side, swooping in on Wizard's car, blocking it, surrounding it.

Wizard, Zoe, and Fuzzy could do nothing.

In the basement radio room at the farm in Kenya, Doris Epper spoke into her mike: "That's great news, Huntsman. Wizard is on his way, too. He just text-messaged me a few hours ago. The mission in Rome was a success. He'll be here in the morning. See you in a couple of hours."

With a spring in her stride, she hurried up the steps to the kitchen. She was relieved that everyone was OK and that their missions had succeeded and she wanted to prepare a nice dinner for when they got back.

She stepped up into the kitchen . . . to find that someone was already there.

"That's wonderful news, Mrs. Epper."

Doris froze.

There before her, sitting casually at her kitchen table, was Marshall Judah. Standing behind him were twelve heavily camouflaged, heavily armed U.S. special forces troops.

Judah's head was bent, his eyes low, his voice laced with menace. "Take a seat, Doris, and let's wait for them together."

West and his subteam returned to Kenya.

On the way, they'd stopped in Spain to refuel, at which point Lily had had another breakthrough with the Callimachus Text. She was suddenly able to read the next entry.

"What's it say?" West asked.

"It's about the Hanging Gardens of Babylon," she said. "It says:

> *"The Hanging Paradise of Old Babylonia.*
> *March toward the rising Sun,*
> *From the point where the two life givers become one.*
> *In the shadow of the mountains of Zagros,*
> *Behold the triple falls fashioned*
> *by the Third Great Architect*
> *To conceal the path he hewed*
> *That climbs to the Paradise*
> *Which mighty Nebuchadnezzar built for his bride."*

West tousled her hair. "Nice work, kiddo. Nice work. Wizard's going to be thrilled."

The *Halicarnassus* landed with a roar on Victoria Station's airstrip just before midnight. It was a classic African night—a swollen full moon illuminated the grassy plains like a floodlight, while the low hills loomed, dark teeth against the moonlit sky.

About a mile from the runway stood the farmhouse, its windows glowing orange. The emergency signal—the lights on the juniper bush in the front garden—was not on.

Sky Monster swung the plane toward the hangar dug into the hill at the end of the runway. As it taxied slowly, everyone grabbed their gear, preparing to disembark.

None of them could know that as they did so, two hundred pairs of eyes watched them closely.

Turbines whirring, the *Halicarnassus* came to a halt just outside the doorway of the brightly illuminated hangar.

A flight of airstairs waited for it there, just outside the open doors. And beyond the airstairs, maybe forty yards away, stood a welcoming party of one: Doris, standing by the hangar doors themselves.

It was impossible for those on the plane to know that she was standing there at gunpoint.

The plane stopped alongside the airstairs at the entry to the hangar, its nose section poking into the actual hangar (it had to cool down outside for a few hours before it could be brought fully inside for storage).

As soon as it had stopped, its forward side door was flung open from within and Big Ears and Lily—eager to see Doris and show her the Zeus Piece—dashed out of the plane and scampered down the airstairs. Big Ears wore his backpack, containing the Piece.

Not far behind them came Pooh Bear and Stretch, escorting Zaeed—now flex-cuffed again. They emerged from the plane into the fresh night air, began stepping down the stairs.

Sky Monster and West lingered in the plane—Sky Monster to do a postflight check; West just to collect all his things: notes, parchments, Hessler's Nazi diary.

It was noisy outside—the *Halicarnassus*'s four massive wing engines still whirred loudly, winding down.

Big Ears and Lily were halfway to Doris.

"Hey, Doris! We did it!" Lily called over the din, but Doris's usually warm face was stony, cold—as though she knew something that she couldn't disclose.

Then she seemed to regather herself, smiled kindly, and called back: "Well done, little Eowyn! What a triumphant return. This is all a bit like Gimli returning to Moria, isn't it!"

At Doris's words, Lily slowed her stride.

Then she stopped completely.

Big Ears paused, turned to her. "What is it?"

Worried, Lily peered fearfully at the dark grassy fields that surrounded the hangar's entrance. Apart from Doris, the area was completely deserted.

"Big Ears, we're in trouble," she said evenly. "We have to get back to the plane. This is a trap."

"How do you know—"

"Just go! Now!" she said with an authority that belied her age.

And abruptly, she spun, grabbing Big Ears' hand, and together—still twenty yards from the plane—they bolted back toward the *Halicarnassus*.

No sooner had they moved than all hell broke loose in the hangar.

Every door on every side of the hangar burst open and disgorged dozens of black-clad American troops.

A maintenance door behind Doris was also thrown open and Marshall Judah rushed out of it, accompanied by a CIEF team led by Cal Kallis.

Kallis pushed roughly past Doris and opened fire on the fleeing pair with a god-almighty fury.

When the gunfire started, different people did different things:

West.

He raced to the forward door of the *Halicarnassus,* to see what was going on.

Sky Monster.

He peered out the cockpit windows—to see Lily and Big Ears running together back toward the airstairs, chased by an oncoming swarm of enemy troops.

Zaeed.

He was at the bottom of the airstairs when the gunfire began, flanked by Pooh Bear and Stretch, his hands still flex-cuffed. But his eyes, far from being wild and crazed, were watchful and focused now.

He'd actually just managed to extract a blade hidden in his pants and saw halfway through his flex cuffs, and was three seconds away from stabbing Stretch between the ribs and commencing his escape when the gunfire had started. At that point, he'd slid the blade back into his pocket and clambered back up the airstairs as they were hammered with bullet impacts.

And Judah.

While his men hurried past Doris, he stopped right in front of her and said, "I told you, no warnings."

And then, without the slightest hesitation, he drew

a Glock pistol, placed its barrel against her head and fired.

West arrived at the forward door just in time to see Doris fall.

"Oh, God, no . . ." he breathed. "No . . ."

He surveyed the rest of the scene in the hangar.

Pandemonium reigned.

A massive American force had emerged from every corner of the hangar. Most of them were on foot, but then West saw three Humvees come blasting out of the grassy fields outside.

The American troops were converging on the big black 747 like an army of ants, their collective movement focused on the two fleeing figures of Big Ears and Lily.

West zeroed in on the running pair.

One thing was clear: they weren't going to make it to the airstairs.

The Americans' angle of fire would cut them off before they got there. And he noted that the Yanks weren't aiming to *kill* them—just stop them from escaping. They knew not to harm Lily.

But Big Ears and Lily did make it to a portable electricity generator wagon just short of the airstairs. The generator wagon was the size of a small trailer. Normally, once the *Halicarnassus* was fully stopped, Sky Monster would get out and attach the generator to it, providing external electrical power. But he hadn't been able to do that yet.

Lily and Big Ears dived behind the generator wagon,

and Big Ears immediately opened fire on his closest pursuers, causing them to halt and duck for cover.

So now West stood at the top of the airstairs, while Stretch and Pooh Bear were huddled at the base of those same stairs, ducking gunfire. Zaeed was in the middle, halfway up the steps, getting away from the action.

And Lily and Big Ears lay crouched—cut off, pinned down by enemy fire—a tantalizing five yards from the base of the airstairs.

West keyed his radio mike. "Sky Monster! Fire her up again! We gotta get out of here!"

"Roger that!" A moment later the great jet turbines of the 747 roared back to life, the thunderous noise drowning out the sound of gunfire.

"Big Ears!" West called into his mike. "I hate to do this to you, but you've got to find a way to get Lily back on this plane! *Now!*"

Huddled behind the generator wagon, Big Ears was thinking fast.

Five yards. That was all it was. Five yards.

Only these five yards looked like a mile.

And then suddenly—with a kind of crystal clarity that was new to him—the situation became clear to Big Ears.

No matter what the outcome of this situation, *he was going to die.*

If he ran for the airstairs, he'd be shot for sure—even if they didn't shoot Lily, they'd nail him.

Alternatively, if he and Lily were caught by the Americans, they'd kill him then, too.

And with that realization, he made up his mind.

"Lily," he said, over the raging din all around them. "You know something. You've been the best friend I've ever had in my life. You were always way smarter than me, but you always waited for me, were always patient with me. But now I have to do something for you—and you have to let me do it. Just promise me, when the time comes, you do what you were put on this Earth to do. And remember me, the dumb grunt who was your friend. I love you, little one."

Then he kissed her forehead and, with his MP5 in one hand, he picked her up with the other, and shielding her with his body . . .

. . . he broke cover . . .

. . . and ran for the airstairs.

The American response was both immediate and vicious.

They opened fire.

Big Ears only needed six steps to make it to the airstairs.

He made four.

Before a crouching U.S. trooper nailed him with a clean shot to the head.

The bullet passed right through Big Ears' skull, exploding out the other side and he fell instantly—crumpling like a marionette whose strings have been cut—falling to his knees midway between the generator wagon and the airstairs, dropping Lily from his lifeless hands.

"No!" Lily screamed in horror. *"Noooo!"*

The Americans charged, moved in on the girl—

—only to be stopped by a curious sight.

At *exactly* the same time, in *exactly* the same way, two figures dived out from the base of the airstairs, each of them holding two MP5 submachine guns, the weapons blazing away in opposite directions as they flew through the air toward Lily.

Pooh Bear and Stretch.

They couldn't have planned the move. There simply hadn't been time. No, they had actually both dived *independently* of each other.

Yet their identical dives had been motivated by the exact same impulse:

To save Lily.

The Arab and the Israeli slid to simultaneous halts alongside Lily, bringing down four Americans each as they did so.

Lily was still kneeling beside Big Ears' body, her cheeks covered in tears.

Still firing repeatedly, Pooh Bear and Stretch each grabbed one of her hands and crouch-ran with her back to the cover of the airstairs.

Up the stairs they stumbled, as the steel side railings of the airstairs were riddled with a thousand dome-shaped bullet impacts.

Off-balance and firing blindly behind them, Pooh Bear and Stretch reached the top of the stairs and flung Lily in through the door, rolling themselves in after her, while above them West jammed the door shut and yelled, "Sky Monster! *Go! Go! Go!*"

* * *

The giant 747 pivoted on the spot, rolling around in a circle until it was re-aimed back up the runway— bullets pinging off its black-armored flanks.

As it completed its circle, it crunched *right over* a Humvee that got too close, flattening the car.

Then Pooh Bear and Stretch took their seats in the *Halicarnassus*'s wing-mounted gun turrets and let fly with a barrage of tracer fire, annihilating the other two Humvees.

Then Sky Monster punched his thrusters and the big black 747 gathered speed—thundering up the runway, its winglights blazing, chased by Humvees and jeeps spewing gunfire; returning tracer bullets from its own turrets—until it hit takeoff speed and lifted off into the night sky, escaping from its own supposedly secret base.

A grim silence hung over the main cabin of the *Halicarnassus*.

West held Lily in his lap. She was still sobbing, distraught over the deaths of Big Ears and Doris.

As the jumbo soared into the night sky, heading for nowhere in particular, everyone who had survived the gun battle in the hangar returned to the main cabin: Pooh Bear, Stretch, and Zaeed. Sky Monster stayed in the cockpit, flying manually for the time being.

With Lily in his arms, West's mind raced.

Big Ears was dead. Doris was dead. Their secret hideaway had been exposed. Not to mention the most frustrating fact of all—when he'd been killed, *Big Ears had been carrying the Zeus Piece.*

Shit.

Up until a few minutes ago, they'd actually *succeeded* on this impossible mission. Against all the odds, they had actually obtained a Piece of the Capstone.

And now . . .

Now they had nothing. They'd lost two of their best team members, lost their base of operations, and lost the one and only Piece they'd ever got.

Hell, West thought, he didn't even know why Lily and Big Ears had suddenly turned and run back to the plane. Gently, he asked Lily.

She sniffed, wiped away her tears.

"Doris gave me a warning. She said our return was

like Gimli's return to Moria. In *The Lord of the Rings,* Gimli the dwarf returns to the dwarf mines at Moria, only to find that the mines have been overrun by orcs. Doris was sending me a secret message. She obviously couldn't say anything directly, so she spoke in a code I'd understand. She was saying that the farm had been taken over by our enemies and to get away."

West was amazed at Lily's quick deduction—and at Doris's selfless sacrifice.

"Nice work, kiddo." He stroked Lily's hair. "Nice work."

It was Pooh Bear who asked what they were all thinking. "Huntsman. What do we do now?"

"I have to talk to Wizard," West said, moving to one of the communications consoles.

But just as he reached it, the console—as if by magic—started blinking and beeping.

"It's the video phone . . ." Stretch said. "An incoming call."

"It must be Wizard," Pooh Bear said.

"No," West said, staring at the console's readout. "It's coming from Victoria Station."

West clicked the ANSWER button and the screen on the console came to life. Filling its frame was the face of . . .

Marshall Judah.

He was sitting at a console inside the hangar back in Kenya, flanked by Kallis and some of his men.

"Greetings, Jack. My, my, wasn't that a narrow escape for you all. Sorry"—he corrected himself—"not exactly *all* of you escaped."

"What do you want?" West growled.

"Why, Jack. How could I want anything from you? I already have everything you can give me: the Zeus Piece, to add to the three Pieces I already possess. Oh, and I am not sure if you're aware of the fate of your friend Epper in Rome. Seems he's fallen into the hands of our European competitors. I do hope he'll be all right."

West tried not to let his surprise show. He didn't know that the Europeans had captured Wizard's team.

"Epper's capture," Judah said, realizing with a grin. "You weren't aware of this."

Shit.

"Why are you calling us?" West demanded. "To gloat?"

"To remind you of your status, Jack. Look at you. Look at what you have achieved. Your band of pissant nations shouldn't have tried playing at the grown-ups' table. At every juncture in our parallel missions, I have comprehensively *beaten* you. In the Sudan. In Tunisia. And now here in Kenya. Can't you see. There is nowhere you can go that I cannot follow. There is nowhere *on Earth* you can hide from me, Jack. My scientists are at this very instant about to uncover the location of the Hanging Gardens and, unlike you, we have long been aware of the importance of the Paris Obelisk—and in two days' time, we will use those measurements to reveal the location of Alexander's Tomb in Luxor: the resting place of the final Piece."

"Are you finished?"

"How about I finish with this: you never had a

chance on this mission, Jack. Let me give you a quick lesson in the law of nations: there are big fish and there are little fish. And the big fish eat the little ones. *You came up against a bigger fish,* Jack, and you got eaten. Your mission is over."

"I'm going to kill you, Judah," West said flatly. "For Doris."

"As if you could, Jack. As if you could."

With that, Judah cut the signal and West found himself staring at a blank screen.

There was silence in the main cabin.

For a long while, no one spoke.

West just stared at the blank screen, his teeth grinding.

"Stretch, try and call Wizard," he said. "See if Judah was telling the truth."

Stretch went to the satellite radio console, tried every channel that Wizard, Zoe, and Fuzzy could be on. He even tried their cell phones.

He received no reply.

"Nothing," he said, returning to the group. "There's no answer from Wizard, Zoe, or Fuzzy. They're off the air."

There was more silence as the full weight of their predicament sank in.

In addition to their terrible losses at Victoria Station, they had now lost three more people—including the one person who had been their greatest source of knowledge on this mission, Wizard.

Stretch said, "Every move we've made, Judah's

known it and followed right behind us. In the Sudan. In Tunisia. Now Kenya."

"Not exactly," Pooh Bear said. "Kenya was different: he got to Kenya *before* we did, not after. He was waiting for us there." Pooh looked hard at Stretch. "Somehow he knew about our base."

Stretch bristled. "What are you implying? Do you think I informed the Americans?"

Pooh Bear's glare suggested that he was seriously considering the idea.

Zaeed piped in: "Unless I'm mistaken, *you* were never invited to join this mission, were you, Israeli? I would say Saladin is perfectly within his rights to question your loyalty."

"This does not concern you!" Stretch said. "Bite your tongue, murderer!"

"An Israeli calls me a murderer!" Zaeed stood up. "Count the innocents *your* country has murdered, you—"

"Quiet!" West called, silencing them.

They all retreated, sat down.

West addressed them. "Judah and his backers now have four of the seven Pieces of the Capstone. And if they get the Artemis Piece from the Europeans—and we must assume they have a plan to do just that— they'll have five.

"At that point, they'll need only two more Pieces to complete the Tartarus Ritual at the Great Pyramid and rule the world. Now, the two Pieces left to find are those of the Hanging Gardens of Babylon and the Great Pyramid itself—"

Zaeed said, "You can forget about obtaining the

Great Pyramid Piece. It is the First Piece, the most highly prized, the pyramidal peak of the Capstone itself. It was buried with Alexander the Great and the location of his tomb will only be revealed at dawn on the final day."

"When the Sun shines through the obelisks at Luxor?" Pooh Bear said.

"Yes."

"Which leaves us the Hanging Gardens Piece," West said.

Zaeed said, "Of all the Wonders, the Hanging Gardens of Babylon have proved to be the most elusive. All of the other Wonders, in one way or another, survived into the modern age. But not the Gardens. They have not been seen since the fifth century B.C. Indeed, observers in the ancient world questioned whether they even existed at all. Finding them will be exceedingly difficult."

West frowned.

Maybe Judah was right.

He honestly didn't know if he could do this.

Not without Wizard. And certainly not when his only companions were a known terrorist, a constantly feuding Arab and Israeli pair, a slightly crazy New Zealand pilot, and one little girl.

The thought of Lily made him turn to her.

Her face was still red from crying, dried tear marks lined her cheeks.

"What do you think?" he asked.

She returned his gaze with bloodshot eyes, and when she spoke, she spoke with a new maturity.

"Before he died, Big Ears made me promise him

something. He asked that when the time came, I'd do what I was put on this Earth to do. I don't really know what that is yet, but I don't want to let him down. I want the *chance* to do what I was put on this Earth to do. Give me that chance, sir. Please."

West nodded slowly.

Then he stood up.

"The way I see it, folks, we have our backs to the wall. We're down on people, on options, and on luck, but we're not out of this game. We still have one option left. We find the one remaining Piece of the Capstone still available to us. The Piece hidden in the only Ancient Wonder never to have been found. People, we have to locate the Hanging Gardens of Babylon."

FIFTH MISSION
THE
HANGING
GARDENS

IRAQ
MARCH 19, 2006
THE DAY BEFORE TARTARUS

NEBUCHADNEZZAR'S PARADISE

OF ALL THE Seven Wonders of the Ancient World, none retains more mystery than the Hanging Gardens of Babylon.

There is a simple reason for this.

Of all the Wonders, only one has *never* been found: the Hanging Gardens. Not a single trace of them has been unearthed: no foundations, no pillars, not even an aqueduct.

In fact, so elusive have the Gardens been throughout the ages that most historians believe they never even existed at all but were rather the product of the imaginations of Greek poets.

After all, as Alaa Ashmawy, an expert on the Seven Ancient Wonders from the University of Southern Florida, has pointed out, the Babylonians were very careful record keepers, and yet their records make *not a single mention* of any Hanging Gardens.

Nor did the chroniclers of Alexander the Great's many visits to Babylon mention any kind of Gardens.

This lack of evidence, however, has not stopped writers throughout the ages from creating all manner of fabulous descriptions of the Gardens. On these facts, all agree:

1. The Gardens were constructed by the great Mesopotamian king, Nebuchadnezzar, around the year 570 B.C., in order to please his homesick new wife, who, hailing from Media, was accustomed to more verdant surroundings;

2. They were built to the east of the Euphrates River; and:

3. The centerpiece of the Gardens was a shrine devoted to the rare Persian White Desert Rose, a species that has not survived to the present day.

At this point, however, the descriptions vary greatly.

Some historians say the Gardens sat atop a golden ziggurat, its vines and greenery overflowing from the building's tiers. A dozen waterfalls were said to cascade over its edges.

Others say the Gardens dangled from the side of an immense rocky cliff face—literally earning the description "hanging."

One lone scholar has even suggested that the Gardens hung from a gigantic stalactite-like rock formation *inside* a massive cave.

An interesting sidenote, however, applies to the Gardens.

In Greek, the Gardens were described as *kremastos,* a word which has been translated as *hanging,* thus the term "Hanging Gardens" and the notion of some kind of suspended or raised paradise.

But *kremastos* can be translated another way. It can be translated as *overhanging.*

Which begs the question: is it possible that those ancient Greek poets were perhaps merely describing an ordinary stone ziggurat whose decorative foliage, left uncut and unkempt, had simply outgrown its tiers and overhung them at the edges? Could this reputed "Wonder" have really just been very very ordinary?

The *Halicarnassus* shoomed through the night sky.

The big black unregistered 747 zoomed out of Africa on a flight path that would take it across Saudi Arabia to one of the harshest, wildest, and most lawless countries on Earth.

Iraq.

It made one stop on the way.

An important stop in a remote corner of Saudi Arabia.

Hidden among some barren rocky hills was a cluster of small man-made caves, long abandoned, with flapping rags covering their doorways. A long-disused firing range stood nearby, ravaged by dust and time; discarded ammunition boxes lay everywhere.

It was a former terrorist camp.

Once the home of Mustapha Zaeed—and the resting place of all his notes on the Seven Wonders of the Ancient World.

Covered by West, Stretch, and Pooh Bear, the flex-cuffed Zaeed scrambled inside one particular cave, where behind a false wall he located a large trunk filled with scrolls, tablets, sandstone bricks, gold and bronze ornaments, and literally *dozens* of notebooks.

It also contained within it a beautiful black jade box no bigger than a shoebox. Before he passed the trunk out to the others, unseen by West's men, Zaeed grabbed the black jade box, opened it, and gazed for a moment at the fine-grained orange sand inside it. It lay flat, undisturbed for many years. It was so fine it was almost luminous.

He snapped the jade box shut, slipped it back into the trunk, and passed it out to the others.

Then on the way out of the hidden space in the wall, he triggered a small electronic beacon.

Zaeed emerged from behind the false wall and presented the trunk to West. "My life's work. It will help."

"It had better," West said.

They grabbed the trunk, hauled it back to the *Halicarnassus,* and resumed their course for Iraq.

Inside the *Halicarnassus,* West's depleted team went about the task of finding the location of the Hanging Gardens of Babylon.

While West, Pooh Bear, and Lily pored over Lily's most recent translation of the Callimachus Text, Zaeed—his flex cuffs now removed—was on his knees, rummaging through his dusty old trunk.

"You know," Pooh Bear said, "it would be nice to have some idea what these Gardens actually looked like."

West said, "Most drawings of the Gardens are little more than wild interpretations of vague Greek sources, most of them variations on the classic ziggurat shape. No one has an actual image of them—"

"Don't speak too soon, Captain West! That may not be so! Here it is!" Zaeed called, pulling a crude rectangle of very ancient cloth from his trunk.

It was about the size of a sheet of letter paper, rough and rectangular. Its edges were worn, ragged, unsewn, like hessian cloth. Zaeed brought it over to the others.

"It's a draft cloth, a simple device used by ancient kings to keep an eye on the progress of their faraway construction sites. The cloth would be taken by a royal messenger to the worksite where the messenger then drew the scene. The messenger would then bring the cloth back to the king, thus showing him the progress being made.

"I found this cloth in a pauper's tomb underneath the town of Ash Shatra, in central Iraq—the tomb of a horseman who had died near the town, having been robbed and left for dead by bandits. Although he was buried as a pauper, I believe he was actually a royal messenger returning to New Babylon with a draft cloth of the Hanging Gardens for Nebuchadnezzar. *Behold* all of you, the only picture, so far as I know, of the Hanging Gardens of Babylon."

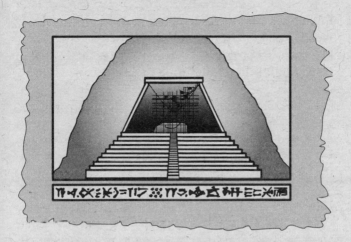

"It looks like an open cave in the mountainside," West said. "Only they refined the natural opening into a magnificent arch."

"What is that upside-down triangle suspended from the ceiling of the cave?" Pooh Bear asked.

"It looks like a gigantic *stalactite* . . ." Stretch said.

West said, "And that structure on the cave floor directly beneath it appears to be a ziggurat, encased in a construction mud mound. You used the mound to build the ziggurat, then you took the mound away after you were finished."

Zaeed eyed West sideways. "If that is a full-sized ziggurat, Captain, then that stalactite must be at least *fifteen stories tall*. It must be immense."

"What are all those crisscrossing lines covering the two structures?" Lily asked.

"I have long pondered those lines, child," Zaeed said. "I believe that they are an ancient form of scaffolding—a multilevel temporary structure made of wooden poles used to build the Gardens. Remember, this cloth is a progress report—it depicts the Gardens being built. I therefore surmise that they are a building tool."

Pooh Bear asked, "Lily. What does the writing say?"

Zaeed said, "My brother, this is not written in the language of Thoth. It's just standard cuneiform, written by a messenger for his king—"

"Lily can read cuneiform," West said. "Go on, Lily."

Lily read the text box: "It says: *Construction continuing as scheduled. Nineteen worker deaths. Sixty-two injuries. Losses tolerable.*"

"Losses tolerable," Stretch repeated. "Doesn't look like the despots of this region have changed much over the ages."

They returned to Lily's translation of the Callimachus Text's sixth entry:

> *The Hanging Paradise of Old Babylonia.*
> *March toward the rising Sun,*
> *From the point where the two life givers become one.*
> *In the shadow of the mountains of Zagros,*
> *Behold the triple falls fashioned*
> *by the Third Great Architect*
> *To conceal the path he hewed*
> *That climbs to the Paradise*
> *Which mighty Nebuchadnezzar built for his bride.*

"Well, it begins straightforwardly enough," West said. "You march due east from the point where the two life givers become one. 'The life givers' is the name the Mesopotamians gave to the Tigris and Euphrates Rivers. This must be a reference to the point where they meet."

"Baghdad?" Pooh Bear asked. "It stands at a point of convergence of the Tigris and Euphrates. Isn't it the site of ancient Babylon?"

"Actually, no," West said, "Babylon lies underneath the modern-day town of Hilla, to the south of Baghdad. And your theory doesn't strictly obey the verse. The two rivers bend very close to each other at Baghdad, but they don't *become one* there. They actually come together much farther south, at the town of Qurna. There they become one big super-river—the Shatt al-Arab—which flows south through Basra before draining into the Persian Gulf."

Stretch said sourly: "I can't believe the Americans haven't found the Gardens already. They must have over a hundred and fifty thousand troops in Iraq right now. They could easily have sent huge forces of men to check out every waterfall in the Zagros Mountains due east of Baghdad, Hilla, *and* Qurna by now."

West paused, an idea forming in his mind. "Unless . . ."

"What?"

"The modern town of Hilla does indeed stand on the ruins of Nebuchadnezzar's Babylon," he said. "But now that I look at it closely, our verse does not refer to 'Babylon' at all. It mentions the Hanging Paradise of *Old Babylonia*. Old Babylon."

"Meaning?" Pooh Bear asked.

"Consider this," West said. "New York. New England. New Orleans. Today, many cities and regions are named in memory of older places. In some ancient texts, Nebuchadnezzar's Babylon is actually referred to as *New* Babylon. What if the Gardens were *never* in New Babylon, but were, rather, built in an older city also named 'Babylon,' but built far from the newer city that adopted its name. The *original* Babylon."

"It would explain why Alexander the Great's biographers never mentioned the Gardens when he passed through Babylon and why no one has found them near Hilla," Stretch said. "They would only have seen New Babylon, not Old Babylon."

"Two Babylons. Two cities," Zaeed stroked his sharply pointed chin. "This is a good theory . . ."

Then suddenly his eyes lit up. "Of course! *Of course!* Why didn't I think of it before!"

"What?"

Zaeed dashed to his trunk and scrounged among the notebooks there.

As he did so, he spoke quickly, excitedly. "If I may take Captain West's theory one step further. Modern logic assumes that the Tigris and the Euphrates follow the *same* courses today that they followed back in 570 B.C. They flow down from Turkey, through Iraq, before joining at Qurna in the southern marshlands.

"Now consider this. Mesopotamia is the birthplace of all flood myths. Why, the tale of Noah and his Ark is but a flimsy retelling of the story of Zisudra and his animal-carrying boat. Why is this so? Because Iraq's flood myths stem from *very real* floods: of the Persian

Gulf breaking its banks and flooding far inland, ripping apart eroded land formations and, on occasion, *diverting* the courses of the two great rivers of the region, the Tigris and Euphrates. A westerner named Graham Hancock has written about this very convincingly in a marvelous book called *Underworld*. Ah-ha! Here it is!"

He produced a battered book, opened it to a page containing a map of Iraq. Prominent on the map were the two major rivers, the Tigris and Euphrates, that joined in a "V" shape in the south of the country:

Zaeed had scribbled the locations of Hilla, Qurna, and Basra on the map.

He explained. "Now. As we continue to do today,

people back in ancient times built their towns on the banks of the two great rivers. But when the rivers diverted onto new courses because of flooding, it follows that those same people would have abandoned the old towns and built new ones, the ones we see on the banks of the rivers today.

"Many years ago, in my search for lost documents relating to the Hanging Gardens, I mapped the locations of *abandoned* towns, towns that were once situated on the banks of the rivers, but which, once the rivers diverted, were simply deserted. From these locations, I was able to reconstruct the *former* courses of the two rivers."

"So where did they converge back then?" West asked.

Zaeed grinned. "See, *that* was what I did not know—that their *point of convergence* was the all-important factor."

With a flourish, Zaeed then flipped the page to reveal a *second* map of Iraq, only on this map, an additional dotted V had been drawn directly beneath the present-day one:

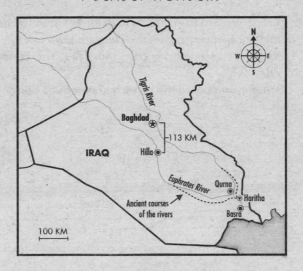

Zaeed pointed at this new river junction—it lay south of Qurna, roughly halfway between it and Basra.

"The rivers," Zaeed said, "used to meet here, at the town of Haritha."

The *Halicarnassus* shot into Iraq, heading for the southern village-town of Haritha.

As it did so, everyone prepared for their arrival—prepping guns, maps, helmets, and tunnel gear.

Alone in his office, with Horus perched on his chair back, West kept one eye on a laptop computer that Wizard had set up soon after their mission in Tunisia had gone to hell.

It was the microwave communications net he had

instructed Wizard to create, to scan for any signals emanating from, or coming to, the *Halicarnassus*.

As they crossed the border into Iraq, the laptop pinged.

Someone on board the plane had sent out a homing signal.

To get to Haritha, the *Halicarnassus* had to skirt the port city Basra.

As it soared over the outskirts of Basra, Sky Monster's voice came over the PA. "Hey, Captain West, you better come up here and see this."

West went up to the cockpit and peered out the windows.

A long column of heavy-duty vehicles was rumbling out of Basra, heading north toward Haritha.

It was a gigantic convoy. Of American military vehicles.

Troop trucks, engineering vehicles, Humvees, jeeps, motorbikes, plus no fewer than ten Abrams battle tanks and several Black Hawk helicopters, prowling overhead.

In all, it amounted to maybe five thousand troops— five thousand regular American troops who, unbeknownst to them, had simply been *handed over* to Judah thanks to the influence of his powerful bosses.

Geez, they had some pull, West thought.

"How can this be?" Zaeed asked, appearing behind West with Pooh Bear.

"How can they be onto us *again*?" Pooh Bear asked.

West just stared at the convoy, trying not to betray his thoughts: *who gave us away?*

"Oh, shit!" Sky Monster exclaimed, hearing something through his headphones. "The Yanks just scrambled fighters from Nasiryah. F-15s. We better find this place fast, Huntsman."

A few minutes later, they arrived above the dusty town of Haritha, situated on the eastern bank of the Shatt al-Arab River about thirty miles north of Basra.

"OK, Sky Monster, swing us due east," West said.

Sky Monster banked the *Halicarnassus* above the town, but as he did so, he and West glimpsed the highway coming from the north, from Qurna—

—and on that highway, they saw *another* column of American vehicles.

It was almost identical to the first—lots of troop trucks, Humvees, and tanks; and another five thousand men, at the very least.

West's mind raced.

"Judah must have had people at Qurna, searching for the waterfalls," he said. "But Qurna is the wrong junction of the rivers. He was searching too far to the north."

"And now—*suddenly*—he knows to come south," Sky Monster said pointedly. "How about that . . ."

West just tapped him reassuringly on the shoulder. "East and low, my friend."

But their position was clear—with a rat in their ranks, they were now caught between *two* converging convoys of overwhelming American firepower.

If they found the Hanging Gardens—which wasn't guaranteed—they'd have to be in and out *fast*.

Within minutes, the jagged peaks of the Zagros Mountains rose up before them, the boundary line between Iraq and Iran.

Numerous small rivers snaked their way through the range's mazelike system of peaks and valleys—descending to the Shatt al-Arab. Waterfalls could be seen everywhere: tall thin stringlike falls, short squat ones, even horseshoe-shaped ones.

There were many double-tiered waterfalls, and several quadruple-tiered falls, but as far as West could tell, there was only one set of *triple*-tiered falls in the area due east of Haritha: an absolutely stunning cascade easily three hundred feet from top to bottom, that bounced over two wide rocky ledges, before flowing into a stream that wound down to the mighty al-Arab. These falls lay right at the edge of the mountain range, looking out over the flat marshy plain of southern Iraq.

"That's it," West said. "That's them. Sky Monster, bring us down anywhere you can. We drive from here. You take the *Hali* to these coordinates and wait for me to call." He handed Sky Monster a slip of paper.

"Roger that, Huntsman."

The *Halicarnassus* landed on the flat cracked surface of a lakebed that hadn't seen water in a thousand years.

No sooner had its wheels touched down than its rear loading ramp dropped open, banging onto the ground, and—*shoom!*—a four-wheel-drive Land Rover came rushing out of the big plane's belly, bouncing down onto the mud plain and speeding off to the east, kicking up a cloud of sand behind it.

For its part, the *Halicarnassus* just powered up again and took off, heading for the secret hangar where Jack West had originally found her fifteen years before.

* * *

The Land Rover skidded to a halt before the towering triple-tiered falls. The roar of falling water filled the air.

"Allah have mercy," Pooh Bear said, gazing up at the falls. At three hundred feet, they were the height of a thirty-story building.

"There!" West called.

A narrow stone path in the rock face led behind the lowest tier of the waterfall.

West hurried along it. The others followed. But when they arrived behind the curtain of falling water, they were confronted by something they hadn't expected.

On every tier of the falls, the water was thrown quite a way out from the cliff wall, propelled by its rapid speed. This meant that the actual *face* of each tier was largely water-free—except for a layer of moss and a constant trickle of dribbling water. It *also* meant that each cliff face was *concealed* by the falls themselves.

And behind the curtains of water was a most curious feature.

Cut into the face of each rock wall was a dizzying network of ultranarrow paths that crisscrossed up them. There were maybe six paths in total, but they wound and intersected in so many ways that the number of permutations they created was huge.

Gazing at the twisting array of pathways on the first cliff face, West saw with dismay the alarming number of wall holes and blade holes that opened onto the paths.

Booby traps.

Zaeed was awed. "Imhotep III. A genius, he was,

but a sinister genius. This is a very rare type of trap system but typical of his flair. There are many paths, with deadly snarcs, but only one of the pathways is safe."

"How do we know which route is the safe one?" Stretch asked. "They all seem to intertwine."

Beside West, Lily was gazing intently at the path system behind the waterfall.

As she looked at it, something clicked in her mind.

"I've seen this before . . ." she said.

She reached into West's backpack and extracted a printout.

It was titled: *Waterfall Entrance—Refortification by Imhotep III in the time of Ptolemy Soter.*

"Well, would you look at that . . ." Stretch said.

The lines on the printed image exactly matched the layout of the pathways on the waterfall.

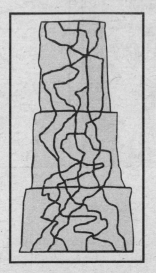

"But which path is the safe route?" Pooh Bear asked anxiously.

"That I don't know," Lily said, deflating.

"Wait a second," West said. "Maybe you do . . ."

Now he rifled through his pack for a few moments, before he said, "Got it!"

He pulled from the backpack . . . a little tattered brown leather-bound notebook.

The diary of the Nazi archaeologist, Hessler.

"Hessler knew the safe path," West said, flicking the pages of the diary until he found what he was looking for.

"Here!" He held the diary open, revealing a page they had seen before:

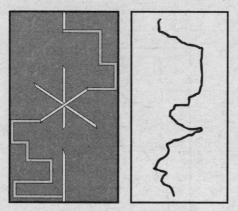

Its title was "Safe Routes."

West smiled.

He brought the right-hand image from this page alongside the picture of the waterfall's paths, and everyone else saw it—the right-hand "Safe Route" matched one of the twisting paths on the waterfall diagram perfectly:

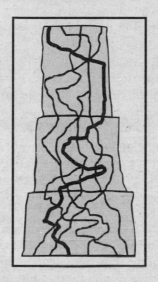

"You know, Captain West," Zaeed said, "you're a lot cleverer than I give you credit for. I shall have to watch you."

"Thanks," West said drily.

As he spoke, he stole a glance at the plain behind them. In the far distance, a high dustcloud stretched across the sandplain, from horizon to horizon—a sandstorm, or perhaps something else . . .

The dustcloud of two massive convoys.

"Come on," he said. "We don't have much time."

* * *

Up the vertical cliff wall they went, following the safe path, with the roaring curtain of water falling behind their backs. Diffused sunlight lanced in through falling water, lighting the way.

West climbed in the lead, with Horus in his chest pouch.

Their path twisted and turned, doubling back and forth as it rose up the cliff face. It was so narrow that the team could only climb it in single file, and it was covered in slippery moss, so their progress was slow. That said, without the map, they could never have figured out the safe route up the falls.

At both of the middle ledges in the waterfall, the path burrowed into the rock face as a tunnel—a tunnel that emerged above the ledge, giving access to the next level.

And so after twenty minutes of careful climbing, they reached the top of the third rock face. There, just below the lip of the uppermost ledge of the falls, immediately beneath a stunning translucent veil of fast-flowing water, the path ended . . .

. . . right in front of a third low tunnel—a passageway that bored directly into the cliff face, disappearing into darkness.

The entrance to this tunnel, however, was different from the lower ones.

It was more ornate, despite the fact it was covered in overgrown green moss.

The tunnel's entry frame—every side covered with hieroglyphs—was beautifully cut into the rock face, in a perfectly square shape. Its smooth walls retained this shape as they receded into blackness.

And on the lintel above the door, obscured by trickling water and moss, was a familiar carving:

West smiled at the carved image. "We're here."

As West and the others evaluated the tunnel entrance,
Pooh Bear followed a short horizontal section of the
path that led to the edge of the waterfall.

Leaning out, he peered around the edge of the
flowing body of water, looking out at the vast sandplain
behind them.

What he saw made his eyes boggle.

He saw the two American convoys—now merged
to become one megaconvoy—thundering across the
plain, kicking up an immense dustcloud behind them.
Choppers hovered above the great column of vehicles,
with one darkly painted Black Hawk out in front.

Ten thousand men, *coming right for them.*

"By Allah," he breathed. "Er, Huntsman . . ."

West joined him, saw the immense American
force, and particularly eyed the dark Black Hawk
leading the way.

He frowned.

That chopper actually didn't look . . .

He pursed his lips in thought.

The world was closing in on him, and he was fast
running out of options.

"Come on, Pooh," he said. "We can't stop now."

They rejoined the others at the tunnel entrance,

where Stretch said, "If this trap system is anything like the others, there's no way we can get in and out before the Americans arrive."

"If I may be so bold," Zaeed said slyly from behind them. "There *might* in fact be a way . . ."

"What way?" Stretch said suspiciously.

"The Priests' Entrance. The Nazi's diary mentions it, and I have come across this phrase in my own research. Such an entrance is usually a small one, unadorned, used by the priests of a temple to tend to its shrines even after that temple has been closed off. As a royal retreat, the Gardens almost certainly contained temples in need of tending."

"A back door," West said.

"Yes. Which means we can enter through this door and exit out the other end, via the Priests' Entrance."

"*If* we can find it," Stretch said.

"If we don't get this Piece," West said, "Doris and Big Ears and Noddy will have died for nothing. I'm not going to let that happen. I'm getting this Piece."

And with that he turned, and gripping Lily's hand, he started for the tunnel behind the waterfall.

Pooh Bear fell into step close beside him, and stole a whisper: "Huntsman. That lead chopper, the dark Black Hawk out in front of the convoy, did you see it?"

"Yes," West's eyes remained fixed forward.

"That isn't an American chopper."

"I know."

"Did you recognize the markings? It was—"

"Yes," West whispered, glancing back at Stretch. "It's an Israeli chopper. Somehow the Israelis knew our location, and I think I know how. Thing is, it looks like they're trying to get here *ahead* of the Americans." He threw another deadly look at Stretch. "Israel always looks after Israel. Come on."

And with those words, they entered the trap system that guarded the Hanging Gardens of Babylon.

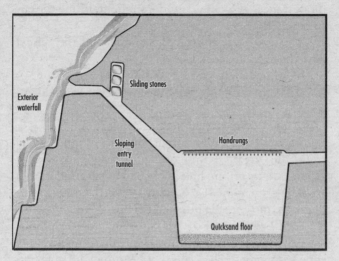

THE ENTRY TUNNEL AND THE SAND CAVERN

The flashlight on West's fireman's helmet carved a saberlike beam through the darkness of the tunnel.

His team followed him, silhouetted by the daylight that penetrated the waterfall behind them. They also wore helmet lights. Horus flew out in front.

The tunnel was perfectly square in shape, its walls hard, carved from solid rock. And it sloped steadily downward, away from the daylight. Shadowy square recesses were cut into its ceiling, concealing God-only-knew-what. The waterfall behind them roared loudly, a constant *shhh*—

The first trap struck.

With a heart-stopping *boom,* an enormous five-ton drop stone fell out of a recess in the ceiling—just inside the entrance—blocking out the sunlight, filling the entire tunnel!

Then, to their horror, the gradient of the tunnel gave the massive block life.

It immediately started sliding *down* the slope—toward them—forcing West's team forward and downward.

"Move!" West called.

They all started running down the tunnel, away from the great sliding stone, sidestepping warily around all the ceiling holes they had to pass under.

The great stone slid quickly forward, chasing after them, an unstoppable pursuer, driving them toward—

A cliff edge.

A hundred feet down the slope, the tunnel simply ended at a gaping black abyss. The tunnel did not seem to continue in any way beyond the dark void. This, it appeared, was the absolute end of the tunnel.

The stone kept rumbling down the tunnel behind them.

West fired a flare into the dark void—

—to reveal that they were standing at one end of a gigantic subterranean cavern shaped like a giant cube, easily fifty meters long and at least ten stories high.

Their problem: their tunnel opened onto this cavern right up near the *ceiling*.

The sliding stone kept coming.

Then, by the glow of the hovering flare, West saw *the floor* of the great cavern a hundred feet below him.

It was flat and bare, made of sand.

But there was something wrong about it—it was *too* flat, *too* bare.

West kicked a nearby stone off the edge and watched it sail down to the floor of the cavern.

The stone hit the floor.

It didn't bounce.

It just landed with a splonk, *embedding* itself in the goopy sandlike surface. And then it went under, seemingly *swallowed* by the semiliquid surface.

"Ah-ha, quicksand," Zaeed said, impressed. "The *entire* floor is quicksand . . ."

"God, you're just like Max," West said, snapping round to check on the fast-moving stone behind them—thirty feet away and about to force them into the quicksand-filled chamber.

"This trap system doesn't waste any time, does it."

But then, turning back to the massive square cavern, he saw the answer—a long line of hand bars had been dug into its ceiling; a line that ended at a matching tunnel at the opposite end of the cavern, 160 feet away.

Of course, more dark and deadly trap holes were interspersed between and above the hand bars.

"Lily, here. Jump onto my chest, put your hands around my neck," West said. "Zaeed. You got any intel on these hand bars?"

Zaeed peered back at the sliding stone. "I found a reference once to something called the High Ceiling of the Sand Cavern. It said, 'Walk with your hands but in deference to he who built it, avoid those of its Creator.' Imhotep III built this system, so I'd avoid every third handgrip."

"Good theory," West said, "but since I don't trust you, why don't you go first and test it out. Now *move.*"

Zaeed leaped out onto the hand rungs, swinging himself along them, avoiding every third one.

Once he'd survived the first few yards, West scooped up Lily. "Everybody, follow us."

And so with Lily gripping him around the neck, West reached up and grabbed the first hand bar . . .

. . . and swung out over the ten-story drop to the quicksand floor.

It was an incredible sight: five tiny figures, moving in single file, all hanging from their hands, swinging fist over fist across the ceiling of the immense cube-shaped cavern, their feet dangling ten stories above the floor.

The last in the line was Pooh Bear, who leaped off the doorway ledge a bare moment before the five-ton sliding stone came bursting out of the tunnel, filling the entire passage before falling clear out of it!

The huge square stone thundered off the edge . . . and tipped . . . and went sailing down the sheer wall of the cavern before it splashed into the quicksand with a great goopy *splat.*

Then the stone settled in the quagmire and sank below the surface—grimly, slowly—never to be seen again.

* * *

West gripped each hand bar firmly, swinging himself and Lily down the length of the cavern. Horus flew alongside them, hovering nearby—seemingly amused at their difficult method of travel.

Following Zaeed, West avoided every third hand bar, which was just as well. Zaeed had been right. West tested the ninth hand bar and it just fell from its recess, dropping all the way to the deadly floor.

He was halfway across when he heard the voices. Shouts. Coming from the entry tunnel.

The first chopper—the Israeli Black Hawk—must have dropped its men directly onto the path at the top of the falls.

West reasoned that they were probably commandos from the *Sayeret Matkal*, the very best of Israel's elite "Sayeret" or "reconnaissance" units. The Matkal were crack assassins—ruthlessly efficient killers who, among other things, were widely acknowledged as the best snipers in the world. Stretch's old unit.

Now they were coming in.

Fast.

"Everybody!" West called. "Get a move on! We're about to have some really nasty company!"

He started double-timing it across the hand bars—swinging like a monkey hand over hand—high above the deadly floor.

Then suddenly from the entry tunnel there came the familiar heavy *whump* of a sliding stone dropping from the ceiling—followed by shouts and the sound of rapidly running feet.

The Israelis had set off a second sliding stone.

West kept moving across the high cavern, swinging by his hands.

Out in front, Zaeed reached the mouth of the opposite tunnel, swung into it. West followed seconds later, swinging his feet onto solid ground. He turned to help the others—

—only to see a red laser dot appear on his nose . . . a dot that belonged to a sniper rifle in the opposite tunnel, a sniper rifle held by one of the Israeli commandos, bent on one knee.

A voice came over West's radio frequency: *"Stay right where you are, Captain West. Don't move a muscle."*

West was hardly going to obey—but then, as if it could read his thought, the dot shifted slightly . . .

. . . so that it now rested on the back of Lily's head.

"I know what you're thinking, Captain. Don't. Or she dies. Cohen! These hand rungs. The safe sequence."

Right then Stretch landed on the ground beside West. Pooh Bear was still huffing and puffing behind him, crossing the hand rungs with difficulty.

Stretch glanced sideways at West as he spoke into his mike: "Avoid every third rung, Major."

The Israelis moved quickly, leaping out from the entry tunnel, grasping the hand bars, moving across the high ceiling of the cavern.

There were six of them, and they all emerged from the entry tunnel ahead of the sliding stone—it just rumbled out of the tunnel harmlessly behind them, dropping into the quicksand pool.

But they also moved in a brilliantly coordinated fashion—so that at any moment, one of them hung one-handed and always had his gun aimed at Lily.

Within a few minutes, they were across the cavern and surrounding West's little team.

The Israeli leader eyed West menacingly.

Stretch made the introductions. "Captain Jack West Jr. . . . this is Major Itzak Meir of the Sayeret Matkal, call sign: *Avenger*."

Avenger was a tall man, broad-chested, with hard green eyes that were entirely lacking in nuance. For him, black was black, white was white, and Israel always came first.

"The famous Captain West." Avenger stepped forward, relieving West of his holstered pistol. "I've never heard of a soldier enduring so much failure, and yet still you keep picking yourself up, dusting yourself off, and coming back for more."

"It's never over till it's over," West said.

Avenger turned to Stretch. "Captain Cohen. Congratulations. You have done a fine job on an unusually long mission. Your work has been noted at the highest levels. I apologize for surprising you in this way."

Stretch said nothing, just bowed his head.

Pooh Bear, however, was livid.

He glared at Stretch. "Accept my congratulations, too, Israeli. You performed your mission to the letter. You led them to us and you *sold us out* just in time to hand them the last available Piece. I hope you're satisfied."

Stretch still said nothing.

Lily looked up at him. "Stretch? Why . . ."

Stretch said softly, "Lily. You have to understand. I didn't—"

Avenger grinned. "What is this? 'Stretch?' Have you been renamed, Cohen? How positively sweet."

He turned to Pooh Bear. "Alas, everything you say is true, Arab. The last available Piece is to be ours, one Piece of the Capstone that will give Israel all the leverage it needs over the United States of America. Now, Captain West, if you would be so kind. Lead the way. Take us to this last available Piece. You work for Israel now."

But no sooner had these words come out of his mouth than there was a great explosion from somewhere outside.

Everyone spun.

West swapped a glance with Pooh Bear.

They all listened for a moment.

Nothing.

Silence.

And then West realized: silence *was* the problem. He could no longer hear the constant *shhh* of the waterfall up at the entrance to the tunnel system.

The shooshing had stopped.

And the realization hit.

Judah had just used explosives to divert the waterfall—*the entire waterfall*! He was opening up the entrance for entry: mass forced entry.

*   *   *

In fact, even in his wildest dreams, West still hadn't fully imagined the scene outside.

The waterfall had indeed been diverted, by a series of expertly laid demolition charges laid in the river above it. Now its triple-tiered rock face, crisscrossed with paths, lay bare and dry, in full view of the world.

But it was the immense military force massing around the base of the dry waterfall that defied imagining.

A multitude of platoons converged on the now-tranquil pool at the base of the triple-tiered cliff face. Tanks and Humvees circled behind them, while Apache and Super Stallion choppers buzzed overhead.

And commanding it all from a mobile command vehicle was Marshall Judah.

He sent his first team in from the air—they went in fast, ziplining down drop-ropes suspended from a hovering Super Stallion direct to the top tier of the dry falls, bypassing the paths.

Guns up and pumped up, they charged inside.

From their position at the far end of the quicksand cavern, West and his new group saw the Americans' red laser-sighting beams lancing out from the entry tunnel, accompanied by fast footsteps.

"American pigs," Zaeed hissed.

Then suddenly—*whump*—the Americans' footfalls were drowned out by a much louder sound: the deep ominous grinding of a third sliding stone!

Gunfire. The Americans were firing their guns *at* the sliding stone!

Shouts.

Then running—frantic running.

Seconds later, the first desperate American trooper appeared on the ledge on his side of the cube-shaped cavern.

He peered around desperately—looking left and right, up and down—and he saw the quicksand floor far below; then he saw the hand rungs in the ceiling. He leaped for them—swung from the first one to the second, grabbed the third—

—which fell out of its recess and sent the hapless commando plummeting ten stories *straight down*.

The man screamed all the way until—*splat!*—he landed in the gelatinous floor . . . at which point he started screaming in a whole new way.

The screams of a man caught in the grip of a force he cannot resist, a man who knows he is going to die.

His five teammates arrived at the tunnel's edge just in time to see him get sucked under, his mouth filling with liquid sand. Now trapped on the ledge, they glanced from the deadly hand rungs back to the sliding stone, then down to the quicksand.

Two tried the hand rungs.

The first man reached the sixth rung—which felled him. The second man just slipped and fell all on his own.

The other three were beaten by the sliding stone.

It burst out of the tunnel behind them like a runaway train and collected them on the way—hurling them all out into the air, sending them sailing in a high-curving arc ten stories down before they all landed together with simultaneous sandy splashes.

As the massive stone itself landed, it smacked one of the American soldiers straight under the surface. The other two bobbed on the gluggy surface for a few seconds before they too were sucked under by the hungry liquid floor.

West and his group saw it all happen.

"That won't happen again," West said to Avenger. "Judah sent that team in to die—a junior team without instructions, without warnings. He was just testing the trap system. When he comes in, he won't be so foolish."

The Israeli major nodded, turned to two of his men. "Shamburg. Riel. Make a rearguard post here. Hold them off for as long as you can, then catch up."

"Sir!"

"Yes, sir!"

Avenger then grabbed Lily from West, held her roughly by the collar. "Lead the way, Captain."

They hadn't taken ten steps down the next tunnel before they heard gunfire from the two rear guards.

Sustained gunfire.

More Americans had arrived at the sand cavern—having probably completely disabled the sliding stone mechanism by now.

Two men wouldn't hold them off for long.

THE GIANT STAIRWAY

After passing through the short tunnel, West led his expanded group into another cube-shaped chamber—about fifty feet high, wide, and long—only this time, his tunnel opened onto the chamber from the *base,* not up near the ceiling.

Its doorway opened onto a railless stone path that hugged the chamber's left-hand wall. A quicksand pool lay to the right, filling the rest of the floor.

The low stone path, however, led to something quite astonishing.

Seven giant stone steps that rose magnificently upward to a doorway cut *into* the ceiling of this chamber. Each step must have been at least seven feet high, and they all bristled with holes and recesses of various shapes and sizes, some of them door-sized, others basketball-sized, every one of them no doubt fitted with deadly snares just waiting to be triggered.

To the left of the giant stairway, flush against it, was the same stone wall that flanked the path. It was also dotted with various-sized trap holes. To the right of the stairs, there was nothing but empty air.

The intent was clear: if you were thrown off the stairs, you fell all the way down to the floor, made entirely of quicksand.

"It's the *levels,*" Zaeed said.

"What?" West said.

"Remember the progress report I found, the sketch of the Gardens under construction? These steps weren't originally steps at all. They were the steplike *levels* that led up to the main archway of the cave. Imhotep III converted them into this ascending stairway trap."

"Clever."

Zaeed said, "If I'm right, the Hanging Gardens of Babylon lie beyond that doorway in the ceiling."

Avenger pushed West forward—while maintaining his grip on Lily. "Captain West, please. Time is of the essence. Lead the way."

West did so, taking on the giant steps.

He encountered traps on nearly every one.

Blasts of quicksand, trap doors, upward-springing spikes designed to lance through his grasping hands, even a one-ton boulder that rolled suddenly across the fifth step.

But through skill and speed and quick thinking, he got past them all, until he finally stepped up into the opening in the ceiling, emerging on a dark platform that he sensed opened onto a wider, infinitely more vast space. And so he lit a flare and held it aloft and for one brief moment in time, standing alone in the darkness, Jack West Jr. beheld a sight no one had seen for over two thousand five hundred years.

Standing there before him, in all their incredible glory, were the Hanging Gardens of Babylon.

THE HANGING GARDENS OF BABYLON

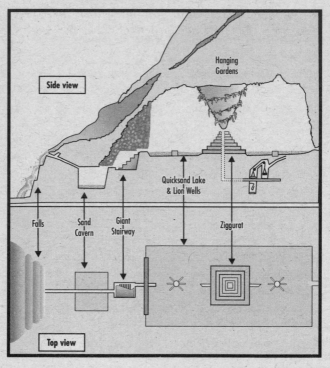

He needed eight more flares to illuminate the gargantuan cavern fully.

It was better described as a *super*cavern, for it was the size of twenty football fields laid out in a grid. It was perfectly square in shape, and its floor was made up entirely of quicksand—giving it the appearance of a vast flat *lake* of yellow sand.

And rising up from this sand lake, in the exact center of the supercavern, was a fifteen-story ziggurat—the variety of stepped pyramid common in ancient Mesopotamia.

But it was the natural feature that lay above the ziggurat that inspired sheer *wonder*.

An absolutely immense limestone stalactite hung from the ceiling of the cave directly above the ziggurat. It was so huge, its mass so great, it dwarfed the ziggurat. Perhaps twenty-five stories tall, it looked like an inverted *mountain* suspended from the ceiling of the supercavern, its pointed tip reaching down to meet the upwardly pointed peak of the ziggurat on the ground.

But this incredible natural feature had been modified by the hand of man—thus lifting it out of "incredible" and into the category of "wondrous."

A pathway had been hewn into its outer flank—in some sections it was flat and curving, while in others it took the form of short flights of steps. This path spiraled up and around the exterior of the great stalactite, rising ever higher, heading for the ceiling of the cavern.

Dotting this path were nearly one hundred semicircular archways, each archway containing vines and shrubs and trees and flowers—all of them overgrown to excess, all hanging out and over the edge of the stalactite, dangling precariously three hundred feet above the world.

It defied belief.

It was stupendous.

A truly hanging garden.

The Hanging Gardens of Babylon.

As the others joined him, West noticed the wall soaring into the upper reaches of the supercavern immediately above and behind them.

While it was made of densely packed bricks, West could make out at its edges the traces of another *earlier* structure, a structure that had been trapezoidal in shape and huge—three hundred feet high—like a giant doorway of some sort that had been filled in with these bricks.

West grabbed Zaeed's sketch from his pocket—the drawing of the great stalactite (shrouded in scaffolding) visible from outside the mountain *through* a window-like trapezoidal archway:

At that moment, he remembered a reference from the Nazi Hessler's diary. He pulled the diary from his jacket pocket and found the page:

1ST INSCRIPTION FROM THE TOMB OF IMHOTEP III

WHAT AN INCREDIBLE STRUCTURE IT WAS, CONSTRUCTED AS A MIRROR IMAGE, WHERE BOTH ENTRANCE AND EXIT WERE
    ALIKE.
IT PAINED ME THAT MY TASK—WHAT
    WOULD BE MY LIFE'S MASTERWORK—
    WAS TO CONCEAL SO MAGNIFICENT A
    STRUCTURE.
BUT I DID MY DUTY.
WE SEALED THE GREAT ARCHWAY WITH A
    LANDSLIDE.
AS INSTRUCTED, THE PRIESTS' ENTRANCE

REMAINS OPEN SO THEY MAY TEND THE
SHRINES INSIDE—THE PRIESTS HAVE
BEEN INFORMED OF THE ORDER OF THE
SNARES.

"*'We sealed the great archway with a landslide,'*" West
read aloud. "Imhotep bricked up the archway and then
triggered a landslide to cover it. But he wasn't done.
Then he diverts a river outside to cover the whole thing.
My God, he was good . . ."

"The third great architect was indeed a master,"
Zaeed said, coming alongside West.

Beside them, the others were arriving and taking in
the awesome sight.

Lily's mouth hung open.

Stretch's eyes were wide.

Even Avenger was impressed enough to fall silent.

It was Pooh Bear who summed up their mood: "So
this is why they call them *Wonders*."

But they weren't there yet.

The wide lake of quicksand still lay between them
and the ziggurat—the only means of getting up to the
Hanging Gardens.

Halfway between them and the ziggurat, seemingly floating on the surface of the sand lake, there
stood a small roofed structure that looked like a
gazebo. Made of stone, it was hexagonal in shape and
roughly the size of a single-car garage, but it had no
walls, just six pillars holding up a heavy-looking stone
roof.

A dead-straight path barely an inch above the surface of the lake stretched out from their position directly toward this hexagonal gazebo—only to end abruptly a hundred feet short of the structure.

The path reemerged nearer to the gazebo, its submerged center section presumably having been consumed by the quicksand sometime in the distant past.

As West looked more closely, he saw more paths.

Radiating out from the hexagonal sides of the gazebo, creating a star-shaped pattern, were six stone paths that were also virtually level with the surface of the lake.

Each of these paths also ended abruptly about fifty feet out from the gazebo.

"How do we get across?" Pooh Bear asked. "The paths have long been swallowed by the quicksand lake."

"Can't we just follow the straight path?" Avenger said. "Surely it continues just beneath the surface."

"Yes. Let's do exactly that and why don't you lead the way, you stupid fool Israeli," Zaeed said.

Avenger frowned.

"He means, walk that way if you want to die," West said. "It's a trap for the unwary and uninformed. This looks to me like a false-floor trap—the biggest false-floor trap I've ever seen. There must be a safe route just underneath the surface of the lake, but you have to know the route to use it and we don't."

"I think we do," a quiet voice said from behind him. Lily.

Everybody turned to face her.

"We do?" Pooh Bear said.

"Yes," Lily said. "It's the second 'safe route' that the German man wrote down. The first was the safe pathway up the waterfall. This is the second. That's why he put them together."

She took Hessler's diary from West and flipped back a couple of pages, to reveal the page they had looked at only half an hour before, entitled "Safe Routes":

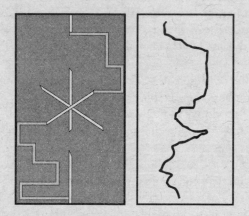

But whereas before they had been looking at the *right*-hand image, now it was the left-hand one that concerned them.

Sure enough, it matched the view before them exactly.

Only it revealed a path hidden beneath the quicksand lake—a circuitous path that skirted the walls of the cavern, crossed through the hexagonal gazebo, and ended at the top of the page, at the base of the ziggurat.

West nodded at Lily, very impressed.

"Nice work, kiddo. Glad we've got someone here who's got their head screwed on right."

Lily beamed.

Suddenly Avenger's earpiece burst to life and he spun around to see his two rear guards enter the Giant Stairway cave behind and below them.

"Sir!" one of them said over the radio. *"The Americans are crossing the first cavern! There are just too many of them! Under cover of sniper fire, they brought in pontoons and extendable ladders to cross the cavern at its base! They just had too much firepower for us! We had to retreat! Now they're coming!"*

Avenger said, "OK. I'll send Weitz back to guide you up the Stairway. Once you're up, set up another rear-guard position at the top. We still need every second we can get."

Avenger turned to West. "It's time for you to test your little girl's theory, Captain. I hope for your sake she's right. Move."

And so, following the map, West took a hesitant step off the main path, heading *left,* out over what appeared to be pure quicksand, and . . .

. . . his boot landed on a solid surface, on an unseen pathway hidden a couple of inches below the oozing surface of the lake.

Lily exhaled in relief.

West tested the lake on either side of the path—and found only goopy quicksand of uncertain depth.

"Looks like we found the pathway," he said.

After a quickly sketched copy of the safe route was made and left for the rear guards, the group ventured gingerly out across the sand lake, led by West.

They followed the map, seemingly walking on water, on nothing but the flat surface of the wide quick-sand lake, heading way out to the left, then stepping along the left-hand wall, before cutting back toward the center of the lake and arriving at the central gazebo.

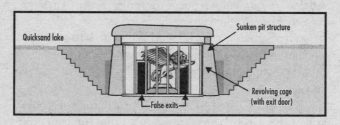

THE GAZEBO

The "gazebo" structure surprised them all.

For unlike the hidden path, its floor was *not* level with the surface of the lake. It was sunken twelve feet *below* the level of the lake, a stone rim holding back the sea of quicksand around it.

It was also solid as hell—thick-walled and sturdy.

A short and narrow flight of stone steps led down into this pit—which like the gazebo itself was also six-sided, with doors cut into every one of its sides. The structure's thick stone roof loomed over it all, a few feet above the rim, resting on its pillars, like a dark thundercloud just waiting to do its worst.

Curiously, just *inside* the walls of the hexagonal pit, forming a kind of inner wall to the structure, was a cylindrical bronze cage—also twelve feet high, made of imposing vertical bars, and crisscrossing bars across its top.

But while the pit had six doors, the circular cage had only one: which currently opened onto West's entry steps, allowing entry to the pit.

"Ah, a rotating cage . . ." Zaeed said. "Once you enter the pit, the cage rotates, and you have to pick the correct exit door. But entering the pit will trigger the trap—hence you must survive the trap in order to cross."

"Like that drowning cage in Tunisia," Pooh Bear observed.

Last of all, in the exact center of the pit, mounted on an ornate podium, stood a magnificent statue carved out of black limestone.

It was a statue of a winged lion, depicted on its hind legs in midspring, both forepaws raised high; its wings flared out behind it. It stood five feet tall, and its angry eyes were made of dazzling red rubies.

"The Well of the Winged Lion . . ." Zaeed said to West. "The Nazi knew of this, too."

They found the applicable page in Hessler's notes:

2ND INSCRIPTION FROM THE TOMB OF IMHOTEP III

ONLY THE BRAVEST OF SOULS
SHALL PASS THE WELLS OF THE WINGED LIONS.

BUT BEWARE THE PIT OF NINGIZZIDA.
TO THOSE WHO ENTER THE SERPENT LORD'S PIT,
I OFFER NO ADVICE BUT THIS:
ABANDON ALL HOPE,
FOR THERE IS NO ESCAPE FROM IT.

*Winged Lions. Common Assyrian Statue
Found in Persia/Mesopotamia.
Ningizzida: Assyrian God of Serpents &
Snakes.
Possible Ref to the HG of Babylon???*

"The Nazi was right," Zaeed said, "it *was* a reference to the Hanging Gardens—"

Suddenly, a burst of gunfire rang out from the Giant Stairway Cavern behind them.

"Sir! The first American squad has reached the Stairway!" the rear guards reported. *"Holding them off but more are on the way—and we can't hold them back forever."*

"Delay them as long as you can, Shamburg," Avenger said. "We still need the time."

He turned to West. "What is this trap?"

West hesitated. "I think Zaeed is right. The cage moves in a rotating circle, bringing its gate into alignment with the correct exit door of the pit, which according to the map, is that one directly opposite us—"

"Find out," Avenger said, shoving West forward. "Schaefer, go with him. Cover him."

Covered at gunpoint by the Israeli trooper named Schaefer, West stepped cautiously out from his steps, through the cage's gate and out onto the sunken floor of the gazebo's pit.

Imhotep's ancient warning about the well repeated over and over in his head: *only the bravest of souls shall pass.*

And then suddenly, four steps in, just as West and his companion stepped out into the center of the pit beside the statue of the lion, the well's lethal mechanism sprang into action.

What happened next happened very, very fast.

Screeeeech!—with an ear-piercing shriek of metal on metal, the circular cage suddenly started *turning,* revolving laterally within the larger hexagonal pit, thus exposing its lone gate—for brief moments—to all six of the stone doorways surrounding the pit.

But then came the worst part.

Shhhhh!—thick gushing waterfalls of quicksand started *pouring* into the pit from above! Channels in the pit's rim had opened, allowing the quicksand lake above it to invade the pit. The pit began to flood, the quicksand level quickly rising to West's knees . . . and continuing to rise!

And instantly, with the turning of the cage and the influx of quicksand from every side, West lost his bearings completely.

Which, he realized, was precisely the intent of the trap.

You were *meant* to panic, you were *meant* to be disoriented . . . and so exit via the wrong doorway, where presumably worse things awaited—

His Israeli companion panicked.

As one of the revolving cage's gates came into alignment with one of the pit's stone doorways, the frightened Corporal Schaefer raced through it—

—into a narrow stairway similar to the one they had descended to get into the pit.

Only this narrow stairway went nowhere. It had no stairway.

It was just a tiny space, barely bigger than a coffin standing vertically.

Then, with shocking suddenness, an eight-foot-high bronze plate, fitted with a barred grille at head height, slid across *into* the doorway behind Schaefer, sealing him inside the narrow space . . . and suddenly a special waterfall of quicksand began to flood into his tight vertical coffin.

As the sand rained down on his head, Schaefer screamed. It only took seconds for his little space to fill, and West watched in horror through the little face grille as the sand consumed Schaefer, filled his screaming mouth and swallowed him whole.

The screaming stopped.

Now completely alone, West breathed, *"Fuck me . . ."*

The wider pit continued to fill with sticky quicksand—rising past his waist.

And seeing Schaefer die had made him completely lose his bearings. He didn't know which was the right exit door. He was starting to panic himself.

Only the bravest souls . . .

Only the bravest . . .

Don't panic, Jack. For God's sake, don't panic—

And then he heard Lily scream.

He spun, saw her behind the bars of the moving cage—Avenger and the others had retreated back up their entry steps, but Lily was crouched on the stairs, peering through the doorway, trying to see West.

"Daddy . . . no!" Lily yelled.

And suddenly, amid all the mayhem, all the pouring sand and the turning of the cage, time stood still for West.

Daddy?

Did she just say "Daddy"?

And in that single flashing instant, a wave of adrenaline surged through him—a feeling that he had only ever felt once before, inside that volcano in Uganda, exactly ten years previously, when he had held her in his arms as a crying baby.

I . . . Am . . . Not . . . Going . . . To . . . Die . . .

I am not going to let her down.

Clarity returned.

Only the fucking bravest . . .

And it hit him: *brave men don't panic. They remain calm in the face of danger.*

Right.

He spun, his mind now hyperalert, thinking not panicking, no longer rattled by the elaborate deathtrap he found himself in.

No sooner had he done so than the answer came.

In fact, it was Lily's shout that provided the answer.

According to the map, the correct exit door was the one directly opposite *her* door.

Lily, West realized, was his advantage. Most tomb robbers would not leave someone behind in the entry doorway—they'd all walk into the pit together, go for the rubies on the winged lion, trigger the trap and lose their bearings, and then die.

"Don't give up on me, kiddo!" he called. "I'm not dead yet!"

He started wading powerfully across the pit, past the lion statue, over toward the stone doorway opposite Lily's door. He arrived there as the swirling pool of sand reached his chest.

The cage rotated, bringing its gate into alignment with that door.

Gate and door became one.

West surged through it, pushing through the quicksand, and found himself standing in a tight coffin-sized space just like the one Schaefer had entered—and in a single horrifying instant, he knew that he'd made a terrible, terrible mistake.

No, he hadn't.

It wasn't an enclosed space at all—there was just a sharp right-angled bend in the passageway here, a bend that led to a set of narrow steps which themselves led . . . upward!

West clambered up those steps, out of the deadly pool of quicksand, and emerged in open space, on a low path again, *safely on the other side of the well.*

As he crawled onto the path, he must have depressed a trigger stone that reset the trap, because suddenly the cage rotated back to its original position and the pit drained of quicksand.

Across the top of the well, he could see Avenger.

"You're all going to have to come across!" he called. "It'll seem disorienting, but I'll stand at the correct door. Just come to me."

And so the rest of the group all crossed the well safely.

It took two trips, and each time the pit filled with quicksand and its cage revolved dizzyingly, but knowing the correct exit they all just forged across the quicksand and exited the pit before it had even risen to knee height.

When she emerged out the other side, Lily leaped into West's arms and hugged him tightly.

"Don't leave me," she whispered.

He held her firmly. "No matter how bad it gets, kiddo, I'll never leave you. Always remember that."

Thus reunited, they pressed on and following the submerged path on the other side of the gazebo, they arrived at the ziggurat that lay in the very center of the supercavern.

And there, looming above the ziggurat like some kind of otherworldly spaceship, suspended from the cave's ceiling, impossibly huge, was the great stalactite that was the Hanging Gardens of Babylon.

They climbed the ziggurat quickly.

Very quickly. In fact, there was not a single trap on the structure's ceremonial stairway.

At first, West was surprised by this, but then he realized that this was the first Ancient Wonder they had actually *entered* on this mission.

All of the other Pieces they had encountered so far—those of the Colossus, the Pharos, the Mausoleum, the Statue of Zeus, and the Temple of Artemis—had all been *removed* from their original structures. They had all been guarded by trap systems built *after* the original structures had been lost or destroyed.

Not so the Gardens.

They alone remained in their original condition. And therefore the Piece they contained also remained *in its original resting place*.

But what West also realized as he climbed the ziggurat was that Imhotep III had shown *respect* for the

Wonder he was defending: sure, he had surrounded it with booby traps, but out of deference to its original architect he hadn't laid any traps on the Wonder itself.

Gunfire continued to ring out from the two Israelis stationed on the Giant Stairway, still holding off the American force.

West and his group arrived at the peak of the ziggurat, and found themselves standing seven feet below the jagged point of the stalactite.

It was truly mind-bending to stand beneath such an enormous natural formation. It was just too big, too *immense* to comprehend. It was like standing underneath an ocean liner hanging from its stern, its bow pointed right at your nose.

Directly above them, a right circular shaft bored up into the tip of the stalactite, driving up into its core.

But there was also a notable feature below them.

The peak of the ziggurat was flat and square—about fifteen feet by fifteen feet—but taking up nearly all of its floorspace was a wide square hole that disappeared *down* into the ziggurat, into inky darkness.

Ladder handholds ran down into this square well-like shaft, and, of course, the square shaft was perfectly aligned with the round one in the stalactite directly above it.

Zaeed bent to read an inscription on the rim of the ziggurat's square well shaft.

"It is the Priests' Entrance," he said to West. They both glanced at Avenger.

The Israeli commander did not seem to recognize the term—or its importance—and by some unspoken agreement neither Zaeed nor West felt the need to enlighten him.

West, Pooh Bear, and Stretch unloaded their caving equipment from their packs and started constructing a large tripodlike ladder over the square shaft.

Within minutes, they had an A-shaped ladder standing astride the square shaft and reaching up to the tip of the stalactite above it.

"Move." Avenger nudged West forward.

West climbed the ladder, and disappeared up into the borehole carved into the great stalactite.

This tight vertical shaft had ladderlike handholds, too, making progress quite easy.

But it wasn't for the claustrophobic. Glistening wetness trickled down its close, tight walls.

Guided by the flashlight on his fireman's helmet, West climbed cautiously upward until he emerged in a flat man-sized tunnel that led out to the exterior of the stalactite.

There he stepped out onto the path that spiraled up the outside of the Gardens.

By the light of his previously-fired flares, he beheld the supercavern from above. The view was breathtaking. He saw the ziggurat far below him, its steps fanning outward, with the quicksand lake all around it, and—in the middle of the lake—the Well of the Winged Lion, with its starlike series of paths radiating out from it.

Interestingly, he saw that the Well had a twin on the *other* side of the ziggurat—complete with an identical semisubmerged path.

He recalled Imhotep III's words: the Gardens had been *constructed as a mirror image, where both entrance and exit were alike.*

There must be another exit out that way, he thought. And now that he thought about it, he realized that Avenger and the Israelis knew of this exit: *that was how they intended to leave all along, without being caught by the Americans.*

So Avenger wasn't entirely ignorant about this place—

"Come on, Captain," Avenger said, arriving at West's side, rousing him from his thoughts. The rest of his team came up behind him, guiding Lily and Pooh Bear with them. "You're not done yet."

West led the group up the path that spiraled around the stalactite.

Everything was moist, all the overgrown foliage was like that found in a rainforest: plants and mosses that needed moisture rather than sunlight to live.

At times the going was difficult, since some of the bushes had grown out and over the path and hung off the edge, out over the drop.

Although it pained him to do it, West hacked through the fabled plants with a machete, to carve the way.

Higher and higher they went, into the upper reaches of the supercavern.

The great quicksand lake and the ziggurat fell farther and farther away from them. The drop down to the lake was now a clear four hundred feet, dizzyingly high.

At one point along the path, they came across a surprising splash of color: a beautiful cluster of roses. White roses.

"How can they survive here without sunlight?" Pooh Bear asked.

West was thinking the same thing, when he saw the answer: a series of tiny boreholes cut into the rocky ceiling of the cavern. They were barely a few inches wide, but they seemed to emit *light*—natural light. The little boreholes must have reached all the way to the surface of the mountain.

West noticed that the roses would catch daylight from some of the holes for a few moments every day—enough to keep them alive and regenerating.

"The Persian White Desert Rose," he breathed. "Extinct. Till now."

"Come on." Avenger shoved him on, oblivious to the monumental discovery. "I'll put some of them on your grave."

They pressed on.

On a couple of occasions the path delved *into* the stalactite—crossing through its core. Whenever it did this, the path met and crossed the claustrophobic vertical bore shaft that West had climbed into at the bottom. The shaft, it seemed, bored all the way up through the great stalactite. On these occasions, the group would just jump across the narrow shaft.

THE CATWALK AND THE MOST HOLY SHRINE

At length, they came to the point where the stalactite met the ceiling of the supercavern.

Here, a rotten wooden catwalk stretched out from the stalactite across the rocky ceiling.

The ancient catwalk threaded itself through several U-shaped beams that hung from the ceiling, and it stretched for about 160 feet before it stopped just short of a very large recess in the ceiling.

Hand rungs continued from there, heading out

across the ceiling and up into the dark recess. To hang from the hand rungs meant dangling by your hands high above the quicksand lake five hundred feet below.

"This is it," West said. "This is where all roads end."

. "Then go," Avenger said. "You may even take the Arab with you—although I shall keep the girl with me as insurance."

West and Pooh Bear ventured out across the ancient catwalk, high above the supercavern.

The wood creaked beneath their feet. Dust and debris fell off the catwalk's underside, sailing all the way down to the sand lake. Twice the entire catwalk lurched suddenly, as if the entire assembly was going to fall.

They reached the end of the catwalk.

"I'll go first," West said, eyeing the hand rungs. "I'll trail a return rope as I go. If the Piece is up in that recess, we'll need a rope to send it back."

Pooh Bear nodded. "I want to kill them all, Huntsman, for holding a gun to her head."

"Me, too. But we have to stay alive. So long as we're breathing, we'll still have a chance to do exactly that," West said. "The key is to stay breathing."

"Be careful."

"I'll try, buddy."

And with that, West grasped the first hand rung, and swung out onto it, five hundred feet above the world.

Against the spectacular backdrop of the mighty Hanging Gardens, the tiny figure of Jack West Jr., swinging hand over hand across the rungs in the ceiling of the supercavern looked positively microscopic.

Fluttering near him, watching over him as always, was Horus.

Trailing a return rope from his belt—a rope that went all the way back to Pooh Bear—he came to the large recess in the ceiling.

It was shaped like a trapezoid, with steep inwardly slanting walls tapering upward to a point. More hand rungs ran in a line up the slanting wall—so that it was now like free-climbing up an overhang, with your legs hanging beneath you.

But it was the focal point of the recess—the highest point—that seized West's attention.

It was a square horizontal ledge cut into the rock, about the size of a large refrigerator.

In stark contrast to the rough rocky surface of the rest of the recess, it was ornately decorated—with gold and jewels, making it look like a shrine.

From his current position, West couldn't see inside it. He scaled the hand rungs on the near side of the recess, supporting his entire body with only his arms.

He arrived at the ledge, did a strenuous chin-up to raise his head above its rim.

And his eyes widened.

Sitting there before him, mounted proudly inside this exceedingly difficult to reach altar, was a medium-sized golden trapezoid.

The Hanging Gardens Piece.

It was one of the middle Pieces, about the size of a laundry basket. Too big for one man to carry by himself. He pulled out his pressure gun, fired a piton into the rock wall, and looped his rope around it.

"Pooh Bear," he said into his mike. "Can you come over here? I need your help. Avenger: send some of your people to the other end of our rope to catch this when we send it back."

Pooh Bear joined West—after a precarious climb—and together they managed to pull the Piece from its holy alcove and, placing it safely in a pulley harness that hung from the return rope, they sent it whizzing back down the return rope to the catwalk.

Nestled in its harness, the Piece slid down the length of the rope, arrived back at the catwalk where Avenger caught it with gleaming greedy eyes.

"Have you got it?" West's voice said over the radio.

Avenger replied: "Yes, we have it. Thank you, Captain West, that will be all. Good-bye."

And with that Avenger cut the return rope at his end and let it swing out over the void.

* * *

From his position, West saw the rope go slack, leaving it hanging only from its piton at his end.

"Oh, shit! *Shit!*" He swung past Pooh Bear, moving fast down the hand rungs in the slanting wall of the recess, reaching the bottom—the flat ceiling of the supercavern—just in time to see Avenger and his men run to the far end of the catwalk and toss three hand grenades behind them.

The grenades bounced along the rotten wooden catwalk.

And detonated.

The ancient catwalk never stood a chance.

The grenades exploded—and with a pained shrieking, the catwalk fell away from the ceiling . . .

. . . and sailed in a kind of slow motion all the way down to the sand lake, five hundred feet below.

West watched it all the way, knowing exactly what this meant.

With the catwalk gone, he and Pooh Bear had no way to get back to the stalactite.

The horror of their predicament hit home.

Lily and the Piece were in the hands of the escaping Israelis, the Americans were banging on the door, and now . . . *now* he and Pooh were stranded *on the ceiling* of the biggest cave he had ever seen with no way or hope of getting back.

After watching the destruction of the catwalk with grim satisfaction, Avenger scooped up Lily. He turned to head back down the stalactite's spiraling path.

"We won't be needing Captain West or the Arab anymore. Nor"—he drew his pistol—"will we be needing you, Mr. Zae—"

But Mustapha Zaeed, his animal instincts ever alert, had already seen what was coming.

By the time Avenger had his pistol drawn, Zaeed had already broken into a run—dashing off down the path and into one of its cross tunnels.

"He won't get far. Come. Let's get out of here." With Lily in his grasp, he led his men down the path.

"Huntsman," Pooh Bear gasped. "I'm . . . er . . . in some trouble here . . ."

West rushed back—swinging with his hands across the rocky ceiling—to check on Pooh Bear in the recess.

Pooh was heavier than he was, with far less arm strength. He wouldn't be able to hold himself up for long.

West swung alongside him. "Hang in there, my friend. No pun intended." He quickly tied the now-loose return rope around and under Pooh's armpits—allowing Pooh Bear to hang from it without effort.

As for himself, West could hang from his mechanical arm longer—but not forever.

"The Israelis?" Pooh Bear asked.

"They destroyed the catwalk. Took the Piece and Lily. We're stranded."

"If I ever catch him, I'll throttle Stretch," Pooh Bear said. "You know, for a moment there I actually thought he might have become one of us. But I was wrong. Dirty betrayer."

"Pooh, right now, I'd just be happy to get out of here alive."

The Israeli team charged back down the stalactite, with Lily and the Piece in their possession.

As they reached the tip of the great stalactite, they saw their two rear guards come running into the supercavern.

"Sir! The Americans have breached the Giant Stairway! Repeat: the Americans have breached the Giant Stairway! We couldn't hold them off any longer!"

"You held them off long enough! We have the girl and we have the Piece," Avenger replied, grinning. "Meet us at the ziggurat and proceed to the other side. We're going out that way!"

Stretch ran behind Avenger, saying nothing, his teeth clenched, his eyes vacant and distant, lost in thought.

The Israeli team reached the bottom of the stalactite—just in time to see Zaeed disappear down the square shaft in the top of the ziggurat: the Priests' Entrance.

Avenger didn't care.

Although killing the terrorist would have brought him much kudos back home, Zaeed wasn't his concern here.

He had to get out.

Only then, as he clambered down the A-frame ladder at the base of the stalactite and stepped down onto the ziggurat, he saw the Americans enter the supercavern.

They came rushing in from the Giant Stairway entrance. But it wasn't the superlarge force of men he was expecting, it was just ten men.

And oddly, they *didn't* venture out across the quicksand lake.

No.

Rather, this small group started free-climbing up the sheer wall *above* that entrance, the wall that had filled in the old Grand Archway.

And there they—

"Oh, no . . ." Avenger breathed.

—started planting explosives, heavy-duty Tritonal 80/20 demolition charges.

The Americans worked fast, laying their charges and then getting the hell out of the way.

The result when it came was as spectacular as it was destructive.

With a colossal series of *booms,* the demolition charges went off.

* * *

The rock wall filling up the Grand Archway of the Hanging Gardens of Babylon was ripped apart by twenty simultaneous blasts. Great starbursts of rock sprayed out from it.

But the charges had been directional, forcing the bulk of the debris to be flung toward the outside world. Only a few smaller boulders landed in the quicksand lake.

Giant holes were opened in the rock wall.

Shafts of sunshine blazed in through them.

And daylight flooded into the supercavern for the first time in two thousand years, illuminating it gloriously—and in the brilliant light of day, the Gardens took on a whole new level of splendor.

Then these many holes collapsed, forming one great 200-foot-wide hole and through the resulting opening, following hard on the heels of the sunlight, came the American helicopters, roaring into the supercavern with a fury.

Wwest couldn't believe what was happening.

First, he'd been left for dead up in the recess by Avenger.

And now he could only watch in stunned awe as the entire cavern beneath him was flooded with light.

Six, then seven, then eight American choppers— Black Hawks and Apaches—banked and buzzed around the immense cavern, hovering above the ancient ziggurat, rising alongside the great stalactite, searching for the enemy, searching for the Piece.

The roar of their rotors in the cavern was deafening, the wind that they generated, swirling.

Then West saw one of the Black Hawks rise up directly beneath him, saw the circular speed blur of its rotors, and he thought, *If I fell now, at least death would be quick.*

But the Black Hawk hadn't seen him and Pooh Bear—it was peering *at the stalactite,* searching . . .

It moved closer to the stalactite, for a better look, and suddenly it wasn't directly beneath West anymore.

And West saw a way out of his predicament. It was totally crazy, but it might work . . .

He sprang into action.

"Pooh Bear, get a handhold. I need that rope and piton."

Pooh Bear obliged, grabbed a hand rung, while—

one-handed—West disengaged the piton and wound in the rope. It was about fifty feet in length.

Then he said, "OK, Pooh, now let go of the hand rung and grab my waist."

"What!"

"Just do it."

Pooh Bear did. Now he hung from West ... as West hung from his superstrong mechanical hand, gripping a hand rung.

And then West let go.

They dropped from the ceiling.

Straight down.

They shot like a bullet past the tail of the Black Hawk ...

... and as they did so, West hurled his piton—still attached to the rope—*at* the Black Hawk's landing wheels!

Like a grappling hook, the steel piton looped around the rear landing wheels of the helicopter ... and caught.

The rope played out before—*snap!*—it went taut and suddenly West and Pooh Bear were *swinging,* suspended from the helicopter's landing gear, swooping in toward the giant stalactite!

The helicopter lurched slightly with their added weight, but it held its hovering position, anchoring their swing.

They swung in a long swooping arc right over to the path on the flank of the stalactite, where West and

Pooh Bear dismounted deftly and released the rope, back in the game.

"Never thought I'd be happy to see Judah arrive," West said. "Come on! We've got to save Lily."

They charged down the path at breakneck speed.

Chaos. Mayhem.

Blazing sunlight.

The roar of helicopters, and now . . .

. . . hundreds of American regular troops flooded in through the newly opened Grand Arch.

Avenger's Israeli team danced down the far side of the ziggurat and raced out over the quicksand lake on that side. As West had seen before, this side was the mirror image of the entry side: it also featured a concealed path just below the surface with a hexagonal well in its center.

Avenger's team reached the well, raced down into it in two subgroups, beheld another statue of a proud winged lion.

Avenger and the two Israelis carrying the Piece went first. The trap sprang into action. Quicksand flooded in. The one-gate cage revolved. But they sloshed through the sand and emerged from the other side with little difficulty.

Stretch, the other two Israeli commandos, and Lily went next.

Again the trap initiated. Quicksand poured into the hexagonal well. The cage rotated. They sloshed across it, knee deep.

And suddenly Lily tripped and fell.

The rising quicksand had caught her feet and she stumbled to all fours with a squeal.

The sand grabbed her, sticky and foul.

She screamed in terror.

Stretch and the other two Israelis spun, saw her struggling. They were almost at the exit doorway and the cage's rotating gate was about to let them out.

Avenger called from the doorway, "Leave her! We have the Piece! She was only a bonus! It's the Piece that matters, and if we don't get it out, this will all have been for nothing! Move!"

The two commandos with Stretch didn't need to be told twice. They sloshed toward the gate and slipped through it.

Stretch, however, paused.

With quicksand flooding in from every side and the cage turning dizzyingly around him, he looked back at Lily.

The little girl was struggling against the rising quicksand pool, whimpering vainly with the effort. The sand had wrapped itself around her like a constricting snake, it was up to her neck now, consuming her, dragging her under.

"Cohen!" Avenger called. "*Leave her!* That's an order!"

And with a final look at Lily, Stretch made his fateful decision.

Flanked by the flying Horus, West and Pooh Bear were bolting down the spiraling path on the stalactite when suddenly the foliage beside them was ripped apart by helicopter gunfire.

One of the American Apache choppers had swung into a hover right next to them and was now lining them up in its minigun sights!

They dived into a nearby cross tunnel just as the Apache's six-barreled minigun whirred to life—and came to the vertical borehole that ran up the center of the rock formation.

"They're *firing* at the Hanging Gardens of Babylon!" Pooh Bear exclaimed. "Have Americans no respect for history!"

Moments later, they emerged from the same borehole at the lowermost tip of the stalactite, having slid all the way down it with their hands and feet braced against its walls.

West jumped down onto the peak of the ziggurat, snapped round to check on the progress of Avenger's fleeing Israeli team.

"Jesus, no . . ." he breathed.

He spied Avenger and four of his men just as they disappeared through an exit tunnel at the far end of the supercavern, having navigated the quicksand lake and the well on that side.

Stretch wasn't with them.

Nor was Lily.

And then West saw the well.

Peering under its canopied stone roof, he could see that the hexagonal well was just then overflowing with quicksand—*completely* filled.

"Oh, no. *No* . . ." West stared at the scene in horror.

Worse still, at that very moment, two American Black Hawk helicopters were landing on the star-shaped paths surrounding the well.

Troops charged out from the choppers, converging on the well from opposite sides.

Marshall Judah himself stepped out of one of the choppers, directing the operation.

"Oh, Lily . . ." West breathed, frozen, stunned.

At the hexagonal well, a CIEF trooper called to Judah: "Sir, you better come and see this."

Judah strode to the edge of the well.

And he was surprised by what he saw.

There, pressed *right up* against the roof bars of the cage inside the well—her face upturned, with only her mouth and nose and eyes protruding above the surface of the quicksand pool that now filled the well, breathing shallowly and desperately, her lips puckered, was Lily.

Judah wondered how on God's earth she had got into this lifesaving position.

The cage—and the well—must have been at least fourteen feet deep. Caught in the grip of the sand, she could never have reached up and grabbed the cage's roof bars and lifted herself out—

There must be someone else in there, he figured. *Holding her up.*

Then Judah saw it.

But only barely, it was so small.

He saw the tip of a *gunbarrel* protruding an inch above the surface of the quicksand pool right next to Lily's upturned face. It was the tip of a sniper rifle's gun barrel—an ultralong Barrett M82A1A sniper rifle.

Only this gun barrel was not being used for its original purpose.

It was being used as a snorkel by whoever was holding Lily up from below!

It wasn't until he had the well trap reset and drained of quicksand that Judah fully appreciated the scene underneath Lily.

As the quicksand drained away, he beheld Stretch, standing on top of the statue of the winged lion that stood in the center of the well, his own face upturned, breathing through the barrel of his disassembled Barrett sniper rifle, with Lily balancing on his shoulders in a perfect ballet toe pose!

Stretch had indeed made his decision.

It would turn out to be a very good one, but for another reason entirely: for Judah would take him and Lily away alive.

Avenger and his team of Israeli commandos would not be so lucky.

For at the secret rear entrance to the Hanging Gardens, a CIEF squad led by Cal Kallis was waiting for them.

And Kallis had strict orders *not* to be merciful.

Avenger and his Israelis—thinking they had got away with the Piece—emerged from the underground tunnel system to see their extraction helicopter lying nearby, charred and smoking, destroyed, its pilots shot dead.

They also found themselves surrounded by Kallis's team.

The Israelis were quickly disarmed. Then, slowly and deliberately, Cal Kallis executed them all himself—one by one, shooting each man in the head, killing Avenger last of all, smiling meanly the whole time. This was the kind of thing Kallis *enjoyed*.

Then he took the Piece from their dead hands and flew away, leaving the corpses for the desert birds to feast upon.

And so West watched, helpless, as Lily and Stretch were bundled into Judah's helicopter—

—at which moment, a wave of gunfire smacked down all around him, from two Apache attack choppers that appeared suddenly from behind the stalactite.

Horus squawked.

West moved too late.

But Pooh Bear didn't.

And he saved West's life—yanking him out of the line of fire and down into the square-shaped well shaft of the ziggurat.

Down on the floor of the supercavern, Judah snapped round to see the cause of the commotion.

He glimpsed the two tiny figures of Pooh Bear and West up on the peak of the ziggurat—saw Pooh pull West down into the well shaft that descended into the ziggurat, the shaft known as the Priests' Entrance.

"Jack . . ." Judah whispered. "Alas, you've served your purpose. You're no longer a protected species. Time for you to die."

Judah returned to his heavily armed Black Hawk, with Stretch and Lily as his captives. The chopper lifted off and zoomed out of the cavern.

It was quickly followed by the other choppers: the Apaches and the Black Hawks. The American troops covering the liquid floor of the cavern also pulled out, exiting through the blasted-open Great Arch.

Once all his people were out, Judah—still eyeing the top of the ziggurat, the last place he had seen West alive—gave his final order.

"Fire into the stalactite. Bring it down on that ziggurat."

His pilot hesitated. He wasn't one of Judah's hand-picked CIEF people. "But sir . . . this place is historica—"

"Fire into the stalactite now or I will have you thrown out of this helicopter."

The pilot complied.

Moments later, three Hellfire missiles lanced out from the missile pod of the Black Hawk, their three matching smoketrails spiraling in toward the giant rock formation . . .

. . . and they hit.

Shuddering explosions. Starbursts of rock and foliage.

And then, a momentous groaning sound as—

—the great stalactite slowly peeled off the ceiling of the supercavern, tilting precariously before . . . it fell away from the ceiling.

It sounded like the end of humanity. The sound was deafening.

Great chunks of rock were ripped away from the ceiling as the upside-down mountain fell away from it and crashed down onto the ziggurat.

The tip of the stalactite slammed down against the

peak of the ziggurat and the ziggurat—itself the size of a ten-story building—was just *crushed* like an aluminum can, compressed horribly downward, *totally* destroyed.

Then the great rock formation tipped sideways like a slow-falling tree and splashed down into the quicksand lake on the inner side of the supercavern.

The stalactite hitting the lake had the impact of an aircraft carrier being dropped from a great height into the ocean. An enormous wave of rolling quicksand fanned out from the impact zone, slapping hard against every wall of the supercavern.

Then slowly, very slowly, the stalactite—the fabled Hanging Gardens of Babylon—came to rest, on its side, half-submerged in the wide quicksand lake, just another broken rock formation in a world of broken things.

Thus, the American force left the foothills of the Zagros Mountains with everything they had come for in their grasp: Lily *and* the Piece.

And somewhere underneath all the wreckage and destruction they left behind—with no possible chance of survival—were Jack West Jr. and Pooh Bear.

SIXTH MISSION
ISKENDUR'S TOMB

FRANKFURT, GERMANY
LUXOR, EGYPT
MARCH 19, 2006
THE DAY BEFORE TARTARUS

At the same time that the Hanging Gardens of Babylon were crashing into oblivion, Wizard, Zoe, and Fuzzy were being transported via limousine—under armed guard—from the airfield at Frankfurt Military Base into the city of Frankfurt.

After they'd been captured in Rome, Wizard and his team had been taken by Learjet to Germany. Having been held overnight at the base on the outskirts of Frankfurt, they were now being taken to the headquarters of the European coalition: the Messe Tower in central Frankfurt.

The Messe Tower is one of the tallest skyscrapers in Europe. It stands fifty stories high and is known for one singular feature: its peak is a magnificent glass pyramid. More importantly—but far less well known—this pyramid has been "sectioned" horizontally just like the Golden Capstone.

But when a pyramid surmounts a shaftlike column like a tower, it becomes something more again: it becomes an obelisk.

The ultimate symbol of Sun worship.

Conspiracy theories abound that the Messe Tower, the Canary Wharf Tower in London, and the old World Financial Center in New York—all built in the shape of giant glass obeslisks—formed a modern triumvirate of "superobelisks" built by the two Sun-worshipping cults: the Catholic Church and the Freemasons.

Wizard thought about these theories as he, Zoe, and Fuzzy were brought, handcuffed, to the uppermost floor of the Messe Tower.

They stood inside its spectacular pyramid-shaped pinnacle. Its slanting floor-to-ceiling glass walls revealed a 360-degree view of Frankfurt and its surrounding rivers and forests.

Francisco del Piero was waiting for them.

"Maximilian Epper! My old seminary classmate. Oh, how the Church lost a great mind when it lost you. It's good to see you again, my old friend."

"I'm not your friend, Francisco. What is this about?"

"*What is this about?* What it's *always* been about, Max: power. The eternal struggle for one man to rule over another. Call it Europe *v.* America. Call it the Church *v.* the Freemasons. Call it a battle between elites: between my European sponsors and Marshall Judah's grubby gang of influential American billionaires, a group of high-ranking Masonic businessmen known as the Caldwell Group. It doesn't matter. It is all one and the same. A ceaseless battle for power that has lasted generations, all of it coming to a head tomorrow, at a once-in-five-thousand-year event, an event which can grant absolute power: the arrival of the Tartarus Sunspot."

Wizard glanced at Zoe. "Now you can see why I never went through with becoming a priest." To del Piero: "But Judah has four of the Pieces. You have one, and the last two remain unaccounted for."

"Max. It is not who holds the Pieces *now* that matters, but who holds them when Tartarus arrives," del Piero said. "And we will have all the Pieces soon enough. Thanks to your courageous Captain West, we now know that the Tomb of Alexander lies in Luxor—its location to be revealed by the focused rays of the rising Sun shining through the obelisks at the Luxor Temple. Judah knows this, too.

"But when he and his renegade CIEF troops arrive at Luxor, we shall be waiting for them. As I say, it is not who holds the Pieces now that matters, but who holds them when Tartarus arrives. *We* shall hold them when Tartarus arrives."

"We?" Wizard said.

"Oh yes, I don't believe you've met my young friend and greatest ally . . ."

Del Piero stepped aside to reveal a small boy, with dark hair, darker eyes, and really dark, frowning eyebrows. Just in the way he stood and glared at Wizard, the boy had a disconcerting air of superiority about him.

"Max Epper, meet Alexander, son of the Oracle of Siwa, expert in the Language of Thoth and the vessel of Tartarus."

"Hello there," Wizard said.

The boy said nothing.

Del Piero said, "He has been groomed since the day he was born—"

"The day you stole him from his mother's arms . . ."

"He has been groomed since the day he was born for tomorrow's event. His command of Thoth is unrivaled. His understanding of the ceremony unmatched. This boy was born to rule, and I have personally inculcated in him the mindset of the perfect ruler. He is strong, he is firm, he is wise . . . and he is *uncompromising,* intolerant of the weak and the foolish."

"I thought all the greatest rulers governed *for* the weak," Wizard said, "not over them."

"Oh, Max, I love your idealism! So noble yet so fundamentally flawed. How about this theory: the strong rule, the weak get ruled over. Some are born to rule; most are ruled over. After tomorrow, you will be in the latter group."

Zoe looked at the boy, Alexander. He returned her gaze coldly, without emotion.

"Hey kid," she said. "You ever played *Splinter Cell* in dual-player mode?"

Del Piero frowned, not understanding. But the boy knew what *Splinter Cell* was.

"It is a game. Games are tools by which we the rulers keep the masses entertained and amused," the boy replied. "Games are for fools. I do not play *games*."

"Is that right? Some games teach us lessons that we can use in our everyday lives," Zoe said. "Have you ever thought about that?"

"I do not have an everyday life."

"You want to know what I learned from playing *Splinter Cell* in dual-player mode?"

"Enthrall me."

"It's always nice to know someone's watching your back," Zoe said. "My question for you, Alexander, is this: when the going gets tough, who's gonna be watching *your* back?" A dismissive nod at del Piero: "Him?" A disdainful glance at the guards arrayed around the room: "Them?"

"And who, may I ask, watches your backs?" del Piero shot back.

"Jack West Jr.," Wizard said firmly.

"Hmm, the famous Captain West." Del Piero nodded. "Although following his exploits in Paris yesterday, I fear you might be a little behind on current events. Your friend, Mr. West, turned up in southern Iraq today, where he uncovered no less than the Hanging Gardens of Babylon."

"Go Jack . . ." Zoe said.

But Wizard frowned. He didn't know about West's last-gasp mission to Iraq—nor was he aware of its origins in the American ambush in Kenya and the loss of the Zeus Piece, Big Ears, and Doris.

"I hate to dampen your celebrations, Ms. Kissane," del Piero said, "but I fear Captain West encountered an American force of nearly ten thousand men in Iraq. What actually happened, I do not know. All I know from our intercepts is that they clashed."

"And . . ." Wizard couldn't hide his concern.

Del Piero threw Wizard a transcript of a communications intercept, dated only fifteen minutes previously. It read:

TRANS INTERCEPT
SAT BT-1009/03.19.06-1402
A44-TEXT TRANSMISSION
FROM: UNKNOWN SOURCE/AIRBORNE ORIGIN (IRAQ)
TO: UNKNOWN DESTINATION, MARYLAND (USA)
VOICE 1 (JUDAH): HARITHA MISSION IS A SUCCESS.
     WE HAVE THE H-G PIECE IN OUR POSSESSION, *AND*

THE GIRL. EN ROUTE TO EGYPT NOW. WILL ARRIVE LUXOR 0200 HOURS LOCAL TIME, 25 MARCH. IMPERATIVE THAT WE BE THERE AT DAWN TO TAKE MEASUREMENTS THROUGH THE REMAINING OBELISK AT LUXOR TEMPLE.

VOICE 2 (USA): WHAT OF THIS COALITION OF SMALL NATIONS? WHAT NEWS OF THEM?

VOICE 1 (JUDAH): ENCOUNTERED THEM AT THE H-G. MET WITH MINIMAL RESISTANCE. WEST DEAD. DATA FROM BIOMETRIC TRACER CHIP IN HIS CERE-BELLUM CONFIRMS THIS. IS THE NEXT STAGE READY?

VOICE 2 (USA): IT IS. THE EGYPTIAN GOVERNMENT HAS BEEN INFORMED OF YOUR IMPENDING AR-RIVAL IN LUXOR. THEY ARE BEING MOST COOPERA-TIVE, ALBEIT FOR A PRICE. THE PLATFORM AT GIZA HAS BEEN ERECTED TO YOUR SPECIFICATIONS AND THE ENTIRE PLATEAU HAS BEEN CLOSED TO THE PUBLIC UNDER THE GUISE OF REPAIR WORK.

VOICE 1 (JUDAH): THANK YOU. RECOMMEND OPERA-TION CONTINUE FROM HERE IN UTMOST SECRECY. HAVE ONLY A SMALL FORCE MEET ME IN LUXOR TO CARRY OUT THE MISSION THERE: 100 MEN, NO MORE. WE DO NOT WANT TO ATTRACT TOO MUCH ATTENTION.

VOICE 2 (USA): IT WILL BE DONE.

Wizard's face fell as he gazed at the terrible words: "WEST DEAD."

"Judah has too much confidence," del Piero said, stepping forward. "When he and his men arrive in Luxor, their 100-man force will encounter a European force three times that size. You can mourn the loss of Captain West another time, Max, for your part in this drama is not yet done—I still have another use for you.

"It is time for you to join me on the final leg of this journey, a journey that will end with Alexander fulfilling his destiny. It is time for us to meet Judah's force in Egypt and steal his Pieces. It is time to go to Luxor."

An hour earlier.

As the stalactite containing the Hanging Gardens of Babylon crashed down onto the ziggurat underneath it, down in the tunnels of the Priests' Entrance, Jack West and Pooh Bear were running headlong down a long stone passageway whose roof was *caving in* close behind them! The collapsing roof seemed to be chasing after them like the chomping jaws of an ever-gaining monster.

As soon as he'd heard the impacts of Judah's missiles hitting the Gardens, West had realized Judah's intention.

"He's trying to crash the Gardens onto us!" he said to Pooh Bear. "Run! *Run!*"

And so they'd bolted. Fast, with Horus fluttering above them.

Down the vertical shaft of the Priests' Entrance—avoiding some traps along the way—until it had opened onto this horizontal passageway.

Then the stalactite had landed on the ziggurat, and the structure had started collapsing behind them—which was how West, Pooh Bear, and Horus came to be here now, hurdling traps, running in total desperation from the collapsing ceiling and crushing death.

It was also why they almost ran right into the next trap.

It came upon them with startling suddenness—a narrow but exceedingly deep pit with hard blackstone walls and a quicksand floor. In fact, though much smaller, it was very similar to the first quicksand pit they had traversed earlier: their entrance was right up near the ceiling, opposite a matching exit on the far side; a set of about thirty hand rungs joined the two openings.

One big difference, however, was the intricate engravings on the walls of this pit. They were *covered* with images of snakes—and in the very center of the main wall, one supersized image of a serpent wrapped around a tree.

"Ningizzida, the serpent god . . ." West said, seeing the serpent image. "The Pit of Ningizzida . . ."

But then movement caught West's eye and he saw a figure standing in the far exit doorway having just traversed the pit.

The figure turned, saw West, and grinned meanly.

It was Mustapha Zaeed.

West glanced from the collapsing tunnel behind him to Zaeed.

"Zaeed! What's the sequence of the hand rungs!"

Zaeed eyed West slyly. "I fear I have run out of advice for you, Captain! But I thank you for breaking me out of Guantanamo Bay. You have enabled me to continue on my quest for the Capstone. Although I will give you one piece of knowledge that I imagine the good Professor Epper neglected to tell you: for Tartarus to be tamed, your girl must be sacrificed. Thank you and good-bye. You are on your own now!"

And with that, the terrorist vanished, disappearing down his passageway, leaving West and Pooh Bear stuck on their ledge, with their collapsing tunnel rushing forward fast!

"Huntsman!" Pooh Bear urged. "What do we do!"

West spun, saw the collapsing tunnel behind them. It was certain death to stay here.

He turned to see the wide deep pit before him, the Pit of Ningizzida, and a flashing memory raced across his mind, a page from the Nazi diary:

> BUT BEWARE THE PIT OF NINGIZZIDA.
> TO THOSE WHO ENTER THE SERPENT LORD'S
>   PIT,
> I OFFER NO ADVICE BUT THIS:
> ABANDON ALL HOPE,
> FOR THERE IS NO ESCAPE FROM IT.

So it was also certain death to enter the Pit.

Certain death vs. certain death.

Some choice.

"Screw it," West said. "Grab the rungs . . . Go!"

And out they swung, over the deep quicksand pit, *just as* a billowing blast of dust exploded out from the collapsing tunnel behind them.

The eighth hand rung broke in West's grasp . . . and he fell.

Pooh Bear avoided it—but the tenth one got him, and he also dropped, down into the quicksand, joining West in the Pit from which there was no escape.

West and Pooh Bear landed in the quicksand with twin goopy splashes.

West made to lie on his back, to spread his body weight and thus avoid sinking . . . when abruptly, four feet below the surface of the quicksand, his feet struck the bottom.

They could stand in here . . .

So he and Pooh Bear stood, chest deep in the deep pit.

The walls around them were slick and sheer, made of diorite.

"This isn't so bad . . ." Pooh Bear said. "I don't see why Imhotep said this was escape-proof—"

It was precisely then that the *ceiling* of the pit—the flat section of stone containing the hand rungs—began to *lower* itself. Its great square bulk fitted the pit's four walls perfectly.

The intention was clear: the lowering ceiling—itself a two-ton slab of stone—pushed you down *into* the quicksand, drowning you.

It was only a lightning quick swoop from Horus that saved her from the descending ceiling. As the trap sprang into action, she darted like a rocket for the exit tunnel and zoomed into it just as the lowering ceiling rumbled past the tunnel, closing it off.

From her position here, she could see the ceiling's operating mechanism on the *top* side of the descending slab—the ceiling was suspended from a pair of thick chains, which themselves hung out from a wide shaft in the roof. They clanked loudly as they lowered the deadly ceiling.

Just then in the Pit, Pooh Bear spotted movement.

Saw the spotted body of an outrageously enormous python come slithering out of a wall hole and dive into the quicksand pool!

"Huntsman!"

"I know, there are three more on this side!" He called up at the ceiling: "Horus! Reset the bucket! Reset the bucket!"

There were three more wall holes arrayed around the Pit . . . and they too were spewing forth the long, speckled bodies of pythons.

"Ningizzida . . ." West said, staring at the snakes. "The Assyrian serpent god, also known as the God of the Tree of Life: Christianity basically stole him and placed him in the Garden of Eden as the snake who tempts Eve to eat the apple from the tree."

The ceiling was halfway down and closing fast.

The snakes slithered across the surface of the quicksand pool, moving with intent.

One wrapped itself around West's right leg and reared up around him, jaws bared wide. West, since he had no gun to shoot it with, just jammed an X-bar into its wide-open mouth. The snake froze in confusion, its mouth held bizarrely open, hyperextended, with no way of dislodging the X-bar in it. It slithered off West's body, shaking its head violently, disappearing into the sand.

"Horus!" West yelled. "What are you doing up there?"

Horus zoomed up the chain shaft, following the ceiling's mighty chains as they stretched upward, bent over a large bronze pulley, and then *descended* back down another wider shaft.

Folding over the pulley, the chains shot down this new shaft, where at their other end they upheld . . . a gigantic clay bucket. It was easily ten feet wide: the world's biggest bucket. And next to it flowed a healthy little waterfall, pouring out of a man-made drain.

Right now, the bucket hung askew, at right angles, tipped over on some hinges, its open top facing sideways. If it had been sitting in the upright position, it would have *received* the flowing water from the waterfall . . . and filled up . . . and hence via the chains, *hauled up* the movable ceiling in Ningizzida's Pit.

Known as a "water-based mechanism," this was the standard operating system behind all Egyptian moving-wall traps.

It was an ingenious system devised by the first Imhotep, and was remarkable for its simplicity. All it needed to work were three things: gravity, water . . . and a pulley.

When West had grabbed the wrong hand rung, he had triggered a catch which had tipped the (full) bucket.

Now, when *filled* with water, the great bucket perfectly counterbalanced the ceiling slab. But when up-turned, the bucket emptied, and thus the ceiling—now outweighing it—lowered.

There was a second trigger stone on the floor of the Pit—the "reset" switch—which, when eventually hit by the lowering ceiling stone, would right the giant bucket, and allow it to fill again, thus raising the ceiling back to its resting position, ready to strike once again.

As such, there truly was no escape from Ningizzida's Pit. It offered no tricks, no riddles, no secret exits. Once you were in it, you did not leave.

Unless you had a companion like Horus.

Flying fast, Horus swooped up the chain shaft, past the pulley, and down toward the big clay bucket.

There she landed and hopping around, searched for the reset catch that righted the giant tub.

In the Pit, the ceiling was still lowering fast. It was only seven feet above the surface now and closing quickly.

The pythons circled, moving in on West and Pooh Bear.

Without warning, one dived under the surface—and reappeared slithering up Pooh's body with frightening speed! It constricted violently, trying to crack his spine—just as Pooh Bear swiped hard with his KA-BAR knife and the python froze in midaction. Then its head fell from its body.

The ceiling kept descending.

Five feet.

West was very worried now.

Four feet.

The pythons cut and ran—fleeing for their wall holes, knowing what was about to happen.

Three feet . . .

"*Horus . . .*" West yelled.

In the bucket shaft, Horus searched patiently, just as she had been taught.

And she found the reset catch: a little hinged hook that, when released, righted the empty bucket.

Horus bit into the hook with her tiny beak . . .

Two feet . . .

West called: "Horus! Come *on!* You can do this! Just like we practiced at home!"

One foot . . .

He and Pooh Bear now had only their upturned faces above the surface of the quicksand.

Six inches . . .

"Take a deep breath, Pooh," West said.

They both sucked in as much oxygen as they could hold.

In the bucket shaft, Horus continued to bite at the reset hook. It wouldn't budge.

* * *

In the Pit, the lowering ceiling met the surface of the quicksand . . . and touched it, pushing West and Pooh Bear under—

—just as Horus got a good grip on the hook with her beak . . . and *lifted it*!

The response was instantaneous.

With a silent lurch, the great empty bucket rolled upward on its hinges, offering its open mouth to the cascade of water pouring down above it.

The bucket immediately began to fill with water.

And with the added weight, the great clay bucket now began to *lower* on its chains . . .

. . . which by virtue of the pulley now pulled the ceiling of the Pit upward . . .

. . . raising it off the quicksand pool!

West and Pooh Bear burst up from underneath the quicksand, gasping for air.

As the ceiling above them rose, they grabbed the two hand rungs nearest the exit end, and allowed the ceiling to hoist them all the way up the Pit.

Hauled up by its water mechanism, the ceiling slab returned to its original position, and West and Pooh suddenly found themselves hanging in front of the exit tunnel—where Horus now sat proudly, staring triumphantly up at West.

He swung into the tunnel, crouched before her, gave her a much-loved rat treat.

Horus gobbled it up whole.

"Thank you, my friend, nice work," he said. "You saved our bacon. Imhotep didn't count on grave robbers having friends like you. Now let's get the hell out of here."

Through the Priests' Entrance they bolted—West, Pooh Bear, and Horus.

Ten minutes later, they emerged from an inconspicuous cleft in a rocky hillside, a barren desolate hillside that faced onto a barren desolate valley that appeared to have no natural exits. The valley was on the Iranian side of the Hanging Gardens, far from the waterfall entrance on the Iraqi side.

But it was so inhospitable, so bleak, that no human being had had any reason to come here for two thousand years.

West froze as a thought struck him.

There was no sign of Mustapha Zaeed.

He wondered where Zaeed had got to. Had he at some point on this journey called his terrorist pals and told them to pick him up here?

West thought about that: perhaps Zaeed had triggered a locator signal when they'd stopped by at his old hideout cave in Saudi Arabia. West knew Zaeed had grabbed other things while they were there, including the beautiful black jade box filled with fine sand.

He considered the rogue signal that he'd picked up on the *Halicarnassus* on the way to Iraq. He'd first believed it had been sent out by Stretch, alerting the Israelis to their location.

But something Avenger had said to Stretch inside

the Gardens now made West revise that belief. When he had first appeared, Avenger had said to Stretch: "I apologize for surprising you in this way."

Stretch hadn't known of the impending arrival of Avenger's team.

The Israelis had been tracking him *and he hadn't known.* Now West believed that the Israelis had been tracking Stretch from the very start via some other kind of bug—probably a surgically implanted locator chip that Stretch never knew he'd been carrying.

Granted, the signal from the *Halicarnassus* could also have been sent by Zaeed—alerting his allies to his whereabouts—but West doubted that.

He actually had another theory about that rogue signal, a theory that made him sick to his stomach.

But now, right now he worried that by breaking Zaeed out of Guantanamo Bay he had unleashed an unspeakable terror on the world.

Zaeed wasn't going to abandon his quest for the Capstone, not when he knew where the final Piece could be found, not when it was so close. The terrorist wasn't out of this race yet. He would reappear before the end.

West radioed Sky Monster and arranged to rendezvous with the *Halicarnassus* on some flat ground at the far end of the valley, then he and Pooh Bear headed out across the valley on foot.

They never saw the lone figure crouched on the rocky hill high above them watching them as they did so.

Never saw the figure pursue them at a careful distance.

Later, West, Horus, and Pooh Bear strode up the rear loading ramp of the *Halicarnassus,* dirty, bruised, and beaten.

Inside the main cabin, West paced, thinking aloud. Pooh Bear and Sky Monster just watched him.

"Every move we've made, Judah's known it ahead of time," he said. "We arrived in the Sudan, and he showed up soon after. Tunisia, the same. And in Kenya, hell, he got there *before* we did. He was waiting for us. And now Iraq."

"It's like he's had a beacon on us all along," Pooh Bear said. "A tracing signal."

West pursed his lips, repeated Judah's taunt from before: "*'There is nowhere you can go that I cannot follow. There is nowhere on this earth you can hide from me.'* I think he's had a tracking beacon on us all along."

"What? How? *Who?*"

West looked hard at Pooh Bear.

"Four missing days, Pooh. Four missing days from my life."

"What are you talking about, Huntsman?" Sky Monster asked.

"Zaeed had a chip in the head, implanted while he was imprisoned in Cuba, making him forever traceable by the Americans. I can't account for four days of my life, Pooh, four days *when I was exclusively in American hands.*"

West stood up abruptly and grabbed the AXS-9 digital spectrum analyzer—the same bug detector that he had used before to test for the locator chip in Zaeed's head.

He flicked it on, and fanned it over Pooh's entire body. Nothing. No bugs.

Sky Monster was next. Also nothing. As expected.

West looked at them both . . .

. . . before he turned the wand on himself, running it up his entire body.

Legs: nothing.

Waist: nothing.

Chest: nothing.

Then the spectrum analyzer came level with his head, and it started beeping off the charts.

Pooh Bear and Sky Monster gasped, speechless.

West just closed his eyes, cursing himself.

All the time he'd thought there had been a traitor in their midst—in particular, Stretch or Zaeed—but there had been no such traitor.

It had been *him*.

He had been the one leading the Americans to their location every single time.

Four days of his life: those four days he had spent in that American military hospital after his accident in the war-game exercises at Coronado.

Four days during which the Americans had tagged him with a microchip, so that they could keep track of him over the ensuing years.

Why? Who knew—because he had talent, because they wanted to keep track of *everyone,* friend and foe alike.

West couldn't believe it. Australia was a close ally of America's. And this was how the U.S. treated it. America, it seemed, treated its allies no differently than its enemies. No, it was simpler than that: America treated *everyone* outside the U.S. as a potential enemy.

He thought about Judah. Somewhere amid Judah's equipment there was a GPS-equipped computer with a map of the world on it and a little blinking blip that represented Jack West Jr.—a blip that had represented him *for nearly fifteen years.*

The Americans had known about the safehouse in Kenya since Day One.

Likewise they had known about the mine in the Sudan from the moment he'd got there; it was the same for the Tunisian coast—which only West and Wizard knew about. It also meant that Judah and the Americans would know it was West who had busted Zaeed out of Guantanamo Bay. They wouldn't have liked that.

West strode across the cabin, watched in stunned silence by Pooh and Sky Monster. Over by the rearmost console, he picked up the EMP gun that he had used before to neutralize the locator chip inside Zaeed's neck.

He pointed it at his head like a man about to shoot himself—

—and he pressed the trigger.

At that very moment, inside a U.S. Black Hawk helicopter landing in Basra, a technician at a portable GPS-equipped computer snapped up.

"Colonel Judah, sir! Jack West's locator signal just dropped out."

"Where was he when the signal disappeared?"

"Judging by the GPS, still in the vicinity of the Hanging Gardens," the tech said.

Judah smiled. "That tracer's biometric, grafted onto the living tissue of his brain. If West dies, the tracer chip dies with him. He must have been wounded by the collapse of the ziggurat and held on this long before he died. Rest in peace, Jack . . . never knowing that you led us every step of the fucking way. Fortunately, we don't need you anymore. Kallis. Feed the men, replenish their arms, and set a course for Luxor."

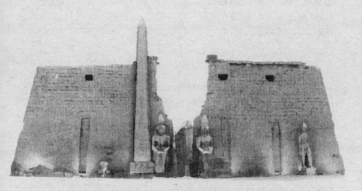

LUXOR TEMPLE, EAST BANK, LUXOR

**HATSHEPSUT'S MORTUARY TEMPLE,
WEST BANK, LUXOR**

In the early hours of the morning on the day the Tartarus Sunspot would turn to face the Earth, three hundred European troops lay in wait around Luxor International Airport, ready to ambush the American force arriving in the southern Egyptian city that night.

Bisected straight down its middle by the River Nile, Luxor is a fairly large town. Heavily dependent on tourism, on its East Bank one will find the Karnak and Luxor Temples, two of the most impressive sites in Egypt. The Luxor Temple sits right on the bank of the river, separated from it by a splendid riverside drive called the Corniche.

On the West Bank of Luxor, one will find a cluster of high brown mountains and jagged dry hills that rise up from the desert floor. The very first valley of these dusty hills is the famous Valley of the Kings—the extraordinary collection of deliberately plain tombs that were once filled with all the riches of the pharaohs. It is the home of Tutankhamen's Tomb, Rameses the Great's tomb, and hundreds of others. Even today, every few years a new tomb is unearthed.

On this Western Bank, you will also find one of the most mysterious sites of ancient Egypt: Hatshepsut's mortuary temple, constructed by the brilliant woman pharaoh, Hatshepsut.

Built into a great rocky bay in the mountainside,

Hatshepsut's mortuary temple is composed of three gigantic colonnaded terraces, all stretching backward—like three god-sized steps—each flat tier connected to the next by a colossal rampway.

From its dominant position at the base of the cliffs, it stares proudly back at Luxor, facing the rising sun. The size of three football fields, it is unique in all of Egypt.

It is also notorious.

In November 1997, six Islamist terrorists armed with machine guns massacred sixty-two tourists in rank cold blood at the site. The terrorists hunted down the unarmed tourists over the course of a terrifying hour, pursuing them through the Temple's colonnades, before committing group suicide themselves.

Luxor is steeped in history, both ancient and recent.

Luxor's airport, however, is on the eastern bank, and the American CIEF planes landed in the darkness, one after the other, their lights blinking—two C-130 Hercules cargo planes, and landing lightly after them, one sleek Learjet.

It was a small force, just big enough to safely convey the Pieces in its possession but small enough not to attract too much attention; as Marshall Judah had stated in his intercepted transmission.

As usual, the Egyptian government, desperate for American approval and money, had allowed their entry into the country with not a single question asked.

But the Egyptian government did *not* know of the 300-strong European force that was at that moment surrounding Luxor's airstrip, aiming their weapons at the arriving Americans.

Father Francisco del Piero sat in a big Toyota Land Cruiser parked just outside the airport, waiting for his French and German troops to make their move. With him were Wizard, Zoe, and Fuzzy—handcuffed and immobile, also waiting tensely.

Also in the Land Cruiser with them was the boy, Alexander, and safely in a large steel trunk, one Piece of the Golden Capstone: the Artemis Piece, recently removed from the main altar of St. Peter's Basilica.

On the runway, two desert-camouflaged Humvees sped out from the cargo hold of the first Hercules and skidded to twin halts beside the Learjet—the jet that held the Pieces.

A line of troopers emerged from the Lear, guarding a smaller group of men who carried among them five Samsonite cases of varying sizes. These men started loading the Samsonite cases onto the rear tray of a third Humvee—a black one—that had just arrived.

The Pieces.

The Europeans sprang their trap—in a kind of surreal unearthly silence.

They leaped from the shadows—French and German commandos—black-clad ghosts wearing night-vision goggles and running with submachine guns pressed to their shoulders, the muzzles of those guns spitting forth silenced tongues of deadly fire.

The CIEF troops at the Lear never stood a chance. They fell in a hail of blood and bullets, dropping to the tarmac. Likewise, all the drivers of the Humvees were ripped to shreds by the charging French and German commandos.

It was over in minutes.

As various "Clear!" signals were given, del Piero drove out onto the runway.

He joined the European troops gathered around the black Humvee parked beside the Lear.

With a smile of supreme satisfaction, he strode over to the Humvee's rear tray, opened it, and unclasped the lock on the nearest Samsonite case—

—to discover that it was filled with worthless bricks and a single Post-it note:

Careful, Father del Piero.
Don't let any blood get on you.
Judah.

Del Piero's eyes went wide.

He whirled around—

—just as an absolutely *devastating* burst of coordinated sniper fire whistled all around him—sizzling and popping past his ears—and in a single terrifying instant, *every one* of the ten troopers standing around him was hit by separate sniper rounds, their heads all exploding in simultaneous bursts of red, their bodies crumpling like rag dolls.

Only del Piero was unhit. Only he remained standing. The burst of fire had been so well aimed, so well coordinated that this was clearly deliberate.

Blood, bone, and brain matter had sprayed everywhere, splattering all over del Piero's face.

At which moment, the *thousand-strong* American CIEF force that had been lying in wait in the mudbrick houses and sewers of Luxor *behind* the European ambush force moved in.

They were merciless, ruthless—as ruthless as the Europeans had been to their own men. Even those European troops who surrendered were executed where they stood.

None were left alive—except for del Piero and the four other people who had been inside his Land Cruiser:

Wizard, Zoe, Fuzzy, and the boy, Alexander.

It was at this time that the *real* American air convoy arrived at Luxor.

The first one had been a decoy, its men expendable: live bait to draw out the waiting European force.

Now with the airport secured, Judah arrived in a second Learjet, flanked by a couple of F-15s and tailed by no less than six massive Hercules cargo planes.

The air convoy landed, one plane after the other, their landing lights blazing through the clear night air.

Judah's Lear swung to a halt beside the first "decoy" Learjet . . .

. . . where del Piero still stood like a thief caught with his hands in the till, covered now by American CIEF troops and surrounded by the bloodied corpses of his own men.

Judah just strolled casually out of his private jet, appraised del Piero coldly, before nodding at the blood on the priest's face.

"Father del Piero. My old teacher. It's good to see you again. You didn't heed my warning. I told you to be careful about the flying blood."

Del Piero said nothing.

Just then, a figure appeared behind Judah: an old, *old* man, gnarled and hunched. He had a bare blotch-speckled scalp and wore a leather coat and thick Coke-bottle glasses that obscured his evil little eyes.

Judah said, "Father, I don't believe you've met

Hans Koenig. He's been a guest of the United States since 1945 and has been searching for the Capstone for a *very* long time."

Del Piero gasped. "Koenig and Hessler. The two Nazi explorers . . ."

"Colonel Judah!" Cal Kallis called from the rear of the Land Cruiser. He stood by the boot of the big four-wheel drive, having opened the steel case there, revealing the Artemis Piece. "We have the Europeans' Piece. We also have the boy . . . and a couple of West's people."

Kallis held Alexander out in front of him. His men covered the handcuffed Wizard, Zoe, and Fuzzy.

Judah grinned. "Why, Father del Piero, what possible reason could you have for bringing these good people along on your mission? I imagine it will be exactly the same reason I will keep you with me."

Del Piero's eyes went wide with fear.

Judah enjoyed it. "What does the Bible say? Do unto others as you would have them do to you. How ironic."

He beheld the boy. So did the Nazi, Koenig.

"So this is him. The son of the Oracle. Alexander, I believe," Judah bowed respectfully. "My name is Marshall Judah, from the United States of America. It's my honor to make your acquaintance."

The boy—completely fearless—returned his gaze evenly, but said nothing.

Judah said, "It's also my honor to present to you, for the first time, your sister."

With that, Judah stepped aside, to reveal, standing shyly behind him, with her legs nervously crossed and her head bowed: Lily.

In the predawn, a dense low mist hung over Luxor.

Through the unnatural haze moved a convoy of heavy vehicles, their headlights casting beams of light.

It was Judah's CIEF force, rushing toward the Luxor Temple.

The Temple sat beside the Nile—with its immense pylon gateway guarded by two colossal statues of Rameses II, seated on identical thrones, and its obelisk standing proudly but alone out in front, its twin long since removed to Paris.

The convoy of vehicles included Humvees, Jeeps, motorcycles, a single Apache helicopter overhead, and in the middle of it all, a long lumbering flatbed semi-trailer, on which sat a large folded up crane.

At the Temple, under the glare of floodlights, Judah's force raised the mobile crane alongside the still-standing obelisk, in the exact spot where the obelisk's identical twin had once stood.

The crane was a cherry picker, not unlike those used by electricity workers to fix power lines, with a basket at its summit big enough for three or four men. Judah, Kallis, and Koenig were raised in it.

"Herr Koenig," Judah said. "You have your copy of your colleague's diary?"

The old hunched-over Koenig held up his own secretly made copy of Hessler's diary. "As always, Herr Judah," he hissed.

As they rose up the flank of the existing obelisk, analyzing the many hieroglyphs on its sides, Koenig flipped to the relevant page in the diary:

FROM THE SECRET GOSPEL OF ST. MARK

AT DAWN ON THE DAY OF JUDGMENT,
THAT FINAL HORRIBLE DAY,
AT THE ONLY TEMPLE THAT BEARS BOTH
    THEIR NAMES,
THREAD THE POWER OF RA THROUGH THE
    EYES OF GREAT RAMESES' TOWERING
    NEEDLES,
FROM THE SECOND OWL ON THE FIRST
TO THE THIRD ON THE SECOND . . .
. . . WHEREBY THE TOMB OF ISKENDUR WILL
    BE REVEALED.
THERE YOU WILL FIND THE FIRST PIECE.

At the summit of the lone obelisk they found three carved owls, seated side by side. There, just as West had done on the Paris Obelisk, Judah extracted a little plug stone from a carving of the Sun above the second owl. He found a second plug on the other side, and removed it too—

—to reveal a borehole running horizontally *through* the obelisk, from east to west . . . again, just as West had found in Paris.

Judah then had his crane basket brought over to where the summit of the *other* obelisk—the one now in Paris—would have stood.

"You have the measurements, Herr Koenig?"

"To the millimeter, Herr Judah."

And so, using a caesium altimeter and a digital inclinometer to get the angles and the height absolutely correct, they erected a pipelike cylinder on a tripod in their basket. They erected it horizontally, angling it according to their measurements, impersonating the borehole of the missing obelisk, the borehole that would have sat above the third owl on that obelisk.

They had got it just right when the orange rim of the Sun peeked over the eastern horizon and dawn came on the Day of Tartarus.

The *power* of the rising Sun was instantly noticed by all.

On this day, the Day of Tartarus, it was hotter, fiercer. It practically *burned* through the hazy low-hanging mist in dazzling horizontal shafts creating minirainbows in the air.

Then it struck the uppermost tip of the obelisk— and the high needle of rock seemed to shine majestically—before the beam of sunlight slowly began to descend down the obelisk.

The American force watched it in awe.

From his basket, Judah watched it in triumph.

From his position down in one of the Humvees, Wizard watched it in grim silence.

Then the sunlight struck the borehole on the existing obelisk *and shone directly through it* . . .

. . . whence it continued on, shooting right into the pipe on Judah's crane . . .

. . . and suddenly the great shaft of sunlight combined with the unnatural mist to become a tiny laserlike beam of multicolored sunlight.

The rainbow-colored laser beam lanced out from the Temple, shooting in a dead-straight horizontal line *westward,* out across the Nile, out over the fields on the west bank, out toward . . .

. . . the great bay of brown cliffs that protected and defended the Valley of the Kings.

No.

It was more precise than that.

The beam of light came to rest on the structure built *into* that bay of cliffs—a structure unique in all of Egyptian architecture, featuring two great rampways and three glorious colonnaded tiers.

Hatshepsut's mortuary temple.

The CIEF force made swift progress.

The dazzling beam of sunlight had illuminated a lone archway at the far left of the lowest tier of the great structure.

There a door was found, so well concealed that it appeared to be part of the wall itself. But above it was a familiar symbol that until today had been attributed little significance:

At the sight of the carving, Marshall Judah's eyes shone with delight.

Judah's men were through the door in no time.

Traps awaited them.

A passageway filled with vicious swing traps— long swing blades that swooped out of slits in the ceiling and chopped one man's head off.

Then a partially submerged chamber, the knee-deep water of which concealed leg-chopping blades. Fortunately, from his research, Koenig knew the safe route.

Until Marshall Judah emerged from a stone doorway and stood on a platform that overlooked a gigantic subterranean cavern.

It wasn't as big as the supercavern that contained the Hanging Gardens of Babylon, but what it lost in size, it made up for in artistry.

Every stone wall had been fashioned by human hands. There was not a single rough surface in the place.

It looked like an underground cathedral, with soaring high walls, a curved ceiling, and four immense sacred lakes arrayed in such a fashion that they created a wide raised path in the shape of a giant †. Great pillars of stone held up the superhigh ceiling.

At the junction of the "†"—the focal point of the great underground hall—was a raised square platform, flanked on all four corners by obelisks. On this high platform lay an ornate glass sarcophagus.

"Ornate" was barely sufficient to describe it.

It was crafted of gold and glass, and it lay underneath a high canopy crafted entirely of gold. The pillars of the canopy were not straight, but rather they rose in a bending, spiraling way, as if they were solidified vines.

"The coffin of Alexander the Great . . ." Koenig breathed.

"It was said to be made of glass," Wizard confirmed.

"Wait a second. This looks familiar to me . . ." Judah breathed.

Beside him, Francisco del Piero—like the others, his hands were cuffed—bowed his head in silence, tried to be invisible.

Judah turned to Koenig.

"Take some measurements with the laser surveying equipment. I want to know the length, height, and breadth of this hall."

Koenig did so.

After a minute, he reported: "It is six hundred thirty feet long, and five hundred thirty-five feet wide at the widest point of the †. Height of the cavern above the central junction is . . . four hundred thirty-three feet."

Wizard snuffed a laugh.

Koenig turned. "What is so funny?"

"Let me guess," Wizard said, "that canopy over the sarcophogus, the one with the twisted columns, it's ninety-five feet high."

Koenig did the computations with his laser surveying gear . . . and turned to Wizard in surprise. "It is ninety-five feet in height *exactly*. How could you know this?"

Wizard said, "Because this cavern has the exact same dimensions as St. Peter's Basilica in Rome."

Judah swung to face del Piero, who shrank even lower, if that was at all possible.

Wizard went on. "If everything in the Roman Catholic Church is a reinvention of Egyptian Sun worship, then why should St. Peter's be any different. Its dimensions are simply a replication of this sacred place: the resting place of the most prized Piece of the Capstone, the top Piece."

They proceeded to the great altar at the focal point of the T-shaped hall, where they beheld the gold-and-glass coffin.

Through the glass, they saw only white powdery dust—the remains of the greatest warrior ever known, the man who had ordered the Pieces of the Capstone to be scattered around the then-known world and hidden within the Seven Ancient Wonders.

Alexander the Great.

A bronze Macedonian helmet and a lustrous silver sword lay upon the layer of white dust, along with a bronze chest plate.

And sticking up from the middle of the dust layer—as if it had once been laid upon the dead man's chest, only to see that chest erode over the course of two millennia—was a tiny apex of gold.

A tip of a small golden pyramid.

The top Piece.

Without preamble, Judah ordered the coffin opened, and four of his men stepped forward, grabbed a corner each.

Del Piero started forward. "For pity's sake, do take care!"

The men ignored him, removed the glass lid of the coffin roughly.

Judah stepped forward, and with everyone watching tensely, reached in, dipped his fingers into the remains of Alexander the Great, and pulled from them . . .

. . . the top Piece of the Golden Capstone.

Pyramidal in shape, with a base the size of a square paperback book, it radiated power.

More than that.

It radiated a power and an artistry and a *knowledge* beyond anything mankind had ever devised.

It was beyond man, beyond the limits of human knowledge.

The crystal in its peak glittered like a diamond. Its crystal array bored down the spine of the gold minipyramid, reappearing at the base.

Judah gazed at it adoringly.

He now held in his possession *all seven* Pieces of the Golden Capstone, something no man had done since Alexander the Great.

He grinned.

"It's time to capture the power of Ra. Tartarus will arrive over Giza at noon. To Giza, and a thousand years of power."

THE GREAT PYRAMID

GIZA

GIZA, EGYPT
MARCH 20, 2006
THE DAY OF TARTARUS

THE GREAT PYRAMID AT GIZA

It is perhaps the only structure on Earth known by name to every single member of the human race.

The Great Pyramid.

The most common misconception about the Seven Ancient Wonders of the World is that the three pyramids at Giza comprise a single Wonder.

This is not the case.

While Khafre's and Menkaure's additional pyramids are certainly impressive monuments, only one pyramid is known as the *Great* one: that of Khufu (or Cheops, as the Greeks called him). It is this pyramid alone that comprises the Wonder.

In a word, it is breathtaking.

Its dimensions are staggering: 460 feet high, while each of its base sides is 469 feet long. With the addition of its missing Capstone—lost in antiquity—perfect symmetry would be returned and it would once again resume its original height of 469 feet.

It is estimated to weigh over 2 million tons, and yet, despite this unimaginable bulk, it contains within its mass the most intricate and beautiful passageways, all built with an exactness that defies belief.

It has outlasted pharaohs and kings, tribal wars and world wars, earthquakes and sandstorms.

Devotees of the Pyramid swear that it possesses unusual powers: it is said that no bacteria can grow inside the Great Pyramid. It is said that flowers planted inside it grow with unusual vibrancy. It is claimed to heal sufferers of arthritis and cancer.

Whatever one's beliefs, there is something about this man-made mountain that draws people to it, that entrances them. It defies times, it defies imagination. To this day, it is still not known exactly how it was built.

It is the only man-made structure in history to defy the ravages of Nature and Time, and indeed the only one of the Seven Ancient Wonders known to have survived to the present day.

It is a building without equal in all of the world.

The Great Pyramid of Khufu lorded over outer Cairo, absolutely dominating the landscape around it.

Apartment buildings constructed by men four thousand five hundred years after it had been built looked puny beside it. It stood at the point where the lush river valley of Cairo met the edge of the Western Desert, on a raised section of cliffs called the Giza Plateau.

Beside it stood the pyramids of Khafre and Menkaure—also magnificent, but forever inferior—and before it, crouching, eternally at rest, lay the mysterious Sphinx.

It was almost midday and the Sun was rising to the high point of its daily arc. It was hot—very, very hot—even for Cairo: 120 degrees Farenheit and rising rapidly.

Reports from around the world had reported oppressively warm weather across the globe: China, India, even Russia—all had reported unusually high temperatures on this day. Many reported instances of people collapsing in the streets.

Something was wrong.

Something to do with the Sun, the TV commentators said. A sunspot, the meteorologists said.

495

In the United States, all the morning news shows had made it their story of the day and were looking to the White House, waiting for an address from the president.

But no such address came.

The White House remained mysteriously silent.

In Cairo, the Egyptian government had been most accommodating to Judah's force.

The entire Giza Plateau had been closed to civilians and tourists for the day—all its entrances were now guarded by Egyptian troops—and an advance team sent by Judah overnight had been given free rein on the ancient site.

Indeed, while Judah had been at Luxor that morning, his advance team had been working diligently, preparing for his arrival. Their work: an enormous scaffold structure that now shrouded the summit of the Great Pyramid.

It was a huge flat-topped platform, made entirely of wood, three stories high, and completely enveloping the peak of the pyramid. It looked like a big helicopter landing pad, square in shape, 100 feet long on each side, and its flat open-air roof lay level with the bare summit of the Pyramid. Indeed, the platform had a hole in its exact center that allowed the peak of the Pyramid to protrude up through it . . . and thus allow Judah to perform his preferred Capstone ritual.

The platform's vertical support struts rested upon the steplike sides of the Pyramid, as did two tall cranes that rose high into the sky above the platform. Inside the baskets of these cranes were CIEF troops armed with Stinger missiles and antiaircraft guns.

No one was going to interrupt this ceremony.

**THE GREAT PYRAMID
ON THE DAY OF TARTARUS**

At 11:00 A.M. exactly Marshall Judah arrived on a CH-53E Super Stallion helicopter, surrounded by twelve CIEF troops led by Cal Kallis, and carrying with him in the back of the chopper *all seven pieces* of the Golden Capstone of the Great Pyramid, ready to be restored to their rightful place.

The Super Stallion swung into a low hover above the platform and in the swirling hurricane of wind it created, the Pieces were unloaded on wheeled trolleys.

Flanked by the heavily armed CIEF commandos, Judah stepped out of the helicopter, leading the two children, Alexander and Lily.

Wizard and del Piero came after them, handcuffed and guarded—brought along by Judah for no other reason, it seemed, than to observe his triumph over them.

Zoe, Fuzzy, and Stretch (who had also been reunited with the team when Judah had revealed Lily) were being held in a second helicopter traveling behind the Super Stallion—a Black Hawk—that landed at the base of the Great Pyramid. They were being held for another reason: to control Lily. Judah had told her that if she disobeyed him at any time, Zoe, Stretch, and Fuzzy would be killed.

* * *

On the short helicopter flight from Cairo Airport to the pyramids, Lily had found herself seated beside Alexander. A brief conversation had ensued:

"Hi, I'm Lily," she said.

Alexander gazed at her airily, as if he was deciding whether or not to bother replying. "Alexander is my name . . . my young sister."

"*Young?* Come off it. You're only older than me by twenty minutes," Lily said, laughing.

"Nevertheless, I am still the firstborn," Alexander said. "To the first, go certain privileges. Such as respect."

"I bet you probably get out of doing your chores sometimes, too," Lily said.

"What are chores?" the boy asked seriously.

"Chores," Lily said in disbelief. "You know, things like cleaning out the horse poo in the barn. Washing up the dishes after dinner."

"I have never cleaned a *dish* in my life. Or a *barn*. Such activities are beneath my station."

"You've never done any chores!" Lily exclaimed. "Man, you're lucky! Wow, no chores . . ."

The boy frowned, genuinely curious. "Why do you do such things? You are highborn. Why would you even *allow* yourself to be dragooned into performing such tasks?"

Lily shrugged. She'd never actually thought about that. "I guess . . . well . . . while I don't really like doing them, I do my chores to contribute to my family. To be a part of the family. To help out."

"But you are *better* than they are. Why would you want to help such ordinary people?"

"I like helping them. I . . . I love them."

"My sister, my sister. We were born to rule these people, not to help them. They are beneath you, they are your inferiors."

"They are my family," Lily said firmly.

"To rule is lonely," Alexander said, as if this was a phrase he had been told a lot and learned by rote. "I expected you to be stronger, sister."

Lily said nothing after that, and minutes later, they arrived at the Great Pyramid.

And so it was that at 11:30 A.M. on the Day of Tartarus, thirty minutes before the blazing sunspot rotated in direct alignment with the Pyramid, a ceremony began on the summit of the Great Pyramid at Giza, an ancient ceremony that had not been performed in over four thousand five hundred years.

Standing on the platform, Judah clipped himself to a long safety rope, to take care of his fear of heights.

He gazed at the bare summit of the Great Pyramid, saw the ancient verse carved into it:

> *Cower in fear, cry in despair,*
> *You wretched mortals*
> *For that which giveth great power*
> *Also takes it away.*
> *For lest the Benben be placed at sacred site*
> *On sacred ground, at sacred height,*
> *Within seven sunsets of the arrival of Ra's prophet,*
> *At the high point of the seventh day,*
> *The fires of Ra's implacable Destroyer will devour us all.*

Beside this carving, in the exact center of the bare stone summit, there was a shallow indentation carved in the shape of a person. The "head" of this person-sized indentation was weathered and worn, but it was clearly that of Anubis, the jackal-headed and much-feared god of the Underworld.

And in the heart of this Anubis indentation—in the *exact* center of the summit and thus the center of the entire pyramid—there was a small dish-shaped hole the size of a tennis ball. It looked like a stone cru-cible.

Judah knew the purpose of the crucible. The Nazi archaeologist, Hessler, had too:

THE RITUAL OF POWER

> AT THE HIGH ALTAR OF RA,
> UNDER THE HEART OF THE SACRIFICIAL
>   ONE
> WHO LIES IN THE ARMS OF VENGEFUL
>   ANUBIS,
> POUR INTO THE DEATH GOD'S HEART
> ONE DEBEN OF YOUR HOMELAND.
> UTTER THOSE ANCIENT EVIL WORDS
> AND ALL EARTHLY POWER SHALL BE YOURS
> FOR A THOUSAND YEARS.

Pour into the death God's heart
One deben of your homeland . . .

A "deben" was the ancient Egyptian measure of weight. It equaled 3.5 ounces.

Judah pulled a glass vial from inside his jacket. In it was some amber-colored soil, soil that had been taken from the Utah desert, deep inside the United States—soil that was unique to the United States of America.

Judah poured exactly 3.5 ounces of the soil into the crucible. One deben.

Eyeing it proudly, he called to his men, "Gentlemen! Erect the Capstone!"

One Piece after the other, Judah's people began erecting the Golden Capstone.

The largest Piece—the Pharos Piece—went on the bottom and the human-shaped indentation in its golden underside perfectly matched up with the Anubis indentation on the summit of the Pyramid.

The Pyramid's summit was also fitted with a low channel cut into it from one side—since the Capstone lay flat on its peak, this channel provided a tight crawl-way that would allow the "Sacrificial One"—one of the children—to crawl *into* the indentation when the time came.

As each new Piece was laid on it, the Capstone began to take shape.

It was truly magnificent—glittering and powerful—a golden crown to an already stupendous structure.

And of course, the line of crystals running down through the center of the Capstone pointed directly at the heart of Anubis.

Judah coordinated the operation, his eyes wide with delight.

And then the final Piece, the pyramidal top Piece, the Piece he had obtained from Alexander's tomb only that morning went on . . .

. . . and the Capstone was complete for the first time in nearly five millennia.

The Great Pyramid of Giza stood whole once more, as it had originally appeared in 2566 B.C.

It was 11:50 A.M.

Ten minutes till the Tartarus Rotation occurred.

Judah turned to face the two children.

"And so it falls to me to make a historic choice," he said. "Which child to sacrifice to the power of the Sun . . ."

"Sacrifice?" Alexander said, frowning. "What are you talking about?"

"It is what you were born for, young man," Judah said. "It is what you were put on this earth to do."

"I was put here to rule—" Alexander threw a confused look at del Piero.

"I fear you have been misinformed," Judah said. "You were put here to decode the Word of Thoth, then to die for the eternal benefit of Father del Piero and his friends. Although I'm sure they would have worshipped you fervently *after* your death, if that is any consolation. I'm assuming Father del Piero must have failed to mention this."

Alexander's eyes flashed to del Piero, blazing with fury.

Lily just remained silent, her head bowed.

"So. Who to choose?" Judah mused.

"Her," Alexander said quickly. "She didn't even know of her own importance. At least I did."

Judah grinned at this. "Is that so?" Then he said, "No, boy. I like her, because she's quiet. You're not. Which means you're elected."

And with that, Judah scooped up the boy and thrust him into the tight channel underneath the Capstone, forcing him at gunpoint to crawl through it and lie down inside the arms of Anubis, beneath the assembled Capstone, his heart directly *underneath* the Capstone's crystal array while also directly *above* the dish-shaped crucible containing the soil of America.

The boy sobbed all the way.

At 11:55, Judah stepped into position.

He held in his hands the Ritual of Power—which he had taken line by line from the surface of each of the Capstone's seven Pieces.

"Everyone, prepare for the ceremony! Five minutes!"

It was then that one of the CIEF spotters in the northern crane spied a tiny black dot high in the eastern sky . . .

It looked like a plane of some sort, approaching fast, *descending*.

A 747 . . . a black one.

The *Halicarnassus*.

The *Halicarnassus* zoomed out of the sky at near-supersonic speed, nose down, wings pinned back, all its guns pointed forward.

Sky Monster was at the helm, yelling, "Yee-ha! Come and get it, motherfuckers! Pooh Bear—you ready to rock'n'roll?"

In the revolving gun turret on top of the plane's left wing, Pooh Bear replied, "Let's do some damage."

Sky Monster said, "Let's hope Wizard's retro system is up to the challenge or else this could be a disaster of gargantuan propor—shit! *Incoming!*"

The CIEF sentries on the cranes had launched two Stinger missiles at the incoming 747.

The missiles streaked upward from the Great Pyramid, shooting toward the inbound jumbo jet, but Pooh Bear nullified them both—he got one missile to lock onto a chaff bomb, and the other he destroyed with an interceptor missile of his own, a French-made FV-5X Hummingbird, designed by the French in the 1990s for the Iraqi Army, specifically to nullify American Stinger missiles. When West had found the *Halicarnassus,* it had been fitted with ten brand-new Hummingbirds.

The CIEF sentries then started firing their anti-aircraft guns.

Tracer bullets raced up into the sky—there were so many they *filled* the sky—but Sky Monster banked the *Halicarnassus* brilliantly, avoiding the laserlike streaks while at the same time, Pooh Bear returned fire and unleashed a Hellfire air-to-ground missile of his own.

The Hellfire shoomed out from a pod on the *Hali*'s underbelly and spiraled down toward one of the American cranes and—

—*smashed* into it and detonated.

The crane's basket was blasted into a million pieces, its occupants and their weapons vaporized.

Judah and all the others on the platform spun at the nearby explosion.

The other crane continued to fire up at the incoming *Halicarnassus,* unleashing a thousand rounds of AA ammunition and another Stinger missile—which Pooh Bear just blasted out of the sky a moment later.

Then Sky Monster yelled, "Pooh! *Hang on, buddy!* Here we go!" Then to himself he whispered, "Please God, Wizard, tell me you got this right . . ."

It was then that, roaring down toward the Giza Plateau like an out-of-control missile, Sky Monster lifted the *Hali*'s nose up slightly and *jammed* all his thrusters back . . . throwing the *Halicarnassus* into a deliberate stall . . . so that now it looked like a stallion rearing up on its hind legs, its nose up, its tail down . . .

. . . at which point, Sky Monster held his breath and punched the *second* collective on his console, a thruster collective marked: RETROGRADE THRUST SYSTEM.

* * *

What happened next startled everyone on the Pyramid's summit—everyone except Wizard.

The *Halicarnassus*—dropping through the sky in a graceful flat stall, nose up, tail down—emitted a noise deeper and louder than a thousand thunder claps.

BOOOOOOOOM!

The colossal noise came from the eight Mark 3 Harrier retrograde thrust engines that had been incorporated into its armored fuselage.

By Wizard.

The result was sensational: the massive all-black *Halicarnassus* stopped in midfall, as if it was suspended from giant descender cables, and to the sound of its deafening retrograde thrusters, it swung into a perfect hover, 200 yards off the ground and only *a few hundred yards from the Great Pyramid*!

Sky Monster brought her closer, bringing the big hovering plane's left forward door alongside the platform on the summit of the Pyramid.

It was an absolutely astonishing sight—the massive black jumbo jet, bristling with guns and missile pods, hovering with its nose close to the summit of the Great Pyramid of Giza.

From the platform itself, the *Halicarnassus* loomed large, superhuge, like an angry bird god descended from heaven itself to wreak its fury.

The initial spell broken, the surviving American crane swung around to unleash a new burst of AA fire, now from point-blank range.

But Pooh Bear, on the *Hali*'s left wing, was quicker on the draw and also at point-blank range.

He loosed a withering burst of fire—a hyperfast *barrage* of gunfire—that shook, shattered, and blasted apart the crane, turning its occupants into fountains of spraying blood and the crane into Swiss cheese.

On the platform, Judah's eyes boggled.

He checked the Sun, checked his watch: 11:59:29.

Thirty seconds.

"Hold them off!" he called to his men. "Hold them off! We only need *thirty seconds*!"

Consumed with the spectacular arrival of the *Halicarnassus,* Judah never noticed a *second* airborne craft zeroing in on the Pyramid, a very small craft that came zooming in low and fast from the Western Desert.

It was a man, possessed of carbon-fiber wings.

The tiny man-shaped figure soared low over the desert, before at the last second, he rose up swiftly— rising up the slanting side of the Pyramid as if it were an aerial ramp—and landed with a graceful upward plonk, up onto the far side of the Capstone, on the side opposite the attention-grabbing *Halicarnassus.*

It was Jack West Jr.

Back from the dead, and pissed as hell.

West landed with his wings outstretched and with two big .45 caliber Desert Eagle pistols in his hands. The instant his feet touched the platform, his guns started blazing, taking down four CIEF troopers with four shots.

Then he punched a release clip on his wing harness and the carbon-fiber wings fell off his back, freeing him, making him even more deadly.

He ran out onto the platform, guns up.

At the same time, in response to the spectacular arrival of the *Halicarnassus,* four CIEF helicopters lifted off from their positions at the base of the Great Pyramid: three Apache attack birds and the mighty Super Stallion that Judah had used to bring the Pieces to Giza.

A fifth chopper—a Black Hawk—made to follow them, but it seemed to hesitate on the ground as a scuffle occurred inside it.

Then, a few seconds behind the others, it lifted off and headed for the battle going on at the top of the Pyramid.

* * *

**THE GREAT PYRAMID
ON THE DAY OF TARTARUS II**

Pandemonium reigned on the platform.

With the *Halicarnassus* looming alongside it like a ship from outer space, and Pooh Bear blazing away from the plane's powerful left-side gun turret, all the American CIEF troops on the platform were either getting shot or diving for cover behind Samsonite crates or the Capstone itself or to the lower levels of the open-sided structure.

In the chaos, Wizard hurled himself on top of Lily to protect her.

Del Piero charged across the platform and slid to the ground beside the little channel, to reach for Alexander, still inside the Capstone.

"Not so fast, Father!" a voice said from behind him. Del Piero turned—

—to find himself staring into the barrel of a Glock pistol held by Marshall Judah.

Bam!

The pistol went off and the priest's brains splattered the golden flank of the Capstone.

With a core group of CIEF men surrounding him, Judah stood before the Capstone—cleverly putting it between him and Pooh Bear's guns—and with a glance at his watch, looked to the sky.

At that moment, the clock struck noon and it happened.

It looked like a laser beam from Heaven.

A dead-straight beam of dazzling white light lanced down from the sky, from the surface of the Sun, and accompanied by a tremendous *boom,* it slammed into the Capstone atop the Great Pyramid.

The Capstone, in reply, *caught* this ray of hyper-intense energy within its crystal array—so that the beam remained in place, giving the impression that the Pyramid was now *connected* to the Sun by a super-long and perfectly straight ray of glowing white energy.

It was a stunning image: the Pyramid—surmounted by the great wooden platform, with the *Halicarnassus* hovering alongside it and with helicopters buzzing and banking around it—*absorbing* the blazing white beam of pure energy that was lancing down from the sky.

It was incredible, impossible, otherworldly.

But it was also oddly *right.* It was as if this was what the Great Pyramid at Giza, dormant and mysterious for so many centuries, had been designed to do.

* * *

The platform was ablaze with light and sound.

Here at the epicenter of the great Sun ray, the glow was almost blinding. And the noise—it was all-consuming: the colossal boom of the great Sun ray combined with the roar of the *Halicarnassus*'s retro-thrusters and the turning of its regular engines (which were level with the platform) drowned out all other sound.

And in the midst of all this stood Marshall Judah, before the Capstone. He raised one arm toward the Golden Capstone, palm up, and then in an ancient language not heard in thousands of years, he began to recite an incantation.

The power ritual.

The power ritual was seven lines long.

As Judah began to recite it, several things were happening:

Pooh Bear.

He was waging his own private war with the four CIEF helicopters. He had knocked out one Apache helicopter with gunfire and had just fired a Hellfire missile at the rising Super Stallion. The missile slammed into the front windshield of the Super Stallion just as the big chopper came level with the platform.

The CH-53E exploded in a giant ball of flames—and lurched in midair, before it fell, dropping alongside the platform, its swirling rotor blades missing the lower levels of the platform by inches before the whole chopper *smashed* down in a crumpled heap on the sloping southern flank of the Great Pyramid itself.

It now lay at a fifty-two-degree angle—the slope of the Pyramid—at the spot where the platform's struts met the Pyramid, its body crumpled and broken but its rotors still buzzing in blurring circles of motion.

Judah had recited two lines by this time . . .

Pooh Bear swung around in his gun turret and had just zeroed in on the CIEF Black Hawk when—to his surprise—he saw the Black Hawk fire a missile into the back of one of its own Apache attack birds.

It was then that Pooh saw the pilots of the Black

Hawk: Zoe and Fuzzy. In the confusion earlier, they'd escaped their bonds, stolen the Black Hawk, and leaped into the fray.

But then suddenly a CIEF trooper leaped up onto the *Halicarnassus*'s wing, trying to take out Pooh Bear's turret guerrilla-style. Pooh couldn't turn the turret in time. The man had him, raised his Colt rifle—

Bam!

The CIEF trooper was hit in the back of the head by a long-distance sniper shot, a shot that had been fired by—

—Stretch, sitting in the side door of the stolen Black Hawk, holding a sniper rifle.

Pooh saw the Israeli, alive and with the good guys, and he smiled for the briefest of moments.

Judah had recited four lines . . .

West.

He was waging *his* own private war against the eight men guarding Judah at the Capstone: six CIEF troopers, Koenig, and Kallis.

He strode forward, eyes fixed, face set, both of his guns held outstretched in front of him.

The old warrior in Jack West—a warrior Judah had helped create—had returned . . . and he was a mean motherfucker.

West shot four of the troopers—all right between the eyeballs. One shot, one kill. Another he grabbed from behind, snapping his neck, before using the dead man's body as a shield to receive fire from Cal Kallis while emptying the dead man's M4 into two others. Then the wily old Nazi, Koenig, lunged at him from the side with a knife, but he received two rounds to the nose for his trouble, the force of the shots sending the old Nazi flying clear off the platform.

Judah finished the sixth line . . .

"Hold him off!" he called to Kallis as he began the last line.

That left West facing Cal Kallis—who now stood between West and Judah—in the midst of the maelstrom of light, wind, and sound.

It was a standoff from which there could be only one winner.

But there was also one more figure at work in all this chaos.

Beyond the mayhem happening on the platform, unseen by anyone, the exit door above the left wing of the *Halicarnassus* opened and a figure emerged from it, skulking low, moving swiftly, holding something small in his hands.

He scurried out from the doorway and onto the wing. Then he leaped down from the front of the wing onto the wooden platform, heading—again unseen— in the direction of Wizard and Lily.

West and Kallis faced each other.

Then they moved, at exactly the same time, lifting and firing their guns simultaneously, like a pair of Wild West gunslingers—

Click! Click!

They were both dry.

"Fuck!" Kallis yelled.

"No . . ." West breathed.

For he knew that it didn't matter now.

Judah also knew. Their eyes met, and West's face fell.

He was too late.

By a bare few seconds—no, a bare few *yards*—he was too late.

With a smile of insane delight, by the light of the Tartarus Sunspot on the Day of the Rotation, Marshall Judah uttered the final words of the ritual of power and looked triumphantly to the heavens.

Nothing happened.

Granted, West wasn't sure what *should* have happened. Should the sky darken? Should the Earth shake? Should Judah turn into some giant all-powerful dragon? Should West's gun turn to dust?

Whatever was supposed to happen to show that the United States of America had just earned itself a thousand years of undisputed worldly power, it didn't manifest itself in any visible way.

And then West saw that, indeed, nothing *had* happened.

For there, scuttling on all fours away from the Capstone on the other side of the platform, having crawled over the corpse of the CIEF trooper who was supposed to be guarding the channel that led under the Capstone, was the boy, Alexander.

He hadn't been in the sacrificial spot when Judah had completed the ritual . . .

So the ritual hadn't taken effect.

Judah saw it, too, and he shouted, "No! *No!*"

The boy clambered to the edge of the platform, turned back—and seeing del Piero's dead body, he leaned out over the side of the platform, lowering himself to the level below.

West's view of Alexander disappearing over the edge was cut off by the flash of Cal Kallis's KA-BAR knife rushing toward his eyes.

West ducked and the blade went high. He then rose quickly and punched the knife from Kallis's hand before nailing the CIEF trooper square in the nose with the best punch he'd ever thrown with his all-metal left hand—

The blow connected . . .

. . . and had no effect on Kallis at all.

The big CIEF trooper just grinned back at West through bloody teeth.

Then he replied with three *awesome* punches of his own—all vicious, all hard, all to West's face.

Once, twice, three times, each blow sent West staggering backward.

"You feel that, West! You feel that!" Kallis roared. "I've been waiting all fucking week for this! But I had to keep you alive, to let you lead us to each site. But not anymore. My boys got your Spanish friend in the Sudan! But I was the one who offed your dumb Irish lad in Kenya! He was still alive after you left, you know—a gurgling bloody mess. I was the one who put a bullet in his brain to finish him off."

A fourth blow, then a fifth.

On the fifth punch, West's nose broke, exploded with blood, and his boots came to the edge of the platform and he teetered there for a moment, glanced quickly behind him.

Immediately below him, twenty feet down, was the crashed Super Stallion—its blades spinning like a buzz saw *directly* beneath him!

Kallis saw them too. "But while I enjoyed snuffing out the Irish kid, I'm glad I'm the one who gets to kill *you*. See you in Hell, West!"

And with that, Kallis unleashed the final crushing blow.

Just as West himself lunged desperately forward, his left arm lashing out, extending fast—a final last-gasp all-or-nothing strike.

His blow struck Kallis a nanosecond before Kallis's blow struck him.

Phwack!

Kallis froze in midaction—

—with West's artificial left fist, his *metal* fist, lodged deep in the center of his face, having thundered right *through* his nose. The blow had been so powerful, it had *dented* Kallis's nose three inches inward, breaking it in several places. Blood had sprayed everywhere.

Incredibly, Kallis was still conscious, his eyes bulging, his entire body twitching, but his limbs were no longer responding to his brain.

He wouldn't be alive for long.

"This is for Big Ears," West said, yanking Kallis around and hurling him off the edge of the platform.

Kallis fell—thirty feet, straight down—and in his very last moment of consciousness, he saw, to his horror, the spinning rotor blades of the Super Stallion rush up to meet him . . .

He inhaled to scream, but the shout never came. In a single split second, Cal Kallis was diced into a thousand bloody pieces.

On the other side of the platform, Wizard had watched in horror as West had fought Kallis.

He wanted to help, but he also didn't want to leave Lily.

But then he saw Jack surprise Kallis with that lethal punch, saw the foul explosion of blood from the back of Kallis's head, and he suddenly felt like they might just have a chance—

Wizard was struck viciously from behind . . . by the figure who had emerged from the *Halicarnassus*.

He fell, and his world began to darken at the edges.

Oddly, the last thing he heard before he fell into blackness was Lily shouting to someone: "No! Forget Alexander! Take me instead!"

His face a mess of blood and dust, West rose from the edge of the platform and turned to head back to the Capstone—

—only to find himself staring into the barrel of Marshall Judah's Glock, just as del Piero had. He froze.

"You should be proud, Jack!" Judah called. "This is all your doing! *You* led us to this juncture! But all the while you were working for me! There is nothing you can think of, nothing you can do, nothing you have, that I do not already possess! Why I even have your little girl to use for the ritual! Tragically, you won't live to see her fulfill her destiny! Good-bye, Jack!"

Judah tightened his trigger finger . . .

"That's not true!" West shouted above the din. "I do have one thing you don't have! Something that was once yours!"

"What?"

"Horus!"

At that instant, a blurring flash of brown streaked through the air, cutting across Judah's face, and suddenly Judah screamed, his face spraying blood. He threw his hands to his eyes, still half-holding the gun.

Horus swooped clear of the screaming Judah, clutching something in her talons . . . something white and round and trailing a ragged bloody tail.

It was Judah's entire left eye, including the optic nerve.

Horus had ripped it clean from its socket!

Judah dropped to his knees, wailing, "My eye! My eye!"

At the same time, with his good eye, he saw the Capstone and yelled with even more anguish: "Oh, God, no . . . !"

West spun too—and he also saw the nightmare scenario take physical form.

For there, standing at the Capstone, having taken Lily from Wizard and ushered her at gunpoint into the sacrificial cavity in the base of the Capstone *and* having refilled the crucible inside the cavity with exactly one deben of the fine-grained sand from his black jade box, was Mustapha Zaeed, now reading from Judah's notebook, *performing the ritual of power*!

It was Zaeed who had crept unseen from the wing-door of the *Halicarnassus* earlier, having stowed aboard the plane in Iran after the confrontation at the Hanging Gardens.

It was he who had followed West and Pooh Bear to the rendezvous with Sky Monster and crept aboard the plane through its landing gear, unnoticed—assuming correctly that West would go to Egypt to confront the Americans one last time.

Once on board, Zaeed had crept to his old trunk and pulled from it his prized black jade box, filled with the fine-grained sand, sand that he had kept for so long in his secret cave in Saudi Arabia—sand unique to the Arabian Peninsula, sand that would bring to the Muslim world a thousand years of unchallenged power.

Now, here, on the platform, it was he who had struck Wizard from behind. As he'd done so, he had spotted Alexander lowering himself over the edge nearby, and he'd been about to grab the boy to perform the ritual, when suddenly Lily had said, "No! Forget Alexander! Take me instead!"

And so Zaeed had.

Now he only had to utter seven lines.

It took him fifteen seconds.

And there, atop the Great Pyramid of Giza, under the blinding sun ray from the Tartarus Sunspot in the roaring wind and the blazing heat, to the horror of everyone else watching powerlessly, Mustapha Zaeed—his voice resonating with evil reverence—uttered the final words of the ritual of power.

This time, West had no doubt that the ritual had been performed correctly.

It sounded like the end of the universe.

Flaring light.

Clashing thunder.

The very earth shook.

What followed next made man's most spectacular fireworks shows look positively puny.

The dazzling white beam of light reaching down from the Sun pulsed brilliantly, as if it were doubling in intensity.

An unearthly thunderclap boomed, causing West's ears to ring, and a white-hot ball of superbrilliant energy thundered out of the sky, racing down the length of the vertical beam before rushing headlong *into* the Capstone . . .

. . . where the Capstone received it within its crystal array.

Inside the Golden Capstone, the energy burst rushed down through its seven layers of crystals—at each layer refining the beam into an ever-smaller, ever-more-intense thread of superluminous light.

And then this superthin beam struck Lily in the heart.

The little girl convulsed, hit by the light beam. The beam, however, seemed to pass *right through* her chest and strike the soil in the crucible.

With a blinding flash, the soil was instantly transformed to cinders.

Seen from the outside, the Capstone shone with blinding brilliance as it received the energy burst, before with a terrible *whump,* the white-hot ball disappeared into it, and the phenomenon abruptly ceased and all was quiet, save for a deep humming that came from the Capstone and the drone of the *Halicarnassus*'s engines.

West could only stare at the Capstone and wonder what had happened to Lily inside it. Could she have survived such a phenomenon? Or had Zaeed been right when he'd said she would die in the ceremony?

Zaeed stood beside the Capstone, his arms raised in triumph, his face upturned to the sky. "A thousand years! A thousand years of Islamic rule!"

He rounded on West, eyes glowering, hands spread wide.

"The ritual is done, infidel! Which means my people are unconquerable! Invincible! And you— *you*—will be the first to feel my wrath!"

"Is that so?" West said, jamming a new clip into one of his Desert Eagles and aiming it at Zaeed.

"Fire your weapon!" Zaeed taunted him. "Bullets cannot help you anymore!"

"Finc," West said.

Bam!—he fired.

The bullet hit Zaeed square in the chest, sending him jolting backward. Blood sprayed outward and the terrorist dropped to the ground, to his knees, his face the picture of shock and confusion.

He stared at his wound, then up at West.

"But . . . how . . . ?"

"I knew you were on my plane after the Hanging Gardens," West said. "I knew you'd try to stow aboard. How else were you going to get here? You've been chasing this all your life, you weren't going to stay away. So I let you stow aboard."

"But the sand . . ."

"While you were hiding in the belly of my plane, I took the liberty of changing the sand in your black jade box," West said. "It's not the soil of Arabia anymore. What you put inside the Capstone was the soil of *my* homeland. You just performed the ritual of power for my people, Zaeed, not yours. Thanks."

Zaeed was thunderstruck. He looked away, considering the consequences. "*Your* soil? But that would mean . . ."

He never finished the sentence, for at that moment life escaped him, and Mustapha Zaeed dropped to the platform, dead.

There came a sudden pained shout—*"WEST!"*—and West spun to see Marshall Judah lunging toward him, blood and flesh dangling from his ripped-open eye socket, and an M4 assault rifle in his hands, taken from one of his dead CIEF troops.

It was point-blank range.

Judah couldn't miss.

He jammed down on the trigger.

* * *

The gun literally exploded in Judah's hands.

It wasn't a misfire, or a jam. It was a total outward explosion. The gun broke outward in a thousand pieces and fell crumbling from Judah's hands.

Judah frowned, confused—then he looked up in horror at West and said, "Oh my God . . . you . . . *you* have the power . . ."

West stepped forward, knowing that the gun could not hurt him. "Judah. I could forgive you for what you did to me, putting that chip in my head. I could forgive you for the beatings you gave Horus. But there's one thing I cannot forgive: killing Doris Epper. For that you have to pay."

As he spoke, West picked up the end of Judah's long safety rope, unclipped it from its anchor near the Capstone.

Judah stepped backward toward the edge of the platform where the *Halicarnassus*'s wing loomed. He held his hands up. "Now, Jack. We're both soldiers and sometimes soldiers have to—"

"You executed her. Now I'm going to execute you."

And West threw his end of the safety rope past Judah . . . into the still-rotating jet engine of the *Halicarnassus,* hovering immediately behind Judah.

Judah spun as the rope flew by him, saw it enter the yawning maw of the engine.

Then he saw the future, saw what would happen next and his one good eye boggled with fear.

He screamed, but his scream was cut short as the enormous turbine swallowed the rope . . . and sucked *the rest of the safety rope* in after it.

Judah was yanked off his feet, doubling over as he was sucked backward through the air. Then he entered the engine and—*thwack-thwack-CHUNK!*—was chewed alive by its hyperrotating blades.

And suddenly the summit of the Great Pyramid was still.

Seeing the awesome blast of light from the Sun and the deaths of their summit team, the CIEF force at the base of the Pyramid fled, leaving West and Wizard up on the platform, alone.

Moments later, Zoe's Black Hawk landed on the platform and Zoe, Fuzzy, and Stretch came rushing out of it—at the same time that Pooh Bear leaped onto the platform from the *Halicarnassus*'s wing.

They all arrived on the platform to find West—watched by Wizard—crawling underneath the Capstone to check on Lily.

West belly-crawled through the tight channel carved into the stone beneath the Capstone.

He came to Lily, found her lying motionless inside the human-shaped cavity in the Capstone's lowest Piece. Her eyes were closed. She seemed calm, at peace . . . and not breathing.

"Oh, Lily . . ." West scrambled forward on his elbows, desperate to get to her.

His head came alongside hers. He scanned her face for any movement, any sign of life.

Nothing. She didn't move at all.

He deflated completely, his entire body going limp, his eyes closing in anguish. "Oh, Lily. I'm sorry. I'm so sorry."

He bowed his head, tears rolling from the corners of his eyes, and said, "I loved you, kiddo."

And there in the cavity, in the golden glow of the Capstone, lying before the body of the happy little girl he had guarded and raised for ten whole years, Jack West Jr. wept.

"I love you, too, Daddy . . ." a soft voice whispered weakly.

West snapped up, his eyes darting open, to see Lily staring back at him, her head rolled onto its side. Her eyes were milky, dazed.

But she was alive, and smiling at him.

"You're alive . . ." West said, amazed. "You're alive!"

He scooped her up in his arms and hugged her firmly.

"But how . . . ?" West asked aloud.

"I'll tell you later," she said. "Can we please get out of here?"

"You bet," he breathed. "You bet."

Minutes later, the *Halicarnassus* powered up and lifted vertically into the sky, rising on its eight massive retro thrusters.

Once it was high enough, it pivoted in midair and allowed itself to drop, nose-down. It fell briefly, plummeting toward the ground, before it engaged its regular engines, using the short vertical fall to get up to flight speed. Its main engines firing, it swung up at the last moment and soared away from the Pyramids on the Giza Plateau.

* * *

The Great Pyramid was left standing there behind it, with the half-destroyed platform shrouding its summit, and the American helicopters and cranes lying smoking and broken on its flanks. The Egyptian government, which had aided and abetted the American ritual, would have to clean it all up.

Importantly, however, the peak of the Pyramid was also once again nine feet shorter than it should have been.

West and his team had taken the Capstone—the entire Capstone—with them.

Inside the main cabin of the *Halicarnassus,* West and the others gathered around Lily, hugging her, kissing her, clasping her on the shoulders.

Pooh Bear embraced her: "Well done, young one! Well *done!*"

"Thanks for coming back for me, Pooh Bear," she said.

"I was never going to leave you, young one," he said.

"Nor was I," said Stretch, stepping forward.

"Thanks, Stretch. For saving me at the Gardens, for staying with me when you could have gone."

Stretch nodded silently, to Lily and also to all the others, especially Pooh Bear. "They don't come often, but every now and then, there come times in your life when you have to choose a side; choose who you are fighting for. I made my choice, Lily, to fight with you. It was a hard choice, but I have no doubt that it was the right one."

"It was the right one," Pooh Bear said, clapping a hand onto Stretch's shoulder. "You are a good man, Israeli . . . I mean, Stretch. I would be honored to call you my friend."

"Thank you, Arab," Stretch said with a smile. "Thank you, *friend*."

When all the backslapping was over, West was eager to understand how Lily had survived.

"I went willingly," she said simply.

"I don't get it," West said.

Lily grinned, obviously proud of herself. "It was the inscription cut into the wall of the volcano chamber where I was born. You yourself were studying it one day. It said:

"*Enter the embrace of Anubis willingly, and you shall live beyond the coming of Ra. Enter against your will, and your people shall rule for but one eon, but you shall live no more. Enter not at all, and the world shall be no more.*'

"Like the Egyptians, we thought it was simply a reference to the god, Horus, accepting death and being rewarded for that with some kind of afterlife. But that was wrong. It was meant to apply to me and Alexander—to the Oracles. It's not about accepting *Death* willingly. It's about entering the cavity willingly.

"If I entered it of my own accord, I would survive. If I went unwillingly, I'd die. But if I didn't go at all, and the ritual was not performed, you would all have died. And I, well, I didn't want to lose my family."

"Even if that meant giving Zaeed power for all eternity?" Pooh Bear said in disbelief.

Lily turned to him, and her eyes glinted.

"Mr. Zaeed was never going to rule," she said. "When he grabbed me, I saw the soil in his jade box." Lily turned to West. "It was a kind of soil I'd seen many times before. I've been fascinated with it for a long time. It has been sitting in a glass jar on a shelf in Daddy's study for years. When I saw it on Mr. Zaeed's box, I knew exactly what it was, and so I knew I wasn't giving Mr. Zaeed any power at all."

Pooh Bear said, "Did del Piero know this, too? Is that why he treated Alexander like a little emperor, ready to rule? Did he want Alexander to enter that cavity willingly?"

"I think so," West said. "But there was more to it than that. Del Piero was a priest, and he thought like a priest. He wanted Alexander to survive the ritual not because he wanted the boy to live and rule, but because he also wanted a *savior,* a figurehead, a focal point for his new ruling religion. A new Christ figure."

Through all this, Wizard sat alone in a corner of the cabin, silent, head bent. Zoe sat with him, holding his hand, equally shocked at the death of her brother, Big Ears.

Lily walked over to them, touched their shoulders.

"I'm sorry about Doris, Wizard," she said with a seriousness that belied her age. "And Big Ears, too, Zoe."

Tear lines streaked down Wizard's face; his eyes were moist and red. It was only on the platform that he had learned of Doris's death at Judah's hands.

"She died saving us," Lily said. "Telling us to get away. She gave her life so that we could escape."

"She was my wife for forty-five years," Wizard

said. "The most wonderful woman I've ever known. She was my life, my family."

"I'm so sorry," Lily said.

Then she took his hand and looked deep into his eyes. "But if you'll take me, I'll be your family now."

Wizard looked up at her through his wet eyes . . . and he nodded. "I'd like that, Lily. I'd like that a lot."

A few hours later, Wizard found West alone in his office at the back of the *Halicarnassus*.

"I have a question for you, Jack," he said. "What does all this mean now? We set out to perform the ritual of peace, but now the ritual of power has been initiated—in favor of your country. Can Australians be trusted to possess such power?"

"Max," West said, "you know where I'm from. You know what we're like. We're certainly not aggressors or warmongers. And if my people *don't know* they've got this power, then I think this is the best possible outcome—because we're the most unlikely people on Earth to use it."

Wizard nodded slowly, accepting this.

"I won't let them know if you won't," West said.

"Deal," Wizard said. "Thank you, Jack. Thank you."

The two men shared a smile.

And with that, the *Halicarnassus* soared into the sky, heading for Kenya, heading for home.

For the second time in ten years, the lonely old farm-house on the hilltop overlooking the Atlantic Ocean was host to an important meeting of nations.

A couple of the faces had changed, but the nine original nations represented at the first meeting had not. Plus, there was one extra nation present this time: Israel.

"They're late," the Arab delegate, Sheik Anzar al Abbas, growled. "Again."

The Canadian delegate—again—said, "They'll be here. They'll be here."

A door slammed somewhere, and a few moments later, Max T. Epper entered the sitting room.

Jack West, however, was not with him.

But he did have a companion: the little girl.

Lily.

"Where is Captain West?" Abbas demanded.

Wizard bowed respectfully. "Captain West sends his apologies. Having succeeded on his mission, he assumed you wouldn't mind if he did not attend this meeting. He said he had some things to do, some loose ends to tie up. In the meantime, may I introduce to you all the young lady to whom we owe a profound debt of gratitude. Ladies and gentlemen, meet Lily."

* * *

At length Wizard reported the events of the previous ten years to the delegates of the coalition of small nations.

Of course, they were aware of some elements of his success: the Earth had not been blasted with superheated solar energy; and America had not become invincible—its continued problems imposing law and order in the Middle East showed that. Word had got out about a spectacular battle atop the Great Pyramid, too, but damage to the structure had actually been minimal and the Egyptian government, ever keen to retain American aid money, had denied the story absolutely.

And so Wizard told the delegates of Lily's upbringing in Kenya, of the chase to locate the seven Pieces of the Capstone, of the inclusion of Mustapha Zaeed in their quest, of their losses—of Noddy, Big Ears, and of his own wife, Doris—and of the final confrontation on the summit of the Great Pyramid with Judah's renegade CIEF force and with Zaeed.

It was only on this last point that Wizard diverted slightly from the truth.

Since it accorded with the state of the world—safe from the power of the Sun, and with no apparent superpowerful ruling nation—he reported that on the summit of the Great Pyramid the ritual of *peace* had been performed, not the ritual of power.

He even informed them of the fate of the boy, Alexander. He had been found after the battle on the Pyramid and placed in the care of some trusted friends of Wizard's, people who would teach him to be a normal boy . . . and who would observe his maturation into adulthood, and keep track of any children he might have later in life.

"And so, ladies and gentlemen, our mission is accomplished," Wizard concluded. "This issue need not be addressed for another four thousand five hundred years. At which time, I am pleased to say, it shall fall to someone else to handle."

The delegates at the meeting rose from their chairs and applauded.

Then, buzzing with excitement, they started congratulating each other and calling home, to relay the excellent news.

Only one of them remained seated.

Sheik Abbas.

"Wizard!" he called above the din. "You neglected to tell us one thing. Where is the Capstone now?"

All fell silent.

Wizard faced Abbas, eyed him evenly. "The disposition of the Capstone was one of the loose ends Captain West had to attend to."

"Where does he intend to hide it?"

Wizard cocked his head to one side. "Surely, Anzar, the fewer who know the resting place of the Capstone, the better. You have trusted us this far, now trust us one more time.

"But let me assure you of one thing: Captain West has now retired from national service. He does not intend to be found. If you can find him, you can find the Capstone, but I pity the man who is tasked with that hunt."

This seemed to satisfy Abbas, and the congratulations continued.

The sounds of celebration would echo from the farmhouse deep into the night.

The next morning, Wizard and Lily left Ireland.

As they boarded a private plane at Cork International Airport, Lily said, "Wizard. Where did Daddy go?"

"As I said, to tie up some loose ends."

"What about after that? When he's done, where will he go?"

Wizard eyed her sideways. "He said you might ask me that—and he told me specifically *not* to tell you. In fact, he informed me that he once gave you a riddle concerning the location of his new home. I suggest if you want to find him, you solve the riddle."

The Toyota four-wheel drive zoomed along the empty desert highway.

In the passenger seat, Lily gazed out at the most inhospitable landscape she had ever seen. Wizard drove, with Zoe in the back. Lily shook her head. If there was any place on Earth farther from civilization, she didn't know it.

Dry, barren hills stretched away in every direction. Sand crept out onto the desert highway, as if eventually it would consume it.

But it was an odd kind of sand, orange-red in color, just like the soil that had been in West's jar.

They hadn't seen another car in hours. In fact, the last living thing they'd seen was a big saltwater crocodile basking on a virtually dry riverbank under a bridge they'd crossed two hours ago.

A sign on the bridge revealed the river to be named, somewhat appropriately, the River Styx, after the river in Hell. A three-way junction a few miles after it offered three options—to the left: Simpson's Crossing, fifty miles; straight: Death Valley, seventy-five miles; while going right would ultimately take them to a place called Franklin Downs.

"Go straight," Lily had said. "Death Valley."

Now, two hours later, she said, "It has to be here somewhere . . ."

She checked her riddle:

My new home is home to both tigers and crocodiles.
To find it, pay the boatman,
take your chances with the dog and journey
Into the jaws of Death,
Into the mouth of Hell.
There you will find me, protected by a great villain.

Lily said, " 'Pay the boatman, take your chances with the dog.' In Greek mythology, when you entered the Underworld, you first had to cross the River Styx. To do that, you paid the boatman, then took your chances against Cerberus, the dog guarding Hades. We've found the River Styx."

Wizard and Zoe exchanged looks.

"And Death Valley?" Zoe asked. "What makes you think that?"

"The next two lines in the riddle, 'Into the jaws of Death/Into the mouth of Hell,' they're from a poem that Wizard taught me, 'The Charge of the Light Brigade.' In the poem, the six hundred members of the Light Brigade charge into 'the Valley of Death.' Death Valley."

Minutes later, a series of low buildings rose out of the heat haze.

The town of Death Valley.

A weatherworn sign at the entry to the town read:

WELCOME TO
DEATH VALLEY
HOME OF THE MIGHTY
DEATH VALLEY TIGERS FOOTBALL TEAM!

"Home to both tigers and crocodiles," Lily said.

Death Valley turned out to be a ghost town—just a cluster of old wooden shacks and farms with long dirt driveways, long abandoned.

They drove around for a while.

Lily gazed out the window, eyes searching for a clue. "Now we need to find a 'great villain' . . . a great villain . . . *There!* Wizard! Stop the car!"

They stopped at the end of an ultralong dirt driveway. It was so long, the farmhouse to which it belonged lay over the horizon.

At the point where the driveway met the road, however, a rusty old mailbox sat on a post. Like many such mailboxes in rural Australia, this one was a home-made work of art.

Constructed of old tractor parts and a rusted oil barrel, it was fashioned in the shape of a mouse . . . complete with ears and whiskers. Only this mouse wore, of all things, a crown.

"A Mouse King . . ." she breathed. "*The* Mouse King. This is it."

"How do you know?" Zoe asked.

Lily smiled at the in-joke. "The Mouse King is a great villain. He's the villain in *The Nutcracker*."

Their car bounced down the dusty dirt driveway. At the very end of the long drive, far from the main road, they found the quiet little farmhouse nestled beneath a low hill, its windmill turning slowly.

A man stood on the front porch, dressed in jeans

and a T-shirt, his metal left arm glinting in the sunshine, watching the approaching four-wheel drive.

Jack West Jr.

Lily bounded out of the car and leaped into West's
arms.

"You found me," he said. "Took you long enough."

"Where have you been?" Lily asked. "What were
these loose ends you had to tie up for a whole month?"

West grinned. "Why don't you come and see."

He led her behind the farmhouse, into an old abandoned mine hidden in the base of the low sandy hill
back there.

"Later today, like Imhotep III did at the Hanging
Gardens, I'm going to trigger a landslide to cover the
entrance to this mine," he said as they walked, "so that
no one will ever know that there's a mine here, or what
it contains."

A hundred yards inside the mine, they came to a
wide chamber and in the center of the chamber
stood . . .

. . . the Golden Capstone.

Nine feet tall, glittering and golden, and absolutely
magnificent.

"Pooh Bear and Stretch helped me get it here. Oh,
and Sky Monster, too," West said. "I also got them to
help me pick up a few other things that we encountered
on our adventures. Wizard, I thought you might like to
keep one or two."

Standing in a semicircle on the far side of the Capstone were several other ancient items, large items.

The Mirror from the Lighthouse at Alexandria.

The Pillar from the Mausoleum at Halicarnassus.

Both last seen in Tunisia, inside Hamilcar's Refuge.

"You didn't get the head of the Colossus of Rhodes?" Wizard asked jokingly.

"I was thinking of going after it in a few months, if you wanted to join me," West said. "I could use the help. Oh, and Zoe . . ."

"Yes, Jack . . ."

"I thought you might like a flower, as a token of thanks for your efforts these last ten years." With a flourish, he whipped something from behind his back and held it out to her.

It was a rose, a white rose of some kind, but one of unusual beauty.

Zoe's eyes widened. "Where did you find this—?"

"Some gardens I saw once," West said, "which, alas, are no longer there. But this variety of rose is really rather resilient, and it's taking in my front garden very well. I expect to develop quite a rosebush. Come on, it's hot, let's head inside, and I'll get some drinks."

And so they left the abandoned mine and went back to the farmhouse, their shoes and boots caked in the unusual orange-red soil.

It was indeed a unique kind of soil, soil rich in iron and nickel, soil that was unique to this area: the north-western corner of what was now the most powerful nation on Earth . . . if only it knew it.

Australia.

ACKNOWLEDGMENTS

First and foremost, I am indebted to a wonderful non-fiction book called *Secret Chamber* by the Egyptologist Robert Bauval. He's the guy who deduced that the pyramids at Giza are laid out in imitation of the constellation Orion's Belt.

It was from reading *Secret Chamber* that I discovered that a Golden Capstone did indeed once sit atop the Great Pyramid at Giza. As an author, it's wonderful when you discover something so big and so cool that it can be the ultimate goal of your story. When I read about the Golden Capstone, I just leapt up and started dancing around my living room, because I'd found exactly that.

I am often asked "Where do you get your ideas?" And this is the answer: I read a lot of nonfiction books. If you read enough, you find gems like this. As a work on the darker side of ancient Egypt, with interesting sections on the Word of Thoth and the Sphinx, I would thoroughly recommend this book to anyone keen on the subject of ancient Egypt.

On the home front, as always, my wife, Natalie, was a model of support and encouragement—reading draft after draft, letting me off doing chores around the house, and most of all, happily allowing our honeymoon in Egypt to morph into a quasiresearch trip!

Honestly, in Egypt I became one of those tourists who is the first off the bus and the last one back to it, and who pesters the tour guide with all kinds of weird questions. For example, at the Valley of the Kings I asked, "Is there a hieroglyph that says 'Death to grave robbers'?" (Sure enough, there is, and the image of it in this book is it!) And neither my wife nor I will ever forget exploring—on our own—the haunting chambers beneath the "Red" Pyramid south of Giza by the light of a perilously fading flashlight!

Special thanks to the good folk at Simon & Schuster for a stellar effort, in particular David Rosenthal and Kevin Smith. This is the first time I've been published by S&S, and I've been extremely fortunate to work with a great group of people who really "got" my work.

Kudos also to my agents at the William Morris Agency, Suzanne Gluck and Eugenie Furniss—they look after me so well! And they're just from the literary section. That's not even mentioning the cool people in L.A. (notably Alicia Gordon and Danny Greenberg) doing film things on my behalf.

I'd also like to thank Mr. David Epper, who generously supported my favorite charity, the Bullant Charity Challenge, by "buying" the name of a character in this book at Bullant's annual auction dinner. Thus his son, Max Epper, is in the book as Professor Max Epper, aka Wizard. Thanks, Dave.

And last to family and friends, once again I pledge my eternal thanks for their support and tolerance. My mum and dad; my brother, Stephen; friends like Bec Wilson, Nik and Simon Kozlina, and, of course, my first "official" reader—my good friend

John Schrooten, who still reads my stuff in the stands at the cricket after all these years. If he starts ignoring the cricket because he's absorbed in the book, it's a good sign!

Believe me, it's all about encouragement. As I've said in my previous books: *to anyone who knows a writer, never underestimate the power of your encouragement.*

An Interview with Matthew Reilly

The Writing of *7 Deadly Wonders*

Q: *7 Deadly Wonders* has some fairly wild concepts in it—like a 747 that can hover, Jack West's mechanical arm, and some gigantic underground structures. What exactly were you trying to achieve with the elements of *7 Deadly Wonders*?

MR: This is an important question. What I've tried to create with *7 Deadly Wonders* is what I would call a "modern real-world fantasy novel." By this I mean, a novel set in the present day, with real countries and real armies—but in which *hyper*-real things happen in hyper-real environments.

So, the *Halicarnassus*, for instance, is indeed a wild (and even perhaps absurd) idea—a 747 that has been modified so it can hover—but it makes for a fun and adventurous story. And Jack's mechanical arm also pushes the boundaries of modern science, but story-wise, it makes Jack very special and different (and it even gives him a little extra strength in the Hanging Gardens!) This is what I mean by "hyper-real."

If you want totally rigid reality in weapons, vehicles. and formal military procedures, authors like Tom Clancy and Nelson DeMille have those areas covered.

With *7 Deadly Wonders* I am trying for a *Lord*

of the Rings–scale adventure with a *Star Wars* feel; a story that is certainly not real, but which when viewed from the very limits of our current technology could be; a story in which the sheer outrageous *adventure* of it all trumps the contraints of reality. That's what I mean by a "modern real-world fantasy".

Q: **How was the writing of *7 Deadly Wonders* different from the writing of your other books?**

MR: It's funny, but for some reason the writing of this book was a more solitary experience than the others—if anything, it felt a lot like the writing of *Contest*. Perhaps that's because the subject matter of the book, the Seven Wonders of the Ancient World, is *so* ancient, *so* distant, *so* alien to us, that I was creating most of the story from pure imagination (rather than from actual sources—some of the stuff on the Wonders is pretty flimsy). As I did when I created the aliens in *Contest*, I just had to create these mystical places, like the Hanging Gardens of Babylon, for example, from scratch.

Q: **What did you try to do differently with this book?**

MR: For me, the key difference between *7 Deadly Wonders* and my previous books is the theme of "family" in it. The team of international soldiers guarding Lily ultimately becomes a family—complete with grandparents (Doris and Max Epper), squabbling brothers and sisters (Pooh Bear, Stretch, Big Ears, and Zoe), and the father-like figure of Jack West.

This was a thematic thing that I started in *Hover Car Racer* and I enjoyed it immensely when I wrote that novel. In the end, when you write an action-thriller novel, you must have characters that you care about, and by creating this quasi-family environment out of a bunch of hard-ass troopers, I felt I'd created a special kind of team that readers would want to cheer for.

I particularly love how Lily renames all the soldiers, changing all their tough-guy call signs into goofy childish nicknames. Having utilized 'serious' call signs in the *Scarecrow* books, I felt it was time to have a bit of fun, and turn this plot device on its head.

Q: Is it true that for this book you created your own language?

MR: I wouldn't go so far as to say that I created a language! What I did do was create an alphabet (not unlike cuneiform) to display the Word of Thoth—but my translation is just from English, not a brand-new language. That would have been way too hard and time-consuming. I'll leave that sort of thing to J.R.R. Tolkien!

It took some time, but it was great fun. I created symbols to match those of our own alphabet, plus rules for proper nouns and special symbols for certain objects (like the Great Pyramid, Alexander the Great, and the Sun, for instance). If anyone has the time and the inclination they can translate all the Thoth references in the book back to English, but be careful, as in the novel, it gets harder, as more symbols are used, and sometimes not from left to right!

After the book has been out a while, I'll put up the alphabet on my website, so that anyone who's interested can see how it works.

Q: **With the exception of Jason Chaser in *Hover Car Racer*, *7 Deadly Wonders* sees the introduction of your first Australian action hero. What made you decide to make Jack West Jr. an Australian?**

MR: It suited the story. Simple as that. I'm often asked why the heroes of my other books are American and the answer is really the same: it suited those stories (it especially suited *Ice Station*).

Q: **You mention *The Da Vinci Code* by Dan Brown a couple of times in the novel. Have you read it? Did it influence you?**

MR: I have indeed read *The Da Vinci Code* and I enjoyed it thoroughly. I actually read it long before it dominated the bestseller lists—when I was touring with *Scarecrow* in 2003, I would recommend it to anyone who would listen!

That said, *The Da Vinci Code* wasn't really an

influence on *7 Deadly Wonders*. The Indiana Jones movies were probably more of an influence. I wanted to create an Indiana Jones–type story, with booby traps and high adventure, but set in the present day. The reason I mentioned *The Da Vinci Code* in the book was really because that novel is now *so* globally known, if you do write a story about Catholic Church conspiracy theories or one which has a scene set in the Louvre, you should probably make a *Da Vinci Code* joke!

Q: ***7 Deadly Wonders* features some pretty dastardly American villains. Is it an anti-American novel?**

MR: I hope it's not interpreted that way. The Americans are just the villains in this book, that's all. They want the power of Tartarus and so they go after it—they just do so a little more ruthlessly than our heroes!

The key to *7 Deadly Wonders* was that the heroes had to be underdogs, underdogs battling the most powerful nation on Earth, and that at the moment is America. America has more guns, tanks, and planes than the next dozen countries combined. For a bunch of little countries to go up against the United States is a big thing, a hard thing. And that, to my mind, makes for an interesting story.

I guess, like many others, I do question the new American 'Imperialism' under George W. Bush, but unlike others I don't dislike America for it. It's a lone superpower in a changed world. It has to figure out how to find its way, just like the rest of us. It will make mistakes. Unfortunately, any mistakes it makes will have a big impact on everyone else on this planet. It will also, it must be said, do much good.

I don't know. I invariably find myself *defending* America when I'm out at dinner with friends. I have many American friends, and I work with some *very* clever New Yorkers and Los Angelinos. Smart people, all of them. I also firmly believe that America is a fantastic social experiment—a land of opportunity, where capitalism is king, and where 280 million people live in relative peace under the rule of law; not a bad achievement at all.

After all that, if some Americans think that just because I made them the villains of this book that I'm anti-American, then what can I do? I'll just have to cop it and know that they're wrong. And hey, the Brits never minded being the villains of *Ice Station*! But then again, I still have not been published in France . . .

Q: Will we see Jack West Jr. again?

MR: We certainly will! I am now well advanced into the sequel to *7 Deadly Wonders*, and Jack is back, as is Lily and the rest of the team. The new story takes place eighteen months after the events in *7 Deadly Wonders* and is even bigger in scale and scope. It turns out that the Tartarus Rotation is actually the triggering event for a far, far larger global event. (Oh, and a nice U.S. Marine named Astro joins our team of heroes on this adventure, so the USA is back with the good guys!)

Q: **You've had a busy year. *7 Deadly Wonders, Hell Island,* and your movie work on *Contest*. How have you survived it all?**

MR: Yes, it has been a busy year! But it's been enormous fun.

I had just finished *7 Deadly Wonders* when the call came from the Federal Government asking if I would write a brand-new short-novel for their Books Alive campaign. Luckily, I had a new idea sitting in the "Story Ideas" drawer of my desk ready to go, so I turned around, sat back down and started writing again!

And yes, at that stage, I'd already planned to direct a pilot shoot of *Contest,* so I was in the midst of preproduction when I was polishing both *Hell Island* and *7 Deadly Wonders*. I'm still not quite sure how I did it, but I figured I could sleep later! Believe me, I'm resting now.

Q: **Shane Schofield appeared in the Books Alive edition of *Hell Island*. Will we see the Scarecrow again in a new novel?**

MR: A few things about *Hell Island*, especially since I didn't do an interview like this in the back of that book.

I really enjoyed doing *Hell Island*, and making it a Schofield book. I think it's a pretty kick-ass story—bold, fast, and *mean*; and yet still short. It was designed to be a kind of "side-adventure" for Schofield; a minor mission that occurred in between books (although technically it occurs after the events in *Scarecrow*). You also have to remember that my fans in the United States and other countries won't see *Hell Island*, as it was a free book given out in Australia only.

Will he appear again? I reckon so. He's a fun character, who's always getting into trouble, and they're the ones I like to write about. The question is, who do I write about next? Schofield or Jack West?

Q: What is the latest movie news?

MR: *Hover Car Racer* is still with Disney. Last I heard, Alfred Gough and Miles Millar were still at work on the screenplay. And of course, I'm hard at work trying to get *Contest* up and running as a feature film.

I had an awesome time directing the pilot of *Contest* earlier this year, which was the first twelve minutes of the book. This included getting a creature shop to build a fully-articulated Karanadon head and filming it in the Stack of the New South Wales State Library. We also filmed in the abandoned train tunnels underneath Sydney, the Royal North Shore

Hospital, and even in the basement of my house! Ah, movie magic.

Q: So, what's next for Matthew Reilly?
MR: Sleep. Rest. And maybe play a bit of golf. It's been a very busy year and I need to slow down a bit. I'm just going to sit on my couch and read a bunch of nonfiction books! Although, if I get *Contest* up and running, then it'll be all systems go and I can sleep next year. . . .

Q: Any final words?
MR: As always, I just hope you all enjoyed the book. I had a lot of fun writing this one and I hope you had just as much fun reading it.

UNFORGETTABLE BESTSELLERS FROM POCKET BOOKS

Blue Valor
Illona Haus
To solve a crime that defies the imagination, a Baltimore cop must take a twisted journey into the dark recesses of a killer's mind.

Saving Cascadia
John J. Nance
Washington state's Cascadia Island is a tranquil Northwest paradise—until a disaster only one man can predict threatens the lives of thousands.

The Pandora Key
Lynne Heitman
She's a tough, sexy private investigator—and she's unlocking explosive secrets form the past.

Live Wire
Jay MacLarty
A high-stakes delivery and a high-risk courier make for an explosive combination.

The Greater Good
Casey Moreton
Even in the top-secret world of Washington politics, some crimes can't be justified.

Thrillers that leave you on the edge of your seat from Pocket Books

Fury
Robert K. Tanenbaum
Butch Karp tackles his most personal case
yet—one in which his family may be only the
first victims of a ruthless terrorist cell.

Kindred Spirit
John Passarella
For twins separated at birth, life can be twice
as terrifying…

Finding Satan
Andrew Neiderman
A man of science and logic will come to
believe—in the power of ultimate evil.

Cobraville
Carson Stroud
A covert CIA mission to infiltrate a terrorist
stronghold in the Philippines goes horribly
wrong—and now one man must pay the price.